"... ...bout
... he said when she said nothing more. His lips curved in a wicked smile. "We can be secret partners."

The low, almost seductive tone of his voice snaked through her like a lightning strike. She felt the thunderous aftermath low in her belly, a shudder of raw, unexpected need.

Agreeing with him would be the worst possible decision she could make. She knew it bone deep. But when she opened her mouth to speak, the word that spilled from her lips was "Okay."

He gave her another narrow-eyed look, as if he suspected she was joking. "Okay?"

This was her chance to back out, she thought. Laugh and agree that she'd been joking.

But she couldn't, she realized. No matter what kind of fluttery things he did to her insides just by being Cain Dennison, he was right about one thing. He did know more about Renee Lindsey's final days than anyone else in town, save the killer himself. If she was serious about getting to the bottom of Renee's murder, she needed his help.

"Okay," she repeated more firmly. "You're right. I need your help. And, frankly, you could use mine, as well."

"I need you, do I?" His smile made her heart flip-flop.

CRYBABY FALLS

BY
PAULA GRAVES

Published in Great Britain 2014
by Mills & Boon, an imprint of Harlequin (UK) Limited,
Eton House, 18-24 Paradise Road, Richmond, Surrey, TW9 1SR

© 2014 Paula Graves

ISBN: 978-0-263-91374-3

46-1014

Harlequin (UK) Limited's policy is to use papers that are natural, renewable and recyclable products and made from wood grown in sustainable forests. The logging and manufacturing processes conform to the legal environmental regulations of the country of origin.

Printed and bound in Spain
by Blackprint CPI, Barcelona

Alabama native **Paula Graves** wrote her first book, a mystery starring herself and her neighborhood friends, at the age of six. A voracious reader, Paula loves books that pair tantalizing mystery with compelling romance. When she's not reading or writing, she works as a creative director for a Birmingham advertising agency and spends time with her family and friends. She is a member of Southern Magic Romance Writers, Heart of Dixie Romance Writers and Romance Writers of America. Paula invites readers to visit her website, www.paulagraves.com.

For my mother, who took me
to Noccalula Falls in Gadsden, Alabama,
when I was just a child, engendering in me a love
of roaring waterfalls and tragic, romantic stories.

Chapter One

The roadside memorial wasn't tattered or faded as so many monuments to the departed were. The simple wooden cross planted in the ground off Black Creek Road gleamed white in the midday sunlight, and the flowers in the resin urn were real, not plastic, still dewy with recent life.

Sara Lindsey crouched beside the small display and touched the big red gerbera daisy in the center of the urn. A chill skittered through her, as if someone had touched the back of her neck with cold fingers, and she nearly knocked herself on her backside turning to look.

Nobody's there, Sara. Get a grip.

Turning back to face the monument, she silently read the name etched there, darkened with black paint by whoever had planted this latest incarnation in the ground. *Donnie Lindsey. Beloved son and husband.*

Today was the third anniversary of the accident. Some days, Donnie's death seemed like a distant memory, as if life since the accident had slowed to an interminable crawl, each minute stretching to hours or even days. And other times, like now, the raw realization that he was gone forever ached and bled like a brand-new wound.

Joyce must be the unseen caretaker, Sara thought. For her mother-in-law, the wound never stopped bleeding. Her grief was a physical thing, a heavy pall hanging over whatever space she occupied these days. How her husband, Gary, lived with her constant state of mourning, Sara couldn't imagine. As painful as her grief for Donnie had been for the past three years, Sara still managed to find moments of happiness within the sadness.

Joyce never seemed to. Grief had aged her a decade in the past three years, her pain exacerbated by the loss of her daughter years before. And as much as she mourned the loss of her children, Joyce craved someone to blame for their deaths.

For Renee's death, there was no closure. Her murder remained unsolved. But for Donnie's death, Joyce had found a target for her silent wrath.

After all, Sara had been behind the wheel of Donnie's truck the night of the accident. And she'd refused to play by her mother-in-law's rules of grieving widowhood, choosing to honor her husband in her own way.

She checked her watch. Almost noon. Joyce, Gary and all of Donnie's childhood friends who still lived near Purgatory would be leaving the cemetery now, heading back to the Lindseys' home for a potluck dinner. This was the second year of what Joyce called "The Remembering," and for the second year in a row, Sara hadn't been able to bring herself to go, even though everyone clearly expected her to make an appearance.

As the widow and part of the reason Donnie was dead, the least she could do was show up and take part in the ritual show of grief, right?

But grief was a private thing for her. She wasn't going to put on a show or stand around and watch others grieve just because people expected it. So she'd come here instead, to the hairpin turn on Black Creek Road, the place where everything had fallen apart, for her own personal memorial. And if she allowed no tears to dampen her cheeks or sobs to escape her throat, there was no one else around to pass judgment on her restrained style of grief.

Bitter much, Lindsey?

With a sigh, she pushed to her feet, grimacing at the lingering pain in her joints, and turned toward the drop-off only a few short yards from the roadside. Donnie hadn't actually died here, at the site of his monument, but nearly forty feet down the gorge that ended where Little Black Creek snaked its way through the foothills of the Smoky Mountains.

Sara wasn't sure how she'd survived the accident. She remembered none of it, not even why she and Donnie had been in Purgatory that night in the first place. She knew Donnie had been following a new lead about his sister's murder, but thanks to the head injury she'd sustained in the crash, she couldn't even remember what the lead had been or how he'd come by it. She'd spent a month in the hospital, missing Donnie's funeral and wallowing in a toxic combination of grief and pain until she'd finally talked her doctors into letting her go before the hospital killed her.

Recuperation had taken a year, and to this day, though she was pretty much back to normal physically, the memory loss lingered like a big, blank hole in the middle of her upended life. And the memory she most wanted to recover was what had happened in those last few seconds before the truck had left Black Creek Road and spun over the cliff edge.

What had caused the accident? Was it something she could have avoided? The question had haunted her for three years.

"Must've fallen asleep and missed the hairpin turn," had been the accident investigator's best assessment. But she'd never been able to picture the accident happening that way. She was so careful behind the wheel. She never drove sleepy or even distracted by the radio or her cell phone, because her first two years as a Birmingham police officer had been spent in the traffic division. She'd seen a lifetime's worth of the grim results of inattention behind the wheel in those two years.

She wouldn't have been driving impaired. And she couldn't imagine how anything but impairment would have led her over that cliff at such a high rate of speed.

She heard a faint rustle in the woods nearby, and the creeping sensation that had followed her down from the scenic overlook where she'd parked intensified until the hair on the back of her neck prickled to attention. She eased around in a full circle, studying her surroundings with the eye of an investigator.

The woods around her bristled with life, leaves fluttering in the late September breeze that ruffled her hair into disarray. She spotted a squirrel shinning up a tree with quick, darting movements, its black eyes scanning the area for threats much the same way her own gaze was seeking some cause for the unsettled sensation that had set her heart pounding and scattered goose bumps across her limbs.

You're alone, she told herself, firmly turning her gaze back to the road and the long walk uphill to the scenic overlook.

Always alone.

With the skin on the back of her neck still twitching as if brushed by invisible fingers, she took one last look at the roadside memorial before heading up the mountain road.

CAIN SHOULD HAVE known Sara Lindsey wouldn't show up for the graveside memorial. From what he'd heard around Purgatory over the past couple of weeks, she hadn't been back to Ridge County more than a handful of times since the accident.

Thanks to being laid up in ICU, she'd missed the funeral. Even her in-laws couldn't fault her for that. But what had kept her away after that?

A hunch had brought him out here to Black Creek Road and the roadside memorial Joyce Lindsey tended with obsessive attention. And sure enough, here she was, the grieving widow crouched beside the gleaming white cross, her head bent, a glossy curtain of dark hair hiding her face from his curious gaze.

She couldn't remember the accident, people said. Unfortunate for her if it was true, because without any memory of what had happened that night, there was no way for her to refute the whispered rumors about what might have led her to drive their truck off the road and down the steep bluff.

There had been no witnesses. Nobody to say, one way or another, whether she'd been reckless or even careless. The hospital wouldn't release the records of the tests they'd done on her, but he knew they'd have checked her blood-alcohol level and probably even done a tox screen, since she'd been found behind the wheel. If anything had turned up, she'd have been charged.

Her husband, on the other hand, had gone through the windshield. He'd been dead before anyone arrived on the scene.

Cain knew that for a fact. Because he'd been the one to find them.

A few yards away, Sara stood and looked around, her shoulders hunched and her eyes narrowed as if she sensed his presence. He stood very still, knowing that motion, more than the color of his clothing, would betray his location. His drab clothing would blend in well enough with his woodsy surroundings, but a turn of the head or a flick of a hand would give away his position in a heartbeat.

She had become a beautiful woman, a combination of age and tragedy carving away any vestige of baby softness from her features, leaving the fine bone structure in full view. A stirring sensation in his chest caught him by surprise, and he averted his gaze without moving a muscle.

After a moment, she seemed to shake off her nervous tension, turned back to the road and started walking uphill toward the scenic overlook located a quarter mile up the mountain.

He watched until she was out of sight around the next curve. Then he pulled out his cell phone and pressed the speed dial for his office.

Alexander Quinn answered on the second ring. He didn't bother with a salutation. "Did you find her?"

"Yes."

"Any clue why she didn't show for the memorial?"

"Oh, she showed for a memorial. Just not the one at the cemetery." That strange flutter he'd felt in his chest earlier recurred. He tried to ignore it.

"I didn't hire you to be cryptic." Though Quinn's voice barely changed tone, Cain knew his boss was annoyed. In fact, something about this case had been making the old spymaster cranky from the moment Joyce Lindsey had showed up at Quinn's detective agency, The Gates, and hired him to look into the deaths of her two children.

"Sorry." Cain started walking along the narrow shoulder, keeping an eye out for cars coming around the blind curve. "I found her at the roadside memorial her mother-in-law maintains."

"Thought those weren't legal in Tennessee."

"What's legal and what's tolerated can be two different things." Cain paused as he reached the small white cross. "From what I hear, Joyce Lindsey sets up a new one almost as fast as the state can remove the old one."

"She's lost a great deal." Coming from almost anyone else, the comment might have been a statement of sympathy. But Quinn was anything but sentimental, and what Cain heard in his voice was unease.

"You think you were wrong to take her case?"

"Cases," Quinn corrected. "She lost two children. But I don't need to remind you of that, do I?"

Cain tightened his grip on the cell phone. "No, you don't."

"She wants justice. I don't blame her for that."

"But?"

"But she seems very sure she already knows the answers," Quinn answered. "I wonder whether she'll accept a truth that conflicts with what she already believes."

"Just a second." Hearing the sound of a vehicle engine approaching around the curve, Cain edged away from the shoulder of the road, taking care not to get too close to the drop-off. A sturdy thicket of wild hydrangea offered a hiding spot; he crouched behind the thick leaves until the truck passed. He caught a glimpse of Sara Lindsey's fine profile before sunlight bounced off the driver's window with a blinding glare. The flutter in his chest migrated down to his lower belly, and he knew instantly what that feeling was.

Desire. Raw, visceral and entirely unwelcome.

"You think she wants us to confirm her beliefs rather than find the truth," Cain continued after the truck was safely past, dragging his mind out of dangerous territory. "For instance, if we find that her daughter-in-law didn't cause the accident—"

"The police looked into the accident pretty thoroughly. They found nothing to prove the widow was at fault."

"So they say," Cain murmured, remembering the flicker of guilt he'd seen on Sara Lindsey's face as she looked back at the small white cross before heading up to the overlook.

"You think they missed something?"

Cain started up the mountain, where he'd left his own

truck parked at the overlook. "Maybe. It would help a whole lot if Sara Lindsey could remember anything about that night."

"How sure are you that she doesn't?"

A three-year-old memory pricked Cain's mind. Sara Lindsey, bloodied and panic-stricken as she lay strapped upside down in the crumpled truck cab. She had looked straight at Cain, but he could tell she wasn't really seeing him. Her breathing had been fast and labored, but she'd managed to find air enough to scream her husband's name in terror, over and over, until she'd gone quiet and still, falling unconscious.

He shut the memory away, not wanting to let it taint his present investigation. "From all accounts, she and her husband had been happily in love since they were both in grade school. Even the people who think she must have caused the accident don't reckon she did it on purpose."

"And the sister's death?"

"We know Renee's death was murder," Cain said grimly. "We just don't know who did it."

"Joyce Lindsey still thinks *you* did it, doesn't she?"

Cain crossed the road to the wider shoulder on the other side while there was no traffic approaching from either direction. "You should have told her you were assigning me to the case. She'll find out sooner or later. Nothing stays secret in a town this small unless you bury it."

"I didn't want to give her the chance to say no."

"She'll just fire you later rather than now."

"We'll deal with that when it happens."

"What's this case to you, Quinn? Why are you misleading a client in order to keep investigating?"

"It's not what the case is to me, Dennison. It's what the case is to *you*."

Cain pressed his mouth to a thin line, torn between

irritation and an unexpected flicker of gratitude. "I've lived this long without answers."

"Too long. You almost turned down a job with The Gates because of what happened here in Purgatory eighteen years ago. Nobody should have to live his life under a constant cloud. Believe me."

Cain almost laughed. Quinn's whole life was lived smack-dab in the middle of an impervious cloud of secrecy and lies. Little of what Cain knew about his boss's life and history was reliable. Quinn had spent two decades in the CIA, fabricating an identity as impossible to penetrate as a Smoky Mountain midnight.

He sighed. "Okay, fine. But how am I supposed to investigate Renee Lindsey's murder when half the town still thinks I did it? Who's going to be willing to talk to me?"

"You had an alibi. There was never any evidence to implicate you. You weren't charged with anything."

"Small-town gossip doesn't deal in evidence and legal outcomes." Cain reached the summit of the hill, where a scenic overlook offered parking for a half dozen vehicles and an observation deck with a panoramic view of the Smoky Mountains. "People know what they know, the truth be damned."

As he unlocked the cab of his Ford F-150, he spared a moment to gaze out across the spectacular mountain vista. The sight tugged at something deep inside him, something he'd have sworn died years ago when he'd shaken the dust of Purgatory, Tennessee, off his boots.

Yet, thanks to Alexander Quinn, here he was again, back in the hills he'd left behind, ready to face a past he'd long been determined to forget.

What the hell was he thinking?

"Don't you want to know who killed Renee Lindsey?"

If Cain didn't know better, he might have imagined a touch of sympathy in Quinn's soft question. But Cain *did* know better. If there was any emotion in Quinn's voice, it was carefully planted there for a reason. To disarm him, perhaps. To get him to spill his own secrets.

To prod him into doing whatever it was Quinn wanted for whatever reason he wanted it.

"Of course I do," Cain answered, keeping his tone businesslike and free of the emotion that burned like a furnace in the center of his chest.

Of course he wanted to know who'd killed Renee Lindsey. In his own way, he'd loved her almost as much as her family had. And when he'd found her body at the base of Crybaby Falls, he'd felt so much rage he'd thought he'd combust. She'd been a sweet girl. A good girl, despite her foolish choices. She hadn't deserved to die for her mistakes.

"Keep me informed." Quinn hung up without saying goodbye.

"Goodbye to you, too," Cain muttered, shoving his phone into his pocket and climbing into the truck cab.

As he belted himself in, he stared through the windshield at the cool blue mountains spreading out in front of him as far as the eye could see. Just over the closest rise, he thought, was Crybaby Falls. He could be there in five minutes. Maybe less.

He tried to quell the thought. He'd spent too many hours haunting the falls all those years ago before he'd left Purgatory behind. Too many hours beating his head against an invisible wall of secrets and lies, grieving the loss of his friend and the colossal unfairness of a world where Renee Lindsey had to die while Cain's bastard of a father got to live. He'd buried the boy he'd been deep in the rocky soil of Mulberry Rise when he left Purgatory behind. He hadn't been back to the falls in years.

But when he reached the turnoff to Old Bridge Road, he

took a right and headed down the narrow, rutted one-lane that would take him straight to the footbridge over the falls.

A WOODEN BRIDGE crossed Warrior Creek mere yards from the top of Crybaby Falls, close enough to the water's surface that a strong rain could raise the creek high enough to swamp the rough wood slats that made up the floor of the bridge. But even though the afternoon sun had surrendered to clouds and a light shower, the rainfall never made it past a slow, steady drizzle, cooling air shrouding the woods in a misty fog that made the trees and rocks look like an alien landscape, full of mystery and danger.

Or maybe it was this landscape in particular. These rocks, these trees, these thundering falls.

Sara tucked her knees up closer to her chest as a rising breeze blew the rainfall under the rocky outcropping providing her with shelter. She wondered, not for the first time, if she and Donnie had stopped here at Crybaby Falls before heading up the mountain the night of the accident. Had they lingered here, Donnie stewing in a toxic blend of grief and obsession? Had she tried to coax him back to the present, to what he still had rather than what he'd lost so many years ago?

She'd tried to understand his driving need for answers. He and Renee had been close, despite the four-year difference in their ages. When Renee had died at eighteen, Donnie and Sara had been high-school freshman, just starting to transition from their innocent childhood flirtation to the complexity of a high-school romance. At fourteen, Sara hadn't known how to comfort her grief-stunned boyfriend.

At twenty-nine, she still hadn't known how to comfort Donnie. And she'd begun to fear what his intensifying obsession was doing not just to him but to their marriage, as well.

They'd both been Birmingham police officers. But

while Donnie had been content in uniform, she'd been pushing her way up the ranks, making detective and settling into a professional life she'd loved, despite the pressures of the job.

Ironic, she supposed, that the strain on their marriage hadn't come from the stress of her work but from her husband's inability to get past that one, tragic moment from his past.

She'd wanted answers, too. But if she'd learned anything in her time as a Birmingham police detective, it was the awful truth that some murders never got solved. Some killers never saw justice.

And she'd had a sinking feeling that Renee Lindsey's murder was going to turn out to be one of those cases that went permanently cold.

"I won't accept that," Donnie had told her as he'd packed his bags for a trip back to Purgatory the morning before the accident that took his life. It was the last moment of her life she could remember before waking up in a Knoxville hospital, drowning in bandages and a relentless tide of pain.

She rubbed her gritty eyes. They'd come here to Purgatory to follow a new lead. That much she knew.

But what new lead? Had Donnie told her? Or had he kept it to himself, the way he'd begun to hide all aspects of his investigation into his sister's murder from Sara, as if he no longer trusted her to listen to his theories with an open mind?

Had she forced him into such secrecy with her growing impatience? She didn't want to believe she'd made him feel he couldn't trust her with his thoughts, but if she was truthful with herself, she knew it was possible. The more she'd settled into her new life in Birmingham, the more distance had seemed to grow between her and Donnie. His mind, his heart, was still in Tennessee. It was as if the world had stopped turning for him fifteen years earlier, when the Ridge County sheriff had shown up at the Lindsey house to break the wretched news of Renee's death.

She had wanted to understand. But his grief wasn't hers, no matter how much she'd wanted to bear it for him.

Had they been arguing in the car? Had she let his anger, her growing impatience, distract her at the wrong moment?

Pressing the heel of her palm to her forehead as if she could somehow quell the throbbing ache behind her eyes, she tried to remember something, anything, from that night.

She'd been driving Donnie's Silverado. His baby. He'd bought the truck used when he'd turned eighteen with money he'd made working at a tourist trap in Sevierville. He'd pampered the old truck as if it were a beloved pet and rarely let Sara drive it, not because he didn't think she was a good driver but because he found such simple joy behind the wheel of the tough old Chevy.

So why had she been driving that night? Had he been impaired in some way? Donnie had never been much of a drinker, but he'd had a beer now and then if he was socializing with friends who drank. The police hadn't checked his blood-alcohol level, as far as she knew, since he hadn't been driving.

They'd checked hers in the hospital, of course, and found no alcohol in her system. She'd have been shocked if they had; she had avoided alcohol like the plague ever since one nightmarish teenage binge on prom night her senior year. When she'd vowed "never again," she'd meant it.

The tox screen had come up clean, as well.

But something had caused her to veer off Black Creek Road, a road she'd traveled nearly every day of her life until she was eighteen. A road as familiar to her as her own face in the mirror. She knew every turn, every twist, every incline and straightaway of Black Creek Road, from the old marble quarry north of town to where the road ended ten miles past Bitterwood to the south. She wouldn't have missed the hairpin turn. Not even at midnight in a snowstorm.

But it hadn't been midnight. The crash had happened a little after nine. And the night had been clear and mild, according to reports.

She hadn't hit an animal. There weren't any signs that she'd swerved or braked to miss an animal, either. There hadn't even been any skid marks to indicate she'd tried to stop their plummet over the cliff.

How the hell could that be? If she hadn't been drunk or incapacitated, why wouldn't she have tried to stop the car from going over the edge?

Somewhere outside her hiding spot came a distinct snap of a twig, loud enough to make her nerves jangle. On instinct, she tugged her knees more tightly to her chest, like a child hiding from detection.

Was this how Renee Lindsey had felt? she wondered suddenly as her pulse sped up and her skin broke out in goose bumps. Had this been the last thing she felt before she'd died?

A man strode into view, moving in quick, powerful strides that exuded barely leashed anger. He was tall and lean, all sinew and muscle.

And dangerous, Sara thought, staring out from her hiding place with her heart in her throat.

This particular man was as dangerous as hell.

Chapter Two

The drizzle had started to pick up, whipping needle pricks of rain into Cain's face as he crossed the wooden bridge over Crybaby Falls. From here, the roar of the cascade drowned out other sounds in the woods, creating a cocoon of white noise that made him feel as if he were the only person left in the world.

He forced his gaze down to the churning maelstrom at the base of the falls, where the power of the water slamming into the rocks below created a perpetual explosion of spray, both constant and ever changing. The official name of the cascade was Warrior Creek Falls, but it had been called Crybaby Falls for as long as anyone could remember and even appeared that way on some local maps.

Legend had it that a young Cherokee maiden in love with a white settler had discovered, soon after her lover's death in battle, that she was carrying his child. She'd hidden her pregnancy from her family until the day she gave birth in the shelter of the rock beneath the falls. But she'd died in childbirth, leaving the tiny infant alone, unprotected against the elements.

The sound of the crying baby had, supposedly, brought the Cherokee tribesmen and their white enemies together for a time, as they joined forces to search for the source of the cries. They found the baby just as he breathed his last.

Touched and chastened by the tragic, unnecessary deaths of mother and child, the Cherokees and the white settlers had made peace.

For a time, at least.

According to the stories, if you came to the falls at night when the moon was bright, you could hear the baby's plaintive cries coming from the rocky shelf behind the falls. A nice story. Dreadfully romantic. And almost certainly pure bunk.

The true history of Crybaby Falls was tragic enough without embellishment. Another pregnant girl had fallen in love with the wrong person and died here for her mistake. But there had been no crying baby, no lesson learned. Only death and grief and a gut-churning failure of justice.

Cain reached the other side of the falls and bent to pluck a sunny golden coneflower from a patch of the wildflowers that grew along the bluff overlooking the falls. Coneflowers had been one of Renee Lindsey's favorite. "They're like lookin' into the sun," she'd told him one day as she plucked one and handed it to him. "They make me feel warm and happy."

He pulled one of the golden petals and let the wind pick it up and swirl it into the churning water below.

She loves me, he thought.

He tossed another petal.

She loves me not.

Renee had once told him he was her best friend, and he had thought at the time she was either lying or sadly short on friends. He hadn't been the kind of kid who made friends easily, for a variety of reasons, some his own fault and some not. And his high-school years had been among the worst years of all.

But something about Renee had drawn him to her. He couldn't say they'd shared much in common, except maybe an inborn impatience with phony people. She was from a family with two parents and two perfect kids, a family with a nice house in town and money in the bank. Her father owned a small chain of stores providing automotive parts and service. Her mother had been a stay-at-home mom, always there for her kids after school.

All Cain had waiting at home, back then, was a mean drunk of a father who liked to knock him around and call him names. Hell, he'd named Cain after the Bible's first murderer because he'd been the only survivor of his mother's attempt to give birth to twins—a fact his father had been only too happy to explain when Cain had come home crying after a nightmarish first day of school. "You earned your name fair and square, boy. Live with it."

Taking someone home after school to study or just hang out was so beyond a possibility that Cain had never even wished he could have friends over. And he knew enough about the real world to refuse all of Renee's hints that he could come home with her sometime.

Lindseys and Dennisons didn't live in the same world. Hell, there'd been some whispers and raised eyebrows when the Lindsey boy, Donnie, had married Sara Lynn Dunkirk, whose daddy was a lifelong Ridge County sheriff's deputy and whose mama was one of those Culpeppers from over in Cherokee Cove.

If the people in Renee's circle could barcly accept a nice, good-natured girl like Sara Dunkirk because of her family connections, what on earth would they have done with Billy Dennison's long-haired, bad-tempered spawn?

He released the last of the coneflower petals and looked over the bridge railing. The thickening clouds overhead had darkened the tree-dense forest, plunging the world around him into premature twilight, but he could still make out the tiny golden petals as the whirling waters sucked them under and regurgitated them a few feet downriver.

He turned away from the falls and started back across

the wooden bridge, watching his steps on the rain-slick wooden slats. When he looked up again, his whole body jangled with surprise.

Standing at the other end of the bridge was Sara Lindsey, her shoulder-length hair dancing around her face in the damp wind. Her body was rigid, her hands clasped so tightly around the rails of the bridge that her knuckles had turned white.

Cain's heart gave a lurch and settled into a rapid, pounding cadence against his rib cage. Low in his belly, he felt the slow, sweet burn of attraction and wished she was anyone else in the world.

That he was anyone else in the world.

"Did you kill her?" Sara asked, her low voice whipped toward him by the wind.

He stared back at her, wondering if he'd imagined the question. Wondering if he was imagining her, standing here at the scene of the crime like an avenging angel.

"No," he answered.

But he couldn't tell if she believed him.

DESPITE THE PASSAGE of seventeen years since Sara had last seen him, Cain Dennison had changed little. The tall, lean boy with wary gray eyes and a feral sort of masculine beauty had aged into a taller, lean-muscled man in his mid-thirties with the same winter-sky eyes and a touch of the wild. Life had etched a few more lines in his face, but those lines only made him seem more mysterious and compelling than she remembered.

Once a bad boy...

He had always been an object of girlhood fantasies, as sweet a piece of forbidden fruit as Purgatory had to offer. Sara herself had not been immune, even as madly in love with Donnie Lindsey as she'd been.

The flicker of heat building low in her belly suggested she still wasn't immune, all these years later.

"Why are you here?" she asked. He'd left town not long after Renee's murder, coming back now and then only to visit his grandmother, who lived near Miller's Knob on the eastern edge of town. According to her father, who'd kept an eye on Cain Dennison's comings and goings ever since Renee's murder, he hadn't been back in town since the accident three years ago.

"Why are *you?*" he countered, a snap in his voice, as if he couldn't quite control the defensive response.

She wasn't sure how to answer that question. Her official reason for returning to Purgatory had been to attend Joyce's memorial day for Donnie, but she'd known before she ever climbed behind the wheel of her Chevy Silverado that she wasn't going to make it to the cemetery.

So why had she come?

I want answers. The thought formed like a lightning bolt slashing through her brain.

But answers to what questions? She couldn't even remember coming to Purgatory the day of the accident. She knew Donnie's motivation—the new lead she couldn't remember. And was it a coincidence the accident had happened the day before the fifteenth anniversary of Renee's death?

But why had she come with him this time? Her boss at the police department hadn't been much help in answering that question; he'd told her she'd given him no reason for asking for a few days off. The demands of her job meant that most of her closest friends had been fellow cops and their families, but apparently she'd failed to inform any of them what she and Donnie had planned to do in Purgatory, either.

And neither her parents nor Donnie's had known they were in town, though Joyce and Gary had told her later, in the hospital, that Donnie had called the night before to tell them he'd be in town for the anniversary of Renee's death.

"I don't know," she finally said aloud. "I guess because it was three years ago today. And tomorrow, it'll have been eighteen years since Renee's death."

Cain looked down at the falls thundering beneath the bridge under their feet, his expression grim.

"Sometimes, I can barely remember what she looked like," Sara continued when he didn't speak. "Isn't that strange? She was Donnie's sister, and I saw her all the time, but when I try to remember things about her, it's all fuzzy and distant, like I'm looking at the past through a frosty windshield. I wish I could blame the head injury from the crash, but the truth is, I don't think I really knew her at all. She was just Donnie's sister, the one who didn't want us to bother her or mess with her things."

"I remember her." The words seemed to spill over his tongue before he could stop them. His gray eyes slanted her way, narrowing as if he'd said something he regretted.

"Do you know who fathered the baby she was carrying?" she asked.

His gaze snapped up to hers again. "No."

She knew it hadn't been Cain's baby. DNA tests had established that much. But short of court-ordering every male who'd ever had contact with Renee to take a DNA test, the question of her baby's paternity had remained as open a question as the identity of her killer.

"She wouldn't say," he added so softly that for a moment, she wasn't sure she'd actually heard him speak. But when he turned to look at her again, he added, "She made it clear she didn't want anyone else to know."

She stepped closer, lifting her face toward him. The rain had almost stopped, but the wind had picked up, blowing damp strands of her dark hair across her face. One strand snagged on her lips, and Cain's gaze dropped to her mouth.

For a moment, his eyes darkened, and something crackled between them like electricity.

Then he looked away again, his gaze drawn back to the waterfall.

"Did you love her?" She hadn't realized she was going to ask the question until it tumbled from her lips.

He turned his head slowly, his eyes narrowing as they met her gaze. "I wanted her. I don't reckon that's the same thing, though." His shoulders slumped after a moment and he turned to put his hands on the bridge railing. "I wanted her to be happy. And she wasn't."

No, she wasn't, Sara thought. She might not have a strong memory of Donnie's sister, but what she did recall was that Renee had been full of life and laughter, even when she was being the imperious older sister—except for those last few weeks of her life.

Sara supposed learning she was pregnant must have been terrifying for a girl like Renee, whose parents had put her on a pedestal and made big plans for her life. College, marriage, a career if she wanted it—the Lindseys had been determined to give their children a charmed life, especially their smart, beautiful firstborn.

Renee would have felt the heavy weight of those expectations and dreaded having to tell her parents the truth.

"She wasn't dating anyone as far as her parents and Donnie knew." Sara wondered if Cain Dennison was willing to be any more forthcoming now, all these years later, than he'd been right after Renee's death. Sara couldn't bring Donnie back, but maybe she could finish what he'd started before his death. Maybe she could find out the truth about what had happened to Renee.

She'd been a good detective once, before the accident. And she had a lot of time on her hands now, while she tried to figure out what to do with the rest of her life.

"I knew she was seeing someone," Cain said. "I just never knew who."

Sara couldn't hide her surprise. "You never told the cops that."

He slanted a look at her. "They didn't ask me that."

"And you didn't volunteer the information?"

"The cops thought she was dating me. Secretly, of course." He laughed, though the sound held little in the way of mirth. "Because Renee Lindsey wouldn't dare date a Dennison in the open."

"But the two of you spent a lot of time together."

"We were friends."

"And I'm supposed to believe that was enough for you?"

He shot her a narrow-eyed look. "Did your daddy send you to interrogate me, Detective Lindsey?"

"My daddy doesn't tell me what to do. And, by the way, it's just plain Mrs. Lindsey now."

One dark eyebrow arched over a pale gray eye. "Since when?"

"I turned in my badge last week."

"Your decision?"

The decision had nominally been hers, but she knew it had been a matter of time before her bosses let her go. She hadn't been able to throw herself into her work the way she'd needed to. Donnie had haunted every inch of the town they'd once called their home, until he was almost all she could think about. Donnie, her questions about his death and her own guilty fear that whatever had happened had been her fault.

"Close enough," she answered.

He cocked his head, his gaze sliding over her slowly, as if to adjust his assessment of her now that he had this new piece of information. "What are you going to do now?"

She shrugged. "I have some savings that didn't get eaten

by the medical bills. Donnie had some life insurance. I've got a little time and space to decide."

"And you came back *here* to do your thinkin'?"

She smiled at the first hint of his mountain accent coming into play. He'd been gone from the mountains awhile, just as she had, but highlanders like the two of them could never completely escape their roots.

"My granddaddy died last winter. He left me his cabin. My dad says there's a lot of work to be done on it, and I should probably just sell it. But I don't have to decide right away." She wasn't sure why she was telling Cain even this much about her plans. He might as well be a stranger to her, and what little she did know about him and his past didn't exactly paint him as a trustworthy confidante.

"And you figure it's as good a place to do your thinkin' as any?"

"Something like that."

He nodded slowly. "Looks like we're both back for a while, then."

"So this isn't a short visit for you?" She felt a flicker of unease. Purgatory, Tennessee, was a place with a long memory, and there were a whole lot of people in this town who still believed Cain Dennison had gotten away with murder.

Her father included.

Carl Dunkirk had never been happy about the sheriff's decision not to pursue Cain as a suspect in Renee's murder. He'd seen Renee's pregnancy by another man to be a damned good motive for murder rather than exculpatory evidence.

If Cain planned to stay here long, he might come to regret it.

"I have a job," he said after a moment, not looking at her.

"Doing what?"

He glanced at her. "This and that."

"Are 'this and that' legal?"

His mouth curved, the first hint of a smile since she'd confronted him. The twitch of his lips carved a dimple in his cheek, sending an odd flutter through the center of her chest. "You think I'd tell you if they weren't?"

She tried a different tack. "I heard you joined the Army when you left town."

"You heard that, did you?"

"It's not true?"

"I didn't say that."

"Did you like the service?"

"*Liked* isn't exactly the word I'd use," he said after a pause. "I guess you could say I found satisfaction in serving my country."

"How long were you in?"

He made a show of looking at his watch. "Fifteen years, two months and three days."

Now she was really surprised. The Cain Dennison she knew—through rumors and stories, anyway—couldn't have lasted a week in the Army. "That's a career."

"I thought it would be, yeah."

"What happened?"

He blew out a long breath. "I guess you could say I didn't see eye to eye with the brass, and I knew it was a battle I couldn't win."

Now that sounded more like the Cain Dennison she remembered.

He lifted his face to the wind, narrowing his eyes. "Looks like the rain's about to pick up again."

She knew a dismissal when she heard one. Cain was done with the conversation.

As she started back up the incline to where she'd parked her truck, she thought over what he'd let slip during their brief encounter. He hadn't exactly been forthcoming, but at least he'd given her a place to start looking.

Renee had been seeing someone secretly, and Cain had known about it, even if he didn't know who. Which meant it was possible someone else knew something about Renee's clandestine affair as well, right?

But who?

Buckling herself in behind the steering wheel, she watched the woods, wondering if Cain would follow. Or did he plan to brave the rain that was already pelting her windshield with increasing fury in order to pay his respects to Renee?

When he didn't appear after a few minutes, she cranked the truck. But before she could change gears, her cell phone rang. Glancing at the display, she saw her mother's number.

She could imagine what her mother would have to say. She'd probably attended the memorial for Donnie, hoping to see Sara there, as well.

Bracing herself, she answered. "Hi, Mom."

Ann Dunkirk's voice held a hint of anxiety when she spoke. "Did you get caught in traffic? You didn't have an accident, did you?"

She closed her eyes, feeling guilty about giving her mother more to worry about. "No. No accident. I just decided to visit the memorial on Black Creek Road instead of going to the cemetery."

"Oh." Ann's pause extended so long that Sara almost began to squirm. "I wish you'd called Joyce Lindsey to let her know."

"I should've." Sara knew her mother was right. She didn't regret missing the memorial, but she shouldn't have been a coward about it. She should have let Joyce know her plans.

She just hadn't been up to dealing with the guilt she felt whenever she talked to Donnie's mother.

"You're still planning to come to dinner tonight? I'm making chicken chili."

Her stomach growled at the thought. "I'll be there."

"Be careful driving in the rain. And don't try to drive while talking on your cell phone."

"Yes, Mom."

As she ended the call and put her phone back in the pocket of her jacket, she saw Cain Dennison exiting the woods about twenty yards away from where she'd come out herself. His head lowered against the now-driving rain, he walked quickly toward a dark blue Ford F-150 parked along the shoulder a quarter mile down the road.

She watched until he'd climbed into the cab of the truck, curiosity keeping her still. There was something about the truck that seemed familiar, she realized. But what? What was tugging at her memory?

He pulled past her as he drove away. If he noticed her parked there off the road, he didn't give any sign. As she started to look away, a flash of red caught her attention. It was a bumper sticker attached to the back of the truck that read, "Never follow the advice on a bumper sticker."

Even as her lips started to curve in a smile, she remembered where she'd seen the truck before—parked at the scenic overlook above the spot where she and Donnie had missed the tight curve and gone down the gorge.

Her smile faded.

So, Cain Dennison had been at the same overlook where she'd parked her car. And now he turned up at Crybaby Falls at the same time she had.

Coincidence?

Not bloody likely.

Chapter Three

"I think her memory loss is genuine." Cain waved off Alexander Quinn's offer of a drink and took a seat in front of the big mahogany desk that occupied most of the back half of Quinn's office. Outside, rain and falling night obscured what would normally be a stunning view of the Smoky Mountains from the window where Quinn now stood, holding a tumbler with two fingers of bourbon in one hand as he gazed out at the gloom.

"Or perhaps she's a talented liar."

"Do you honestly think she'd have risked her own life in that accident in order to kill her husband? I was there at the scene before the paramedics arrived. I know how close she came to dying."

Quinn took a sip of the whiskey and grimaced. "I didn't say she tried to kill him. But she might be covering up what she remembers because she was culpable."

"I think not remembering makes her afraid she's at fault." Cain had spent most of the afternoon going back over his encounters with Sara Lindsey, from his first glimpse of her at the roadside memorial to their wary conversation at Crybaby Falls.

She was grieving, but she didn't like to show it. She was private and self-contained, but in her dark eyes he'd seen the ragged edges of her lingering pain. She missed her husband, grieved for him, but there had also been a hint of frustration in her tone when she'd spoken about his family, about Renee's death.

He knew from his preliminary investigation that Donnie Lindsey had become increasingly intent upon finding out who killed Renee. The passage of years had only intensified his determination, it seemed.

What kind of havoc could his focus on the past have created in his marriage to Sara? She had been a cop, just like Donnie, so she'd have known the odds were against finding the killer after so long. Had she tried to temper his thirst for closure?

Had it created problems between them?

"Is it possible the accident wasn't an accident?" Quinn asked after a few moments. "Whether or not the widow was involved?"

"If the sheriff's department thought it was anything but an accident, they'd have investigated." Cain hadn't been able to make any contacts inside the sheriff's department—a predictable outcome, given his dicey past relationship with Ridge County law enforcement. But everybody in Purgatory knew former Sheriff Will Toomey and Gary Lindsey had been friends since their own days at Purgatory High. If Toomey had even an inkling that the crash that had taken Donnie Lindsey's life was anything but a tragic accident, he'd have continued the investigation instead of accepting the official verdict of accidental death.

"So maybe it's time to set aside your investigation of the widow and start looking into the sister's death instead."

"You know my past with these people. I was a suspect in the murder for a while there, and I know there are folks around here who still aren't convinced I'm innocent."

Quinn shot him a narrow-eyed look. "*Are* you innocent?"

The question surprised him. "Why would you have

ever hired me if you didn't already know the answer to that question?"

Quinn's expression didn't change. "Why would you deflect my question?"

"I didn't kill Renee Lindsey." Cain pushed to his feet and started for the door. "And I don't work for people who play mind games with me."

Behind him, Quinn clapped his hands, slowly and deliberately. Heat rose into Cain's neck, making his ears burn with a toxic combination of humiliation and fury.

He turned slowly, battling both emotions, and made himself look at Quinn. "Is that your way of telling me to pack up my things and get out?"

Quinn picked up his glass of whiskey from where he'd set it on the windowsill. He took a long sip before he spoke. "If I had fired you, there would be no question of my intentions."

"You still want me on this case?" Cain tried to keep the desperation out of his voice, not wanting to reveal to Quinn just how badly he still wanted answers about Renee Lindsey's death. But he could tell from Quinn's expression that he hadn't succeeded. His boss at The Gates was a former CIA man with a long and colorful past in some of the world's most dangerous hot spots. Very little got past him.

"You have the capacity to be a good investigator," Quinn said in a tone that oozed reason and calm. "But you have to scrape that boulder-size chip off your shoulder. You tell me you're innocent, and I want to believe you, but you give off an air of guilt."

"I may not be a murderer, but I'm no Boy Scout."

"Your record in the Army was impressive. Your commanders spoke highly of your courage and skill."

"I'm not in the Army anymore."

"So you're only trustworthy in uniform? But once you step foot in Purgatory, you're nothing but trouble again?"

Cain frowned. "You know what I mean."

"And you know what I mean." Quinn finished off the whiskey and set the glass on his desk with a muted thud. "Did you know Seth Hammond spent over a decade as a con artist? Or that Sutton Calhoun used to steal food from the greengrocer over in Bitterwood when he was growing up? Hell, Sinclair Solano joined a terrorist group and spent five years on the FBI's most wanted list."

Quinn was speaking of men he'd hired at The Gates, Cain knew, men who were now vital members of his investigative team. Cain released a long, defeated sigh.

"What have you done to rival any of those things?" Quinn asked pointedly.

"I killed my mama and my twin brother just by bein' born," he answered bitterly. "Nobody in Purgatory's going to give me the time of day. They think they see too much of my daddy in me. And, hell, maybe there's something to that."

"You had no agency in what happened to your mother or your brother at the time of your birth," Quinn said bluntly, "no matter what your bastard of a father might have told you. And *you* have control over whether or not you behave as your father did. You're not a child. Stop thinking like one."

He never should have come back to Purgatory, Cain thought. He'd had a life in Atlanta, working construction. Making decent money doing honest work. Nobody there knew about his past, about his father or his own failings.

He didn't let anyone get too close, of course, but his track record with friendships hadn't exactly been great, anyway. He didn't mind being alone.

He was used to it.

"Think about what I said," Quinn said after a long, tense silence. "If you still want out of the job, I'll see that you get back to Atlanta."

"But don't expect a reference?"

Quinn shrugged. "There are some things even I won't lie about." He turned back to the window, his posture a clear sign of dismissal.

Cain left the office and wandered down the short corridor into the large communal office shared by Quinn's agents. Even after the official closing time, there were still a few agents at work. He spotted Sinclair Solano sitting on the edge of Ava Trent's desk, his dark head bent low as they conversed in quiet tones. Sinclair looked up and nodded a greeting before he turned his attention back to the other agent.

There was something going on with those two, Cain thought, although they made an effort to keep it under wraps at work.

The new hire was still here, too. Nick Darcy. Guy had a British accent, despite being one-hundred-percent genuine American. At first, Cain had figured he was putting on airs or something, until he learned Darcy had grown up in London because his dad had been the U.S. ambassador to Great Britain. Darcy himself had worked for the State Department, in Diplomatic Security. Cain had no idea, however, why he'd left that job behind to work for The Gates.

Alexander Quinn had put together quite the motley crew. Cain just didn't know where he was supposed to fit.

"Cain Dennison's back in town." Sara watched for her father's reaction to her casual remark. Carl Dunkirk had been a good cop, with a good cop's poker face, but she'd figured out his tells a long time ago.

He leaned back in the kitchen chair across the table from hers. The corner of his left eye twitched, even as he adopted a tone of nonchalant surprise. "Really?"

"But you already knew that."

Her father's lips quirked. "You've gotten too big for your britches, young lady."

She grinned at him, the sensation strangely alien, as if her muscles weren't accustomed to stretching that way. "So, what's his deal?" she asked, giving her own poker face a workout. "Why's he back in town?"

"How'd you know he was back?" Carl asked, ignoring her question. She wasn't the only good investigator in the family.

"Ran into him," she said vaguely.

"Where?"

She supposed it was too late to back out of this conversation now that she'd started it. She glanced toward the stove, where her mother stood stirring her famous homemade chicken chili in a stew pot. "I went to Crybaby Falls," she said in a hushed tone. "He showed up."

Her father's eyebrows joined over the bridge of his nose. "You went there by yourself?"

"I'm a cop, Dad. I was armed, and as far as I could tell, he wasn't."

"You know your father's just going to tell me what you two are whispering about later," her mother said from the stove.

Sara arched an eyebrow at her father. He shrugged.

"Tomorrow's the eighteenth anniversary of her death. I guess Dennison went there for the same reason I did."

"You went to Crybaby Falls?" Ann Dunkirk turned from the stove and gave her a curious look.

"She ran into Dennison there," her father said, shooting Sara a look that was part apology, part resignation.

"Really? I didn't know he was back in town."

"Y'all don't exactly run in the same circles," Sara said.

"I don't think Dennison ever had a circle," Carl said in a flat tone Sara recognized from her teenage years. Apparently his assessment of Cain Dennison hadn't mellowed a bit in the intervening years. "He was too much like his daddy that way. Anybody with sense steered clear of the boy."

"Renee didn't."

Her father just looked at her. She supposed his opinion of Renee's judgment wasn't something he planned to speak aloud. She'd heard it years ago, anyway, listening to her parents' conversation shortly after the murder.

"I told Gary Lindsey the girl was heading for grief," her father had murmured, not realizing Sara was sitting on the stairs around the corner, feeling queasy and unsettled by the news about Donnie's sister. "The Dennison boy has never been anything but trouble, and he's been sniffing around her for months. Gary should've done something."

"Done what?" Ann had asked, her voice gentle the way it always was when she was trying to talk her husband through what she called "the valley of the shadow"—the gut-burning stress that came from dealing with death and depravity on a constant basis.

"Locked her up until she was thirty," her father had growled with a burst of anger. "Had the boy arrested."

"On what grounds?" Her mother had tried to walk the line between sympathy and rationality when dealing with her father's bleak moods. Most of the time she succeeded.

That time, not so much.

"Stalking. Harassment. Statutory rape."

"She was nearly eighteen, Carl. And nobody knew she was pregnant."

"All I could think was, what if it had been Sara?" Her father had broken down then, the sound of his harsh sobs sending chills up Sara's spine. She'd sneaked back upstairs to her bedroom and curled up under the bedcovers, shaken to the core, as much by her father's reaction to Renee Lindsey's death as by the murder itself.

"You still think he did it, don't you?" she asked her father.

Over her father's shoulder, Ann Dunkirk gave her daughter a warning look. Apparently the Renee Lindsey murder was still a volatile subject in the Dunkirk household, all these years later.

"I don't know," Carl answered after a pause. "He was always the most likely suspect."

"Even though he wasn't the baby's father?"

"That might have been the motive." Carl scraped his empty coffee cup in a small circle across the table in front of him. "Maybe she told him about the baby and he killed her in a jealous rage."

"Did you know he was in the Army?"

Carl shot her a skeptical look. "He tell you that?"

She nodded. "You think it's a lie?"

"Hard to imagine that wild buck making it through boot camp."

"The military can sometimes straighten a person out."

"Sometimes. If he wants to change."

Sara put her hand on her father's cup, stopping him from scraping it across the table again. "He struck me as different from the man I remembered."

"Apparently he's been trying to talk to some folks at the sheriff's department about Donnie's accident."

Sara tried not to react, but she could see by the narrowing of her father's eyes that she'd failed. Her mother stopped stirring the chili and turned to face them again.

"Why would he be looking into Donnie's accident?" she asked.

"He was first on the scene, remember?" Sara murmured. She didn't actually remember seeing him; she didn't remember anything about the accident, really. But she'd heard what Cain had done to save her life.

And she'd never even told him thanks.

"You're not entirely surprised to hear that Dennison's

been asking questions, are you?" Carl asked bluntly. "What do you know?"

She sighed and pushed the coffee cup back toward him. "Before I went to Crybaby Falls, I went to the roadside memorial Joyce maintains for Donnie on Black Creek Road."

"She went there instead of the cemetery," her mother told her father before turning her gentle, dark eyes toward Sara. "I called Joyce after we talked earlier. To let her know where you'd been."

Sara felt a flutter of guilt. "I should have called her myself."

"I tried to explain to Joyce that you deal with your grief in private ways. You always have."

"Joyce wasn't happy, I guess."

"Joyce hasn't been happy in eighteen years," Carl said bluntly. "And she never liked that you and Donnie got married."

It was nothing she didn't know already, of course, but hearing her father say the words out loud stung more than she'd anticipated. "Yeah, well. Back to what happened when I went to the roadside memorial—to get there, you can either park on the shoulder, which is practically nonexistent on Black Creek Road at that point, or you can park at the scenic overlook up the mountain and walk back down to the curve. Which I did. When I got back to the scenic overlook, I noticed a truck with a humorous red bumper sticker as I was leaving. Didn't think anything about it, until I saw Cain Dennison driving away from Crybaby Falls in that same truck."

Her father's forehead crinkled. "So you think he followed you to the roadside memorial, then to Crybaby Falls, too?"

"Hell of a coincidence if he didn't."

"Language, Sara," her mother said automatically, then shot her an apologetic grin.

Sara smiled back, though inside, her guts were twisting a little at the news that Dennison had been asking questions about Donnie's death.

Why would he do that? Asking about Renee's murder, she could get, but why Donnie's death? Was he somehow invested in the answers because he was the one who'd found them after the accident? Maybe he felt a sense of responsibility, as if he owed it to Donnie, somehow, to get the answers nobody had seemed able to provide.

"He's working at that new private eye place that's opened in the old mansion on Magnolia Street," Carl said. "The Gates, I think they call it."

"Odd name," Ann commented.

"I think it's probably a play on the whole 'gates of purgatory' thing," Carl said.

"Someone opened a detective agency in Purgatory?" Sara asked, surprised. "How do they get enough business to keep the doors open in a little place like this?"

"Oh," Ann said suddenly, turning to look at them. "I wonder if that's what Joyce was talking about today at the cemetery."

"What did she say?" Carl asked.

"Well, I was telling her how sorry I was about all she and Gary have gone through, losing both their children, and she said something like, she hadn't been able to prevent what had happened to them, but she'd do anything, pay anything, to get the answers about their deaths." Ann slanted a troubled look at Sara. "I didn't want to argue with her about Donnie's accident, but she has to know that's what it was. An accident."

"Mom, I don't blame her for wanting answers. I'd like a few myself. Like why we were even in Purgatory that night to begin with."

"You think maybe she's hired The Gates to look into Donnie's accident?" Sara's father looked thoughtful.

"Well, you said the Dennison boy is working at The Gates, and you said he's asking questions about Donnie's accident. Maybe those things are connected."

"Who on earth would hire Cain Dennison as an investigator?" Sara asked. "I mean, even if he was in the Army and all that, he's still got a pretty sketchy background for private-eye work, doesn't he?"

"From what I hear, the fellow running the place has taken on more than one hire with a checkered past. Heard of a fellow named Seth Hammond from over Bitterwood way?"

The name sounded familiar. "Meth mechanic or something like that?"

"No, that was his daddy, Delbert, who blew himself up about twenty years ago. You might have remembered the name from that. Seth, on the other hand, made quite a name for himself as a con artist before he supposedly went on the straight and narrow."

"Hell of a chance to take, hiring a retired con man as a private eye."

"You think *that's* something, apparently he's also just hired Sinclair Solano."

"That hippie boy from California who became a terrorist?" her mother asked, her eyes widening.

"Actually, he spent most of the time he was on the FBI's most wanted list working for the CIA as a double agent," Sara corrected. The story of the radical turned spy had made every major daily newspaper in the country when the truth had come out about a month ago.

"I guess the CIA connection might explain that hire, then," Carl said. "I hear the guy who runs The Gates is a former spook."

Sara glanced at her watch. It was a quarter past six—any chance there was anybody still answering the phone at The Gates?

Her father's sharp-eyed gaze met hers. "What are you thinking?"

She pulled her cell phone from her pocket. "I'm thinking that if Joyce really did hire The Gates to look into Donnie's accident, someone there might want to talk to the only person who made it out of that wreck alive."

Chapter Four

Sinclair Solano and Ava Trent had left separately ten minutes ago, as if they thought they were fooling anyone. Nick Darcy was still here, on the phone at the other end of the communal office. Cain sat at his own desk, trying to come up with a new reason not to go home, if you could call the rented Airstream he'd parked by his grandmother's cabin a home.

His grandmother, Lila Birdsong, had offered to let him stay with her, but she'd taken in enough strays this month. Her current boarders were a couple of Cherokee girls whose alcoholic parents had arranged for the girls to stay with Lila to avoid the state taking them into custody while their folks went through court-mandated rehab. Lila was a distant cousin, according to all parties involved, though Cain had his doubts. Over the years, his generous grandmother had seemed to find more than her share of distant relatives in need.

And not-so-distant ones, he thought with fondness. If it hadn't been for Lila, he doubted he'd have survived to adulthood in his father's custody.

The phone rang. Darcy looked up from his own call, lifting his dark eyebrows at Cain. The number on the display wasn't a local one, and Cain considered letting the answering service pick up, since office hours were, technically, over.

But what the hell—he could use a distraction from his own gloomy thoughts. He picked up the receiver. "The Gates. Dennison speaking."

"So. You really do work there."

His hand clenched around the receiver as he recognized Sara Lindsey's soft voice. "Been doing a little detecting of your own?"

"You were in the woods, watching me at the roadside memorial, weren't you?"

How had she figured that out? "You going to have me arrested for stalking or something?"

"Don't tempt me."

"How'd you get this number?"

"My father. You know him. Used to be a sheriff's department investigator. Tried to send you to jail more than once."

"Yeah, your daddy and I go way back."

"Did Joyce Lindsey hire you to investigate Donnie's accident?" She sounded as if she didn't believe it was true, even as she asked the question.

"I can't comment on agency clients," he answered carefully.

"Which means yes." There was a long pause on the other end of the line, making him wonder if she'd hung up on him. But a moment later, she added, "I can't believe she hired *you,* of all people."

He didn't respond. Anything he said would break a company rule.

"But she didn't, did she?" Sara added, realization coloring her voice. "She hired the agency. She didn't know you'd be the person they'd send out to investigate."

Well, he thought. *That didn't take long.* If only he hadn't gone to Crybaby Falls…

"Does Joyce think I did something to cause the accident?"

The hint of vulnerability in Sara's voice caught him by surprise. What could he tell her? Anything he said at this point would be a breach of confidentiality.

"Oh, right," she said when he didn't respond. "You can't comment on clients."

"Detective Lindsey—"

"Mrs. Lindsey," she reminded him. "Not a cop anymore, remember?"

He closed his eyes. "I don't have any reason to think you did anything to cause the accident. It was a hairpin turn at night. Anything could have happened—maybe you swerved to miss a deer or a raccoon—"

"I've gone over the police reports on the accident. There's nothing to suggest I swerved. It was like I went straight over the edge without stopping."

"Mrs. Lindsey—"

"Oh, for pity's sake, just call me Sara. Mrs. Lindsey is my mother-in-law." Her voice came out in a frustrated growl that made him smile despite the knot of tension in his stomach. "Speaking of Joyce, what are you going to do when it finally gets back to her that you're the agent doing the investigating?"

"That won't be a situation for me to deal with," he answered carefully.

"Have you found out why Donnie and I were in Purgatory the night of the crash?" she asked.

"No. If you saw anyone that day, nobody's saying."

There was a long pause on the other end of the line before she spoke in a quiet tone. "That's a mystery itself, isn't it? Why would we come to town and not see anyone who knows us?"

"What's the last thing you do remember, before the accident?"

Once again, the other end of the line went quiet.

"Sara?" he prodded, wondering if the call had disconnected.

"I'm not at liberty to share the details of my investigation with you," she answered primly, although he thought he heard a hint of payback in her careful tone.

He stifled a smile. "Fair enough."

"If you want to ask me questions, next time just ask me straight out," she added. "Instead of playing games."

"I thought I did just ask you straight out."

"Good night, Mr. Dennison."

"Cain," he corrected, but she'd already disconnected.

With a sigh, he hung up the phone and looked up to find Nick Darcy watching him curiously.

"You're working rather late," Darcy commented. His odd British-tinged accent made the corner of Cain's mouth twitch.

"Yes, rather," he agreed, unable to resist mimicking Darcy's accent.

One of Darcy's eyebrows notched upward, but that was his only reaction to the touch of mockery, and Cain immediately felt like a heel.

"Sorry," Cain said. "I can be an ass."

Darcy's lips curved slightly. "Indeed."

Cain laughed. "You headed home?"

"Thought I'd have a bite to eat first. You?"

"Not sure."

"I wouldn't mind company," Darcy added as he shrugged on his jacket. Unlike most of the other agents at The Gates, who dressed for comfort and mobility, Darcy dressed like a businessman. Or, more aptly, Cain supposed, he dressed like the State Department employee he used to be.

Cain watched through narrowed eyes as Darcy straightened what looked like a very expensive silk tie, wondering how to respond to the invitation. Did he have an ulterior motive for asking Cain to join him? Was he gay and looking for romance?

Darcy seemed to read his mind. "I'm neither gay nor working any sort of agenda. I simply tire of eating alone in public. In a town such as this, a man dining alone provides an opportunity to stare and whisper without compunction."

"It might be your choice of vocabulary," Cain suggested, grabbing his own well-worn leather jacket and nodding toward the exit. "Remind me to teach you a little redneck, Jeeves."

A town the size of Purgatory, Tennessee, offered few sit-down restaurants to choose from even during regular dining hours. After seven, the choices dwindled to two—the steakhouse on Darlington Road near the old marble quarry and a Lebanese restaurant that had opened since the last time Cain had been in town. He was inclined to go for the steak, but of course, Darcy headed straight for the brightly lit storefront of the Lebanese place, where photos of the old country filled the window display, interspersed with wrapped packages of pita bread, jars of spiced almonds and sticky triangles of baklava providing a mouthwatering visual temptation. The restaurant name—Tabbouleh Garden—gleamed in bright teal neon over the door.

"Ever been here?" Darcy asked as they entered.

"No," Cain admitted. "I've eaten plenty of Middle Eastern food in my time, though."

"Right. You were in the Army, I believe?"

"Yes."

"Afghanistan?"

"And Iraq and Kaziristan before that."

Darcy's eyebrows rose at the mention of Kaziristan. "Before or after the embassy siege?"

"After. You?"

Darcy's expression went dark. "During."

Cain grimaced. The embassy siege in Kaziristan had been a nasty, brutal business. "Diplomatic Security?"

Darcy nodded, looking relieved when a pretty, dark-eyed waitress came to seat them and take their drink order. She looked Lebanese, but her accent came out in a pure Tennessee mountain twang. "Here's your menu," she said with a friendly smile. "What'll y'all have to drink?"

Cain ordered sweet tea, while Darcy asked for water with lemon. "I'm afraid my taste for tea is rather English. I can't accustom myself to the Dixie version."

"No worries," Cain said, stifling a grin. "Though you might not want to call it the Dixie version. The word comes out a little sneering in your fancy accent."

"Dreadfully sorry," Darcy said, and Cain could tell by the glitter in his eyes that he was laying on the accent extra thick.

"You're a wicked bloke, aren't you?" Cain murmured.

"I'm told I have my moments," Darcy concurred.

"So why'd you give up all those fancy State Department perks to come down here to hillbilly country?" Cain asked a few moments later, after the waitress brought them their drinks and took their food orders.

"Why did *you* come back?" Darcy countered.

Before he could formulate an answer, Cain heard a woman's voice call his name. For a second, he thought it was Sara, but when the woman spoke again, he realized the tone was all wrong. Tamping down an unexpected ripple of disappointment, he followed the sound of the voice until he spotted an attractive, slightly plump blonde sitting a couple of tables away. As his gaze met hers, she blushed prettily and smiled.

He excused himself and crossed to her table, knowing he should recognize her. She looked familiar, but it had been a long while since he'd spent much time in town.

"You probably don't remember me—you were a few grades ahead. Kelly Partlow. Well, I was Kelly Denton in high school."

He placed her then. Flute player in the marching band. A freshman to his senior. He'd known her older brother, Keith, better, since several of their high school teachers had insisted on alphabetical seating. Cain and Keith had often been seated either side by side or one in front of the other.

"Right," he said aloud. "Keith Denton's little sister."

She grinned. "Haven't been called that in, oh, ten minutes. How're you doing? I didn't realize you were back in town."

He could tell she was lying about that. He had a feeling everybody and his brother probably knew Cain was back in Purgatory by now. Not much got past the gossipmongers in a small town.

"Just been back a couple of weeks," he said, searching his memory for what else he could recall about Keith Denton's sister besides her flute-playing. "So, you got married?"

She smiled. "Thirteen years ago now, can you believe? I married Josh Partlow—you remember him, don't you? He and Keith hung around together all the time back in school."

Cain had a vague memory of a football player with a wicked sense of humor, but he hadn't exactly hung out with the jocks during his years at Purgatory High.

At his glance at the empty seat across from her, she smiled. "He's outside, talking to some client on his cell phone. He says he hates people who talk on phones in restaurants, but his solution is to spend most of the time at a restaurant outside talking on his phone." She rolled her eyes, though he could tell she wasn't really upset. "He's a lawyer now. Can you believe it?"

He hadn't really known Josh Partlow well enough to know whether a career in law was something he should find astonishing. "Good for him. It's really good to see you, Kelly, but I should get back to my friend—"

"Oh, of course." She blushed again, and he got a glimpse of the cute little teenager she'd once been. "Listen, the reason I hollered at you like a crazy woman is to tell you Purgatory High alumni are holding a get-together this weekend at Smokehouse Grill—you know, that steakhouse out near the quarry?"

"Right," he said, trying not to grimace. A high-school alumni get-together? That had to be one of the lower levels of hell.

"Anyway, if you think you'll still be around this weekend, you should come. Saturday, six-thirty to whenever. We've reserved one of the private rooms at the back of the restaurant, and it's always so much fun to catch up with what everyone else is up to."

"Yeah, sounds great," he lied. "I don't know if I'll be able to make it, but if I can—"

"Oh, do try! It would be such a fun surprise, since you've been away from Purgatory for so long!" She seemed sincere enough, but he could tell from the little sparkle in her eyes that she wasn't unaware of what a stir his presence at the reunion might cause. He hadn't exactly left Purgatory High on good terms, especially since he'd made his escape not long after Renee's death, while a whole lot of folks still wondered if he'd been the culprit.

"I'll see," he answered, keeping his tone noncommittal. "Nice to see you again, Kelly." He made his escape back to the table, where he found Darcy watching him with a look of bemusement. "Small towns," he murmured. "Everybody knows everybody."

"She's rather cute."

"She's rather married."

"She's sitting rather alone in a restaurant, making eyes at you."

"Not because she's looking to cheat on her husband, I assure you." Cain was spared having to continue the conversation by the arrival of their orders. He dug into his falafel plate, relieved that Darcy didn't seem inclined to ask any more questions.

Still, he found his thoughts going back to Kelly Partlow's invitation. If he were behaving like the professional investigator he was supposed to be, the invitation to the high-school get-together would offer an unexpected opportunity to dig around a little more into Renee Lindsey's past. He hadn't been her only friend, after all. She'd had girlfriends, too, hadn't she? And, obviously, the secret lover who'd fathered her child.

The mystery man might be there on Saturday. Any investigator worth his salt would go to the get-together and try to figure out who it might be.

But the thought of revisiting his teenage years was enough to make Cain want to flee town at the earliest opportunity.

"YOU'LL NEVER GUESS who I saw at Tabbouleh Garden!" The voice on the other end of Sara's phone didn't bother to introduce herself, but she knew the voice almost as well as she knew her own. Kelly Partlow was one of the few old friends from her Purgatory days who still stayed in touch, mostly because her husband's legal career had occasionally brought him down to Birmingham on business. Between pregnancies, Kelly often accompanied him, joking that a business trip was as close to a vacation as she was likely to get between her workaholic husband and her three rowdy children.

"What is Tabbouleh Garden?" Sara countered.

"It's a new Lebanese place in town. I thought I told you about that in one of my emails."

She probably had, Sara thought. "Who did you see?"

As soon as she asked the question, she knew the answer. Kelly's excited squeal merely confirmed it. "Cain freakin' Dennison! Can you believe he came back to town? It's all anyone can talk about."

"I'll bet." Sara closed her eyes, leaning her head back against the hard oak headboard of her grandparents' four-poster bed. She'd declined her parents' invitation to stay with them in town, since she'd ostensibly come back to Purgatory in order to figure out what to do with the lovely old mountain cabin her grandfather had left her in his will.

"He was eating dinner with one of those guys who work at The Gates—you know, that detective agency that's opened in the old Buckley Mansion on Magnolia." Kelly released a soft gasp. "Oh, wow, do you think he might work there, too? Cain Dennison, a detective! Oh, my word, now I really hope he shows up!"

"Shows up?" Sara grinned as Kelly's chatter reminded her, once again, just how hard it had always been to keep up with her friend's frenetic mental gymnastics. "Shows up where?"

"Oh, I haven't even told you that! We're having a get-together this weekend. Anybody and everybody who attended Purgatory High. We all hooked up on Facebook a while back and now we do these get-togethers every couple of months. It's a ton of fun!"

For someone like Kelly, maybe, Sara thought. But her friend had always been more of a social butterfly than Sara had. "I'm not sure I'm up for a high-school reunion, Kel."

"Oh, Sara, don't say that! It really is a lot of fun. Not like high school at all. And so many people ask about you, all the time. Couldn't you do it, just for me? This Saturday, six-thirty, at the Smokehouse Grill."

Sara tamped down a shudder as she pictured what a night with her old schoolmates might entail. Still, she hadn't seen Kelly face-to-face in a long time. Since just after she went back to Birmingham after she got out of the hospital, she realized with a start.

She really had hibernated from life for the past three years, hadn't she?

"Just promise you'll think about it," Kelly wheedled.

"I promise I'll think about it," she said.

And she did think about it, an hour later, after she and Kelly got off the phone. Apparently she'd become quite the hermit since Donnie's death, if her parents' not-so-subtle hints at dinner earlier were anything to go by. What could it hurt to drop by, see some of the old gang? If it became too unbearable, she had a car and knew how to drive herself home, right?

She pulled up the calendar on her phone and punched in the time and date before she lost her resolve.

THE EARLIER RAIN had passed through by the time Cain reached his grandmother's place up on Mulberry Rise just below Miller's Knob. Despite the cool night, he wasn't surprised to find Lila Birdsong sitting on the crude wooden front stoop of his Airstream trailer, a colorful crocheted shawl wrapped around her lean, aging body.

His grandmother always seemed to know when he needed someone to talk to, even before he realized it himself.

She scooted over to make room for him on the stoop. "You're later than usual. Long day at the office?" She grinned a little as she said it, her strong white teeth shining in the moon glow filtering through the trees overhead. She knew how odd it was for him to be working in an office setting, even one as atypical as The Gates.

"I went with a colleague to grab dinner. We tried that new Lebanese place in town. I'll take you out there soon. Let you try the baba ghanoush."

"I'll wash your mouth out with soap, young man," she teased.

He grinned back at her, already feeling better. "Where are the girls?" he asked, referring to Mia and Charlotte Burdette, the two girls Lila had recently taken in to care for while their parents were working out their problems in rehab.

"They finished up their homework early, so I let them have the TV remote. I think they're watchin' some singing show." Lila made a face. "I'm too soft."

"You're just right." He kissed her on the temple, making her chuckle. Pulling away, he added, "At the restaurant, I ran into someone I used to go to school with. Well, mostly I knew her older brother. She was a few years behind me." He nudged his grandmother's shoulder with his own. "And before you ask, she's already married."

"Did I ask?" Lila asked, the picture of innocence.

"You were about to."

"She remembered you?"

"I was pretty notorious there for a while, Gran."

She squeezed his knee. "Was she mean to you?"

He smiled again. "No, actually, she was very kind. Rather charming, really, in a slightly scattered way. She invited me to some get-together she and some other Purgatory High alumni have started holding regularly. This Saturday night at the steak place over near the quarry."

"You goin', then?"

He shook his head. "Not a good idea."

"I think it's a real good idea," Lila disagreed. "You're too much a loner, Cain. It ain't good for your soul."

"Gran—"

"How long you gonna let your daddy call the shots in your life? He's been gone a long spell now. Let him go."

He grimaced. "Believe me, I've made my peace with the man."

"Have you now?" Lila pushed to her feet with remarkable agility, as lithe as she'd been thirty years ago. She turned and caught his chin in her hand. "Go to the party. Look at it like takin' medicine. Try the first dose, see if it helps. If it don't, you can skip the second dose." She dropped a kiss on top of his head and walked silently back to her house.

Cain watched her go, his chest tight with the conflict warring inside him. He knew, gut deep, that the party would probably be a disaster if he showed up. But his grandmother was right. He'd spent way too much time alone recently. It *wasn't* good for his soul.

And, if he wanted to look at the idea more pragmatically, going to the party would be a prime opportunity to pick the brains of a few former classmates about what they remembered of Renee Lindsey's last months and days.

Maybe someone at the party knew something he or she had never told anyone before. Maybe the killer himself would be at the party.

There was only one way to find out for sure.

With a sigh, he pulled out his cell phone and put a note in his calendar. *Saturday, six-thirty, Smokehouse Grill.* He closed the phone and stuck it back in his pocket, gazing up at the bright moon overhead.

Look out, Purgatory High, he thought with a grimace of a smile. *The Monster of Ridge County is back in town.*

Chapter Five

Sara spent the days leading up to the high-school get-together cleaning out her grandfather's old cabin and trying to assess whether she'd be able to get a decent price on the real-estate market. The location was secluded, which could be both a plus and a minus. But the cabin's bones were solid, the need for structural repairs less urgent than Sara had feared, and the charm of the old place had already started working on her, tempting her to stick around Purgatory rather than start looking at bigger cities for employment.

"I still have a little pull in the sheriff's department," her father had reminded her that morning when he'd dropped by to see how the clean-up was going. "If you're serious about looking for work here, that is."

Was she serious? She'd fled Birmingham because the ghost of Donnie was everywhere she looked. How could Purgatory be any better? She'd met Donnie here, fallen in love with him here, married him here. His parents still lived in town. Many of his old friends were still around, guys he'd played baseball with, friends he and Sara had shared in common.

His grave was here. The roadside memorial was here. There'd be no escaping his memory in Purgatory, Tennessee.

But maybe that was a good thing. Maybe she'd been

spending too much of her time and energy trying to escape his memory rather than facing the loss and dealing with it.

She thought about Cain Dennison, eighteen years past Renee Lindsey's murder, still visiting the scene of the crime and looking as haunted as if her body had been found that morning.

She didn't want to be that person fifteen years from now, the one who couldn't let go and move on. She was going to go to the party tonight, renew a few old friendships and enjoy herself for the first time in three years.

The evening temperatures had begun to plunge as fall swallowed up summer in big, gulping bites of cold air rolling into the hills from the north, so she grabbed an ice-blue cardigan on her way out to cover the short-sleeved brown dress she'd selected for the evening out. Flats for her feet, of course, not just because she was tall but because her calf muscles had already had their workout for the day, thanks to all the sweeping and mopping.

She arrived at the Smokehouse Grill a few minutes late. The red-haired restaurant hostess directed her toward a large private room at the back of the restaurant and, with a smile, warned her it was a rowdy crowd tonight.

She tried to slip into the room unnoticed, but she'd been away from Purgatory so long that her reappearance was enough to elicit shouts of greeting, excited hugs and even a kiss from Logan Miles, one of Donnie's old pals from his varsity baseball team.

"I swear, you don't look like you've aged a day since high school," Logan said with a sheepish grin as his wife gave him a mostly good-humored punch to the arm.

Sara knew better than to believe him, of course, but when she looked around the room at some of her former classmates, now more than a decade older and many married with children, like Kelly and Josh Partlow, she realized that in some ways, a part of her life had been on hold for a long time.

She and Donnie had discussed children, of course, but they were both working for the police force in Birmingham and parenthood had seemed like something they could defer until they were better established in their careers. Then Donnie had started becoming more and more obsessed with his sister's murder the longer it remained unsolved, and the thought of starting a family became such a distant, unrealistic notion that they'd stopped talking about having children at all.

Now he was gone. There'd be no children. No possibility of restarting the clock and moving forward together into the life they should have had.

"Sara!" Kelly Partlow finally wriggled her way through the crowd to reach her side and give her a fierce hug of greeting. "You came!"

"I came," Sara said with a smile and a nod, pushing her bleaker thoughts to the back of her mind. She'd come here to look forward, not back.

Josh Partlow trailed up behind his wife and smiled at Sara. "Hey there, Dunkirk. Lookin' good."

Sara gave him a light punch on the shoulder, wishing he wasn't eyeing her as if he expected her to self-destruct any second. "Back at you, hotshot. Wow, big crowd."

"Well, I might have let it slip that I'd talked to Cain Dennison about the get-together, and he didn't come right out and say no to coming." Kelly shot Sara a smile that was part sheepish, part naughty.

"You convinced people there's actually a chance he'll show up to a high-school get-together?" Sara arched her eyebrows at her old friend. "Wow, you should sell beachfront property in Kansas or something."

"It could happen," Kelly defended, hooking her hand through Sara's arm and guiding her toward the back of the room where a small buffet of appetizers had been set up by the restaurant. "Oh, by the way, there are a few teachers and other staffers who show up for these things now and then—Mrs. Murphy has been a few times, and Coach Allen and Mrs. Petrelli—so if you have an overdue book from the school library or an uncompleted detention, be warned."

"I'm good," Sara said with a smile, a little overwhelmed by Kelly's chatter but already enjoying herself more than she expected.

"Yeah, you always were the teacher's pet, weren't you?" Kelly made a face. "I don't know how we became friends. I swear, I was your polar opposite in high school!"

"Opposites attract?"

Kelly's attention fixed on something across the room. "So they say."

Sara followed her gaze and spotted a tall, good-looking man in his early forties standing next to a slim, pretty woman with neatly styled blond hair and big blue eyes. "Wow, Coach Allen. Has he even aged?"

Kelly made a face. "And his wife, Becky. We all hate her."

"We hate her?" Sara hadn't known the coach or his wife well, but Becky Allen had always seemed nice enough.

"She hasn't aged, either," Kelly said with an exaggerated sigh. "And she's married to that hunk of a baseball coach we all had crushes on in high school. Lucky b—"

"Sheath those claws, gorgeous." Josh joined them, handing Kelly a glass of wine. "Anything for you, Sara?"

She shook her head. "I'll grab a glass of tea in a minute."

"This is *so* not the place to catch up on everything," Kelly said, sipping her wine, "but we're going to have a sit-down soon, right? You've been gone forever and I want to hear everything about what you're doing now."

"Won't need a sit-down for that," Sara said with a rueful

smile. "I've left the Birmingham P.D. and sold my house in Alabama. So, basically, all I'm doing right now is trying to figure out what's next."

Kelly's eyes widened. "Why did you not tell me this?"

Sara shrugged. "Well, I looked for an 'I just quit my job and uprooted my life' card I could stick in the mail to announce it to my friends, but the Hallmark store was fresh out."

"Are you staying with your folks?" Kelly's eyes widened so much that Sara feared she was about to do herself harm. "Do you need a place to stay? Josh and I can totally make room—"

"Kelly, you have three kids, five dogs, six cats and four goats. Where on earth would I stay?"

"Five goats. One of them was a girl and we didn't realize it," Josh interjected. At Sara's quizzical look, he shrugged. "Look, it had long hair and I don't exactly go around examining goat privates as a rule."

Sara laughed. "Well, as much as I appreciate the offer, I'm staying in my grandfather's cabin up on Sandler Ridge while I clean it out and decide what to do with it. He left it to me when he died last year."

"Is it falling apart?"

"No, actually it's in better shape than I thought—"

"Sara?" A masculine voice interrupted her midthought. She turned to find Jim Allen and his wife standing behind her, both giving her the "How're you holding up?" expression she was beginning to grow sick of seeing on the faces of old friends and acquaintances. "Jim Allen. I don't know if you remember me—"

"Of course, I remember." She made herself smile. "Donnie's favorite coach." Turning to the pretty blonde beside him, she nodded a greeting. "Hi, Mrs. Allen."

"Becky," she said with a laugh. "I'm reaching the age where hearing other grown-ups call me Mrs. Allen is very bad for my ego." She extended a slim, well-manicured hand that made Sara glad she'd taken time to buff the rough edges of her own work-chipped fingernails before coming to the party.

She shook Becky's hand. "Big crowd tonight, huh?"

Jim laughed. "Not a whole hell of a lot else to do in Purgatory, Tennessee, on a Saturday night."

"Good thing the Vols have a bye week," Josh interjected with a grin. "Hi, Coach. Becky."

"Oh, honey, the organizers of these shindigs have some sort of spy in the Tennessee football program if you ask me," Kelly added with a laugh, giving Becky Allen a friendly hug. "They always manage to work these get-togethers around the ball game start times in the fall."

Next to her, Josh gave a sudden start, his gaze directed toward the entrance of the private room. Even as he reached into his pocket and pulled out his wallet, a flutter of gasps filtered through from the front of the room. On the heels of the quiet expressions of surprise, conversation in the room went from a deafening buzz to almost complete silence.

"Well, hell, Kelly," Josh murmured, pulling a twenty from his wallet. "You win."

Following his gaze, Sara saw what had shocked the crowd to silence.

Cain Dennison stood in the doorway, looking like a rabbit in a snare.

OF ALL THE bad ideas he'd ever had, and he'd had some doozies in his day, coming to the Purgatory High School alumni get-together had to be near the top of the list. Everybody in the whole damn room was staring at him as if he was wearing the skins of murder victims instead of his best pair of pants, an honest-to-goodness button-down shirt and a brown leather jacket. His hair needed cutting, he supposed, but he'd combed it neatly enough.

He'd even shaved.

As the stunned silence stretched on well past the point of comfort, he thought about saying, "Wrong room," and heading back out the way he came. But just as he started to open his mouth, a tall, dark-haired woman in a curve-hugging brown dress stepped forward and shot him a quiz-zical look as she extended her hand in greeting. It took a second to realize the brunette bombshell was Sara Lindsey, all dressed up and looking like pure temptation.

Her shoulder-length bob of hair framed her face in soft, tousled curls, and tonight, some of the color was back in her cheeks. Her dress skimmed her body like a caress, with a skirt that swirled in tantalizing sweeps around her well-toned thighs. Beneath the skirt, the rest of her legs seemed to stretch for miles, ending in a pair of simple flat shoes that should have looked plain. On her, they looked sexy as hell.

Her dark eyes crackled with energy as she dared him to shake her hand.

He took her hand, felt the slightly roughened texture of her palm against his, and felt as if the whole world had dropped from beneath his feet.

"Good thing I'm not a gambling woman," Sara mur-mured as he reluctantly released her hand, "because I'd have lost money betting against your coming here tonight."

He fell into step with her as she started walking toward the back of the room, careful to look only at her instead of the staring crowd that slowly began to settle into conver-sation again. The whispers swirling around him invoked his name more often than not, but he decided not to lis-ten. They'd get tired of talking about him eventually, and maybe he could get around to doing what he'd come here tonight to do.

"Kelly Partlow was nice enough to ask me to come. I didn't want to be rude and stand her up."

"Is this part of your investigation?" she asked, her tone edged with hardness. "You think someone here might tell you that I secretly hated my husband and wanted him dead?"

"I don't think you hated your husband or wanted him dead."

"Your client does."

He turned to face her. "I don't think she believes you wanted him dead. I think she's looking for someone to blame for an accident that stole her only living child from her."

She held his gaze for a long moment, then her eyelashes dipped to hide her eyes from him. "I don't have anyone to blame but myself. I was driving. Whatever happened was my fault."

"Accidents happen. Sometimes it's nobody's fault." He touched her arm lightly, but it was enough to snap her gaze up to meet his again.

"Then you're here for another reason," she said, her voice low.

"Maybe I'm here to renew a few old acquaintances. Isn't that why you're here?"

Her gaze dipped again.

He bent his head close to hers so she could hear his whisper. "Or are you here to see if anyone knows who killed Renee?"

She looked up at him, her expression fierce. "Maybe I am."

She was tough. He hadn't realized that about her. Really, before now he hadn't thought much about her at all, beyond the basics. Donnie Lindsey's wife, Birmingham police detective—those were just words, really, identifiers that helped him place her in context with his investigation.

The truth was, he had two pictures of her in his mind. One was the Sara Dunkirk he'd run into occasionally at school, passing in the halls or outside waiting for the bus. She'd been a shy, skinny freshman, and he'd been so wrapped up in Renee back then that he hadn't looked twice at other girls. And even if he had, a skinny fourteen-year-old beanpole like Sara wouldn't have been on his radar at all. That had been the sum total of his memory of Sara Dunkirk until three years ago, when he'd run across the accident scene at the bottom of Black Creek Gorge.

His other picture of Sara Lindsey was a bloody, gravely injured woman in a mangled truck cab, screaming her husband's name in fear and pain. And if there was any image of Sara Dunkirk Lindsey that had stuck in his memory since then, it was that heart-shattering moment of fear when he was afraid he was watching her last, desperate moments of life.

The woman standing in front of him fit neither of those images. She wasn't shy. She wasn't broken.

But she was scarred. He could see the faint white lines of her healed wounds, up close. A jagged streak that snaked down the side of her neck. Surgical scars on her left arm where the surgeons had repaired her broken humerus. There would be other scars, hidden by that snug brown dress, constant reminders of what she'd lost.

He knew what those kinds of inescapable reminders of a painful past could to do a person....

"I can't believe you really came." Kelly Partlow's voice dragged his thoughts back from a morass of self-pity.

He smiled at her. "How could I say no when you asked so nicely?"

Kelly's pretty face dimpled. "You remember my husband, don't you? Josh Partlow?"

"I think we had an English class together," Josh said, extending his hand for a shake.

Josh had also been one of the baseball team members who'd threatened him outside the school shortly after Renee's murder, but if the other man remembered that little detail from their history, he didn't let it show.

A few minutes later, however, when Kelly dragged Sara off to another side of the room to renew some old acquaintances, Josh edged closer to Cain, lowering his voice. "Thanks for not spitting in my face. You'd have been within your rights."

Cain paused in the middle of picking out something to eat from the appetizer buffet to look at the other man. "I've made it a rule to leave bad stuff in the past if I can."

"It's a good rule," Josh said with a nod. "Renee was a sweet girl and everybody was rocked by what happened to her. When you're young and confused and angry, you do stupid things, you know?"

"You look for someone to blame," Cain murmured, remembering his earlier conversation with Sara.

"Yeah. You look for someone to blame."

And he'd been an easy target, Cain knew, walking around Purgatory like a wounded animal, snapping at everyone, even the handful of people who'd tried to reach out to him.

Josh lowered his voice. "Nobody knew your father was the one leaving those bruises on you, man. Every time you came in all black-and-blue, we just figured you'd gotten yourself into another fight. If we'd known—"

Cain shook his head, not wanting any part of this conversation. "Doesn't matter. Doesn't change anything."

"Maybe it would have. If we'd known."

Cain pinned him with a hard stare. "I wouldn't have cared for your pity then any more than now."

Josh held up his hands. "Fair enough."

Cain took a quick, deep breath through his nose,

pushing away the old bitterness. "I'm sorry. That was uncalled for."

"No, don't apologize. I wouldn't care to be pitied, either. And, just so you know, I don't pity you. Frankly, I'm kind of in awe you got through it."

"It wasn't all him, you know." Part of Cain wanted to leave this place as quickly as he could and find somewhere small and dark where he could lick his old wounds in private. But he'd spent a whole lot of years trying to pull himself out of that self-imposed isolation, and coming here tonight had been a big step in that process. Running away now would be like admitting defeat.

And Cain had long ago decided defeat was not an option.

"You're not blaming yourself for what he did, are you?"

Cain shook his head, shooting Josh a faint smile. "I just meant that sometimes the bruises *were* from one of those fights I was always getting myself into. Don't turn me into a saintly superhero."

"Yeah, no." Josh flashed a wry grin. "Saintly superhero never occurred to me, Dennison. Trust me on that."

Cain returned the grin, deciding he might like Josh Partlow after all.

AFTER SPENDING HALF an hour following Kelly Partlow around the private dining room, Sara had begun to think the car accident had robbed her of more than just her memory of the days before and after the accident. She recognized fewer than half of the people Kelly chatted with, despite Kelly's obvious familiarity with them all.

"Oh, honey, you probably didn't know half these people when you lived here," Kelly said with a laugh when Sara confessed her confusion a few minutes later, after they'd paused in the social gadding about to grab another glass of wine for Kelly and a second iced tea for Sara. "Remember,

Josh is a lawyer. He represents half the people in town, including *pro bono* cases. And as the receptionist at his law office, I know them, too. And their families and in-laws and—"

Sara gave an exaggerated shudder. "Enough said."

"And I know some people from these get-togethers," Kelly added. "I've made friends with tons of people who were at Purgatory High before we were there."

Some of whom Renee Lindsey might have known, Sara realized. Maybe the mysterious father of her baby had been someone who'd already graduated rather than someone in her own graduating class.

"Sara, why are you really here?" Kelly asked softly, looking up at her with sharp blue eyes that reminded Sara why they'd really become best friends all those years ago. Kelly might not be an honor roll student, but she'd been as smart as a whip when it came to understanding people. Sara had always liked that about her. Kelly's combination of insight and forthrightness had kept Sara honest, forced her to examine her own motives.

"I'm here to find out who killed Renee Lindsey," she answered bluntly.

Kelly's eyebrows rose. "You think the killer is *here?*"

Sara glanced around to make sure nobody was listening to their conversation. "I don't know. It's possible, don't you think?"

Kelly took a surreptitious look around the room. Her gaze settled on her husband talking to Cain Dennison for a second, then snapped back to meet Sara's, her blue eyes widening. "Oh, my God, you don't think it's Cain Denni-son, do you? I thought he was cleared. Is that why you went and dragged him in here when he looked ready to bolt?"

Sara wasn't sure why, exactly, she'd gone to Cain's res-cue earlier. Maybe because she knew how it felt to be the object of staring eyes and whispered innuendos, at least since the accident. "No, just the opposite," she said quietly. "I don't think he killed her, and he doesn't deserve to be treated as if he did."

"Then who?"

"If I knew that, I wouldn't be here trying to find out, would I?"

Kelly sighed. "I hate to think it could be one of us."

It was almost certainly "one of us," Sara thought. But who?

"I don't like it, either," she admitted. "But it's probable, don't you think? People are often murdered by people they know."

Kelly's lips pressed together in dismay, her gaze sliding around the room again. Suddenly, her brow furrowed, and she gave a soft murmur of surprise.

Sara followed her gaze and spotted a tall, lean man in a Ridge County Sheriff's Department uniform standing in the open doorway of the meeting room. His gaze swept over the room, meeting Sara's briefly before it settled on a couple who stood in the corner, talking to Coach Allen and his wife, Becky. The lawman moved through the buzzing crowd with long, determined strides until he reached the couple, a pretty dark-haired woman in her mid-forties and a balding man maybe a year or two older. They turned and looked at him with a combination of surprise and worry.

"Who's the deputy?" Sara whispered to Kelly.

"Not a deputy. It's the new sheriff himself, Max Clanton."

Sara's stomach tightened. A visit from the sheriff himself, looking so grim, couldn't mean anything good.

A moment later, a terrible wail rose from the corner, and the dark-haired woman sank to her knees, her hands over her eyes. Kelly grabbed Sara's arm, her grip tight. Whispers rippled through the crowd, radiating out from the tight cluster in the corner.

"Their daughter Ariel," someone nearby murmured just loudly enough for Sara to hear. "Someone found her dead at the base of Crybaby Falls."

Chapter Six

Sara's father paced the well-worn carpet in the middle of his den, his jaw working with frustration. He stopped suddenly, pinning Sara to her chair with the force of his gaze. "You don't know where Cain Dennison was before seven o'clock last night, do you?"

"He's not a likely suspect, Dad."

"You don't know that. He's been back in town almost two weeks now. God only knows what he's been up to all that time."

"You want me to find out?"

Carl frowned at her. "You're not a cop anymore."

"Neither are you," she pointed out reasonably, but her answer only deepened his frown.

"Maybe I would be if that new sheriff hadn't come to town."

"He didn't force you out, did he?"

Carl sighed, sinking into the armchair across from her. "No. I just saw the writing on the wall. Everything's technology-based these days. Legwork and good old-fashioned instinct aren't valuable commodities anymore."

"And your instincts are telling you that Cain Dennison killed an eighteen-year-old girl he didn't even know?"

"You don't know he didn't know her."

"And you don't know he did." Sara leaned forward,

putting her hand on her father's arm. "If she hadn't been found at the base of Crybaby Falls, would it even have occurred to you to suspect Dennison?"

"No. But she was. And that's too damned close to what happened to Renee Lindsey."

"I know." She sat back, her own stomach in a tight knot. She'd gone to the get-together the night before hoping to find a new suspect in Renee's murder. But now, she was beginning to wonder if what she'd found, instead, was a brand-new wrinkle to the old mystery.

Could the two murders, eighteen years apart, be connected? The most recent murder victim, Ariel Burke, had been an infant when Renee Lindsey had died. Was it really possible the same person had killed both women? Or had someone copied Purgatory's most infamous unsolved murder to throw the cops off the trail?

"I wish I could tag along for the investigation," she murmured. She saw a similar longing shining in her father's dark eyes.

"You could always apply for a job at the sheriff's department," Carl pointed out.

"Don't give her any ideas." Sara's mother stood in the doorway of the den, her hands on her hips. "Carl, Brad Ellis is here."

Sara glanced at her father. "Brad Ellis from the cop shop?"

"Send him on back," Carl said.

Ann gave her husband a troubled look before she left.

"Is he still with the sheriff's department?" Sara asked.

"Sure am, Scooter," a familiar voice boomed from behind her.

Sara turned to see her father's old partner standing in the doorway, a grin carving lines into his rugged face. Returning the grin, she jumped up to give him a hug.

"I swear, if you weren't already married to the prettiest woman in Ridge County, I'd have a go at you myself."

"And if I weren't married to the best shot in Ridge County, I might take you up on it." He gave her a quick kiss on the cheek, then looked at Carl. His grin faded. "Sarge."

"I take it this isn't a friendly visit?"

Leaving his arm draped over Sara's shoulders, Brad shook his head. "'Fraid not. I need to pick your brain about an old case."

"The Renee Lindsey murder?" Sara asked.

Brad gave her a sharp look. "I really shouldn't say—"

"She was a cop for years. In fact, your new sheriff would be a fool not to snatch her up and make her your new lead investigator." Her father's voice was edged with pride that made Sara's chest swell a little. "Whatever you want to say to me, you can say to her."

Brad gave her a long, considering look, a hint of apology in his eyes when he finally said, "I reckon I'm still thinking of you as that kid with braces and skinned-up knees who used to tag along after your daddy everywhere he went."

"Lost the braces years ago. Wish I could say the same about the skinned-up knees." She waved him toward the chair she'd occupied when he arrived, taking the wide ottoman next to her father's chair.

Brad settled his muscular bulk into the chair and leaned forward as Carl sat across from him. "Y'all know a hiker found Ariel Burke's body at the base of Crybaby Falls last night, I reckon."

Carl and Sara nodded in unison.

"The medical examiner conducted the autopsy this morning. Cause of death was ligature strangulation."

Same C.O.D. as Renee Lindsey, Sara thought. "Is that why you need Dad's help? Because it's so similar to what happened to Renee Lindsey, and Dad was the principal investigator on that case?"

Brad passed one large hand across his mouth, as if he was reluctant to answer. Sara's gut tightened as she realized there was something else, something that made Brad look damned near haunted.

"Ariel Burke was two months pregnant."

Carl spat out a profanity Sara had never heard him use before.

"You're doing a DNA test to determine paternity?" she asked.

Brad nodded. "She broke up with her boyfriend about two months ago, so we're looking real hard at him, of course, but—"

"Has anyone talked to Cain Dennison?" Carl interrupted.

Sara looked at her father. "Dad—"

"First person we questioned," Brad answered. "He alibied out."

"Alibis can be faked."

"He's not the killer, Carl." Brad's voice took on a soothing tone that Sara knew would probably infuriate her father. "Ariel Burke's parents saw her yesterday morning at eleven when she left to go to cheerleader practice at the high school. She was there until just after one. So we know she couldn't have been killed before then. But from one to five yesterday, Dennison was at a training seminar at The Gates. Ten different agents there can account for his whereabouts, and there's video evidence, as well. The M.E. says Ariel Burke's time of death was around four yesterday afternoon. There's no way Dennison was involved."

"It doesn't mean he didn't kill Renee Lindsey."

"It doesn't," Brad agreed. "But right now, we have to look at the possibility that the same person who killed Renee also killed Ariel. The similarities between the murders—"

"Could be a coincidence," Carl finished for him.

"Could be. That's why I'm here. You know more about the Renee Lindsey murder than anyone else. The sheriff wants you to consult on the investigation."

Carl looked at Sara, his expression hard to read. When he spoke, she could hear the conflict in his tone. "I promised Ann when I retired that I'd stay retired."

"You won't be policing. You'll be consulting."

"You don't know what that case did to me."

"I remember," Brad said quietly. "I might not have been on the force when it happened, but I worked with you for nearly fifteen years. I know it haunted you. It haunted the whole sheriff's department."

Sara closed her eyes, remembering the way her father had obsessed over that one unsolved murder, as if he took her death as a personal affront.

Maybe he had, in a way. He'd liked Donnie, treated him like a son. He'd seen the way the murder had shattered Donnie's family, transformed his parents from confident, socially active people to haunted recluses whose only social interactions revolved around memorializing their murdered daughter.

"Okay. I'll consult. But not for a fee."

"The sheriff will insist."

"Tell him to put my fee in the sheriff's benevolence fund."

Brad nodded. "He wants you at the station this afternoon at three. You'll be there?"

"I'll be there."

Brad rose and shook Carl's hand. Sara walked him to the door, her father trailing behind.

Ann eyed them warily as they passed through the kitchen on their way to the front door. For the first time since she'd come back to Purgatory, Sara wondered just how much pressure her father's job had put on his marriage while she wasn't paying attention.

"Rita told me to remind you about next Saturday," Brad said to Sara's mother, who was looking at Sara's father with troubled eyes.

Ann turned her gaze to Brad. "Right. Tell her I'll be there by four." She managed a weak smile.

Brad turned to Sara and gave her a quick kiss on her forehead. "Good to see you back in town, Scooter. Think you'll stick around?"

"We'll see," Sara answered with a smile.

After Brad had gone, she turned to look at her parents. They were staring at each other across the kitchen, tension brewing between them like a mountain storm.

"I can be your go-between," Sara said. "You don't even have to step foot in the cop shop."

Both of her parents turned to look at her. "You were all wrapped up in Donnie and his reaction. You don't remember what it was like for your father," Ann said.

"You're right. I don't." Sara put her hand on her father's shoulder, surprised to feel a tremble in his muscles. She looked up at him, saw the haunted look in his eyes, and felt an answering shiver run through her. "Dad, if this is going to be a problem—"

"I let her down." Carl looked at her, his eyes dark with regret. "I let you down. And Donnie. Don't you think I know what brought y'all here the night of the accident? He was still looking for his sister's killer."

"I thought you didn't know why we were here."

"I didn't know what you were doing while you were here. But you weren't here to see us. And Donnie's parents said you didn't come to see them, either. So there was only one possible reason left."

"Did that poor girl's murder have something to do with Renee's murder?" Ann asked. "Is that why Brad was here?"

"We don't know," Sara answered honestly.

The look her mother shot her way sent a flutter of guilt

rippling through her chest. "You're getting sucked into this, too, aren't you?"

"We need answers," Carl said quietly.

"Can't someone else get the answers? Why does it have to be the two of you?"

Sara looked at her father, feeling helpless. She knew her mother's concern was fueled by the same kind of love that had driven Donnie to seek his sister's killer with relentless abandon.

"If I'd been killed when I was eighteen," she said softly, "would you be able to put my unsolved murder behind you and move on with your life?"

Her mother blanched as if Sara had struck her. "God, Sara."

"That's what Donnie was dealing with. I may not know what it was like with Dad and the case, but I know what it was like for Donnie all those years." She crossed to her mother and took her hands. "I don't remember the night of the accident, and until I get some answers about it, I'm going to keep thinking it was my fault somehow. I know he came here because of Renee's murder. But the details are hidden from me, and I can't live with that."

Ann closed her eyes, emotional pain lining her pretty face. "I don't want to lose either of you."

Sara hugged her. "Dad and I will watch each other's backs. I promise."

Ann's arms tightened around Sara's waist, pulling her closer. "I'm glad you're back in town, for however long you stay. I've missed you more than you know."

Guilt crept back, a reminder of how much she'd closed herself off from everyone she loved over the past three years. She'd come back to Purgatory because she didn't have anywhere else to go, but the longer she stayed, the more she realized just how much she'd missed her little hometown while she was gone.

"I think I'm pretty glad to be back, too," she admitted, giving her mother a quick kiss on the cheek. Letting go, she turned to her father. "Let me be your liaison with the sheriff's department, Dad. It'll give me a good excuse to get in on the investigation, and it'll make Mom happy. Win-win."

Her father managed a grudging smile. "Got it all figured out, have you?"

"She's your daughter," Ann said.

By the time they sat down at the kitchen table for a lunch of soup and sandwiches, the earlier tension had mostly disappeared, and the conversation wandered away from murder to talk of high-school football—Purgatory High was supposed to be a contender for a state championship in their division—and the upcoming Mountain Moms charity hoedown. "Rita roped me into helping with the setup down at the civic center," Ann told Sara with a rueful smile. "I knew I shouldn't have retired early. Apparently it makes me the go-to gal for anything around town that requires a volunteer."

"Don't let her fool you—she's about as excited about that hoedown as Rita is." Carl shot his wife an affectionate smile. "She's everybody's hero, too, because she talked the Meades from up in Kentucky to come down to play for the dancing."

Sara raised her eyebrows at her mother. "Wow, the Meades, huh? I thought they never left that little place of theirs in Cumberland." When she and her brother, Patrick, were younger, her parents had taken them up to the Meade Motor Inn in Cumberland, Kentucky, several times to take in the live bluegrass music. "Remember how Patrick decided he wanted to be a banjo player and join the Meades?"

Her father grimaced. "That banjo cost us a fortune and he never picked it up again after the first try."

"I never made it as a singer, either," Sara said with mock regret. "So how'd you score the coup, Mom?"

"Last time your dad and I were up there, I got to talking to Nola Meade. Seems her kids are wanting to go mainstream with their music once they're old enough to leave the nest, so Nola and Del figured it might be good for their future careers if the family got out of Kentucky now and then to give the kids some exposure. So when Rita tasked me with finding a band for the hoedown, I gave Nola a call."

"Yeah, little Purgatory, Tennessee's going to give those kids a lot of exposure," Sara said with an arch of her eyebrow.

Ann smiled placidly. "Well, see, Beeson Lombard of MuCity Records happens to be a Purgatory native. We went to high school together. So when I called up my old high-school friend—"

"Boyfriend," her father elaborated with a grumble.

"—and told him I was helping organize a Smoky Mountain charity fund-raiser and could get him a hot new country act to listen to if he'd like to show up for the event," Ann continued with a smile, "how could he say no?"

"Oh, you're good at this," Sara said with a grin. "No wonder you get roped into organizing things."

"You're still going to be around this weekend, aren't you?" Ann asked. "You should come. You love the Meades."

"I'll come," Sara said, though it was her desire to please her mother more than her love for the Meades and their bluegrass that made the decision for her. After the stress of the Purgatory High School get-together, and the tragic finale of that particular social outing, Sara wasn't in a hurry to crawl out of her hermit hole again anytime soon.

By the time she headed back to her grandfather's cabin to resume her cleaning, her parents were mostly back to their smiling, affectionate selves, lightening her mood as she navigated the twisting road up to her inherited cabin. She almost felt like her old self for the first time since the accident.

She should have known it couldn't last.

As she topped the last rise and the cabin came into view, she saw a dark blue Ford F-150 truck parked in the gravel drive. Its driver sat on the steps of the cabin's sprawling front porch, his elbows resting on his knees as he watched her park her truck and slide from the cab.

"You lost?" she asked as she slowly approached the porch steps.

Cain looked up at her, eyes squinting against the afternoon sun slanting through the evergreens that cocooned the cabin. "No. I asked for directions."

She stopped in front of him, pocketing her truck keys. "From whom?"

"Your friend Kelly. Apparently she has a matchmaking streak." He gave her a mock stern look. "Not very discriminating in her choice of suitors for you, though. You should talk to her about that."

His tone was light enough, but a darker emotion roiled beneath his words. He hadn't come here for a reason as frivolous as courtship.

"What do you want?"

"The Ridge County Medical Examiner's office is as leaky as an old rowboat," he said, rising to let her go up the steps. He followed her to the door, his footsteps making the old boards creak. "The girl was strangled. And she was pregnant."

She stopped at the locked front door and turned to look at him. "The M.E.'s office isn't *that* leaky."

"My boss knows people."

Right, she thought. *The Gates.* When she had a chance to concentrate on something besides solving Renee Lindsey's murder, she should take a harder look at the new P.I. agency in town. She had a feeling it wasn't quite as ordinary an operation as the people in town seemed to think.

"I can neither confirm nor deny any of that." She turned her back on him as she unlocked the dead bolt, hoping he'd take her words and posture for the dismissal she intended.

He didn't. His hand covered hers as she reached for the doorknob. "Know what I'm wondering?"

She turned to look at him, her heart thudding heavily in her chest. "What are you wondering?"

"I'm wondering whether, once the M.E.'s office gets the DNA results on Ariel Burke's unborn child, they discover Ariel's baby and Renee's baby had the same daddy."

Chapter Seven

Cain could see in Sara's expression that the same thought had already occurred to her. How could it not? Two teenage girls, both pregnant, murdered by strangulation at Crybaby Falls? Sure, there were eighteen years between the murders, but Purgatory wasn't like a big city where murders happened every day.

"Don't jump to conclusions," Sara warned, as if reading his mind. She opened the door and gave a brief, forward nod of her head. He took that as an invitation and followed her into the cabin.

He wasn't sure what he'd expected from the old place, given the time-worn state of its weathered exterior, but inside, the cabin offered a rustic, welcoming warmth. Colorful woven rugs hung like art softened the exposed log walls. The sofa was old, with a patina of use, but when Sara waved him to it, the springs were still good and the cushions just the right balance between soft and firm.

"The last thing you need to do is stick your nose into this case," Sara said without preamble.

"It's what I'm paid to do."

"A lot of cops never stopped thinking you got away with murder eighteen years ago," Sara reminded him as she settled in an overstuffed armchair across from the sofa. She tucked her legs up under her, displaying a distracting

level of limberness that drew his gaze to the toned curve
of her thighs so temptingly displayed by her snug jeans.

He dragged his gaze back up to meet hers. "Your father,
you mean."

"He wasn't the only one."

"Too bad, because I had nothing to do with Renee's
murder."

"Your alibi was shaky."

What was this, an interrogation? Did she think he was
guilty of killing Renee, too? "What did you do, talk your
daddy into letting you look at his files on the case?"

"As a matter of fact, yes. I spent the morning reading
his notes on the case." Her lips tightened into a thin line
of annoyance at his tone.

Good, he thought. *Don't want to be pissed off all by my
lonesome.* "I'd have thought you of all people would have
the details memorized, since she was family."

"I was fourteen when she died. My dad didn't exactly
bring his work home to us. He wanted to keep us separate
from that world."

"But you went and became a cop, anyway."

"Yeah." She plucked at the hem of her T-shirt, the movement stretching the cotton fabric over her firm, round
breasts. He averted his gaze from the tempting sight, waiting for her to continue.

He heard her soft sigh. "Before this morning, most of
what I knew about the case came from Donnie. But he
wasn't capable of being objective about his sister's murder."

"Did he think I was the killer?"

She looked surprised by the question. "No. He thought
his parents were grasping at straws trying to get the police
to keep after you. Renee had only good things to say about
you. She told him people didn't know who you really were,
how nice you could be."

Tears pricked his eyes, catching him off guard. He

looked down at his hands and cleared his throat. "I was home with my father the day she died."

"You didn't mention your father when you talked to the deputies."

"He'd been drunk. He wouldn't have remembered." And even if he had, he would probably have lied to the police just to make Cain suffer. The old man would've gotten a kick out of seeing him stuck in jail for as long as it took the cops to sort things out.

If they managed to sort it out at all.

"You didn't want to try explaining something like that to the cops?"

"If they'd questioned him, he'd have made me pay, one way or another."

The skin around her eyes contracted. Not quite a full flinch, but enough. "I see."

"Don't do that."

"Do what?"

"Feel sorry for me. I chose to stick around here with him. I could have left almost any time I wanted."

"So why *did* you stick around?"

He changed the subject. "Are the cops questioning anyone else about Ariel Burke's pregnancy?"

"Your leaky old rowboat didn't spill that information?"

"Just wondering who'll get railroaded this time. She have a boyfriend?"

Sara didn't answer, but he was beginning to understand what her expressions and physical tics meant. Her eyes narrowed slightly. That meant he was right. Ariel Burke's boyfriends—current and ex—would be getting a visit from the Ridge County Sheriff's Department.

"You said Renee had a secret boyfriend." Sara leaned forward. "And she never told you anything about him? Never hinted who it might be? Clearly she considered you a friend. Donnie said Renee told him you were one of the few people she felt she could trust."

The burning sensation returned to his eyes. He made a show of rubbing his forehead to hide his reaction to her words.

"You didn't know that, did you?" she asked gently.

Apparently she was learning to read him, too. "I knew she trusted me, or she wouldn't have bothered with me at all. Renee showed you how she felt by the things she did, not the things she said."

"So the father of her baby might not have realized how much she cared for him. She might never have told him."

He looked up sharply. "She slept with him. If he knew anything about her at all, he'd have known exactly how much she loved him. She wasn't the kind of girl who did something like that without it meaning everything."

"So you and she never…"

"No. We never." He managed a rueful smile. "Not from my lack of trying. But she didn't love me. Not like that. She told me I didn't love her, either. Not the way I would love the right person someday."

"She was a romantic."

"Yeah, she was."

"Do you know when she met the guy she loved enough to sleep with?"

"I think she was already in love with him before she and I ever became friends." He'd forgotten that fact, he realized. Mostly because she'd never come right out and said so, but it hadn't taken long to realize she was nursing a secret passion for *someone*.

He'd just never learned who that someone was.

"I kept asking her, if she and Mr. Right were so meant for each other, why couldn't she tell me who he was? She'd just give me this serious look and tell me love was complicated and I'd understand someday." He looked up suddenly at Sara, realizing how much he'd revealed to her with very little effort on her part. "You're good, Detective Lindsey. Very good."

Her lips curved slightly. "It helps that you're not my prime suspect."

"Do you have a prime suspect?" he asked, curious.

"Not for Renee's murder."

"What about for Ariel's? A boyfriend, maybe?"

"I need evidence before I start naming suspects."

"I heard she was a cheerleader."

"That's right." Sara nodded.

"Renee wasn't anything like that. She wasn't one of the popular girls. Too quiet for that."

"I remember."

"She had long brown hair. What about Ariel?"

"Blond and cut short for cheerleading."

He looked at her through narrowed eyes. "So, if you were a profiler looking at the two victims, you wouldn't see much in common."

"Except they were pregnant and killed by ligature strangulation at Crybaby Falls."

"Copycat?"

She gave him a considering look. "Maybe. Though a real copycat might have done his killing three days ago on the actual anniversary. To make a statement, I mean."

He rubbed his jaw, realizing at the scrape of his beard against his palm that he hadn't shaved that morning. Falling back into old habits, he thought with an inward grimace. He needed a haircut, too. And he'd been throwing on any old pair of jeans in the morning since he'd been assigned this case, grabbing any ratty T-shirt and ignoring the scuffs on his boots rather than taking care to present a neat and polished outward appearance the way the Army had taught him to do.

Falling back into old habits he'd thought he'd put behind him.

"What are you thinking?" she asked curiously.

He shot her a sheepish grin. "Believe it or not, I was thinking that since I came back here to Purgatory, I've been letting myself go. Forgetting to shave, not spit-shining my boots, waiting too long to do the laundry—"

To his surprise, she laughed. "Reverting to your sloppy high-school self, you mean?"

He liked her laugh, the low, throaty sound sending a pleasant rippling sensation down his spine. He smiled back at her. "I guess maybe so. Don't want to let it go too far, though."

"I had trouble leaving my parents' house to come back here this afternoon because my mama cooks for me every time I go there." She shot him a sheepish look. "My old room still looks the same, even. I could move right back in like nothing has changed."

"But everything's changed."

"Not all for the worse," she said after a brief silence.

"No, not all," he agreed.

She dropped her feet to the floor. "I'm going to make coffee. Want some?"

"Sure. I take it black."

She slanted a smiling look at him. "So do I."

They settled into a surprisingly comfortable silence while Sara brewed the coffee in the adjacent kitchen. The coffeemaker looked ancient, apparently a fixture that had come with her inherited cabin. But the strong, hot brew she delivered into his hands a few minutes later left nothing to be desired. "Good coffee."

"I was surprised myself," she said with a glint of humor as she sat across from him again, cradling her mug between her hands. "I guess new isn't always improved."

"You think I should give up this case and let the cops handle it."

She looked at him over the top of her cup, her dark eyes hard to read. "As much for your own sake as for the good of the investigation."

"I'm not giving up. I can't."

She lowered the cup, cradling it in her palms on her lap. "I didn't think you would."

"So why don't we work together instead of against each other?"

Her brow furrowed. "Together?"

Clearly not an idea she cared for, he realized with a flicker of dismay. He supposed it was one thing to let him into her house and give him a cup of coffee, but another thing altogether to trust him to have her back in an investigation.

Especially the investigation of a murder he was once suspected of committing.

"Never mind," he said as the silence stretched between them. He set his coffee cup on the low table between them. "Thank you for the coffee. I'll be on my way."

She rose with him, following him to the door. When he turned to look at her, she was frowning at him. "I didn't mean to hurt your feelings."

He almost laughed. "Don't worry yourself. My feelings are just fine." He gave a nod and headed out to his truck, a grin spreading over his face at the thought of her concern.

Imagine if she knew some of the things he'd endured growing up.

SARA'S CELL PHONE rang five minutes after Cain drove away. The number was a local one, not familiar. Not Cain's, as she'd hoped, given how lousy she was feeling about the way he'd left.

"Sara? This is Becky Allen. You remember, Jim Allen's wife? We talked at the party the other day."

"Of course," Sara replied, wondering how the coach's wife had gotten her cell phone number.

Becky's next words answered that question. "You mother was nice enough to give me your number. I just wanted to check in with you after what happened at the party the other night. That terrible news just—well, I was just thinking it was so much like what happened to Donnie's sister all those years ago, and hitting so soon after the anniversary of Donnie's death…" Becky trailed off to a soft sigh, as if she couldn't figure out how to say what she wanted to convey.

Torn between irritation at the reminder of all she'd lost and guilt at feeling irritated by honest attempts to be thoughtful, she pasted a smile on her face, though no one was there to see. "I'm fine, Becky, thanks. You're sweet to worry about me, but it's the Burkes who can probably use everyone's concern these days."

"It's just so horrifying. I'm to the point I don't even want my own child to go to Purgatory High now."

"You can't possibly have any kids in high school yet," Sara protested, thinking of how young the coach's wife had looked at the party.

"I do. Jeff is already a senior."

"Wow. Where's the time gone?"

"Beats me," Becky said with a rueful laugh. "Listen, I've got to get back to work, but if you're going to stick around town for long, you should come have dinner with Jim and me. Jim thought so much of Donnie, and I know he'd want to have you over before you head out of town. How long are you staying?"

"Awhile, at least," she answered carefully, thrown by the invitation. While Donnie had been one of Jim Allen's star players on the Purgatory High School baseball team, teachers and students hadn't made a habit of socializing. It wasn't as if they were old friends looking to catch up.

Then again, she hadn't been living in Purgatory since she was eighteen years old, and it was a pretty small town. Both Becky and Jim had been Purgatory students themselves, several years ahead of her and Donnie. Class president, homecoming queen, Miss Purgatory High—all those milestones that constituted royalty in a small town. Jim had been the baseball star, the good-looking kid who'd played a couple of years in triple-A before giving up the dream of a professional career and coming back to marry his high-school sweetheart.

No wonder they both kept themselves looking good. They had a reputation to live up to. Royalty didn't get to let themselves go.

"I'll get with Jim and we'll make a date," Becky said brightly. "Talk to you soon."

Bemused, Sara hung up the phone and turned to survey the cabin, thinking about Becky's question. How long *was* she planning to stick around Purgatory?

CAIN'S GRANDMOTHER'S cabin was only minutes away by truck, a vivid reminder of how small Purgatory, Tennessee, was compared to Atlanta. He could get everywhere in Ridge County faster than he could have driven from his apartment to the construction company where he'd worked. And many places on foot, too, for that matter. Sara's recently inherited cabin, for instance, was just a short hike over the hill from where his Airstream was parked on Mulberry Rise.

He wondered what she was doing right now.

When he pulled up beside the Airstream, he saw his grandmother's old station wagon was gone. A glance at his watch suggested why—it was nearly five on a Sunday, which meant she and the girls had gone to church for

the evening services. For a woman some of the more superstitious folks in these parts considered a white witch,
his grandmother had always been strict about her church
attendance, and if he'd been home when she set out, she
might have given him a stern talking-to about his own
backsliding ways.

He smiled at the thought as he climbed the stairs to his
trailer, but his smile faded when he spotted a plain white
envelope tucked into the space between the door and the
frame.

As he started to reach for it, his recent training kicked
in, and he withdrew his hand, giving the envelope a quick
once-over. Digging in his jacket pocket, he pulled out
his multiblade knife, withdrew the small set of tweezers
tucked into the handle and clamped the envelope between
the two small tongs, tugging it free of the door.

There was no writing on either side of the envelope, and
the flap hadn't been sealed shut. Using the hem of his T-
shirt to hold the envelope, he pulled up the envelope flap
with the tweezers and took a look inside.

A piece of plain paper sat tucked inside the envelope.
Cain pried it out with the tweezers and read the three typewritten lines.

*Look in your grandmother's woodbin. Imagine what
might have happened if I'd called the police.*

Alarmed, Cain slid the note back into the envelope and
carried it with him down the steps and around his grandmother's cabin. Near the river-stone chimney sat his grandmother's woodbin, where she and the girls stored their
firewood. He used his T-shirt to lift the lid of the bin and
looked inside.

At first, he saw only pieces of chopped wood stacked
neatly inside. But a closer look revealed the edge of a plastic bag peeking out from between a couple of the logs. He

reached down and moved aside the top piece of wood, staring in mounting dismay at what lay beneath.

A quart-size resealable plastic bag nestled amid the pieces of wood. Inside the bag, four smaller clear plastic bags were tucked together. Each of the smaller bags contained dozens of crystals the color of pale champagne.

Around these parts, he knew, there was only one thing those crystals could possibly be.

Leaving the bag where it lay, he pulled out his cell phone and hit the first number on his speed dial.

Alexander Quinn answered. "We do get days off, you know."

Under any other circumstance, Cain might have smiled at his boss's dry response. If anyone in the world didn't know the meaning of the term "day off," it was Alexander Quinn. Cain wasn't sure the man even slept.

But Cain wasn't in the mood to smile at the moment.

"I've got a problem," he said into the phone, his gaze still fixed on the bag of crystals inside the woodbin.

"What's up?" Quinn was instantly all business.

"I came home to a note stuck in my door frame that told me to look in my grandmother's woodbin and be glad nobody had called the police."

"And what did you find?"

"I can't be sure until we test it, but I think I'm looking at about fifty grand's worth of crystal meth."

Chapter Eight

Sara pulled up in front of the small, neat cabin on Mulberry Rise, her gaze slanting toward the silver Airstream trailer parked beside it as she put her truck in Park and let it idle a moment.

She hadn't planned to come here when she'd left the house that morning, but when the turnoff to Mulberry Rise loomed in her windshield, dead ahead, her hand had flipped the turn indicator and she'd headed up the mountain as if following some inexplicable instinct.

Cain Dennison was trouble. He'd always been trouble, he probably always would be trouble, forever and ever, amen. But she'd spent a whole night feeling terrible about turning up her nose at his offer to work with her to find Renee Lindsey's killer, so the least she could do was apologize for being so blunt with him.

Except why should she apologize? She hadn't changed her mind—his history with Renee Lindsey made him the wrong person to be leading The Gates' investigation in the first place. She wished she could go ask his boss why he'd made such a confounding decision.

Then again, she didn't exactly see her own connection to Renee as a deal breaker, did she? She'd been married to Renee's brother. She couldn't imagine her mother-in-law,

Joyce, would be happy to hear that she was delving into Renee's murder, either.

As she reached for the gearshift to put her car in Reverse, the front door of the cabin opened and a wiry woman in her seventies stepped onto the shallow stoop. Her gaze turned toward Sara's truck, and she offered a placid smile of greeting.

Stifling a sigh, Sara left the car in Park and shut off the engine. She could hardly rebuff two people in the same family within a twenty-four hour period, could she?

Lila Birdsong wrapped her shawl more tightly around her shoulders as a chill autumn wind blew through the trees, stirring her wispy white hair around her pretty, heart-shaped face. "Sara Dunkirk. Ain't seen you in ages."

"No, ma'am. I've been down in Alabama for a long while."

"My grandson tells me you're back for a spell. Thinkin' of stayin'?"

Sara wasn't sure how to answer that question. "I'm just thinking, at the moment," she said finally, managing a smile. "Is Cain here?"

Lila shook her head. "He headed out early so he could drop the girls off at the high school before going to the office."

"The girls?"

"Mia and Charlotte Burdette. Daughters of a cousin of mine who's smack in the middle of a mess." Her tone darkened. "I took those poor girls in to keep them out of the DCS."

Sara nodded, understanding. Like many child-welfare agencies, the Tennessee Department of Children's Services was perennially overworked protecting children from unsafe or abusive home situations. Keeping children out of the system when possible was the better choice.

"How old are they?"

"Sixteen and seventeen." Lila grinned at Sara. "I reckon they were happy enough havin' Cain drive them around."

Sara could imagine. Even though she'd been in love with Donnie Lindsey since middle school, she hadn't been immune to the bad-boy appeal of Cain Dennison. He'd possessed the feral charms of a wild creature, both beautiful and dangerous.

He still did, she thought, remembering her first look at him in years, standing outside her hiding place at Crybaby Falls. Dangerous, yes, but also sexually exciting.

Lila's smile widened as she beckoned Sara to join her. "I've just brewed up some coffee. Come on in and tell me what's on your mind."

The last thing she intended to tell Cain Dennison's grandmother were the thoughts that had just flashed through her mind, but the offer of coffee sounded good. She followed Lila into the warm cabin and sat in the chair Lila waved toward.

"Cain ought to be back soon enough. He was just going into town for an early meeting." Lila returned to the table with a battered old stove-top percolator that had seen better days. But the fragrant, steaming brew she poured into a couple of stoneware mugs smelled like heaven.

"Thank you." Sara picked up the cup and took a sip. It was hot and strong, the way she liked it.

"No cream or sugar," Lila commented with a smile as she opened the refrigerator that stood in a corner near the table. "Must've been raised by a strong man."

Sara laughed. "Yes, but it was my mother who taught me to like coffee black. My father likes his cream and sugar."

Lila laughed with her as she retrieved a carton of cream from the refrigerator and poured a dollop into her coffee. "I reckon I do, too."

"Cain likes his coffee black, too," Sara commented as Lila returned to the table.

The older woman's eyebrows ticked upward. "So he does. I didn't know you knew him that well."

"I don't, really." Sara avoided Lila's gaze. "I just had coffee with him recently, that's all."

"Hmm," was all Lila said.

Squelching the urge to fill the suddenly uneasy silence, Sara sipped her coffee and wondered why she hadn't turned down Lila's offer of coffee and gone on her way.

"I was real sad to hear about your husband's passing," Lila said a moment later. "And real glad to see you're doing good now. I heard you were banged up pretty bad."

"I was. I'm lucky to be alive."

"Lucky," Lila murmured, as if she disagreed.

"Well, lucky, I guess, that your grandson was hiking the gorge that night. If he hadn't found me when he did, I don't think I'd have survived."

Lila nodded and looked up, her sharp brown eyes meeting Sara's gaze. "I don't think things in this world happen randomly. Do you?"

"I don't know," Sara admitted. "Sometimes things in life seem very random."

"Seem," Lila said with a nod. "That's a real good word. I reckon many things seem to be what they ain't."

"And sometimes they simply are what they are."

"Life ain't simple," Lila disagreed. "Do you know how unlikely it was for my grandson to be there in the Black Creek Gorge so late at night? He hadn't been in Purgatory in years."

"Why *was* he back here that night?" Sara asked, curious.

Lila smiled over her coffee cup. "He'd just left the Army and gotten himself a good job in Atlanta. It was supposed to start the next Monday, but for the first time in years, his time was his own. So he came home. To see me, I imagine, but I think he really came to pay his respects."

To Renee, Sara thought. Three years ago, the day after Sara's car accident, had been the fifteenth anniversary of her passing. "He would have gone to Crybaby Falls," she said quietly.

"Yes."

"But that doesn't explain why he was at the Black Creek Gorge."

"No, it don't," Lila agreed.

Sara waited for her to say more, but Lila just sipped her coffee.

"I wish I'd had the chance to thank him," Sara said when the thick silence filling the kitchen became too uncomfortable.

"I don't reckon he thought he needed thanking," Lila said thoughtfully. "It ain't his way."

"It needs sayin', anyway," Sara said, smiling a little self-consciously as she heard her accent slip into the old, familiar intonations of her mountain upbringing. She'd been away from the hills for years, but some parts of her past a person could never really leave behind.

The sound of a vehicle coming up the mountain road seeped through the cabin's walls, drawing Lila's gaze to the front door. "I guess that'll be Cain comin' back."

Sara felt her heart speed up, just a notch. Just as it might if she heard a black bear approaching in the woods, she reminded herself sternly.

Beautiful but dangerous.

The thud of footsteps on the stoop outside gave her just enough time to steel herself for his entrance. He came through the door, filling its frame almost completely, as if to amplify for Sara's already pounding heart just how big he'd become in adulthood, how tall and broad-shouldered. As a boy, he'd been lean, wiry almost, but his time in the

Army had clearly added brawn and power to his build that his time away from the service hadn't erased.

His storm-gray eyes met hers, wary and watchful. "I thought that was your truck outside. Has something happened?"

"No. I just wanted to talk to you." She glanced at Lila, not ready to say the things she needed to say to him in front of an audience.

He nodded at Sara before bending to give his grandmother a quick kiss on the top of her head. The gesture of affection made Sara's heart contract.

"The girls are safely at school, although they tried to convince me to let them ditch and take them in to work with me," Cain told his grandmother. The smile in his voice made Sara look up in time to catch a toothy grin so infectious, she felt her own lips curving up at the corners. "They said it would be educational. Sort of a 'take your grandmother's wards to work day.' I told them no, of course. Because education's a privilege."

Sara could tell by his intonation that his final words were a well-learned quotation, no doubt from his smiling grandmother.

"And so it is," Lila said, giving him a swat on the back as she rose to her feet. "It was a real pleasure havin' coffee with you, Sara Dunkirk, but I'm afraid I've got chores to get to, so I'll leave you with Cain."

Cain waited until his grandmother disappeared into the next room before he spoke, his tone low and urgent. "Has there been another murder?"

She looked up at his worried expression. "No, I told you, I just came to talk to you."

His gaze went from worried to wary. "I thought you already said about all there was to say."

"That's what I wanted to talk about." She nodded toward

the back door, and he opened it, letting her go out ahead of him.

Outside, the wind had kicked up, swirling fallen leaves around their feet. Sara had forgotten, in the toasty warmth of the cabin, how cold the fall air had become. Winter was coming to the hills, sooner than she liked.

Hugging herself for warmth, she looked up at Cain, finding him no less imposing in the wide open than she had in the close confines of his grandmother's cabin. His expression was shuttered, forbidding, sparking an unexpected quiver in the pit of her stomach.

"You don't want me investigating Renee's death," Cain said. "I plan to do it, anyway. Not sure anything more needs saying."

"I don't want you involved in the investigation because there's no way for you to not be in the way."

His eyebrows rose a notch, and she realized how badly she'd just expressed what she was trying to convey.

"I just mean—"

He cut her off. "I know what you mean."

"No. You don't." She caught his arm as he started to turn away.

He looked down at her hand, then up at her, his eyes narrowed. Beneath her fingers, his arm felt as hard as mountain granite but as hot as the coffee cup she'd cradled earlier between her cold fingers. The combination of unflinching strength and fiery vitality sent a different sort of quiver racing through her, straight to her sex.

She stared up at him, both confounded and aroused. His eyes narrowed further, as if he read her emotions and found them just as confusing.

"I know you're not going to believe me, but I'm as worried about you as I am about the case." As she said the words, she realized they shouldn't be true. The case should be everything. In some ways, indirectly, Renee Lindsey's murder was why she'd decided to come back to Purgatory at all. Her death had been a profound part of Donnie's life, of their marriage and, she feared, of his death, as well. Solving her murder might answer the questions that still kept her up at night, quiet the fears and doubts that robbed her of her peace.

She should care more about finding Renee's killer than she cared about Cain Dennison's well-being. He'd offered to help her with her investigation, and he certainly had more direct knowledge of Renee's last days than she did.

Why wasn't she willing to use him the way he'd so willingly offered to be used?

"Why?" he asked, echoing the question hammering in her head.

"You were run out of town by her death," Sara said, though she knew that answer wasn't adequate. "I don't want it to happen again."

"Why would you care?"

"Fine," she said. "I think you complicate the case too much. You'd make it hard for people to trust my motives if they knew we were working together."

"Now we get to the truth," he murmured.

But Sara knew it wasn't the truth. Not all of it. Not by a long shot.

What the hell was going on with her? She'd been a widow for three years, not all of those spent in mourning black. She'd been asked out on dates, had even gone on a few, but not once, not a single time, had she thought of those men as anything but casual dinner companions. Not even a spark of attraction had fluttered low in her belly with any of those men, and she'd come to accept, even cherish, the idea that she was wed to her husband for life, dead or alive.

How could Cain Dennison, of all people, make her feel as if that part of herself might still be alive and kicking?

"We don't have to be open about our...collaboration," he said when she said nothing more. His lips curved in a wicked smile. "We can be secret partners."

The low, almost seductive tone of his voice snaked through her like a lightning strike. She felt the thunderous aftermath low in her belly, a shudder of raw, unwelcome need.

Agreeing with him would be the worst possible decision she could make. She knew it bone deep. But when she opened her mouth to speak, the word that spilled from her lips was "Okay."

He gave her another narrow-eyed look, as if he suspected she was joking. "Okay?"

This was her chance to back out, she thought. Laugh and agree that she'd been joking.

But she couldn't, she realized. No matter what kind of fluttery things he did to her insides just by being Cain Dennison, he was right about one thing. He did know more about Renee Lindsey's final days than anyone else in Purgatory, save the killer himself. If she was serious about getting to the bottom of Renee's murder, she needed his help.

"Okay," she repeated, more firmly. "You're right. I need your help. And, frankly, you could use mine, as well."

"I need you, do I?" His smile made her heart flip-flop.

She had to get a hold of herself, and soon, she thought, before their secret partnership made her spontaneously combust and make a big mess all over his grandmother's front yard. "You do. I have access to people who, right or wrong, aren't gonna give you the time of day, much less any useful information. I'm the daughter of the primary detective on the case eighteen years ago, and I'm good friends with the deputy who's running the new murder case." As she continued speaking, drawing on her professional credentials, some of the sexual tension that had stretched her close to the snapping point began to ease, and she started to think she could make this secret partnership work after all.

Then he touched her. It was nothing but a brief brush of his fingertips along the length of her arm, but it burned through her like a wildfire.

"You won't regret this," he said.

She had a feeling he was dead wrong about that.

SARA LINDSEY LOOKED around his small, sparsely furnished Airstream with a curious gaze, as if assessing him as she took in the decor. He'd come up wanting, he feared, if she judged him on his temporary abode. He'd done little to make it feel like home, mostly because he didn't want to become too used to the place.

He'd grown up in a ramshackle cabin not much larger than this tiny trailer, and for a long time, even after he'd joined the Army and expanded his horizons, he'd felt too small for the world around him. Too lacking, too unworthy of so much space, so much opportunity.

His father had taught him to think small, to expect the worst. Hell, the man had shown him some of the worst life had to offer, made him think it was all he'd ever have. All he'd ever deserve.

For two short years, Renee Lindsey had made him think differently. She'd liked him. Trusted him.

And he'd begun to dream.

"When Renee died," he said aloud, drawing Sara's gaze back to him, "I thought it was the end of my life."

Sara's dark eyebrows lowered, her brow creasing. "You must have loved her a lot."

"I did. More than I realized, I think." Waving her over to the small sofa that nearly filled the front end of the Airstream, he pulled a ladder-back chair from beneath his tiny kitchenette table and placed it across from her, taking a seat. "I don't think it was the hearts-and-flowers kind of love," he added, smiling at the thought. "Renee knew it, even before I did. She didn't need a lover."

"She already had a lover," Sara murmured. "She needed a friend."

He nodded. "I'd never really had one of those before Renee. People tended to give the Dennisons a wide berth, and they weren't wrong for that."

"Your father had a difficult reputation."

"He'd earned it, fair and square," Cain said, trying to keep the bitterness from swallowing him whole. "Every bad thing you've ever heard about him was probably true. And a whole bunch of things you didn't hear."

Sara's gaze grew troubled. "That bad?"

"Worse."

She closed her eyes briefly, and he felt her pity like a cold touch.

"Don't do that," he said gruffly.

Her eyes snapped open. "Don't pity you?"

"I don't want it."

"Pity isn't an insult. It's just a feeling." She reached across the table. Touched his hand.

As her fingertips lingered there, cold against his skin, he felt a surge of raw desire so powerful it nearly swamped him. He drew his hand away before he lost his senses completely.

Sara pulled her hand into her lap and looked down at the table. "If it makes you feel any better, I'm in awe of you, as well."

"Don't do that, either," he said gruffly. "Don't make me out to be some sort of tragic hero."

"Wouldn't dream of it." Her voice was bone dry.

A smile tugged at his mouth. "No, I suppose you wouldn't."

"I just mean, you're here and you're sane. I came from a great family. I had a great husband. A great life. And sometimes I feel as if I'm living in a world I don't even recognize anymore." She looked self-conscious as she tucked a loose strand of hair behind her ear, not meeting his gaze. He supposed she was no more used to talking about her feelings than he was, especially after being alone for nearly three years.

Then again, maybe she hadn't been alone. Maybe there'd been someone else after Donnie's death. Maybe a lot of someones.

He didn't like that thought. Nor did he like just how much he didn't like that thought.

"Where do you think I should start looking?" Sara broke the thick silence that had begun to descend between them.

"For Renee's murderer?"

She nodded, meeting his gaze again. "You probably knew her better than anyone else, right? So where should I look?"

He licked his lips as the answer occurred to him, knowing she probably wouldn't care for what he was about to say. But she'd asked for his honest assessment, hadn't she? He owed her the truth.

"I think you should try to remember what happened the night of your accident," he answered.

As he expected, her brow creased into a troubled frown. "I'm not sure that's even possible. And more to the point, why would that be the place to start looking for Renee's killer?"

He voiced the suspicion that had been building since he found the crystal meth in his grandmother's woodbin. "Because I'm not sure your wreck was really an accident."

Chapter Nine

A flood of cold swallowed Sara's whole body as Cain's words sank in. She fought the strange paralysis with a shake of her head. "There was no evidence of tampering—"

"I don't know how it was done," he said. "I just think there's reason to believe whoever killed Renee would stop at nothing to keep his secrets."

She clasped her hands tightly in front of her, unnerved by the way they were suddenly shaking. "Nobody knows his secrets. The police don't have a clue who killed her. None of us do."

"Someone thinks it's possible for us to find out," he told her, his voice unusually subdued.

Leaning toward him, she lowered her voice, as well. "What's happened?"

Anger blazed in his eyes when they met hers. "Yesterday afternoon, when I got home from your place, there was a note tucked into my door frame. Plain envelope, no name. Inside was a typewritten note that said, 'Look in your grandmother's woodbin. Imagine what might have happened if I'd called the police.'"

Another chill washed through her. "What was in there?"

"About five hundred grams of crystal meth."

She stared at him. "What?"

"Street grade, if the guys at The Gates are right about it."

The Gates? He'd taken the drugs to work? Had he lost his mind? "You didn't turn it in to the cops?"

"Where they can stash it with all the other pounds of crystal meth they've got stored up from drug busts in these mountains while they haul me and my grandmother in for drug trafficking and send those two poor girls into the DCS system?" He looked at her as if *she* were the one who'd lost her mind. "No, thanks. Quinn can get rid of it just as well as the cops, and nobody gets framed."

"What about fingerprints? Trace evidence?"

"The Gates can handle that, too," he said calmly.

She blew out a long breath, shaking her head. "You like to live dangerously. What if a cop had pulled you over on the way to the office?"

"I'd be in jail. Luckily, that didn't happen."

She had grown up in a household where the law was damned near sacrosanct. But would she have been so quick to call the police if she'd found herself in Cain's situation, with his family background?

Probably not, she had to admit. "The chain of evidence has been completely obliterated."

"We'll find some way to use anything we discover." He sounded less than hopeful.

"You don't think you're going to find anything, do you?"

"Nobody gets away with murder for eighteen years if they go around making it easy for people to find them."

She couldn't argue with that point. Donnie had become increasingly obsessed with finding his sister's murderer in the months and years preceding his death, and he'd gotten nowhere, despite his intimate knowledge of her life, her personality and her circle of friends and acquaintances.

Whoever had killed her had done a good job of covering his tracks.

"Okay," she said finally, "I'll buy that. But how does this attempt at blackmailing you figure into my accident? I was the one who was driving. And believe me on this— I wasn't the one who was asking all the uncomfortable questions around Purgatory. That was Donnie. Anyone who wanted to put an end to his investigation would have gone after him, not me."

"He was with you in the car that night."

He had a point. "But I can't find anyone who knew we were going to be in Purgatory that weekend. When would someone have had the chance to do anything to tamper with the truck?"

"You were in Purgatory the night of the accident, Sara, and you don't remember where you went."

She realized what he was implying. "You think we saw or heard something that very night."

He nodded slowly. "It's possible. Maybe even likely." He leaned toward her, the legs of his chair scraping closer. The warmth of his body washed toward her, tempering the cold that lingered in her limbs. "You want to remember what led up to the accident, don't you?"

She stared at him, realizing with dismay that she wasn't sure she knew the answer. She'd spent the past three years telling herself, telling everyone, that not remembering what happened was worse than remembering she was at fault. But was that true? Wasn't it easier not knowing? If she didn't know what happened, then there was still a chance she hadn't caused her husband's death.

What if she remembered everything and erased any hope that she wasn't at fault? Could she live with that knowledge?

She pressed her hand to her mouth. Her fingers trembled against her lips, to her dismay.

Cain reached across the remaining space between them

to touch her hand, gently tugging it away from her face. "I know it must be scary."

"What if I—" She stopped short, unable to say the words.

"What if you didn't?" he countered, his voice warm. "What if someone tried to kill you and Donnie that night? Don't you want to know? Don't you want justice, if that's the case?"

His callused fingers, warm against her skin, had an unexpected calming effect on her trembling limbs. Strange, she thought as she looked up to meet his gaze, considering how his earlier touch had set fire to her blood. "Of course I do."

"Have you ever tried to remember?"

She stared at him, pulling her arm away from his grasp. "What kind of question is that?"

"I mean, I know you've probably tried to remember. Have you ever gone to someone for help recovering your memories?"

"If you're talking about hypnotic regression, I don't buy into that hokum," she said flatly. "There's a reason why it's not admissible in court."

"I'm talking about hypnosis to relax your mental barriers against remembering what happened. If you did hear or see something, your mind may not want to remember what it was. Maybe it's too painful."

Like doing something that ends in your husband's death? She looked down at her hands. "The doctors said it's possible I'll never remember. And after so much time, they're probably right."

"Did they say there was a physical reason why you couldn't remember? A brain injury?"

"I was in a coma for two weeks."

"But that was medically induced, right? Not a result of your head injury?"

She looked up at him, appalled. "How the hell do you know that?"

He looked apologetic. "It was part of the information your mother-in-law gave Quinn when she hired The Gates to look into her children's deaths."

Of course, she thought. Her parents would have thought nothing of telling Joyce Lindsey the details of Sara's condition. After all, as Donnie's mother, she'd have been considered family.

And Joyce, apparently, thought nothing of sharing Sara's personal medical information with strangers at a detective agency.

"Was Mrs. Lindsey wrong? Is there a medical reason you don't remember anything from that night?"

Swallowing the despair rising in her throat, she shook her head. "No. The doctors told me that my head injury was minor. Mostly scalp lacerations and abrasions. The CAT scan didn't show any damage to my brain."

"But when I found you, you were nearly delirious. Then you passed out cold."

She nodded, remembering the doctors' questions after she woke up. "They think it was a combination of emotional distress and pain. I had a couple of bad compound fractures, and the police think, based on Donnie's time of death, we were down there in that gorge for nearly four hours before you found us."

He winced. "I didn't know that."

"Four hours with a couple of compound fractures would be bad enough. Four hours aware that your husband flew through the windshield and was probably dead—" She shuddered, trying to push the thought from her mind, even now. No wonder she didn't want to remember that night.

"I wish I'd gotten there sooner." Cain touched her again, a light brush of his fingertips against her cheek. The potent urge to lean into his touch was so strong, she had to curl her fingers into the sofa cushion to keep from moving closer.

She couldn't stop a bleak laugh from escaping her raw throat. "I don't think it would have changed much. The coroner says Donnie was probably dead the moment he hit the windshield."

Cain dropped his hand. "Did he make it a habit? Not wearing his seat belt, I mean. Or did the belt fail?"

"That wasn't in the notes Joyce gave you?" she asked, immediately ashamed of the hard edge of her tone. It wasn't Joyce's fault that Sara couldn't provide the answers everybody needed.

"She didn't say," he answered quietly.

Of course she wouldn't have. One of Joyce's best— and worst—traits was her undying loyalty to her family. Renee and Donnie could do no wrong, no matter what they'd done.

She supposed Cain Dennison would find that trait a bit more appealing that Sara did. He'd grown up with a man who'd apparently found endless, unjustified fault in everything Cain had done.

But Cain hadn't had to live with that constant conflict between the truth and Joyce's unreasonable perception of her son. The only way to win Joyce's support would have been to agree with Donnie on everything. And Sara just wasn't wired that way.

"He usually wore his seat belt," she told Cain. "He was probably even more militant about it than I am. He was still in the traffic division, so he saw a lot of bad accidents."

Cain's eyes narrowed. "But he wasn't wearing it that night?"

"No. I don't know why he wasn't."

"So maybe you should find out."

Frustrated, mostly because she knew he was right, she scraped her hair away from her face and tried to come up with a reason to protest. But nothing came to mind. Nothing, at least, that would pass muster with her own sense of justice.

"Do you know anyone who does that kind of hypnosis?" she asked finally. "Is that something y'all do there at your fancy detective agency?"

He smiled at her question, the lines creasing his lean cheeks magnifying his masculine appeal until she felt her insides quiver. "I don't know of anyone at The Gates who could put you under hypnosis," he answered, "but I do know a tough old lady who can."

"ARE YOU TRAINED to do this?"

Sara's wary question didn't seem to faze Cain's grandmother. She slanted the younger woman a look of amusement as she pulled her old cane rocking chair closer to Sara's seat on the sofa. "Believe it or not, Sara Dunkirk, I am not uneducated."

"I didn't mean—"

"I just didn't get my education from your fancy schools," Lila added with a laugh. "My mother taught me what she called 'relaxing magic.' Not magic at all, of course, no matter what you may've heard 'bout us Birdsongs."

"I thought Birdsong was your married name."

Lila's eyebrows twitched. "I sent my man packin' the first time he came home drunk and tried to knock me around," she said with a hint of peppery heat in her voice. "Just like my daughter should've done. Though I reckon things happen as they ought, or Cain wouldn't be here."

Cain wasn't sure Sara, or anyone else, would find his presence in the world a compelling argument for his mother letting her husband knock her around, but he flashed his grandmother a smile, anyway.

"So you sent his last name packing at the same time?" Sara asked.

"No need to keep the name around if the man was gone." Almost as soon as she said the words, Lila sent a worried look toward Sara. "I didn't mean—"

"Different men, different situations." Sara waved off Lila's explanation. "If Donnie had been the kind of man to hit a woman, he'd have been gone the first time, too."

"Seems it's always the good ones that pass too soon," Lila said with a nod, sitting back in the rocking chair and giving a push with her legs. The chair started to gently roll back and forth on its rockers. The rhythmic cadence of floor creaks was part of the relaxation method, Cain knew from experience. He'd spent a lot of his adolescence right here in this room, with his grandmother rocking and humming, as she'd just begun to do. The sounds had done wonders to calm his agitated soul and help him survive the double shots of anger and fear that had dominated so much of his young life.

He could see his grandmother's rocking and humming start to have a relaxing effect on Sara, as well. She sank lower in the comfortable cushions of the sofa, her fisted hands releasing their death grip on each other and falling to either side of her legs.

"Do you know this song?" Cain's grandmother asked Sara, humming a few more bars of an old mountain ballad.

Sara began to hum along with Lila in a warm alto harmony. "'Darlin' Ginny,'" she murmured, a smile teasing the corners of her mouth. "My grandmother taught me that song before I could walk."

"Do you do the old-time ballad singin'?" Lila asked between hums.

"All by myself, no instruments?" Sara laughed. "Not if I can avoid it. I prefer singing harmony. Better suits my voice range."

Cain took his seat in the armchair near enough to Sara and his grandmother that he didn't miss a word of their exchange but far enough back to make him a spectator rather than a participant. His gaze settled on Sara's face, watching the nuances of emotion play over her features as she and Lila conversed. She had a good face, he thought. Good bone structure, his grandmother would probably say, her code words for the kind of pretty that would last beyond the bloom of youth.

Sara was still young, but already he could see in the curve of her cheeks and the shape of her jaw what she would look like twenty years from now if life treated her well. She would still be a striking woman, able to command a man's attention as surely as she was commanding his now.

He didn't remember thinking of her that way when he knew her as a gawky teenager. She had still been aglow with lingering childhood, far too young and innocent for a boy who'd had to grow up way too soon.

But Sara had seen the darker side of life in the intervening years, and it had toughened her. Carved a lot of the tenderness out of her, leaving sturdy bone and sinew in its place.

She continued to hum along with Lila, her eyes closing as she laid her head back against the sofa cushion. Across from her, Lila had pulled a half-knitted scarf from the bag of yarn and needles that hung from the back of the rocking chair, and the soft clack of knitting needles joined the symphony of chair creaks and ballad hums.

"I remember the night of your accident," Lila said quietly a few minutes later. "Fall had brung a chill to the mountains, and the trees was already startin' to turn colors."

"Yes." Without opening her eyes, Sara nodded. "It's always colder earlier up here than down in Birmingham at this time of year. You get spoiled down there, thinking summer's gonna last forever, and then before you turn around twice, you're shiverin' in your boots."

"Up here, you get a little warnin' that winter's comin'," Lila agreed with a nod. "Reckon you didn't get no warnin' of the accident, did you?"

"I don't know." Sara's brow furrowed. "I don't remember."

"But you remember it was colder."

"I think so."

"The day had been a cold one, too. Cloudy like it was gonna rain, but it never did. Not 'til after dark."

"Donnie kept saying we should stay with his parents, but I wanted—" Sara stopped, her eyes snapping open. "I remember that conversation."

"Go on and sit back, sugar. Close your eyes again and just answer my questions, best you can." Lila's fingers never faltered on the knitting needles, and the rhythmic creaks of her rocking chair kept a steady cadence. "Your man wanted to stay with his folks, but you wanted somethin' different?"

"I wanted to get out of Purgatory," she said quietly, settling back against the cushions. "I'm just not sure why."

"Do you remember where you was havin' that talk with your man? In the car? Over dinner in town?"

"Outside." A tiny crease formed over the bridge of her nose. "It was cold and windy, and there was just a hint of rain in the air. I told Donnie I wanted to leave Purgatory, but he said it was gonna rain and we ought to stay with his folks until morning." As she relaxed, Sara's voice had settled into a familiar Appalachian twang, sloughing off the veneer of years in the city to expose her mountain roots.

"Outside where?" Cain asked.

His grandmother shot him a warning look and he swallowed an epithet. He'd promised he'd stay a spectator.

His interjection didn't seem to bother Sara. She said,

"It was a house, I think. We were parked on the street, so I guess maybe we'd gone to see someone."

"Who'd you go see?"

Sara's brow crinkled again. "Donnie had been making trips up here when he'd get a couple of days off in a row, lookin' up folks Renee had gone to school with. People who might remember something about her life at the time of the murder. He looked for Cain, but he couldn't track him down."

That's because he'd been in the Army, Cain thought. Lila would have told Donnie that much if he came around asking, though probably not how to reach him. Cain had been determined to steer clear of his father, and at the time he joined the Army, the old man was still alive.

"Can you take a look around you?" Lila asked quietly. "Just turn yourself around right there where you are, where you remember bein', and tell me what you see."

"It's a neighborhood," Sara answered after a moment of thought. "One of those subdivisions they've built out past the marble quarry. Right close to the city limits."

"Do you know anyone who lives out there?" Lila asked.

Sara's brows lifted. "The Allens, I think. Coach Allen and his wife bought a house out there right before we graduated. I remember because Becky Allen hired Donnie and a couple of other guys on the baseball team to come help them put up a fence to keep their dogs from wandering into the street." She opened her eyes and looked at Lila first, then Cain. "We went to see the Allens that night."

"Are you sure?" Cain asked.

Sara nodded. "I remember. Donnie wanted to talk to the coach because during her senior year, Renee had worked in the athletic department to get some internship credit for college. Donnie wanted to ask the coach if he remembered anyone coming to see Renee when she was working in the office."

"Did he?" Cain asked. He'd almost forgotten about Renee's internship with the athletic department.

"He said she mostly worked hard, kept to herself. Only person he saw her with, for the most part, was you."

He supposed that was probably true. Despite his aversion, at the time, for team sports, he'd come up with excuses to haunt the athletic office while she was working her shift, worried that some popular, good-looking jock would come along and snatch her away if he wasn't on guard.

After her death, he'd had far more painful things to remember about her.

"I wonder why the Allens never told anyone that we'd been by to visit that evening," Sara murmured, her brow creased with puzzlement. "I mean, after the accident, I know the sheriff's department went looking for witnesses. Surely they'd have tried to figure out where we were driving from."

"They did," Cain said with a nod. "They spread word they were looking for people who might have talked to you before the accident."

"And the Allens never came forward?"

"Not that I know of."

"I reckon you've done enough for today," Lila interjected, stilling the creak of her rocking chair and flashing Sara a smile. "But you just come on back whenever you want. I'll be right here, and we can commence rockin' and hummin' again."

Sara reached across to clasp Lila's hand. "You've given me somewhere new to look for answers. I don't know how to thank you."

"You just did, darlin'." Lila put her knitting back in the bag hanging from the rocker and looked up at them brightly. "I'm fixin' greens and pintos for lunch. Either one of you want to stick around for it?"

"That's very tempting," Sara said as she stood, sounding sincere, "but I really need to go see Coach Allen now."

"I'll go with you." Cain grabbed his jacket, kissed his grandmother's cheek and followed Sara to the door.

Chapter Ten

"What do you mean he's not here?" Sara's tone went from friendly to sharp in the span of a second, and considering the annoyance flashing in her dark eyes as she towered over the sweet-faced, middle-aged secretary in the Purgatory High School principal's office, it came as no surprise to Cain that the woman looked visibly shaken.

Sara might not be a cop anymore, but she could still be pretty damned intimidating.

"I'm sorry," the woman said when she finally found her voice, "but he and his assistant coach are in Nashville for a seminar on college-recruiting rule changes. There's so many nitpicky things you have to worry about these days to stay in compliance with the NCAA, our coaches like to stay on top of it. They'll be back here Wednesday morning."

"Maybe you could talk to Becky Allen," Cain suggested as he walked Sara back to her truck.

"She did call me, asking if I wanted to come over for dinner some night. It kind of took me by surprise, actually. It's not like we were great friends with her and the coach." She looked at Cain over the truck cab as she unlocked her door. "My stomach is growling. You hungry?"

"I could eat," he said with a smile, wondering if she'd given any thought to what kind of rumors might spread if people saw the two of them eating together in public.

"I heard there's a new Lebanese place in town. What's it called?"

"Tabbouleh Garden," he supplied.

"Right. Kelly Partlow told me about it." She pulled open her door and slid inside. When he'd settled in the passenger seat, she added, "In fact, isn't that where she ran into you last week?"

"It is." Cain smiled at the memory of Kelly's exuberant invitation to the alumni get-together. "She's a force of nature."

Sara laughed, catching Cain by surprise. It was a big, full-throated, uninhibited sort of laugh, the kind that made him want to laugh along. "She is definitely a force of nature. I sometimes wonder how she and I ever managed to become friends. We're so different."

"Are you? So different, I mean."

Her laughter faded as she turned her curious gaze toward him. "Yeah. Very different. She's a social dynamo—always wanting to be out and about. I prefer a night in, curled up in a chair reading a good book."

He smiled at the picture her words painted. "Literature or pop fiction?"

"Either. I'm not that picky." She buckled her seat belt and started the truck. "So, what's good at Tabbouleh Garden?"

"I had the falafel plate. It was excellent."

"There's a great little place in Birmingham with the most amazing falafel wraps," she said as she pulled out of the high school parking lot and headed the truck toward town. "Donnie never cared much for Lebanese food, but I couldn't get enough of it. Thank goodness one of my fellow detectives loved the place. I could talk him into going there to grab lunch at least once or twice a week."

"What did your fellow detective friend have to say about your leaving the police force?" he asked, curious.

"Garrett retired last year." She glanced at him as she pulled to a stop at a traffic light. "I think that was really the beginning of the end for me. I couldn't seem to connect with any of the other detectives on the squad, and I just didn't have the heart to stick around Birmingham after that."

"So you came home."

Her lips curved in a half smile. "I guess I did."

Tabbouleh Garden was doing brisk lunch-hour business, but Cain and Sara didn't have to wait long to get a table. The same pretty waitress who had served him and Darcy the previous week greeted them at the door and led them to a table in the corner of the room.

The waitress returned in a few minutes with the drinks they'd ordered—tea for him, limeade for her. She took a sip of the drink and gave a low moan of pleasure that sent fire blazing through his blood. "This is the best limeade I've had since Moakley's went out of business. Do you remember Moakley's?"

"Doesn't everybody?" He didn't add that, while he'd certainly heard of the old soda shop where all the kids in town had hung out after school, he'd never actually been there. He'd never had two dimes to rub together in those days. His father had refused to let him take an after-school job, demanding that Cain go straight home to take care of the chores. And going to Moakley's on the weekends was out as well, since his father had liked to keep Cain on a short leash.

"They had the best limeade. And they always put a slice of fresh lime in the cup." She laughed again, and the rippling sound was almost as sexy as her previous moan of pleasure had been. "My brother, Patrick, used to work at Moakley's during the summer, and whenever I was being a bratty pest—which was often—he'd swear the next time

I ordered a limeade at Moakley's, he was going to put vinegar in the cup instead."

"Patrick was a couple of years ahead of me in school, I think."

She nodded, giving him a thoughtful look. "Donnie used to want to set him up with Renee, but Patrick already had one foot out of Purgatory by the time Renee was old enough for him to give her a second look. And Renee was such a homebody." She sighed, her fingers playing at the edges of the menu that sat on the table in front of her. "I'd forgotten that about her."

"She loved this town," Cain agreed. "I think her parents wanted her to go off to college and see the world, but she didn't want to leave Purgatory."

"I wonder how much her reluctance had to do with her mystery lover."

He'd wondered the same thing, especially after her death. "I think Renee was just a mountain girl at heart. She used to love Crybaby Falls especially. She loved the whole romantic, tragic history of the place."

"The myth of the heartbroken Cherokee maiden, leaping to her death with her newborn baby?" Sara grimaced. "Tragic, maybe. Not sure I consider it romantic."

"Even after losing Donnie?" As soon as the words left his mouth, he kicked himself. What the hell was he thinking, asking something so personal? "I'm sorry. That was such a stupid question. Forget I asked it."

"It's okay." She reached across the table and covered his hand with hers. "I'm really a little tired of everyone tiptoeing around me these days."

"At least they don't run the other direction when they see you coming." He grimaced before the last word tumbled from his lips.

Sara's lips quirked at the corners. "Now who's pitying you?"

"That *was* pretty pathetic," he agreed as the waitress headed toward them with their orders.

"You sort of give off this vibe," Sara commented as she picked up her falafel wrap and gave it a considering look. "Like you're daring people to come close enough so you can snap your sharp teeth at them."

He frowned. "I do that?"

"A little." She took a bite of the wrap. Her eyes closed and she released a soft moan of satisfaction.

Heat flooded through his veins as he watched her enjoyment of the food and wondered how responsive she might be to other sensual pleasures. "Good?" he asked.

She nodded, her eyes opening to meet his gaze. "Really good."

"You might want to get your baklava to go," he suggested in a soft growl.

Her dark eyes widened slightly as she clearly understood his meaning. "Does it bother you?" she asked, a smile flitting across her lips. "My open display of pleasure?"

"Bother? Yeah, you could say that." He leaned closer, his heart pounding against his sternum. "But only because we're in public."

Her head cocked slightly. "We don't have to be. In public, that is."

"I think maybe we do." He sat back, fighting the urge to reach across the table and touch her flushed face.

She sat back as well, her expression thoughtful. "I don't have any expectations."

"You should. You're a woman who should always have expectations." He forced his attention to his own food, not ready to follow his baser instincts where Sara Lindsey was concerned. She might think she was a woman who could scratch a sexual itch without worrying about the consequences, but he could never see her that way.

Maybe that wasn't fair to her. Maybe he was being a sexist pig, putting her on some sort of pedestal she didn't ask to occupy.

Maybe he knew, deep down, that he wouldn't be able to walk away so easily himself?

"Do you have expectations?" she asked a few minutes later.

He looked up. "About you?"

"About anyone."

"No."

"Maybe you should, too."

He couldn't quell a wry smile. "I'll take your opinion under consideration."

"Your father really did a number on you."

He looked down at the remains of his lunch, no longer hungry. "I really don't want to talk about my father."

"I remember thinking how cruel he must have been to give you a name like Cain." She looked at him over the rim of her glass as she took a sip of limeade. "The original murderer."

"Well, since I was the only one who survived my birth—"

"You didn't kill your mother."

"He used to tell me, from the time I was old enough to understand, that I'd killed my twin brother in the womb and killed my mother coming out."

"The bastard." Her voice trembled with intensity.

"Yeah, well. Made me grow up tough, I guess."

"No kid should have had to listen to that kind of garbage."

No, he thought, no kid should. But on the whole, he'd preferred the words, which his blessing of a grandmother had taught him to ignore with the power of her love, than the beatings.

Not even Lila's love could prevent the bruises and broken bones.

Sara seemed to read his mood, changing the subject to college football and Tennessee's chances for a bowl bid. They concluded, by the time the waitress brought the check, that everything hinged on the sophomore who'd won the quarterback position in the preseason, and they left the restaurant debating the head coach's controversial choice.

What had been a sunny day was beginning to turn gloomy, storm clouds scudding eastward toward the mountains. "Rain's comin'," Sara said, and Cain managed a weak smile at the broadening of her accent. Back in town a few days and she was already picking up the mountain twang again. He was as guilty of that, he supposed, as she was.

You can take a fella out of the mountains...

"Cain?" Sara broke the silence a few minutes later as she turned off the main road and headed back up the mountain toward his grandmother's place.

"Yeah?"

"This is going to be a strange question, I know, but— do you think it's possible Coach Allen could have been the father of Renee's baby?"

"You're right. That's a strange question."

"I know. I just—don't you think it's strange he never came forward to tell anyone Donnie and I visited him the night of the accident?"

"Yeah, but it's a big leap to go from that to murder."

"I didn't say he murdered her." The first fat raindrops splatted against the truck windshield, and she turned on the windshield wipers. "But could he have been the person Renee was involved with?"

He gave the question a moment of thought. "Jim Allen wasn't much older than us students back then. I guess he was probably young enough to see a pretty eighteen-year-old coed as a viable sexual conquest. If he was the sort to cheat on his wife."

"Donnie once told me he thought Coach Allen and his wife were having trouble. He said he'd overheard something that made him wonder."

"I'm not sure you can base an investigation on something someone overheard nearly twenty years ago." Cain had been the focus of some nasty rumors in his day, based on not much less than what Sara was describing.

"I don't know how soon the cops are going to get a DNA profile on the baby Ariel Burke was carrying. But if it proves a familial match with the baby Renee was carrying—"

"We still don't have a DNA profile to match it to."

"So maybe we need to get our hands on Coach Allen's DNA."

Cain looked at Sara. She had both hands gripped tightly on the steering wheel, her gaze aimed forward toward the rain-slick road. But there was a trembling tension in her profile, reminding him of a hawk that had just spotted prey.

"What do you have in mind?" he asked cautiously. "Taking Becky Allen up on her dinner invitation?"

"If I have to. But there may be a way to get our hands on it while flying under the radar."

"Yeah?"

"Yeah." She turned to look at him, just a quick, vibrant gaze that sent a jolt of desire hurtling through his body. "How would you like to be my date to a charity hoedown?"

ON SATURDAY EVENING as she and Cain entered the Purgatory Community Center meeting hall, Sara discovered how seriously her mother and Rita Ellis had taken the charity fund-raiser's hoedown theme to heart. Normally, the community-center event hall was a bland, rectangular room with a dais at the back and two double doors at the front. Tonight, however, Ann Dunkirk, Rita Ellis and their little worker elves had transformed the place into the inside of a barn.

Bales of hay covered with colorful horse blankets lined the walls in the place of chairs, and the dais at the back, where the Meade family bluegrass band was tuning up for their first set, was adorned with stable doors, hitching posts and a variety of ropes and authentic leather tack.

"Yippie ki-yay," Cain murmured in her ear.

She shot him a warning glance. "It's a bit much, but my mother was part of it, so watch your mouth."

His only reply was a twitch of his lips.

She'd been finding it hard to drag her gaze away from him ever since he drove up to the cabin to pick her up for the dance. He looked downright edible tonight, in his Wrangler jeans, plaid shirt and leather jacket. He'd even worn a well-used John Deere cap that he'd folded and tucked into his back pocket when they entered the meeting hall.

He made redneck look pretty damned sexy.

And maybe if his good looks had been the end of it, she might have found him easier to resist. But he also possessed a solid core of decency he seemed so determined to hide from the world. In her work as a detective, she'd learned that a man's true self always found a way to peek through even the most well-crafted facade. All you had to do was wait for it to make an appearance.

Cain had shown his true self during lunch that day at Tabbouleh Garden, when he'd managed to make her feel wildly desirable at the same time he'd turned down her veiled invitation for no-strings sex.

You're a woman who should always have expectations, he'd told her.

If she thought she'd found him desirable before...

Forcing her gaze away from his deliciously stubbled jaw, she spotted her mother talking to Nola Meade, a tall, rawboned woman in her early forties. Her strong, unadorned features were more handsome than pretty, her silver-streaked brown hair gleaming in the spotlights like warm honey. She held a mandolin tucked in the crook of her elbow like a baby and smiled as she spoke to Ann Dunkirk.

"Those the Meades?" Cain asked, nodding toward the stage.

"You've never heard them?"

Cain's mouth curved. "My tastes tend more toward Skynyrd and Marshall Tucker."

"Just promise you're not going to pull out your lighter and start hollerin' 'Freebird.'" She weaved her way through the milling crowds, heading for the dais. She could tell by the sudden buzz in the crowd that Cain was right behind her.

She should have warned her mother of her plans to bring Cain with her tonight, she realized when Ann's eyes narrowed at their approach.

Sara gave her mother a swift hug. "The place looks amazing."

"It's too much," Ann admitted, keeping her voice low. "Rita can be a bit exuberant."

"It's very festive," Sara insisted. She smiled up at Nola Meade. "Hey there, Nola. How're you doing?"

"Better'n I deserve, hon." Her brown-eyed gaze slid past Sara to snag on Cain standing close behind her. Sara didn't miss the spark of feminine appreciation in the other woman's eyes and couldn't blame her a bit.

"Nola Meade, this is Cain Dennison. Cain, this is Nola Meade, the best mandolin player in the hills."

"Not sure I'd go that far," Nola said with a broad smile. "Nice to meet you, Cain."

"Same here, Mrs. Meade."

"Oh, lord, just call me Nola, unless you want to make me feel old." Nola looked at Sara. "I was real sorry to hear about your husband."

"Thank you. It's been a tough few years."

As Nola made her excuses and turned back to the work of setting up the stage for the family band, Ann caught Sara's arm and pulled her to one side of the stage, away from everyone else. She glanced toward Cain, who was waiting patiently by the stage, making a show of watching the Meades tune up their instruments.

"Do you really think it was a good idea to bring Cain Dennison?"

"He paid for his ticket like everyone else," Sara said quietly.

"Joyce still thinks he had something to do with Renee's death."

"Donnie didn't. He said that Cain was a good friend to Renee."

Ann glanced at Cain again. "Have you taken up with him?"

"Taken up with him?" Sara asked, shooting her mother a look.

Ann lowered her voice. "You know what I'm asking."

Sara sighed. "Cain and I both want to know what happened to Renee."

Ann's dark eyes narrowed. "It's not enough that your daddy's come out of retirement with this terrible new case with the Burke girl—"

"Mom, it's what we do. You know that."

With a sigh, Ann slanted a look toward Cain again. "I think your date is trying to get your attention."

Sara turned and saw Cain watching her, his gaze urgent. She excused herself from her mother and crossed to where he stood. "What's up?"

"One of the coaches from the high school is here, and I overheard him telling his wife that Coach Allen had called in sick the past three days of school."

"Well, hell. I guess maybe that's why he hasn't returned any of my calls." She'd tried several times since Wednesday morning to get in touch with Coach Allen, with no luck. Nor had Becky Allen returned any of her messages.

"That probably means he won't show up tonight."

She frowned with frustration. Talking to Jim Allen had been her main reason for coming to this fund-raiser. In a crowd like this, she'd figured, she would have ample opportunities to get her hands on a discarded cup or plate that might contain enough of the coach's DNA to test against the profile of the baby Renee had been carrying at the time of her death.

Cain caught her elbow in his hand, tugging her with him toward the side of the room. If he was aware of the stares and whispers that followed them, he showed no sign of it. Once they were tucked between a bale of hay and a decorative haystack near a window looking out on the parking lot, he said, "Wonder if he's really sick?"

"You think he's faking it?"

"He has to know you're looking for him by now. You left enough messages."

"And he knows Donnie and I went to see him before the accident."

"Maybe he's afraid you've remembered something."

"All I remembered is being outside his house the night of the accident." Despite her attempts to recreate the relaxation techniques Lila Birdsong had used with her the other morning, Sara hadn't been able to uncover any more of her lost memories. "And he doesn't know I remember even that much."

Cain's hand stroked lightly along her arm, sending prickles of delicious heat darting through her. "Maybe not. But between Ariel Burke's murder and your sudden eagerness to talk to him—"

She looked up at him. "You think he might have killed Ariel as well?"

"I can't ignore the similarities in the murders." Cain lowered his voice to a near-whisper. "After we talked about Coach Allen the other day, I remembered something a guy told me back in high school. It was pure gossip, and I've learned not to spread gossip, since I was the focus of a lot of malicious lies in my own time."

"But?" she prodded when he paused as if he didn't want to continue.

"But back in high school, one of the guys in the crowd I hung with swore up and down that there was a coach at the school who was sleeping around with some of the senior girls. What if it was true? And what if that coach was Jim Allen?"

Chapter Eleven

The start of the bluegrass set rolled through the hall almost as soon as Cain posed his question, enlivening the gathered crowd and raising the decibel level in the community-center hall so high that the only way Sara could have responded was with a yell.

Shooting him an apologetic look, she caught his hand and pulled him closer to the stage, where she joined with the crowd in clapping to the beat of the lively reel the Meade family had chosen to begin their set.

Next to her, Cain gave a shrug and started clapping along as well, his grin suggesting that, rock fan or not, he recognized the Meades could flat-out play. Nola's long fingers danced over the mandolin strings, coaxing riffs as fierce as any rock guitarist could hope for, and her older daughter, Tammie Jane, was defying physics on the banjo.

"They're good!" Cain said in her ear as the Meades finished the first song to applause and started straight into the next. The two younger girls, Tammie Jane and her sister, Dorrie, put down their banjo and fiddle respectively, heading to a pair of microphones. The girls began to sing in crystalline harmony to an old-fashioned two-step, and all around Sara and Cain, the fund-raiser attendees began pairing up to dance.

Sara turned to Cain and held out her hand. "Wanna dance?"

"I'm not much of a dancer," he warned as he caught her hand, pulling her flush to him. "But I'm up for a challenge."

Hiding a grin, Sara slipped her arm around his shoulders, settling her fingers in the silky waves of dark hair that brushed the collar of his denim jacket. He met her gaze, heat blazing in the depths of his gray eyes, and something at her core caught fire and started spreading until her whole body burned with excitement.

She'd been gawky as a teenager in most situations, but the one thing she'd always been able to do was dance. It was as if the music took over her body, erasing her gracelessness for the length of the tune.

Cain hadn't been kidding—he wasn't much of a dancer as they started, but he was a quick study, and he seemed to actually enjoy letting her subtly lead the dance, his gaze deepening each time her legs brushed his or their hips collided as she helped him through the steps that twirled them through the crowd.

But eventually, he took control, tugging her closer as his steps became more certain. Her heart pounded a quickened cadence in response, and by the time the song ended, she was nearly out of breath.

"You're a better dancer than you think," she said, trying to tell herself that it was the lively dance and not Cain's arms around her that had stolen her breath and jumpstarted her pulse. But she knew better.

It had been three years since she'd felt another heartbeat thud against her chest or fingers slide over her arm with sexual intent. And even though what she and Cain had just shared would seem, to others, nothing more than a lively two-step, she knew it was so much more.

It was a question. An invitation. The same invitation

she'd so delicately hinted at a few days earlier over lunch. She saw it in his dark eyes, felt it in the way his hand lingered as he released her and stepped back.

What are we going to do about this thing between us? his eyes seemed to ask, and she didn't know the answer any more now than then.

All she knew was when the next song started, a plaintive ballad of love and longing, they reached for each other without question.

He felt solid. Real. For three years, she'd slept with a phantom memory of the man she'd loved since boyhood, awakening to an empty bed and living on the precipice of an aching chasm between what she'd had and what she'd lost. She'd grieved and, in many ways, moved on with her life.

But could she ever really love another man?

She and Donnie had been inseparable from the tender age of thirteen and she'd never doubted her decision to be with him, even during the stresses and strains that challenged every long-term relationship. Was it even possible to find that kind of love again?

Was she greedy to try?

It was stupid to be thinking about love in Cain Dennison's arms. They barely knew each other. What was stirring between their bodies had more to do with friction and hormones, not intimacy and affection.

But it had been a while since she'd let friction and hormones have their way. And she'd already made it plain to him that she'd be okay if whatever happened between them never led anywhere else.

She started to look up at him, to see if she could read what he was thinking in those gunmetal eyes, but before her gaze reached his face, it snagged on a pair of newcomers who had just entered the community center. A hard chill washed over her, driving out the earlier heat, and she stiffened in Cain's embrace.

He pulled back to look at her. "What?"

As he started to turn his head to see what she was looking at, she tightened her grip on him. "Don't turn around. Joyce and Gary Lindsey just came in."

His expression shifted subtly from curiosity to dismay. He dropped his hands away from her body. "I'll go."

No, she thought, desperate to feel the heat again, anything but this disheartening blend of grief and shame. She grabbed his hand again and gave a tug. "There's a side exit between the punch bowl and that big scarecrow." Sara led him to the door and they slipped out into the darkness.

With the door closed, the music faded to a soft whisper of sound. Cain stepped away from her, withdrawing his heat and, with it, any shelter against the cold night air. Autumn was fading in the mountains, and winter was on the way, slithering like a promise of ice down her spine.

Sara wrapped her arms around herself and stared at him, not sure what to say or do now that she had him all to herself. What came out when she opened her mouth was a simple statement. "Winter's coming."

He held her gaze a long moment, as if trying to read what was going on behind her eyes. *Good luck,* she thought with bleak amusement. *Hell if I know myself.*

He reached out almost tentatively, as if he expected her to run at his first touch. When she didn't flee, he ran his hands gently up and down her arms as if to warm her. "You can go back in there now, you know. I'll go on home and Joyce doesn't even have to know I was here."

No, she thought again. She didn't know what she wanted to do, what was the right thing to do, but she knew she wasn't ready to let him leave. She lifted her chin, the decision made. "You know small towns. It won't take a minute before someone tells her all about it."

"I don't want to make things harder for you. For either one of you."

Sara put her hand on his chest, flattening her palm over his heart. "I know."

He covered her hand briefly with his own, then started to step away, once more robbing her of his heat.

She caught his hand as the music coming from inside the hall changed again, to a plaintive lament that seemed to resonate in her own hollow chest. "Don't go."

"Sara—"

"Dance with me again."

He gazed at her in consternation, and she could tell he knew as well as she did that what she was suggesting was akin to lighting matches in a pool of gasoline. He closed his eyes briefly, as if struggling to make the right decision. When he opened them again, the fierce hunger in his gaze shot straight to her sex, setting her nerves vibrating like a tuning fork.

"You like to play with fire, don't you, Sara Dunkirk?" he murmured, tugging her close.

She melted into his embrace, letting the music work its magic on her normally graceless body. The tune was an old one, a mountain lover's plaintive song of love given freely and ripped away, and it made her feel equal parts melancholy and restless.

"This isn't why we came here tonight," he murmured, but he didn't make any effort to end the seductive glide of his body against hers.

"I know."

"You know how wrong I think this is," he added, not sounding as if he thought it wrong at all.

"It's a terrible idea," she agreed in a tone that suggested she, too, thought no such thing.

There was no reason to move from where they swayed under the weak golden light of the parking lot lamps, but before she realized it, they were swallowed by the shadows pooling near the cool brick wall of the community center. The music grew fainter, her pulse more thunderous in her ears as he pressed her into the wall. Though the bricks were cold and hard against her spine, all she felt was a fierce, shuddering thrill as he pinned her there with his long, lean body.

"If you don't want this, say so now," he whispered, his mouth inches from hers. His breath fogged the air between them, softening his features as he gazed at her with feral intent.

She curled her hand around the back of his neck and tugged him closer, lifting her face to him.

The first brush of his mouth to hers was exploratory, almost tentative. But when she darted her tongue against his upper lip, he twined his fingers with hers, trapping her hands against the brick wall as he slid his tongue over hers, drawing out her passionate response until she was gasping for air and sanity.

His mouth danced lightly across her jawline and over to her ear, nibbling lightly on the sensitive lobe before he whispered, "Let's get out of here." He released her hands and stepped back, leaving her feeling so boneless and weak she had to fight to keep from sliding down the wall into a puddle at his feet. Slowly, his gaze warm with sexy confidence, he held his hand out to her. "You coming?"

As soon as humanly possible, she thought, unable to stop a grin from spreading over her features at the naughty thought as she took his hand.

On trembling legs, she followed him across the parking lot to his truck.

WHAT THE HELL do you think you're doing, Dennison? Even as his heart pounded a fierce cadence of desire, his foggy brain struggled to regain control over his senses. He was driving Sara Lindsey back to her little mountain cabin as fast as his truck could go, to hell with traffic laws or anything resembling good sense. When he got there, he fully intended to strip her naked and explore every inch of that tantalizing body that had teased him all night beneath the layers of cotton and denim that had hidden it from his view. He was damned well determined to give her the best sex of her life.

Even if it was the worst idea he'd ever had in his whole sorry, misbegotten life.

"We're crazy, aren't we?" she asked, her tone still as breathless as it had been when she'd asked him not to leave outside the community center. He still heard the same tone of sexual excitement that he'd seen echoed in her dark gaze, but threaded through the arousal was a bleaker tone, a hint of fear and regret.

Tamping down the selfish urge to brush aside those reservations, he made himself slow the truck as it started the climb up the mountainside to her cabin. "Probably," he admitted.

She was silent long enough for them to reach the edge of her property. Cain pulled his truck in behind hers where it sat parked in the gravel in front of the cabin and shut off the engine. The ensuing silence felt heavy and thick with unspoken thoughts.

Sara turned to look at him, and any intention to do the right thing shot straight out of his brain when he saw the fire blazing in her hungry gaze. Reaching for her, he dragged her toward him, laughing helplessly as her seat belt foiled him.

Sara grappled with the clasp until it opened, freeing her to launch herself into his grasp in a tangle of arms and legs and searching lips.

He settled her between his body and the steering wheel, and if the wheel digging into her rib cage caused her any discomfort, she didn't show it, straining closer, her legs straddling his until he felt the fiery heat at the juncture of her thighs press intimately over his own straining erection.

Her thighs clenching, she rose slowly up his body and back down, deliberately creating friction between them. In the pale glow of the dashboard, he caught a glint of pure, wicked pleasure in her eyes as he was unable to stop a groan from escaping his mouth.

"That," she whispered against his mouth, "is what it feels like to discover you're still alive."

The sentiment behind her words stung him, even as she slid her tongue against his, drawing him into another deep, heart-stopping kiss.

He struggled against the power of his lust for her, knowing she'd just told him something important and profound. Gently pushing her away until she winced a little at the press of the steering wheel against her back, he cradled her face and made her look at him. "What do you mean, to discover you're still alive?"

She made a face at him, impatience trembling in her touch as she tried to draw him back to her. "Nothing. I didn't say anything."

Wrestling with the selfish desire to take her at her word, he kept her from bending in for another kiss. "No, you said this was what it feels like to discover you're still alive."

With a growl of frustration, she slid away from his lap. He felt the absence of her soft heat like an ache, and not just the physical kind. A hollow sensation filled his chest as well, as if she'd removed something vital from inside him when she moved to her side of the truck cab.

"I haven't been with anyone since Donnie," she said. The words sounded hushed, as if spoken in the hallowed privacy of the confessional.

Cain had spent more time than he liked wondering if she'd broken her mourning with another man, but hear-

ing her say the words aloud, he couldn't say he was surprised to learn she'd been faithful to his memory. She'd
loved Donnie Lindsey since they were kids, and losing
him couldn't have been something she'd get over easily.

"I guess it sort of felt like my life has been in limbo,"
she added when he didn't say anything. "I still felt married to a man who was dead. I guess it made me feel as if
I was there with him, in death."

"And so this—" Cain waved his hand in the space between them "—is sort of like a limb coming back to life?"

She shot him a grin that was pure temptation. "Well,
yes, if by limb you mean—"

He shushed her with two fingers against her lips. "When
a limb comes back to life, there's usually a good bit of pain
before it's all over."

The smile that curved against his fingers faded, and
her eyes took on a serious light. "It's better than feeling
nothing."

The sorrow in her voice echoed in his hollow chest, ex-
acerbating the empty ache that had set up shop there when
she drew away from him. He didn't let himself examine
the sensation too closely, not ready to think about what it
might mean that he felt her pain so keenly himself.

"I think we shouldn't do anything we can't take back,"
he said, steeling himself against any attempt she might
make to change his mind. "I meant what I said the other
day. You should always have expectations about something
as important as who you sleep with."

"I meant what I said, too," she said quietly. "You should
have expectations, yourself."

"Did you really expect anything good from what we
were about to do?"

She turned her face forward to gaze through the front
windshield at the darkened cabin. "I wasn't thinking about
what happens next."

"You should. We both should."

"I'm not reckless by nature," she admitted. "I'm not used to feeling so out of control."

"Well, at the risk of stretching a metaphor until it snaps, a limb that's fallen asleep usually flails around a bit until all the feeling comes back."

She groaned softly on her side of the cab, slanting a look at him that made him smile for the first time since they'd stopped kissing. "Stop. You've definitely tortured that metaphor enough."

He couldn't stop himself from pressing the back of his knuckles against her cheek. "I'm done."

She caught his hand, her touch gentle but not inviting anything more than the small display of affection. "Thank you. And not just for putting the metaphor out of its misery."

"It's okay if you don't want to work together on this case anymore."

She shook her head. "We're adults. We can be professional, right?"

"Right," he agreed, even if there was a hint of doubt still lingering in the back of his mind. He'd have to make their professional alliance work, even if it killed him, because if the past few weeks in Purgatory had proved nothing else to him, it was that he couldn't open nearly as many doors in this town as he needed to in order to get the answers he wanted. Sara was his key to a whole lot of information currently not available to him, and he didn't know if he'd get anywhere on the case without her.

"Will you stick around to see I get inside safely?" she asked, opening the passenger door. She shot him a sheepish smile that made his legs tingle a little. "You can take the cop out of the big city..."

He grinned. "I've got your back, Detective."

She walked slowly up the stairs to the front door, her

body swaying slightly with each step, as if she could still hear phantom strains of music in the cold night air. She turned at the top of the porch and gave a little wave. He waved back, his chest squeezing into a hot, tight knot at the almost girlish vulnerability he glimpsed in her moon-lit features.

He waited until she unlocked the cabin door and slipped inside before he started the engine. When the lights came on inside the cabin, Cain put the truck in Reverse and started to pull out.

Suddenly the front door opened and Sara hurried out, waving frantically as she ran down the stairs.

Cain jammed the truck into Park and rolled down his window as she hurried up to his door. "What's wrong?"

"Someone broke into the cabin and trashed the place," she said, fear mingling with anger in her blazing dark gaze. "And I think they took all the notes I've made on the case so far."

Chapter Twelve

The large front room of the small cabin was a mess. Sofa cushions had been ripped up and tossed around, the stuffing covering the hardwood floors like the aftermath of a fiberfill snowstorm. The sheer, back-breaking work it was going to take just to get the cabin back to where she'd gotten it over the past couple of weeks was enough to make Sara want to cry.

The damage the intruder had inflicted to photographs and mementos that couldn't be replaced, however, made her seething mad.

"That's the only photograph I have of my great-grandmother Dunkirk," she told Cain with a wave toward the black-and-white photo that had been pulled from its smashed frame and ripped into three pieces. "That broken vase there was made by my uncle Cyrus shortly before he went to Vietnam and died in battle."

Cain remained silent as he looked around the room, taking in the destruction. After a moment, he turned and put his hand on her cheek. "I don't even know what to say to you."

Despite her earlier determination to keep their relationship on a professional footing, she didn't resist when he pulled her into his arms. Pressing her cheek against the solid heat of his chest, she let herself have a quiet moment of mourning for what she'd lost that couldn't be replaced.

But after a minute, she lifted her head and squared her shoulders. "My guess is that what happened here is connected to our investigation."

"Maybe not. Maybe some meth head broke in looking for money and ended up trashing the place just for the hell of it."

"My laptop computer is sitting right there on my desk. There's fifty dollars in an unlocked drawer in that same desk. I put it there to pay the guy I hired to power wash the outside of the cabin next week. And the only thing I can tell was taken was a file folder I left sitting on that desk this afternoon. It contained a compilation of all the notes I had on Renee Lindsey's murder, including the ones Donnie put together before he died."

Cain grimaced. "I'm so sorry."

She pressed her lips in a tight line, struggling to maintain her composure. At the moment, she was in the mood to throw a few things around, herself. Starting with the bastard who broke into her cabin and made this disheartening mess.

"I don't suppose you have copies of those notes?" he said after giving her a moment to calm down.

"Actually, I do. At least, copies of Donnie's notes. I digitized the handwritten stuff after his death, when I was stuck home recuperating from my own injuries." She managed a grim smile, though humor was the last thing she was feeling at the moment. "Gave me something to do with my brain and my hands at a time I really, really needed a distraction."

"What about the other stuff in the stolen folder?"

She shrugged, trying to remember what else there might be. "Mostly it would have been notes I took over the past few days. I like to write things down longhand when I first make a set of notes. I got used to doing it that way when I was working as a police detective, and I never got out of the habit. I find that writing my notes in longhand helps me slow down and let my mind ferret out all the details of my observations. Typing goes too quickly."

"And you haven't had a chance to type up your long-hand notes and put them on your computer?"

"Not the ones I took in the last couple of days." She tried to remember what hadn't yet been saved to her computer. "Mostly it would be the stuff about Coach Allen and our speculations about his potential relationship with Renee."

Cain frowned. "If Coach Allen is the one responsible for what happened here at your cabin—"

"Then he knows we're on to him."

Cain rubbed his jaw as he took another look around the place. "There's something strange about this mess. Don't you think?"

"As a matter of fact, yes," she agreed, following his gaze around the room. She'd understood it almost from the moment she walked into the cabin, despite the paralyzing effect of shock at the sight of so much destruction. "There wasn't any effort to make this look like a common robbery. Not even the most obvious things were taken out of here. And all the destruction is—"

"Personal," Cain finished in unison with her.

"Exactly."

"I doubt there's going to be any evidence to find," he said, looking around, "but you should probably get the break-in on the record with the cops."

The question caught her by surprise. "Cain Dennison, suggesting a call to the police?"

He grinned. "Wonders never cease."

"If you want to clear out before they come, I'll under-stand."

His smile faded. "You want me to leave?"

"No," she said quickly, wanting nothing of the sort. "I just figured you'd want to, considering your history with the Ridge County Sheriff's Department."

"Lotta years ago," he said with a shrug. "Maybe it's time to start acting like an innocent man instead of always looking over my shoulder."

Sara bypassed emergency services and called the station directly, telling the night-shift desk sergeant what was going on. He told her he could have deputies at her cabin in about fifteen minutes, unless she thought there was any chance the intruders might be still lurking about. In that case, he could get them there faster.

"No, I think the intruder's gone for the night." At least, she hoped so, she thought as she hung up the phone. She might be armed and well-trained, but sooner or later she'd have to sleep. And clearly, her defenses weren't exactly shored up at this cabin. She'd locked the doors, but someone had still managed to find a way in.

"What are you thinking?" Cain asked.

"Just wondering how the intruder got in. The front door was still locked when I got here tonight." She headed into the other rooms of the small cabin, checking windows to see if they had provided the point of entry. She also checked the top of the bedroom closet to make sure her gun case was still locked. It was, and the Walther PPK was still snuggled safely in its foam mold. She locked the case, double-checked that all her extra ammunition was still in the boxes stored next to the case and headed back into the hall.

Cain stood in the middle of the hall, looking through an open door with his brow furrowed. "Is this the basement?"

"It's a root cellar."

"Is there a way down there besides this door?"

She nodded, already heading for the front door as she realized how the intruder must have gotten inside the cabin. She stopped long enough to grab a flashlight from the drawer of her desk in the front room and headed outside, Cain on her heels.

On the western side of the cabin, a door set into the ground led into the cellar. Normally, a padlock closed the door hasp to keep out intruders, but the lock lay a few feet away in the grass, snapped in two.

"Point of entry," she said flatly.

"You'll have to add a dead bolt to the door from the cellar." Cain put his hand on her arm, nudging her back toward the cabin. Sara didn't resist, as the cold wind blowing down from Sandler Ridge had a bitter edge.

She rubbed her arms to tamp down a sudden chill once they were back inside the cabin. "How does anybody know to look for me here? I haven't exactly been advertising my living arrangements."

His dark eyebrows notched upward, but he said nothing.

"Oh. Right." She pushed her hair back from her face in frustration. "Small-town gossip."

"This ain't the big city, sugar," he drawled.

But she'd felt safer in the city than she felt right now, she realized with dismay. And she was about to be spending the night here with no way to lock the door from the cellar.

Anyone could break in again, couldn't they?

"Maybe you shouldn't stay here tonight," Cain said, apparently reading her mind. "I'm sure your parents would be happy to have you stay over."

She shook her head. "You have no idea how tempting it is right now to run home to Mom and Dad. But if I do, I'll never get my life back. I can't keep running back home and hiding under my childhood bed."

Almost as soon as she'd blurted the words aloud, she wondered why on earth she was saying such an intimate, revealing thing to a man who had been little more than a stranger only a week ago.

Who was still a stranger, a few hot kisses notwithstanding.

If her confession made him uncomfortable, he didn't show it. "Then call someone to come stay here with you. At least for tonight."

Squaring her shoulders, she shook her head. "I don't need a bodyguard. I'm a trained cop, even if I'm not working at the moment." She shot him a wry look. "I'm armed and dangerous."

"You're armed?" His skeptical gaze roamed her body. "Right now?"

"Well, not at this moment. My Walther's locked in the bedroom closet. But I'm a good shot, and I have plenty of ammo."

"Have you checked to make sure your weapon's still here?"

She nodded. "When I checked for signs of forced entry."

"You know, to open that padlock, someone would have needed a bolt cutter. Was there one lying around this place before?"

She had been over every inch of the cabin while trying to assess its condition. She hadn't seen a bolt cutter or anything that could have snapped the padlock. "No."

"So someone knew you'd be gone tonight and how to get in." His eyes narrowed. "How many people in town would know those things?"

Her heart sank as she once again considered the drawbacks of life in a small town. "Really, almost anyone. My grandfather was one of those people who never met a stranger. He'd bring people into the house all the time, just to sit a spell and talk or show off his latest hunting rifle or how many cans of tomatoes he'd put up out of the garden for the winter."

"You really need to reconsider staying here alone tonight."

Before she could argue, her cell phone rang. "Hello?"

"Hey, Sara, it's Brad Ellis. I just got a call from the station—what's this I hear about somebody breaking in to your cabin?"

BEING THE DAUGHTER of a former sheriff's department investigator clearly had its perks, Cain thought as he watched three deputies scour Sara's place for clues while she talked quietly in the kitchen with Lieutenant Ellis, who'd been her father's partner before his retirement.

Cain really wasn't sure why he was sticking around at this point—she certainly didn't need him to keep her safe, at least not while her place was crawling with deputies.

But sooner or later the deputies would leave, even Ellis, and she'd be alone again.

And a lot more vulnerable than she seemed willing to admit.

He didn't doubt she was smart and tough. He didn't doubt she could use that Walther she had locked in her closet as well as she claimed. But there was no good reason for her to go it alone tonight.

Not when he could stay with her and watch her back.

Unfortunately, she had made it clear that she intended to handle the threat on her own. Her dark eyes had warned him silently against even offering his help. She apparently saw the situation as a challenge, something she had to face on her own in order to maintain her self-respect.

So he hadn't offered to stay.

But that didn't mean he wasn't going to watch her back, whether she wanted him to or not.

After ascertaining that Cain could offer no information about the break-in, the deputies had stopped paying any attention to him, making it easy for him to slip out the front door unnoticed. He stepped into the chilly night air and tucked the collar of his jacket up higher to protect his neck from the brisk wind.

He'd been worried the deputies had blocked his truck in, but they'd left him a narrow lane of escape. Not that he intended to escape far.

He backed through the gap and down the narrow drive until he reached the road. It had been a few years since he'd wandered around this part of Sandler Ridge, but if his memory hadn't failed him, there was a turnabout fifty yards up the road where he could park and watch for the deputies to leave. With the trees starting to lose their summer foliage, he'd probably even have a decent view of the cabin, a good enough view, at least, to see when the lights went out and he could safely move closer and settle in to keep vigil for the night.

His cell phone rang not long after he parked, the trill jarring in the stillness of the truck cab. He glanced at the display. Quinn, of course. Who else would be calling him at this time of night? "What's up, boss?"

"I understand there was a break-in at Mrs. Lindsey's cabin."

How the hell did he know that? "There was."

"Anything of value taken?"

"All her notes on the Renee Lindsey murder. Fortunately for her, she has backups."

"Unfortunately for us all, now someone knows everything she knows about the case."

"If it's any consolation, that isn't a whole lot." Cain grimaced in the dark, thinking about how bloody little they did know that wasn't already public knowledge, more or less. "By the way, I almost ran into Joyce Lindsey tonight. How long do you suppose it's going to be before Joyce Lindsey figures out I'm the investigator you sent to work her daughter's murder case?"

"Not long, I'm afraid. So you'd better find out as much as you can before that happens," Quinn said reasonably. "Speaking of which, anything new going on?"

"We're still trying to get Jim Allen's DNA to test."

"*We* are?"

"Sara Lindsey and I." Cain looked toward the cabin, where the first of the three sheriff's department cruisers was backing out of the driveway.

"She's working with you now?"

"We have the same goal. And she has inside connections I couldn't dream about."

Quinn sighed softly on the other end of the line. "Are you sure you really have the same goal? It wasn't long ago that we were wondering whether she could have been responsible for her husband's death."

"She wasn't. She wants the truth as much as any of us."

"Just remember, you're my employee, not hers. Don't let her agenda change yours."

"Understood." He ended the call.

Down the road, the other two cruisers left Sara's driveway. Cain turned his gaze back to the cabin, wondering how long it would take Sara to wind down for the night.

Not that it mattered. He wasn't going anywhere.

"I'M FINE, DAD. I nailed the door from the cellar shut, so I don't have to worry about anybody else coming in that way. And I'll get a dead bolt for the door tomorrow." Tucking her cell phone under her chin, Sara finished picking up the last of the mess in the front room, tossing the ruined remains of the sofa cushions in the trash. As tired as she was, she hadn't been able to bear the thought of waking up the next day to the mess that had greeted her when she walked through the door earlier that evening.

If nothing else, she supposed, the break-in was speeding up her timetable for making a decision about what to do with her grandfather's cabin. If she was going to sell it, there wasn't much point in worrying about a new sofa, was there?

"I still think you should come stay with your mother and me," Carl said, worry darkening his voice.

"Dad, I lived alone in Birmingham for three years. Believe me, that's a hell of a lot more dangerous than spending tonight in this cabin." She wasn't sure she was speaking the truth, but she knew with certainty that running home to her mommy and daddy was a step backward, not forward.

"Do you know what the intruders were looking for?" her father asked.

So Brad Ellis hadn't let him in on that part of the investigation. She supposed she should be grateful her father's former partner had bothered to hold anything back at all.

She kept her answer purposefully vague. "They just took some papers. Nothing really valuable." Not in monetary terms, anyway.

"What kind of papers?"

So much for vagueness. "Notes and stuff."

"On Renee Lindsey's murder?"

"Yeah."

Her father was silent for so long she started to wonder if the call had cut off. But as she opened her mouth to say her father's name, he spoke in a low, tense voice. "I haven't been given permission to tell anyone this, but I'm not going to keep it from you, since you have a vested interest in the case. Brad told me they got a rush job done on the DNA in the Ariel Burke case."

Sara paced toward the front window, her heart in her throat. "The comparison to the DNA of the baby Renee was carrying?"

"Yes." Her father's voice deepened to a growl.

"And?"

"The fetuses definitely shared a father."

Chapter Thirteen

Sara had suspected the DNA would show a match. She'd even expected it. But hearing her father say the words aloud hit her like a body blow. Groping for one of the kitchen chairs, she took the weight off her suddenly wobbly knees. "Can the DNA tell you anything about the father?"

"We just know that he's Caucasian. I guess if the county could afford to do a more detailed analysis, we might be able to narrow down what part of the world his ancestors came from, but what we really need is a suspect. Without that, the DNA doesn't do us much good."

She started to turn away from the window, but a glint of reflected light outside caught her eye. Pushing the curtains open, she peered down the hill and saw a truck parked across the road from the cabin, mostly hidden by the shadows. Only the faint glint of moonlight on the chrome of the front bumper gave its position away.

Cain Dennison's truck, she thought. Hadn't he left hours ago?

"Why don't I come by and give you a hand with the clean-up?"

"Dad, that's not necessary—"

"Is it a crime to want to see your daughter? Just humor me."

She couldn't hold back a smile. "Fine. In the morning,

though. I'm going to bed." *Eventually,* she added silently, her gaze still fixed on the truck parked at the bottom of her driveway.

"Call me when you wake up in the morning," he said firmly.

"Will do. Love you, Dad. Give my love to Mom, too."

Ending the call, she peered through the window, trying to get a better look at Dennison's truck. She ended up hunting down her grandfather's ancient pair of binoculars to see if Dennison was still inside.

He was, she saw with a quick adjustment of the binocular lenses. He sat in the driver's seat, his head tipped back against the headrest and his eyes closed. For a heart-stopping second, she began to wonder if he was still alive, but then he suddenly moved, his face screwing into a frown. After a moment, his expression relaxed.

He planned to stay out there all night, she realized. Playing sentinel for her.

Torn between gratitude and exasperation, she went to her bedroom to grab a jacket. If he was going to play body-guard for her tonight, he could damned well do it inside a warm cabin.

"You know the story of Crybaby Falls, don't you?" Renee's voice floated to him across the wooden bridge. He'd moved ahead, walking off his anger, while she'd lingered to pick wildflowers that grew in a riot of color near the edge of the falls.

"You mean the Cherokee woman who threw herself off the bridge because her man was killed in battle?" He turned a scoffing look her way. "My grandmother says that's bull. No self-respecting Cherokee woman would be that stupid."

Renee made a face at him. "You don't have a romantic bone in your body, do you?"

I could, *he thought, taking in the simple beauty of her, standing at the other end of the bridge looking at him with her head cocked and her eyes thoughtful. I could be as* romantic as you want. As romantic as you need.

"*I'm pregnant," she said.*

It took a second for the words to slice through the haze of his desire. And even when they registered in his foggy brain, he couldn't believe he'd heard her correctly.

"You're what?"

She walked slowly across the bridge, coming to a stop a couple of feet away from him. The expression on her face was somewhere between sad and hopeful as she pressed her hand against her still-flat belly. "I'm pregnant. And I'm going to keep the baby."

Cold enveloped his body, starting in his limbs and rising upward to his chest, where his heart thudded a hard, slow rhythm of dismay. "Who?"

She shook her head. "I'm not telling anyone. It's for the best."

"But he owes you—"

"Maybe he does. But he's not going to give me what I need. I've finally realized it." *She touched his hand where it lay on the railing of the bridge.* "You're so smart, Cain. Too smart to let romantic notions lead you astray. It's why you'll never have a broken heart."

His heart felt shattered at the moment, but he supposed she was right about one thing. He'd never put his hopes in having her. Desires, yes. Dreams, perhaps. But never hope.

"What did he say when you told him?" *he asked.*

"I didn't. You're the only person I've told."

"Then how do you know what he'll do about it?"

"He doesn't have room in his life for my baby. Not anymore. I won't make him choose." *Renee's lips curved in a faint smile. "It would be needlessly cruel to ask him to pick which one he wants."*

A sharp knocking noise jerked Cain out of his doze. Bright light angled through the window of his truck cab, piercing his eyes and making him squint to see the dark-haired woman standing outside his window.

Renee, he thought, and then checked himself when he saw Sara Lindsey's brown eyes staring back at him through the window.

"You planning to stay here all night?" she asked through the glass.

He sat up straighter and started to roll down the window. But she was already coming around to the other side of the truck. Leaning across, he unlocked the passenger door to let her in.

She pulled herself into the seat beside him, one dark eyebrow cocked. "You were going to stay out here all night?"

"You said you didn't need anyone to watch your back." He rubbed his jaw, feeling the beginnings of a beard. "You didn't say anything about someone sticking around to watch your house."

Her lips twitched at the corners. "Sorry I startled you. When I knocked on the window, I mean."

"It's okay. I was having a dream…." He frowned, straining to remember snippets from the dream. It seemed important somehow. "A memory, really. Something from the last time I saw Renee before her death. We'd met at Crybaby Falls. We met there a lot—it was just about her favorite place on earth."

"Oh, right. The whole romantic suicidal Cherokee-princess thing."

"Yes." He rubbed the lingering sleep out of his eyes, his mind wandering back to that gloomy day at the top of Crybaby Falls. "That was the day she told me she was pregnant."

Sara turned to look at him. "Why didn't you ever tell anyone about her pregnancy?"

"She asked me not to. Not until she could tell her parents. I guess she never got the chance." He stifled a yawn. "But I think I just remembered something important. Something she said about the baby's father."

"Something you didn't remember before?"

"It's not so much that I didn't remember before. I just didn't give it the same importance as I do now. And you have to remember, back then I was trying to keep my own backside out of jail."

"So you weren't exactly volunteering information?"

"No."

"But the pregnancy was a motive for murder. If the father knew—"

"He didn't know. She didn't tell him."

"She didn't tell him?" Sara sounded surprised.

"I know we've been assuming the pregnancy was the motive for Renee's murder—"

"Ariel's, too," Sara interjected.

He looked at her. "We don't know those pregnancies are even connected."

"We do now." She told him about the call from her father. "The DNA was a sibling match to Renee's fetus."

As the full implications sank in, a shiver ran through him, not unlike the chill he'd experienced that day eighteen years ago on Crybaby Bridge. "My God. I mean, we suspected it was possible, maybe even probable—"

"I had the same reaction," she confessed, tucking her thick sweater more tightly around her. The night had grown frigidly cold, Cain realized. They should be inside her warm cabin, not sitting out here in his truck.

"I don't know about you, but I'm about to turn into a

block of ice. Think you could handle someone watching your back from inside your nice, warm cabin?"

At her nod, he started the truck's engine and drove up the gravel drive, parking behind her truck. He followed her up the porch steps and waited for her to unlock the door.

Inside, the cabin was warm and much cleaner than he'd left it, he saw.

"Sorry, the sofa is a loss, but grab a chair. Are you hungry?" Sara shrugged off her sweater, revealing a figure-hugging long-sleeved T-shirt that skimmed the top of her jeans, giving Cain a peek at her bare belly and the curve of her hips as she reached into the cabinet for a skillet. "I'm not much of a cook, but even I can handle a midnight omelet."

"I could eat an omelet." He pulled up a chair and sat at the kitchen table, where he could watch her work. "How long did it take to clean up the mess?"

"A couple of hours." She put the pan on the eye to heat and retrieved a carton of eggs from the refrigerator. "Two or three?"

"Two is great." As he watched her expertly crack the eggs, he realized she might be underselling her culinary skills.

"How sure are you that Renee didn't tell the baby's father about her pregnancy?" she asked.

"Pretty sure. She died the next day." He remembered something else from that day, something he'd forgotten until the dream brought it back. "And she said something really strange that day. She said she wasn't going to ask him to choose."

"Choose what?" Sara looked at him over her shoulder. "Between her and some other girl?"

"I guess I always assumed that's what she meant. But what she actually said was that there was no point in asking him to pick which one he wanted."

She turned to face him, her eyes narrowing. "Which *one?*"

He nodded. "That's what she said. Which one."

"What do you think she meant?"

"I don't know," he admitted. "I guess maybe, thinking of what she said and how she said it—what if she wasn't the only girl her mystery man got pregnant?"

"Were there any other pregnancies at Purgatory High around that same time?"

He shook his head. "Not that I remember. But maybe it wasn't anyone at Purgatory High."

Sara frowned suddenly. "Jim Allen has a seventeen-year-old son."

"You're right," he said, suddenly feeling queasy.

"Which means Becky Allen and Renee would have been pregnant around the same time." She turned to look at him. "And maybe Renee found out about Becky's pregnancy."

"It would have changed the whole equation."

"If she thought he was in an unhappy marriage, maybe she was foolishly romantic enough to think she could win him away from Becky," Sara said in a hushed tone. "But married with a kid on the way?"

"She must have realized then that he'd already made his choice," Cain finished for her, so many of Renee's cryptic remarks finally starting to make an awful sort of sense.

Sara turned slowly back to the stove and continued preparing their omelets in silence. Cain could tell from the stiffness of her spine that what they'd just discussed had disturbed her deeply.

"I didn't want to believe it was Jim Allen," she said after a moment. "I figured after my session with your grandmother, when I didn't remember anything else, that I was maybe conflating days in my head. Maybe I was remembering a visit that didn't happen the night of the accident."

"But you were gung ho to confront him. You wanted to get his DNA."

"I think I wanted to exonerate him," she admitted, removing the skillet from the stove eye and cutting off the flame. She turned around to look at him, her expression grim. "I still want to believe there's another answer. Donnie thought so highly of the coach."

"There are other seventeen-year-old kids in Ridge County. I guess it could have been some other guy with a kid on the way. Or even someone who already had a child. Renee wouldn't have wanted to drag a man away from his family, especially if there was another kid involved."

Sara shook her head. "We have to deal in the facts, not in what I want to believe. The fact is, Renee was working in the athletic office for Jim Allen. The fact is that Jim hadn't been married long at that point—he and Becky were practically newlyweds. And I told you Donnie thought the Allens had been having marital problems back then."

"So maybe the coach thought his marriage was on the rocks and got himself all tangled up with Renee, who was only a few years younger than him. And just the kind of sweet-natured, romantic girl who could mistake sympathy for love and need for commitment."

"But then Jim learned Becky was pregnant, and everything changed." Sara grabbed a couple of plates from the cabinet over the sink and spooned the omelets onto them.

"Maybe he told Renee about Becky's pregnancy before she had a chance to tell him about hers."

"And Renee realized she couldn't ask him to choose between her child and his child with his wife."

Cain took the plates from her and set them on the table while she retrieved forks. "Renee might have loved him enough to take a chance that he'd leave Becky for her, but once a child was involved—"

Sitting in the chair across from him, Sara poked at her

omelet, looking as if the last thing she wanted to do was eat it.

Cain reached across the table, covering her hand with his. "I know you don't want to think Coach Allen did something so terrible. But we have to follow this lead as far as it takes us."

She looked at him thoughtfully, her expression suddenly hard to read. "If we're right about Jim Allen being the father of Renee's baby, then he's also the father of Ariel Burke's."

"And he almost certainly killed them both." Cain looked down at the omelet, his appetite long gone. He shot her an apologetic look and pushed the plate away. "I'm not as hungry as I thought."

"Me, either." She sat back in her chair, looking shell-shocked. "But why would he kill Renee? If she had no intention of telling him about the baby, how would he have even known? Could she have changed her mind?"

Cain gave it a moment of thought. Renee had seemed so resigned to having her child without any help from the father. He'd believed her when she'd said she didn't intend to tell him about the baby.

Could something have changed her mind?

"She said she wasn't going to tell anyone who the father was," he said finally. "She meant it."

"So how did the baby's father find out?"

"I don't know."

Sara pushed to her feet as if propelled by some burst of energy her slim body could no longer contain. The grim look of resolve in her dark eyes sent a shiver of alarm rocketing through him.

"Where are you going?" he asked as she started toward the front door of the cabin.

"To get answers." As she passed the antique desk by the door, she paused long enough to open the lap drawer and pull out a gleaming Walther PPK in a pancake holster. She clipped the holster to the back waistband of her jeans and grabbed a thick wool jacket from the coat tree on the other side of the door.

"And where do you plan to get those?" he asked, catching up with her before she opened the door. He closed his hand over hers on the doorknob, pulling her to face him.

Her eyes sparked flashes of fire as she met his gaze. "From Jim Allen, of course."

Answering heat fluttered low in his belly but he pushed the sensation aside. "You can't go there in the middle of the night, wave that gun in his face and demand answers."

"How stupid do you think I am?" She tried to pull her hand away from his grasp, but he tightened his grip.

"I don't think you're stupid. I think you're desperate for answers and you think Jim Allen can give them to you."

"What if he can?" Her question came out in a tone more vulnerable than he expected. He saw her own frustration flicker over her expression at the trembling undertone of her own voice. "I can't just keep sitting around, doing nothing. I have to know what happened."

"To Renee? Or to you and Donnie?"

"To all of us." Her voice escaped in a raspy whisper. "To me. I have to know why I drove us off that bluff."

He pulled her into his arms, curling his palm around the back of her neck. She resisted briefly, then relaxed into his embrace, her cheek warm against his shoulder.

A few moments later, her hands began to move lightly over his back, a hypnotic, seductive rhythm that charged the atmosphere around them. Not even his best intentions could stop his body's instant, obvious response to her touch.

She lifted her head, gazing up at him with fierce intent. "You should have let me know you were outside sooner," she whispered.

His pulse thudded in his throat. "So you could send me home?"

"So I could let you in," she whispered, rising until her lips brushed his. Her lips parted, her tongue darting against his upper lip.

He opened his mouth to her kiss, slid his hand over the curve of her hip to pull her closer so she could feel what she did to him. His tongue tangled with hers, tasting coffee and the underlying sweetness of her passion.

She pushed him toward the living room, reaching the ruins of the sofa before she seemed to realize that whatever she was looking for couldn't be found there. The look of puzzlement in her eyes as she took in the ruins of the sofa was so comical he couldn't hold back a laugh.

She swung her gaze to him. "I don't have a sofa anymore."

"You have a bed."

She turned a delightful shade of pink. "It was my grandparents' bed," she said in a hushed tone. "I can't have sex with a guy in my grandparents' bed!"

He laughed harder, frustration giving way to an almost painful level of affection for the blushing woman who stood in front of him. "It's okay. I'm not going to suggest the floor. Your grandmother probably used to mop it or something."

She gave his arm a light punch. "Funny."

He cradled her face between his hands. "I could go back outside to the truck."

"No. We'll figure out something." She looked so adorably conflicted, he almost kissed her again. But kissing her was what had gotten them into this muddle to begin with.

"Got a sleeping bag? I could lay it over what's left of that sofa and sleep there tonight."

She eyed the sofa with skepticism. "Are you sure?"

"Positive."

She gave his hand a quick squeeze. "Be right back."

He walked around the living room, trying to cool down the fire her touch had set blazing in his gut while muffled rustling noises filtered down the hallway where she'd disappeared. By the time she returned carrying a sturdy sleeping bag folded over her arm, he felt a reasonable level of control over his libido, though the look of helpless consternation on her still-pink face threatened to set him on fire again.

"I'm sorry." She thrust the sleeping bag into his hands. "I guess I'm not as sexually liberated as I thought."

He tried not to laugh again. "If it makes you feel any better, I wouldn't exactly feel right about having sex with a woman in my grandmother's bed, either. Mostly because she'd box my ears."

"You're very understanding."

He couldn't stop himself from touching her cheek. Nor was he able to keep the hunger from his voice as he whispered, "I'm very patient."

Her dark eyes blazed back at him. "Good." She rose toward him, slanting her mouth across his with a fiery intensity that nearly undid all his good intentions.

Dragging her mouth away, she stepped back and flashed a wicked smile. "Don't be too patient."

Too much patience, he thought as he watched her disappear into the bedroom, would not be the problem.

Daylight slanting through the narrow space between her bedroom curtains nudged Sara awake, dragging her from a dream she couldn't exactly remember but knew she hadn't wanted to end. For a second, the sound of movement in the front of the cabin made her whole body jerk into a knot, until she remembered how her eventful night had ended.

Had she really turned down sex with Cain Dennison

because she couldn't bring herself to do it in her grand-parents' bed?

Bringing her knees up to her chest, she buried her hot face in her hands. Why did something as natural and nor-mal as sex make her feel like a scared teenager all over again? She wasn't a virgin, hadn't been for over a decade. She and Donnie had shared an exciting, fulfilling sex life together; even during the more stressful period of their marriage, sex had never been an issue for them.

Maybe that was the problem. She'd had a lot of great sex, but always with just one man.

Forget falling in love again—what if she couldn't fig-ure out how to please another man?

A knocking sound from the front of the house sent her nerves jangling. Was that the door?

Footsteps sounded in the hall, and a couple of sharp raps on the bedroom door. "Sara?"

She grabbed the jeans she'd discarded the night before and tugged them on. "Yeah?"

"Your dad's at the front door."

Cold flushed through her body. "Oh, damn! He said he'd call first." She shrugged into her bra and threw a sweater over her head on her way to the door.

Cain stepped back as she jerked open the door. "You knew he was coming this morning and didn't think to warn me?"

"I forgot," she said, shooting him a look of apology. "But he said he'd call."

"I'd suggest making my escape out the back, but he can't miss my truck parked out there." He sounded damned near panicked, she realized.

She closed her hands over his upper arms, holding him in place. Stifling the sudden urge to laugh, she made him look at her. "It's okay. I'm well past the age of consent."

"But he's armed."

She couldn't stop a chuckle from escaping her aching throat.

"Oh, yeah, laugh it up," he muttered. "You're not the one he's going to chase down with a shotgun."

She was still chuckling a little as she opened the door to her father's repeated knock. But the grim expression on Carl Dunkirk's face drove out any thought of humor. He barely gave Cain a glance, stepping inside on a cold blast of wind and putting his hands on Sara's shoulders.

Her stomach dropped like a chunk of lead. "What's wrong? Is it Mom?"

Her father shook his head. "Your mother's fine. It's Jim Allen."

Cain stepped closer, all signs of his earlier mortification gone. "What about him?"

Carl finally let his gaze settle on Cain, a hint of curiosity flickering across his face before his expression went deadly serious again. "A student found him in his car in the high-school parking lot about an hour ago. Looks like he shot himself in the head."

"He's dead?" Sara asked, torn between surprise and dismay.

Carl looked at her, regret gleaming in his eyes. "Not yet. But the doctors don't think he's going to make it."

Chapter Fourteen

Westridge Medical Center's sleek facade brought back memories for Sara. Just not the ones she most needed to recover. As she and Cain followed her father through the front doors of the Knoxville hospital, the faintly antiseptic smell of the place hit her like a gut punch, and she stumbled over the large rug that stood in front of the sliding glass doors.

Cain's hand slipped under her elbow, keeping her from falling further off balance. She shot him a queasy smile, and his eyes widened a notch, but he didn't comment. He kept his hand curved around her elbow as they hurried to catch up with her father's long, quick stride.

The receptionist directed them to the waiting area of the emergency wing, where they found a couple of uniformed deputies milling near the coffee carafe and Lieutenant Brad Ellis sitting next to a teary-eyed Becky Allen and her three shell-shocked children. Becky was dressed in dark red scrubs, Sara noticed. Work attire? She had a faint memory that Becky had been working at a doctor's office when she married Coach Allen.

As Sara's father went to talk to Brad, Cain gave Sara's arm a light nudge and nodded toward Becky and her children. "Did you know Mrs. Allen was a nurse?"

"She used to work at a doctor's office in Barrowville," she answered quietly. "I guess she still does."

"Do you know what kind of doctor?" Something in Cain's tone made her look up at him. He was still looking at Becky, her eyes narrowed.

"I don't remember. Why?"

"I was just wondering how Jim Allen could have learned about Renee's pregnancy. Or Ariel Burke's, for that matter."

"You think he learned from his wife?"

"We should find out who Becky works for. And if it turns out to be an ob-gyn, we need to find out if Renee and Ariel were patients."

The quickest way to get that answer, Sara supposed, was to ask Becky herself. But she was clearly distraught at the moment, in no condition to be interrogated about her employment.

Sara had never really considered the coach or his wife to be anything more than acquaintances. She certainly had no idea why she and Donnie would have gone to see the Allens the night of the accident. Coach Allen had been Donnie's friend, not hers, and she'd never gotten the feeling that the coach's wife saw his students as anything but people who took his time and attention away from his family.

Still, the woman had just taken a sharp shock to her system, and so far, there didn't seem to be people gathering around them to offer comfort. The news was too fresh, she supposed, and people couldn't exactly drop everything to come be with her.

"I should go talk to Becky," she told Cain. "I should probably go alone, though."

He nodded, giving her elbow a light squeeze, as if he realized how much she was dreading what she was about to do. And she *was* dreading it. It brought back too many raw memories of waking up in this very hospital, two weeks after her accident, and learning that those disjointed, terrifying nightmares she couldn't remember from her time in a coma were nothing compared to the truth of all she'd lost.

She walked over to the row of connected chairs where Becky and her children sat, not sure what she should say. "I'm sorry" seemed entirely inadequate. She'd never been the kind of person who could sit for hours offering sympathy and a willing ear. She was a doer. A fixer. Dealing with a problem, for her, meant seeking out concrete, physical needs and meeting them as well as she could.

"Sara." Becky spoke before she could come up with anything to say. She reached her hand toward Sara, and Sara took it, giving it a gentle squeeze.

"How're y'all holding up?" she asked, knowing as soon as she spoke the words that it was about as lame a question as she could have thought to ask.

"As well as we can. I just—" She looked at her two youngest children, a pained expression in her reddened eyes. Lowering her voice, she added, "I just don't understand why this happened."

Sara looked at Jeff, the older boy. Like his mother, he was teary-eyed and shell-shocked, but when she suggested he take the two younger children to the gift shop to look for a get-well card for their father, he took his brother and sister in hand and did as she asked.

"Thank you," Becky said quietly. "I couldn't really talk very freely around the babies. They're never going to understand what their father has done. I don't understand it myself."

"You had no idea he was troubled enough to do something like this?"

Becky shook her head, wiping her eyes with a wadded tissue. "Not something this drastic, no."

"But you knew he was worried about something?" Sara pressed as gently as she could.

After taking a long, deep breath, Becky met Sara's gaze.

"He was worried. And secretive. It started in earnest the night of the last Purgatory High get-together dinner. You remember it? You were there."

"The night the sheriff broke the news about Ariel Burke."

She looked stricken, and Sara wondered if she knew about Ariel's pregnancy. Did she suspect that Jim was the father of the baby?

Did she fear he'd been the person who'd killed her?

"Was she one of his students?" Sara asked carefully. At a school as small as Purgatory High, coaches often taught classes as well as coached teams. Coach Allen had taught history when Sara had been a student there.

"Not a student, no," Becky said in a subdued voice.

"But he knew her?"

"Star of the cheerleading squad? Oh, yeah, he knew her." The bitterness in Becky's voice was razor sharp. She looked up suddenly, as if realizing what she'd just revealed.

Sara was torn between pushing ahead for more information and letting Becky Allen deal with her grief in private. Even though she'd frequently questioned grieving family members about homicide cases during her time as a detective in Birmingham, something about Becky's raw pain and humiliation made Sara want to pull her punches.

She glanced toward her father and saw him still conversing with Brad Ellis. But Cain wasn't anywhere in sight.

Turning back to Becky, she opened her mouth to excuse herself for a moment. But before she could speak, Becky caught her arm in a surprisingly tight grip and bent her head toward Sara.

"There's something I have to tell you," she said quietly, her fingers digging into Sara's arm so hard it was beginning to be painful. "There's something you need to know, something I should have told someone long before now. But Jim asked me not to."

Forgetting about Becky's painful grip, Sara leaned forward. "What is it? Is it something to do with Jim?"

"With Jim. And with you and Donnie." Becky's face crumpled. "Jim told me not to say anything, that getting involved would just make life harder for us, and it wasn't like there was anything we could have told anyone that would have changed anything."

"Is this about the night of the accident?" Sara asked. "About Donnie and me coming to visit you and Jim earlier that evening?"

Becky's eyes widened with surprise. "Oh, my God, you remember?"

"Not everything," Sara admitted. "I don't actually remember seeing you that night. I just remember standing outside your house. I think it was not long after sunset, and Donnie and I were arguing about something."

Becky's brow furrowed. "Arguing about what? About us?"

"You and Jim?" Sara shook her head. "No. Why would you think that?"

"No reason. I guess maybe I'm just looking for some clue to what Jim did this morning. He never really told me why we weren't supposed to talk about that night. Just said it would be messy for us to get involved. He was trying to get a raise at the school, and I was trying to get voted president of the Ridge County Women's League at the time, and he said someone might accuse me of giving you too much to drink that night."

"I don't drink," Sara said. "And certainly not when I might be driving."

"I know you didn't drink that night. I'm just saying what Jim said people would say." Becky's lips pressed into a tight line of teary frustration. "You sound like you suspect him of something else. Is it because he shot himself? You think he's feeling guilty about something?"

Sara didn't have a chance to answer. Jeff Allen had returned from the gift shop with his younger brother and sister. She got up, making room for the children in the chairs beside Becky. "I'll see if anyone has an update," she said with a final pat to Becky's shoulder.

She crossed to where her father and Brad Ellis were still conversing in low tones. They looked up with grim expressions as she joined the huddle. "Anything new?" she asked.

"He's still alive," Brad told her, sparing a quick glance toward Becky and the kids. "Apparently he's not a great shot, lucky for him. But it's still too soon to know if he's going to make it."

"How did this happen?" Sara asked. "Who found him?"

"One of the kids on his baseball team, Davy Lavelle. Poor kid's completely freaked out, as you can imagine."

"Was there a note?"

"Not that we've been able to find," Brad admitted. "We haven't gone to his house yet—we figured we'd wait until we knew more about his condition before we disturb Becky that way."

"I think you need to get his DNA," Sara said flatly.

Brad's brow furrowed. "His DNA?"

Sara's father looked at her through narrowed eyes. "You think he may have fathered Ariel Burke's baby, don't you?"

She nodded. "And Renee Lindsey's, too."

"What would make you suspect Jim Allen of all people?" Brad glanced across the room at Becky and the kids, and Sara could imagine what he was thinking. Even red-eyed and in shock, Becky Allen was still as beautiful now as when she'd been Purgatory High's homecoming queen and snagged the heart of the cutest guy on the baseball team. Maybe even more beautiful, as time had only enhanced her classic looks. Why would a man with a woman like that at home ever think of straying?

She didn't know the answer. She only knew that in her

experience as a cop, she'd learned that a good-looking wife at home was no guarantee a man wouldn't cheat.

"Did Cain Dennison put that idea in your head?" her father asked.

"I'm capable of coming up with ideas without help," she said more sharply than she intended.

Her father's eyebrows notched upward at her tone. "Fair enough."

She shot him a look of apology. "I remembered something about the night of my accident that made me question whether Jim Allen might be hiding something." She told them about her memory of arguing with Donnie outside the Allens' home. "And Becky just now confirmed that we were there that night."

"You're kidding me." Her father looked dumfounded. "We begged people to come forward with information about what the two of you were doing in town that night. Nobody did. And you're telling me Jim and Becky knew all along where you'd been?"

"Becky told me Jim convinced her not to tell. He said it was because they didn't need to get mixed up in a police investigation, with him being a teacher at the high school and her running for Women's League president."

"That's no sort of reason." Brad shook his head.

"Did you remember why you were there?" Carl asked, his hand closing over her shoulder, warm and firm.

She shook her head. "And I didn't really get a chance to ask Becky before her kids came back from the gift shop."

"I didn't realize you and Donnie were friends with the Allens," Brad said, slanting a look toward Becky Allen.

"We weren't. That's what's strange about it." Movement in her peripheral vision caught her eye, and she spotted Cain standing near the exit. He gave a slight nod in her direction. "Excuse me a minute," she said, already moving away from her father and Brad.

"Didn't think I should just be loitering around the waiting room, annoying your father and drawing attention," Cain said quietly as she walked outside with him. Nodding toward a bench a few feet away, he led the way, and they settled there, warmed by a shaft of mild sunshine. "What did Becky have to say?"

"More than I expected," she admitted, telling him what Becky had revealed about the night of her accident. "It was so strange, hearing her talk about an event she so clearly remembered. And I can't remember any of it."

"Maybe if you could go back to their house or something…"

"On what pretext?"

"Maybe to pick up some things for Becky. Sounds like Jim has a chance of surviving, but if he does, he'll be here for a long haul. Not just because of the injury, but for psychiatric evaluation, too."

"Actually, why don't I offer to take the kids home? At least the two little ones. Being here, seeing Jeff and their mother in so much turmoil, has to be scaring them to death. I could stay with them until Becky can arrange for someone to watch them." And while she was there, she could have a look around, see if anything jogged her memory.

Cain nodded. "Good idea."

"Meanwhile, find out where Becky works," she added, lowering her voice as a couple of women dressed in scrubs passed them on their way into the hospital. "There has to be some way that Jim Allen found out about Renee's pregnancy. If Becky worked for Renee's doctor, that might be how."

"Are you sure you're okay to go to the Allens' place by yourself?"

She slanted a look at him, surprised by his cautious tone. "I was a cop for years, you know. I reckon I can take care of myself. Or are you talking about the baby-sitting part?"

His lips curved slightly at her final question, but the smile faded quickly. "Actually, I was thinking about the fact that you still have a big gap in your memory of the night your husband died, and part of that missing time was apparently spent in that house you're about to go looking through. What if you do remember something? Something you don't want to remember?"

Her stomach turned a queasy flip at the thought. He had a point, she knew. If there was no physical reason why she shouldn't be able to remember the missing hours from that night, as the doctors had told her, why wasn't she remembering it?

What had she experienced that her subconscious didn't want to deal with?

"Maybe you shouldn't go to Becky's house alone," Cain said quietly.

"I can't exactly make the offer to watch her kids, then ask if I can take a friend." She straightened her back and stood. "I'm fine. I'll get the kids settled and distracted from their worries, and then if I get a chance, I can look around. See if anything triggers any memories."

Cain rose as well, his fingers brushing her arm. A tingle of raw physical attraction jolted through her at his brief touch, but eclipsing even that was a sweet, bracing warmth that seemed to flow between them.

It felt like more than just sexual attraction, she realized. It felt like a real connection. Something that might have a chance of lasting, if that's what she wanted.

Was it what she wanted?

"If you need me, call," he said quietly.

"I'm not going to need you," she said, making herself pull away from his touch. They were getting too close too quickly. She wasn't ready to feel something powerful enough to change her life.

Was she?

Cain's eyes narrowed. "Is something wrong?"

She shook her head, swallowing a sudden flood of fear. She reentered the E.R. and headed toward the bench where Becky still sat with her scared-eyed children, sparing a last, quick glance at Cain, who peeled off toward her father. He met her gaze, his expression troubled, before he turned away.

Sara turned her attention to Becky. "Still no word from the doctors?"

Becky shook her head. "They said it might be a while before we know anything new."

"Why don't I take the younger kids back to your house?" Sara suggested, taking the empty seat next to Jeff. "They could probably use a break from the stress. I could get them settled down watching a movie or something and stay with them until you can arrange for someone to be with them more permanently."

Becky cocked her head, her blue eyes soft with gratitude. "You don't mind doing that?"

"I don't mind. I might need driving directions, though. I haven't been over in that area in a while."

"Of course." While Sara dug in her purse for a pen and piece of paper, Becky asked her two younger children, Gracie and Jonah, if they would like to go home for a while. "Miss Sara is an old friend of your daddy's and mine, and she can take you home and let you watch movies."

"I could pop some popcorn, too, if you like," Sara offered, handing the pen and paper to Becky to write down directions to the house.

The offer didn't evoke any excitement from the two younger kids, but they got up willingly enough when Sara rose to leave.

"Don't let them get into the candy at the top of the cabinet in the kitchen," Becky warned. "I'm saving that for Halloween."

"Got it." With an encouraging smile toward Becky and her older son, Sara led the two younger children outside and across the access road to where her truck was parked. She shot a quick look at Cain as she passed him on the way out, and he answered with a slight arch of his eyebrows.

Once she got the two kids strapped into seat belts on the bench seat behind her, Sara took the interstate south toward Purgatory. While she drove, she contemplated what route to take once she got to the Purgatory exit. There were quicker ways to reach the Allens' house in Quarry Heights, but she decided on Black Creek Road once she took the turnoff toward town. The mountain road was by far the most winding and treacherous, but for whatever reason, the night of the accident she and Donnie had chosen to take that road.

Maybe taking that road now would jog her memory.

The best route to the interstate highway that would take them back to Birmingham was Madison Park Boulevard, not Black Creek Road, so it wasn't likely they'd been heading out of town that night. But they hadn't called her parents or his to let them know they were in town and were planning to stay. And as far as anyone had ever been able to discover, they hadn't booked a room at any of the handful of motels in the area, and the cops had gone as far away as Knoxville and Chattanooga to check. Apparently they'd planned to stick around that night.

But to do what?

She tried to picture herself behind the wheel of Donnie's old truck, the one she'd been driving the night of the accident. She'd have been driving down this road, coming from the opposite direction. Instead of bright sunlight filtering through the trees overhead, there would have been little more than the pale glow of moonlight.

What had she seen? What had driven her off the road? And what had any of it to do with Jim Allen?

Chapter Fifteen

Cain had turned thirty-six in June. He'd spent years in the Army, years out in the world, making his own way and being his own man.

So why the hell did he feel like a tongue-tied teenager when he thought about talking to Carl Dunkirk?

The fastest way to find out where Becky Allen worked, short of asking the woman herself, was to ask someone who knew her. And Carl Dunkirk knew everybody in Ridge County, probably better than they liked. He'd been a deputy for decades, working a job where knowing other people's business was part of the job description.

But he'd also been one of Cain's biggest detractors back when Renee Lindsey's body had first shown up at the base of Crybaby Falls. He'd hounded Cain—much to the delight of Cain's father—certain that Renee's friendship with him had been her downfall.

Hell, maybe it would have been, eventually. Cain had never understood himself why she seemed so determined to hold on to their friendship. She had been the kind of girl who could have done big things in life if she'd wanted to.

Renee hadn't needed someone like him holding her back, but whenever he'd tried to take a step away from her, she'd refused to let him go.

"You have something to say?" Carl's deep voice drew

Cain's mind out of the past. He looked up to find Sara's father watching him with wary eyes. Brad Ellis had gone to talk to Becky Allen, he saw, leaving Carl standing alone near the admitting desk.

Cain took a step closer, amused by how awkward he felt approaching the older man. He felt eighteen all over again, antsy and guilty, even though he'd done nothing wrong. Well, nothing but trying to get the man's daughter into bed. And hoping he'd get a chance to try it again.

Though Sara's sudden withdrawal had caught him flat-footed. Was she having second thoughts about following through on what they'd started the night before?

Taking care to hide his thoughts, he lowered his voice. "Do you know where Becky Allen works?"

The question seemed to catch Carl by surprise. His eyebrows lifted. "Why?"

"I noticed she's wearing scrubs. Does she work at a hospital?"

"She works for Dr. Reed Clayton over in Barrowville."

"Private practice?"

Carl nodded. "Only OB-GYN in the county."

Cain released a long, slow breath. "Has she worked there long?"

"For years." Carl's gaze narrowed. "Why do you ask?"

"Was she working there eighteen years ago?"

Carl didn't answer immediately, but Cain saw the wheels turning behind his dark eyes. "Yes," he answered in a tone so grim it made Cain's gut twist in a knot.

"Was Dr. Clayton Renee's ob-gyn?"

Carl nodded slowly. "Probably Ariel Burke's, too."

"Someone should check on that." Cain rubbed his hand over his jaw, turning his gaze toward Becky Allen, who was holding her son's hand tightly as she quietly answered whatever questions Brad Ellis was asking.

"You think that's how Jim Allen found out the girls were

pregnant. You think he was the father of those babies."
Carl's gravelly voice drew Cain's gaze away from Becky's
tearstained face.

"Yes. We need that DNA sample."

"I'll talk to Ellis."

A couple of men dressed in the dark-pants-and-white-
shirt uniforms of the Ridge County EMS strode toward
the door, their heads together in conversation. Brad Ellis
rose from the waiting-area sofa and hurried to intercept
them before they reached the exit.

When Carl crossed to join them at the door, Cain went
with them. They reached the others just as Brad was asking, "Was he ever conscious at any point of the rescue?"

"Just briefly, right after we got there," the taller of the
two emergency medical technicians answered, his blue-
eyed gaze flickering toward Cain briefly. His eyebrows
notched upward, and Cain realized the EMT had been
a classmate years earlier. One of Josh Partlow's buddies
on the football team, he thought. Couldn't remember the
name.

"Did he say anything at all?" Carl asked. If Brad Ellis
minded the older man butting in on the interrogation, he
didn't show it.

"Gotta say, it was pretty weird," the shorter EMT admitted with a shake of his head. "Guy shot himself in the
head. Those don't usually turn out to be talkers. I guess he
lucked out and aimed poorly. Small caliber, too—anything
bigger and we'd have been waiting for the undertaker."

"What did he say?" Cain asked. Both Carl and Brad
Ellis shot him questioning looks, but he ignored them.

"He said, 'She's crazy. Don't let her hurt her.'"

Brad Ellis looked puzzled, but Carl's dark gaze met
Cain's. "She?"

"That's it, but he said it twice," the taller of the two

men said. "Then he lost consciousness and we scooped and ran."

"Thank you," Ellis said quietly, looking at Carl. After the two EMTs left, he lowered his voice. "Do you know what this is about, Carl?"

Carl looked across the room at Becky Allen, his expression grim. "I'm afraid I'm beginning to."

SARA HAD NO conscious memory of having been at the Allens' house before, but a sense of déjà vu dogged her steps up the neat stone walkway into the pretty split-level brick-and-clapboard house in the middle of Alabaster Circle. Behind the house, a sprawling backyard ended at a fence about twenty yards from a shallow bluff that overlooked Warrior Creek.

Less than a mile down that creek, Sara knew, Warrior Creek spilled its rushing waters over Crybaby Falls.

So easy for Jim Allen to walk the mile along the creek bank to the falls, she thought. Renee Lindsey had loved Crybaby Falls, Cain had told her. She was a romantic, stirred by the notion of tragic love. Had she been the one to suggest Crybaby Falls as their secret meeting place?

What about Ariel Burke? Had Jim Allen remembered his secret trysts with Renee Lindsey at the falls and coaxed young, foolish Ariel to meet him there as well?

"Can we watch *Scooby-Doo?*" Jonah asked before they'd gotten through the front door.

Sara looked at Gracie, the older of the two. At eleven, she was on the cusp of adolescence and showed every sign of being as beautiful as her mother. She was also the more solemn of the two, the weight of tragedy darkening her soft green eyes as she met Sara's questioning gaze. "It's okay," she said. "Mama lets him watch it all the time."

"*Scooby-Doo* it is," Sara said, locking the door behind them.

Gracie got the DVD from a cabinet in the living room and put the disk in the player while Jonah settled in front of the coffee table, his small fingers flicking over the chess set that took up half the glass surface. He picked up pieces and put them back, his brow furrowed as he looked down at the board.

Gracie punched a couple of buttons on the remote and the movie came on. Jonah picked up the black king from the board and clutched it in his little fist as he settled back to watch the movie.

Gracie detoured to Sara's side, her green eyes full of heartbreaking maturity. "Daddy plays the black pieces," she said quietly. "He's teaching Jonah to play." She blew out a deep sigh that broke Sara's heart into a dozen little pieces. "He was, I mean."

Sara wanted to put her arms around the little girl and hold her so tightly that nothing bad could happen to her again, but Gracie was sending off all sorts of "don't touch me" signals. Sara settled for flashing her a gentle smile. "He will again. As soon as he comes back home."

Gracie looked up at her as if she saw right through Sara's bravado. But she said nothing else, just crossed to sit by her brother on the sofa. Sara saw her sneak her hand toward the chessboard, nab the black queen and curl her own little fist around the piece.

Blinking back stinging tears, Sara retreated into the kitchen. It was a large, airy room, full of warm colors and homey smells. At one end of the room, a rectangular table filled a large breakfast nook. Sara wandered over there and sat down in one of the side chairs, trying to remember.

She and Donnie had been here, in this house, that night. Why couldn't she remember it?

She tried to picture Jim Allen sitting at the head of the table. He had always been a friendly man, a man who spoke easily, joked freely and told great stories. A charming man. A man who never met an adversary he couldn't turn into a friend.

What was that story he'd told her one time, about the pig farmer and the Bible salesman—

She sat up straighter. He'd never told her a story like that before. She'd never been close with him. So why did she remember hearing him tell that joke so clearly?

"Miss Sara?" The sound of Gracie's voice sent a jolt of raw adrenaline racing up Sara's spine.

She quelled a jerk of surprise and managed to smile at the solemn-faced little girl. "Yes?"

"My kitten is all grown up now. You want to see her?"

A flash of memory flitted through Sara's mind. A tiny white kitten with just a hint of chocolate on her nose, paws and tail. "Sure," she said, rising to take the small hand Gracie extended toward her.

Gracie led her up the short flight of stairs to the second level and into a small room with lavender walls and a small bed with a frilly white comforter dotted with tiny purple violets. On the pillow, a sleek Siamese cat blinked sleepy blue eyes at their arrival.

"She was little the last time you saw her," Gracie said, picking up the cat and curling her arms around her. "Isn't she pretty?"

The cat purred with contentment, sliding one paw up to curl around Gracie's neck. Sara smiled, remembering how much she'd always liked cats as a girl. She'd missed having pets when she and Donnie lived in Birmingham, but their jobs had made it impossible to give a pet the attention it deserved.

"She's beautiful," Sara said, hearing Donnie's voice whispering in her ear as surely as if he were standing right there in the room with them.

He *had* been, she remembered with a start. He'd been standing right there in Gracie's room beside her as the little girl—three years younger on that fateful night—had showed off her new kitten to them while her parents set the table downstairs.

"When this is over," he'd said softly, "we're going to get ourselves a cat. I promise, we're going to slow things down and get our lives back."

Tears burned her eyes as she reached out to stroke the cat's dark ears. The rumble of the cat's purr vibrated against her fingertips as she met Gracie's soft gaze. "Gracie, you remember meeting me before, don't you?"

Gracie nodded. "You and your husband. He was nice."

Sara smiled. "He was."

"Mama said he died. I'm real sorry."

Sara squelched the urge to stroke the child's soft cheek. "Thank you."

Gracie blinked hard, as if she were fighting off tears. "I'm going to go check on Jonah. He might do something naughty if I don't watch him. Mama says you have to keep an eye on him all the time or he'll get into all sorts of things he shouldn't." She set the cat back on her pillow, where it curled up and settled back down for a nap.

Sara followed her downstairs, feeling as if she were floating on a sea of ice. Chill bumps raced up and down her arms and legs as she left the little girl in the living room with her brother and returned to the kitchen.

She sat at the table, clutching the edge as the mental ice shattered into a thousand little pieces, each fragment a snippet of memory. This table. This room. The kitten, Gracie's gap-toothed grin, little Jonah's newly skinned knee—"He's as clumsy as his daddy," Becky had told them with a rueful smile—and the look of worry in Jim Allen's eyes as Donnie started asking a lot of inconvenient questions after dinner.

Questions about his relationship with Rence.

Sara hadn't been expecting the third degree any more

than Jim had, and she'd tried to coax Donnie into leaving, aware that an ambush was no way to get the answers he was seeking. All he'd done was alienate Jim Allen and turn Becky into a nervous mess. She'd fluttered around, playing the consummate hostess, trying to soothe the unexpectedly roiling waters.

"Miss Sara?" Jonah Allen's quiet voice jerked her back to the present. She blinked away the memories, meeting the little boy's red-rimmed eyes.

"Yes?"

"I'm hungry."

Sara looked at her watch and realized it was nearly noon. "What would you like?"

"Chicken noodle soup?"

"I can handle that," she said with a smile, pushing to her feet. She quelled the tremble in her knees and crossed to the cabinet to see where the Allens might keep their canned soup. "What about Gracie?"

"I'm not hungry," Gracie called from the living room.

"Well, pretend like you are. What would you want?"

Gracie was quiet for a moment, then she said, "I guess chicken noodle soup for me, too."

She looked down at Jonah, who was watching her with curious eyes. "You need something else?"

"Is my daddy going to die?"

Sara felt her heart shatter. Kneeling, she put her hands on his shoulders and looked him straight in the eye. "I know he's in a very good hospital with some very good doctors." Westridge was one of the best hospitals for trauma cases in the state. If Jim Allen had any chance of surviving his self-inflicted wound, he was in the right place to make it happen. "And he's a strong guy, right? Big, tough guy."

Jonah nodded. "He's like a superhero."

"That's right. So you keep thinking about that, okay?

Your daddy's going to fight as hard as a superhero to get better and get home to y'all. Right?"

Jonah nodded. "Right."

Sara watched him head back into the living room, hoping she hadn't just given him false hope. Then she turned back to the pantry and started searching for the canned soup.

Opening the door of the cabinet over the sink, she found not cans but several small bags of hard candy. They were stored in plain plastic bags, tied up with shiny foil twist ties. There were a variety of colors—red, green and some pale yellow ones that made Sara's lips purse at the mere sight. She picked up the bag of yellow candies and removed the twist top. A sharp scent rose from the bag and stung her nose.

Lemon drops, she thought, another memory bolting through the mists of her fragmented memory.

"I made them myself," Becky had said with a too-bright smile as she offered the cut-glass bowl full of sugar-crusted lemon candies, the desperate hostess trying to bring order to the chaos Donnie had created with his sharp questions for Jim.

Uncomfortable with Donnie's sudden aggressive demeanor herself, Sara had smiled an apology and taken one of the candies. But after one taste of the too-tart piece of candy, she'd discreetly slipped hers into a napkin and into the trash can nearby.

Donnie, however, had eaten his lemon drop with unnerving calm, looking like a shark toying with his hapless prey. Sara had never seen that side of her husband before, and it had been utterly unnerving.

"She helped you grade papers," Donnie had continued, refusing to be deterred by the trappings of decorum. "Renee spent a lot of time with you, didn't she? After hours when everybody else was gone." Donnie's tone had been as sharp as a hunter's arrow.

Sharp enough to cut through flesh and bone.

Jim had blanched, Sara remembered, but Becky... Becky had looked almost pleased. Her expression had been placid enough, but there had been satisfaction gleaming in her cool blue eyes, as if she were secretly enjoying her husband's discomfort.

She knew, Sara thought, her stomach knotting. Becky knew about Jim's affair with Renee. And she'd enjoyed seeing her husband squirm.

Donnie hadn't been the only predator in the room that night.

Chapter Sixteen

Not staring at Becky Allen was harder than Cain expected. But he didn't want to spook the woman, especially when all he had at the moment was speculation.

"We can't overlook the fact that Jim Allen shot himself," Brad Ellis said in a hushed tone. "Even if she told him about the pregnancies, it doesn't mean she knew he was the father or that either one of them would take that information and kill those girls."

"We don't even know if this suicide attempt is related to either murder," Carl admitted.

"Are we sure it's a suicide attempt?" Cain asked quietly.

The two older men looked at him. "You think someone else shot him?"

"I'm not sure of anything." He slanted a look toward Becky Allen. She was staring at the door to the E.R. bay, as if waiting for a doctor to come out and give her news. "How much longer before someone can confirm Ariel Burke was a patient of Dr. Clayton's?"

Ellis rubbed his chin. "The Burkes were out when I called. And Dr. Clayton's office won't tell us anything about any of their patients without a warrant."

"The girl is dead."

"Doesn't seem to make a difference to doctor-patient confidentiality."

Frustrated, Cain put his hands on his hips and felt a slight vibration under his right forefinger. He tugged his phone from his front pocket and saw that he'd missed a call from Sara. "I need to get this."

He headed outside and dialed her back, but the call went directly to voice mail. He left a message and went back into the waiting room.

He found Deputy Ellis and Carl Dunkirk talking to a man in surgical scrubs. He reached the small huddle as the green-clad doctor shook his head. "It's going to be days before we can try to bring him out of the coma. Just because the gunshot didn't kill him doesn't mean the brain injury won't finish the job. And I wouldn't get your hopes up about his being able to remember much if anything about what happened."

"Is it possible the wound wasn't self-inflicted?" Carl asked.

The doctor gave him an odd look. "I'm not an expert on forensics. I will tell you that there was stippling around the entry wound, so I'd guess the muzzle was within six inches of his head when it fired."

But that didn't mean he was the one who pulled the trigger, Cain thought, glancing across the room at the waiting area, wondering if Becky was watching them. What would she make of this powwow between cops, doctors and the Monster of Ridge County?

Jeff Allen still sat on the sofa, his lean body hunched forward in misery.

But Becky Allen was nowhere in sight.

He scanned the waiting area, looking for Becky's blond hair and maroon scrubs, but she wasn't there.

He grabbed Carl Dunkirk's arm, making the older man wheel around in surprise. Dunkirk scowled at him. "What?"

"Becky Allen's not in the waiting room."

Dunkirk's gaze followed the same route Cain's had—first to the sofa, where Jim Allen's eldest son sat in quiet misery, then around the room, returning finally to Cain. "Did you see where she went?"

"No."

Dunkirk strode across the room toward Jeff. Cain fell into step, murmuring a warning. "Don't scare the kid, Mr. Dunkirk."

Dunkirk's step faltered, and he turned to look at Cain. "Is that what I did to you?"

For a second, Cain was back in the interview room at the Ridge County Sheriff's Department, sweating and shaking as he waited for Dunkirk to stop staring at him and start asking questions. He'd already been one big nerve, aching from the loss of his friend and scared by the fury he saw on the deputy's face.

Before he found the words to answer Dunkirk's question, the older man put his hand on Cain's shoulder. "I'm sorry. We all wanted answers, and you seemed like the obvious one."

"And we could be wrong about Jim and Becky Allen, too," Cain warned softly.

"But you don't think we are, do you?"

Cain shook his head. "Just keep it cool with the kid. He's not likely to know anything about it, is he?"

Dunkirk glanced at Jeff. "No, he's not."

They continued toward the boy at a slower pace, sitting on either side of him. When Dunkirk spoke, his voice was gentle. "How're you holding up, Jeff? You need something to drink? Maybe something to eat?"

Jeff shook his head, looking miserable. "Mom offered to grab something while she was out, but I just don't think I can eat anything."

"Where'd she go?" Cain asked.

Jeff looked up at him, his expression puzzled. "Do I know you?"

Cain shook his head. "I know your dad. From the high school."

Jeff's lips curled in a faint smile. "Everybody seems to know Dad from the high school."

"Small towns," Cain said with an answering smile. "Did your mother go home?"

"I think so. She said something about needing to get some insurance forms at home, and asked if I'd be okay to stay here alone." He lifted his quivering chin. "I'm going to have to be the man of the house until Dad comes home. Might as well start now."

Dunkirk rubbed Jeff's shoulder gently. "You're doing good, son. Your daddy's going to be real proud when he hears about it." His eyes met Cain's over the boy's head.

"We just talked to the doctor over there," Cain said. "I get the feeling he thinks your dad's a real fighter."

"He is," Jeff said with a firmness his shaking hands belied. "He's the toughest guy I know."

"We'll make sure the doctor comes and talks to you in your mom's absence," Dunkirk said, pushing to his feet. He nodded for Cain to follow.

Cain caught up at the E.R. admitting desk. "Do you think she really went home?"

Dunkirk shrugged. "Maybe. Probably." His brow furrowed suddenly, and he started to look around the room again. "Where's Sara?"

He must have missed seeing her leave with the kids, Cain realized. He and Brad Ellis had been deep in conversation around that time. "She took the two younger Allen kids home to get them away from all this stress."

Dunkirk's frown deepened. "Is that all?"

Clearly, he knew his daughter well. "She wanted to

take a look around, see if being back there would jog her memory. About the night of the accident."

"And what if it does?" Dunkirk asked, his tone grim. "What if Becky walks in right in the middle of a memory flash and figures out that Sara is remembering something that could incriminate her or Jim?"

Cain swallowed a curse and checked his phone. No new calls from Sara since the one he'd missed, not even an answer to the message he'd left. He tried her number and got voicemail again.

He met Dunkirk's gaze. The older man nodded. "Go. I'll get Ellis to send a cruiser for backup. Meanwhile, I'll see if we can rush that DNA match."

"Okay."

"Stay in touch," Dunkirk called after him.

Cain hit the door at a run, dodging foot traffic and slow-moving vehicles as he raced across the parking lot to his truck.

SARA TIGHTENED HER grip on the bag of lemon drops, a fuzzy feeling in her head, as if a thousand little bubbles were popping behind her eyes. The world seemed off-kilter, knocked a hair off its axis so that everything spun a fraction of a second too fast.

She could taste the tartness of the candy lingering in her memory, the sour burn that had made her roll it out into her palm and into a napkin before the sugar crystals finished melting on her tongue. Donnie was the one who liked tart foods; she preferred smoother, richer treats like good chocolate or salted caramels.

Had the Allens known that about Donnie? Had they given him something in the lemon drops that had made him tipsy? Is that why she'd been driving the Silverado that night?

She rubbed the sudden ache in her head, trying to

remember what had happened next. He'd eaten the lemon drop as he'd grilled Jim Allen, asking about his relationship with Renee. He'd heard the rumors, he told the coach, about his yearly affairs with senior girls at the high school. "Like clockwork," Donnie had said, his words hard and precise.

Except they hadn't been precise, had they? At first, perhaps, but as the scene in the living room had escalated, Donnie's movements had become loose-limbed and agitated, his words slurring and finally becoming little more than gibberish.

She'd been terrified, she remembered, afraid that his obsession about his sister's murder had finally driven him over the edge. That he'd finally snapped from the grief and anger, and it had struck her, as she grabbed his flailing arms and pulled him out to the truck, that she wasn't sure what to do next. Should she take him home to his parents, whose grief had driven them far too close to madness as it was? Should she try to drive him back home to Birmingham, even though his wild-eyed ranting was starting to scare her?

In the end, she remembered, she'd thought about her father. Her father would know what to do.

But they hadn't made it that far, had they?

Sara tightened her grip on the bag of candy, lifting it to the light, as if she could see through the pale opaqueness of the hard lumps of sugar to the poison at their centers. Were these the same candies?

"You can't eat that!" Gracie Allen's voice was tight with alarm. Sara turned to see the little girl standing in kitchen doorway, her eyes wide as she stared at the bag of candy in Sara's hand. "That's only for the bad people!"

Sara blinked. "For the bad people?"

"The people who want to hurt us," Gracie explained, her gaze never leaving the candies. "You have to put it up.

Mama says we can never, ever touch it because it's only for bad people."

The knot in Sara's gut tightened. "Your mother made these?"

Gracie nodded. "She says sometimes there are bad people who want to hurt us, and so we have to have a magic potion to stop them."

"And where does she make the magic potion?"

"In the darkroom."

"The darkroom?" Another memory flitted through Sara's reeling mind. Jim Allen's voice, amused.

"We call it her secret dungeon laboratory," he'd told them with a smile when one of the kids had mentioned the photographic darkroom he'd built for Becky in the basement. "She says she's developing photographs for her night-school class, but we all think she's really building Frankenstein's monster in her spare time."

"Can I see the darkroom?" she asked Gracie.

The little girl's face blanched. "No, only Mommy can go to the darkroom! There's bad chemicals down there."

"Oh. Okay." Sara flashed the child what she hoped was a reassuring smile, even though her own stomach was aching so much she wasn't sure how much longer she'd be able to keep down the big cup of fast-food coffee she'd downed on the drive to Knoxville.

Bad chemicals, she thought, thinking of the crystal meth Cain had found in his grandmother's woodbin. Meth was volatile and dangerous, but easy to cook.

Had Becky put the drugs there as a warning for Cain to stop nosing around Renee Lindsey's murder?

Sara tried to clear her mind, not wanting her darkening thoughts to scare Gracie. "You'd better go make sure Jonah's okay, don't you think? I'll put the lemon drops back where I found them."

Gracie looked relieved as she turned and went back to

the den. Sara looked at the bag of candy, her eyes narrowing as she thought about what had happened to Donnie not long after he'd eaten one of the lemon drops.

To put it mildly, he'd started tripping out.

So, a hallucinogen? Something that could be cooked in a home lab?

Sara's head was starting to hurt from the effort of piecing together the sudden overflow of memory fragments into something that made sense. Why had Becky drugged Donnie and tried to drug her as well? Why not just poison them?

Was it possible that Jim Allen had no idea what his wife was up to?

Most poisons that would act fast enough to kill would show up in tests. At least, the toxins that could be easily created in a home lab. What about hallucinogens, though?

LSD was a possibility, though what she could remember of Donnie's agitation seemed a lot more violent than she'd ever seen in someone tripping on acid. DMT— dimethyltryptamine—could be cooked in a home lab if you knew what you were doing, though it was usually smoked, not ingested, because the body metabolized DMT too easily, eliminating the high.

She rubbed her aching forehead, starting to lose focus. She'd let the lab guys worry about what was in the lemon drops. Right now, she had to figure out whether or not it was even possible that Becky Allen had killed Renee Lindsey and Ariel Burke.

They'd assumed a male assailant in both of those deaths because manual strangulation wasn't an easy way to kill an adult. Sara could picture Jim Allen being able to overpower both girls without much trouble; he was a tall, muscular man. But was Becky large enough and strong enough to overpower those two girls?

Probably. Though she was as slender as she'd been back

in her own cheerleading days, Becky was nearly as tall as her husband, and staying in shape had kept her fit and strong. Being a tall woman herself, Sara supposed she could hold her own with Becky Allen, but Renee Lindsey had been petite, and based on the photos of Ariel Burke that Sara had seen since her murder, she hadn't been a big girl, either.

If Becky had surprised them in some way and overpowered them quickly, then yes. She could have strangled both girls to death.

Sara crossed to the living-room doorway to check on the children. Both of them were engrossed in the movie, though Jonah was hugging a ragged-looking blanket to his chest and looking a little more worried than the *Scooby-Doo* gang's shenanigans would require.

Poor babies, she thought with a sinking heart. *If I'm right about your mother, your whole life is about to be turned upside down.*

She returned to the kitchen and took a look around, trying to remember more about the night she and Donnie had come to dinner with the Allens. She'd had no idea he was planning to confront Jim Allen. It had come as a shock to her as well as to the coach and his wife. Donnie had been keeping a lot of his investigation into his sister's death secret from her by then, putting a strain on their marriage.

Before the inquisition began, however, they'd been having a normal sort of conversation with the Allens, hadn't they? She had a vague memory of talking about what had been happening at the high school since their graduation, what teachers had left and what students had grown up to become teachers. Of course, Jim had also mentioned that Becky had been taking photography classes at the junior college up in Barrowville and how he'd built her the darkroom in the basement so she could develop her own photographs.

Sara had wanted to see the darkroom, she recalled. She was something of an amateur photographer herself, but she'd never tried developing her own film, and the idea had intrigued her.

But Becky hadn't wanted to show her the darkroom, claiming it was a mess.

Or had her reluctance to let Sara take a look around had anything to do with something that could incriminate her?

She needed to find that darkroom. Now.

Jim had said it was in the basement. So where was the door to the basement?

She didn't think she should ask the children. Based on Gracie's reaction to seeing Sara holding the lemon drops, Becky had put the fear of God into the children about her secrets. If she had some sort of drug-cooking lab downstairs in her darkroom, she would certainly make sure her kids never went down there to look around.

She wandered past the living-room entrance and into the narrow hallway. A short row of steps led up to the second level, where the bedrooms were, but there was a door in the wall to her left a few feet in front of the steps.

She tried the doorknob. It rattled in her hand, locked.

That was promising.

She reached into the pocket of her jeans and pulled out her key chain. From the leather tool pouch she kept on the chain, she withdrew a simple lock pick she'd bought years ago when she first joined the police force. The ability to pick a lock was a rudimentary skill for police officers, and while the doorknob lock might be effective in keeping the Allen children from going down to the basement, it proved no problem for Sara. The door lock disengaged, and she eased the door open as quietly as she could.

The basement was inky dark, and if there was a light switch on either side of the stairway, Sara didn't find it as she crept her way into the dark basement below.

At the bottom, she fumbled with her key ring until she found the small pen light attached. She snapped the light on, and the weak beam illuminated a narrow path in front of her. She swept the light around until she spotted a red bulb with a chain attached. Crossing to the light, she tugged the chain and red light spread in a circle around the center of the basement.

The setup was, at first glance, like almost every dark-room Sara had ever seen. A long table filled the center of the room, stocked with bottles of developer, pickling vinegar that Sara supposed acted as a stop bath, and fixer. Four flat plastic trays lay lined up in a row on the table, currently dry, with tongs lying next to them, and near the end of the table was a stack of black-and-white photographic paper.

But it was the large cabinet behind the table that drew Sara's attention, due to the shiny silver padlock that held its doors shut. What on earth would Becky be hiding in that cabinet that would require a padlock?

She needed to talk to Cain and let him know what she'd stumbled on. If she was making too much out of her suspicions, he'd talk her down. But if she was right…

Pulling her cell phone from her pocket, she turned it on and found, to her dismay, that her battery was critically low. She should have charged it in the car on her way to the hospital, she thought with a grimace, pocketing it as she turned to head back up the stairs to the Allens' landline.

But before she reached the bottom of the stairs, the door opened, daylight pouring into the basement in a blinding flash. A tall, slim silhouette stood at the top of the stairs, the unmistakable shape of a gun clutched firmly in her right hand.

Sara's heart skittered into high gear.

"I really, really wish you hadn't done this," Becky Allen said.

Chapter Seventeen

Sara still wasn't answering her phone. Cain didn't know whether or not he should worry—for all he knew, she was one of those people who put her phone on vibrate and never felt it when it buzzed.

There was a lot he didn't know about her, if he was honest with himself. But he wanted to know everything.

Like what she did to relax. What kind of music she liked. What foods were her favorites. What she was really thinking when she turned those dark eyes on him and seemed to stare right into his soul.

He knew she was a smart woman. He knew she was tough and capable. But she didn't know that Becky Allen was on her way home. And she didn't know, as Cain did, that it was possible Jim Allen hadn't been the one holding the gun that had come perilously close to killing him.

The drive from Knoxville to Purgatory took a little over thirty minutes, driving as fast as he dared. At most, Becky Allen had a ten-to-fifteen-minute head start on him.

Would it be enough to put Sara's life in danger?

In desperation, he tried her cell phone one more time. Once again, the call went straight to voice mail. The fast shunt to voice mail suggested she was either on the phone or had shut off the phone altogether.

Pulling to a stop at the intersection where Sequoyah

Highway crossed Old Quarry Road, Cain called The Gates, bypassing Quinn's direct number in favor of the agents' office. Ava Trent answered on the second ring. "The Gates."

"Ava, it's Cain Dennison. I need an address."

SARA TOOK A slow step backward as Becky Allen descended the stairs, the small black pistol gripped in her right hand leveled at Sara's head. "What on earth are you doing?"

Becky reached the ground level. "You're remembering, aren't you?"

"Remembering?" Sara played dumb.

"I'm not stupid." She nodded at the bag of lemon drops Sara still held. "You remembered those, didn't you?"

Sara gave up any pretense. Becky clearly wouldn't buy the ignorant act. Besides, she wanted answers, even if they were the last answers she ever got. "Donnie ate one of these lemon drops. And then he started acting strangely."

Becky almost smiled. "I wasn't sure they'd work. That's why I paid one of the addicts I know to bleed your brakes while we were at dinner. Just in case."

Sara's gut tightened painfully. "You bled the brakes?"

"Enough to make them soft. You know these mountain roads. One wrong move…"

My God, Sara thought, sickened. "Why? Because Donnie suspected that Jim had killed Renee?"

"Because he knew that I was the only way that Jim could have known she was pregnant."

"You found out from Dr. Clayton. You told Jim."

"I didn't tell Jim." Becky's whisper of a smile hit Sara like a punch in the gut. "He was as surprised as everyone else when he learned about the baby."

"He wasn't the one who killed her, was he?"

Becky laughed. "He doesn't have the backbone for it. He would have wanted to do right by the girl. Claim the kid as his own. Humiliate me in front of the whole town."

"You couldn't let that happen."

Becky's chin rose like a dagger. "No, I couldn't."

"And Ariel Burke?"

Becky's lip curled in disgust. "He never learned. Not from Renee, not from the others—"

"The others?"

"You think he never messed around with any other homecoming queens between Renee and Ariel?" Her expression darkened. "Every girl in Ridge County goes to Dr. Clayton. Only gynecologist in the county—you know how that works. Do you know how many times one of those cute little things came through the doors, looking for birth control or a pregnancy test, and every damned time I had to wonder, was Jim doing her, too?"

"Why didn't you just leave him?"

Becky looked at her as if she'd lost her mind. "You know this town. You know how fast the rumors would have flown. It would have turned into one big joke—the jock stud hero who still has what it takes get into the pants of cute little coeds versus the aging shrew of a wife who can't even keep him faithful for more than a month at a time."

"What did you give us?" Sara shook the bag of candy.

A flicker of pride gleamed in Becky's eyes, sending a shudder rippling down Sara's spine. "I just gave you lemon drops."

"Donnie started tripping almost as soon as we got out to the truck." The fragmented images that her brain had been piecing together for the past few hours had started to form a coherent memory of the night of the accident. "He hit me in the mouth, hard enough to stun me as we reached the hairpin curve. Donnie never raised a hand to me in his life." She gave the bag of lemon drops an angry shake. "What did you dose him with?"

"DMT," Becky answered finally, her tone almost bored. "Ayahuasca, to be specific. Mixed into lemon sugar syrup and allowed to harden. It's a big favorite with hard-core users."

"Not as volatile to cook as meth," Sara murmured, her gaze wandering around the basement, taking in the boxes stored on shelves at the back of the basement. Not hard to turn a darkroom into a drug lab, she knew, with the right equipment and ingredients.

Becky smiled. "I have kids. You think I'm going to cook meth?"

"You did, though. Didn't you? Enough to try to black-mail Cain Dennison into backing off his investigation."

"You can't prove that."

"It doesn't matter." Sara gave a wave toward the lab equipment. "What else do you deal in? Magic mushrooms, maybe? GHB?"

"I dabble in this and that. Girl's got to make a decent living, and God knows Jim's never going to make anything coaching high-school baseball." She laughed without a hint of humor. "He promised he was going to make it in the majors. If I just hung in there with him, he said, we'd be set for life. Yeah, that really worked out."

"Jim never asked where the extra money was coming from?"

"Jim doesn't want to know."

"Is this why he shot himself?" Sara waved her hand toward the boxes in the back of the basement. "Or did he find out you were the one who killed Renee and Ariel?"

"He was careful, after Renee." Becky shook her head. "It put a scare into him, finding out she was pregnant after her death. He'd assumed she was on contraceptives. Idiot."

"What happened with Ariel?" Sara asked, stalling for time. Right now, Becky held all the leverage in the palm of her right hand. Sara had left her own weapon in the lockbox in the bed of her truck, safely away from the Allen children.

"She told him she was on birth-control pills. No condom required."

"She lied?"

"She had a prescription. I checked. But she wanted more than a few tumbles in the back of his truck out on some dirt road in the middle of nowhere. She thought a baby would make him leave me for her." Becky flicked the pistol toward Sara, motioning for her to move deeper into the basement.

Sara stayed put. "Would it have? Made him leave you, I mean."

"Doesn't matter, does it?"

"Were you the one who broke into my cabin last night?"

Becky just looked at her.

"You heard I was helping out Brad Ellis with the investigation, right? You must have wondered if I had remembered anything about that night. So you broke in and took my notes."

"I broke in to scare you," Becky said bluntly. "Make you think you were in danger. Make you go away again. But you just dug in your heels, didn't you?"

"I'm not a foolish little teenager in love," Sara answered. "I don't scare easily."

"That's too bad for you." Becky gestured more emphatically with the barrel of her gun. "Go to the back of the basement. There's a drop cloth back there. I want you to spread it out and stand in the middle of it."

Sara's heart skipped a beat. "Easier to clean up the mess?"

Becky just looked at her without answering.

"The kids will hear the gunshots."

"I told them I'll be doing some hammering down here. Making a nice surprise for their daddy when he wakes up." Becky shook her head. "He's not going to wake up, but they don't have to know that. Not for a while."

"I'm supposed to just go along with what you ask? Make it easier for you to kill me and cover it up?" Lifting her chin with raw determination, Sara shook her head, trying not to think of everything she'd be leaving behind. There'd been a time, not so long ago, when the thought of following Donnie into the next world wouldn't have seemed like such a bad outcome.

But that's not the way she felt now. She had her parents. Friends like Kelly and Josh. Good old Brad Ellis and even Joyce and Gary Lindsey, who could finally have a little closure in the deaths of both their children, if she managed to get out of here alive to tell them what happened.

And there was Cain. Tough-shelled, softhearted Cain, who made her feel all the prickly, painful, wonderful sensations that came with rediscovering her life. She wanted to see if there was really such a thing as a second chance at happily ever after. She wanted to prove to Cain that he was worthy of finding his own happy ending, too.

She wanted it almost more than she wanted her next breath.

But she couldn't have any of those things if she was bleeding to death on the floor of Becky Allen's basement. She had to find a way to turn the tables and get the upper hand.

But hell if she knew how to get past a loaded .38.

THE ALLENS LIVED on a cul-de-sac surrounded by dense woods and butting up to Warrior Creek. The proximity to Crybaby Falls didn't escape Cain as he parked behind Sara's truck on the street.

There was a compact green Honda sedan parked in the driveway. Cain walked up the drive and touched his hand to the Honda's hood. Still hot. She hadn't beat him here by much.

He headed up the flagstone walkway to the neat little

house with the perfectly manicured lawn and six neatly trimmed azalea bushes flanking the brick and concrete stoop.

The Allens cared about appearances. Enough to kill to maintain them?

He started to knock on the door but hesitated, considering his options. The door was likely to be locked, though he could get past that obstacle if necessary. But could he get inside without alerting Becky Allen that he was there?

His cell phone rang, sending an electric jolt down his spine. He silenced it quickly by answering. "Dennison."

"It's Carl Dunkirk. I'm headed your way."

He wondered how Dunkirk got his cell-phone number, then realized the man used to be a cop. He had resources nearly as good as Cain's. "Has something happened?"

"Brad Ellis finally got hold of Ariel Burke's former boyfriend. Turns out the last time he saw Ariel was the morning before she was killed. And guess who she was talking to?"

"Jim Allen?"

"Becky Allen." Dunkirk's voice darkened. "I'm about ten minutes out. You'd better wait for me."

A muted cracking sound came from somewhere inside the house, setting Cain's nerves rattling. "No time," he growled, slamming the phone shut and trying the doorknob.

To his surprise, it wasn't locked.

THE SHOT CAME without warning, slamming into the wooden shelf behind Sara's head, sending splinters of wood flying into her hair and face. One sharp sliver slashed her cheek, but she barely felt it, her whole body a knot of jangling nerves.

"Get the drop cloth," Becky ordered. "Now."

Hell, no, Sara thought, lifting her chin. She couldn't see a way out of this basement alive, but she'd be damned if she made it easier for Becky to kill another woman and get away with it unscathed. "You might as well shoot me now and get it over with. I'm not going to cooperate with you."

"No fear of death? Not even a little?" Becky took a couple of steps closer, cocking her head as if examining Sara the way she might look at a bug under a microscope. "Losing Donnie do that big a number on you? Maybe you're looking forward to joining him up yonder, huh?"

"I don't want to die," Sara said with as much calm as she could muster. "But I told you, if I'm going to die today, I'm not going to do a damned thing to make it easier on you."

"I can always go upstairs and get the kids. Let them come down here and get the drop cloth for me. I'll tell them it's a game we're playing. All they have to do is get the drop cloth and go stand there in the middle of it, and they'll do it without question. They trust me. I'm their mother."

Bile rose in an unexpected rush up Sara's throat as Becky's meaning filtered through the rush of adrenaline still flooding her system. "My God, Becky. They're your children."

"They're Jim's children. And he's the biggest mistake I've ever made." Becky's lips curled with disgust. "I remember, I was so happy when I found out I was pregnant with Jeff. I thought it would solve all those little problems we'd been having after Jim washed out of pro ball. Then I overheard that stupid little girl telling that Dennison boy about the baby. And I knew. I'd seen Jim with her, you see. And he'd tell me he was just listening to her troubles, that I was being paranoid, but I knew. I could smell her on him sometimes, you know. Basil and lemon. In his hair, on his shirt. On his skin."

"That's not Jeff's fault. Not Gracie's fault or Jonah's—"

"They're constant, sickening reminders of who I shackled myself to. I thought he was a good choice. He was going places." Becky laughed again, the sound harsh with regret. "The only place he was going was right back here to Purgatory, where he could screw pretty little high-school girls and pretend he was still the hottest stud on campus."

A faint noise, coming from somewhere upstairs, seeped past the sound of Becky's voice, sending a dart of alarm skittering down Sara's spine. Had one of the kids gotten curious and decided to come looking for their mother?

Please stay upstairs, babies, she thought with rising desperation, trying not to let her attention wander away from Becky's face. *Whatever happens, stay upstairs.*

Becky's finger slid to the trigger, giving Sara just enough time to duck when another bullet smacked into the shelf behind her.

"Get the drop cloth. Now. Or I'll call the kids down here. I swear to you, I will."

Sara stared back at her, trying to assess Becky's intentions. Was she bluffing? Or was she really willing to kill her own children? Was this her way of tying up all the loose ends of her out-of-control life? First take out Jim, then her children? Freeing herself to go out and start a new life under a new name somewhere far, far away from here?

She wasn't sure. But she couldn't take the chance. If she cooperated, there was a chance Becky wouldn't harm her children.

Sara turned and walked slowly toward the shelves at the back of the basement. "Where's the drop cloth?"

"In that box with the blue lid." Becky sounded impatient.

Sara opened the box and pulled out a neatly folded plastic sheet.

"Bring it out here to the middle of the floor and unfold it."

Sara did as Becky asked, her heart pounding with growing terror. She didn't want to die. The will to live coursed through her like electricity, lighting up her nerve endings and flowing into her veins like pure adrenaline.

But she was out of options.

A flash of movement behind Becky caught her eye. The door to the basement was opening. Had curious little Gracie decided to check up on her mother?

Sara looked desperately at Becky, trying to gauge her chances at overpowering her without getting herself or one of the children killed.

Not great.

Behind Becky, the door creaked. Becky's attention snapped away from Sara for a split second, giving her the tiniest of openings.

She took it, throwing herself at Becky and tackling her to the floor just as Becky pulled the trigger.

A THIRD BARK of gunfire greeted Cain before he could get the basement door open, sending a jolt of pure terror rocketing through his body. He ducked on instinct but picked up speed, barreling down the stairs.

He hit the landing, stopping just long enough to take in the sight of Sara wrestling with Becky Allen on the basement floor. Nearby, a plastic drop cloth covered the floor, the edges nearest the women rumpled from their struggle.

Cain moved forward quickly, stepping on Becky Allen's gun hand. She cried out, a roar of pain and frustration.

With the threat of gunfire neutralized, Sara went into full-on cop mode, jerking the pistol from Becky's trapped hand and sending it sliding across the floor well out of reach.

"Help me roll her over," Sara said bluntly, looking up at Cain with a mixture of relief and some darker, richer emotion he couldn't quite discern. He did as she ordered, using blunt force to hold the struggling, cursing woman down while Sara crossed to a nearby shelf and grabbed a roll of heavy-duty duct tape.

While he straddled Becky's thighs to keep her immobile, Sara quickly secured Becky's hands behind her back. She taped up her ankles as well, pulling her feet up to hogtie her in place.

The sound of footsteps wandering around above drew Sara's sharp glance toward the basement door. "Keep her here. I have to stop the kids from coming downstairs."

Cain watched her hurry up the stairs, his chest filling with a heady blend of admiration and affection. Sara might consider herself tough as nails, and in a lot of ways she was, but she was softhearted enough to try to protect those poor kids a little longer from the harshness life was about to throw their way. She was an amazing woman, and he hoped like hell he could find a way to convince her to take a chance on a man like him.

He turned his attention to Becky, who was growling profanities at him as she struggled to free herself from his iron grasp. If he'd had any doubts that Becky Allen was directly involved with Renee Lindsey's death, they were gone. He'd put together the clues—the gunshots, the drop cloth on the floor—and what little he'd made out of the muted conversation he'd heard coming through the basement door to get a pretty clear picture of what was going on.

Strangling Sara Lindsey to death wouldn't have worked the way it had with Renee and Ariel. Becky hadn't had the luxury of surprise, and Sara was as tall and strong as she was, unlike the two teenage girls she'd caught unaware. That's why she'd gone with the pistol.

"You were going to kill her on the drop cloth. Minimize the mess. But why kill her at all?" he asked.

Becky's answer was a profane indictment of his parentage.

"Hey, I've called my old man worse," he said with a

grim smile. "Just one more question. Did you shoot your husband, too?"

Becky fell silent beneath him.

He'd take that as a yes, he thought, his mouth curling into a grimace, his gaze rising to the open door at the top of the stairs. He could hear Sara's soft voice filtering down from somewhere above, mingling with the querulous replies of the Allen children.

He closed his eyes, aching for those kids. Their lives would never be the same. He just prayed they had someone in their lives the way he'd had his grandmother. They were going to need it.

"JIM'S PARENTS ARE taking custody of the kids," Sara's father told her a couple of hours later when she emerged from her interview with Brad Ellis to find him pacing in the hallway outside. He wrapped her up in a fierce hug, dropping a kiss on the top of her head.

"Anything new on Jim's condition?" she asked, curling her arms tightly around his waist and rubbing her cheek against his shirt, wrapping herself in the familiar, comforting smell of him. She might be over thirty now, but there was still nothing in the world quite like a father's love to make the big, bad world seem a little less scary.

"They're cautiously optimistic he's going to make it. The jury's still out on how much brain damage he might have sustained." Carl released her from the hug but kept his arm draped over her shoulders. "You free to go?"

"Almost. Brad's got to type up my statement and let me sign it." She hoped Brad was a speed-typist. She was feeling pretty shaky now that the adrenaline flood that had kept her moving had finally started to ebb. "Have you seen Cain?"

"Not since I got here."

Brad Ellis emerged from the interview room, clapping

Carl on the shoulder and giving Sara's arm a light pat. "I'll get this statement typed up and back to you in no time."

"Do you know if Cain Dennison is still being interviewed?" she asked as Brad turned to go.

"He was released about fifteen minutes ago. He didn't have as much ground to cover as you did, I guess." Brad headed toward his office down the hall from the interview room.

Sara frowned. She needed to talk to Cain, but she supposed it was silly to think he'd stick around the cop shop to wait for her. She knew his aversion to police stations.

And she'd made it pretty clear to him, earlier in the hospital, that she wasn't ready to pursue the connection that had been growing between them.

How was he supposed to know that she'd changed her mind?

Her father nudged her toward a nearby bench. "I called your mother to let her know what was going on," he warned her as they sat to wait for Brad. "She's not very happy with either of us."

Sara sighed, dropping her head against her father's shoulder. "I guess this wouldn't be a good time to tell her I'm planning to stick around Purgatory and apply for a job with the sheriff's department."

"I think she's been expecting that ever since you got sucked into this murder investigation," her father said, his voice threaded with pride. "I know I was. You're a cop at heart. You always have been. I knew that the first time I caught you sneaking peeks at my case files."

Brad Ellis returned a few minutes later with a pen and a printed statement. He drew an X where he wanted her to sign, though she knew the protocol as well as he did. She scratched her signature in the appropriate place and handed the pen back to him.

"You'll be hanging around Purgatory a little longer,

won't you?" Brad asked, giving her a knowing look. "In case we have more questions?"

"Yeah, I'll be around," she said with a smile.

She and her father walked down the long corridor toward the front exit, where she'd parked her truck in visitor's parking. To her surprise, Cain Dennison was waiting for her there, his long arms draped over the top of her tailgate. He nodded to her father, but his gaze locked with hers, blazing with intent. She felt an answering tug low in her belly.

"Thanks for coming, Dad," she said, tearing her gaze away from Cain long enough to give her father a fierce hug. "I'll drop by the house later so Mom can reassure herself I'm okay."

Her father gave her cheek a quick stroke, nodded back to Cain and headed toward his own truck, leaving her alone with Cain.

"Let's get out of here," Cain said.

Epilogue

The roar of Crybaby Falls grew in strength as Sara and Cain wound through the overgrown trail toward the creek. He leaned a little closer. "You hungry? Maybe we can grab something to eat a little later."

She darted a look at him, a smile curving her lips. "Together? In public?"

He smiled back, not mistaking the teasing tone in her voice. "I like to live dangerously."

"Don't take this wrong, but I'd much rather get takeout. I can't think of anything I want to do more than put my feet up and not move until Monday."

"Just 'til Monday?"

"I'm planning to apply for a job at the Ridge County Sheriff's Department." She stole a glance at him, as if wondering how he'd take the news. He'd been vocal enough about his troubled relationship with law enforcement, so he could hardly blame her for her apprehension.

His attitude toward the police had evolved over the past few weeks, he supposed. Especially if Sara was the one wearing a badge. "You'll be an asset to the department."

She shot him a grin, looking ridiculously, endearingly pleased.

Ahead, the trees began to thin out as they neared the top of the falls. He took her hand and gave it a tug. "Let's do this, Deputy."

"Do what?" She quirked her eyebrows, looking intrigued. He just smiled and motioned with his head for her to come along with him, leading her across the bridge over Crybaby Falls.

They picked their way down the slightly treacherous incline that flanked the falls. He could tell by her look of curiosity that she'd never ventured to this part of the falls. Few people did—the path was steep and scary-looking, and only daredevils and fools ever took the chance.

He'd been one of those people, both daredevil and fool. Mostly, he'd been a kid who'd felt he had nothing to lose, and the challenge had seemed impossible to resist.

He'd learned, however, that the descent was less treacherous than it looked, and worth the slight risk once he'd discovered the treasure that lay at the end of the journey.

"Oh," Sara murmured, her voice soft with surprise.

Ahead of them, the path curved toward the falls, where a set of natural stone steps led toward a hidden cavern behind the flow of water.

"Did someone make these?" she asked as they started down the steps.

"Either the Cherokees or God. Take your pick." The steps ended where the floor of the cavern leveled off to a stone shelf sheltered by the roaring curtain of water that hid them from the world outside.

"I had no idea this place existed," Sara breathed, her smile widening as she took in the full splendor of this inside view of the falls.

"Not many people do." Cain led her to an outcropping along the back wall of the cavern that formed a makeshift bench. He settled her onto the outcropping and took a seat beside her. "My grandmother showed me this place, back when I was a kid. I think it was her way of teaching me that I couldn't let fear and anger stop me from finding the beauty in this world. I think maybe more people knew about this place back then. But after Renee's death…"

"Not many people come to the falls anymore."

"Nobody but me. And teenagers looking for a thrill." Smiling, he reached down and pulled her feet into his lap. Removing her shoes, he began rubbing her feet. A look of pleasure suffused her face, and he felt an answering response building low in his belly.

"You're turning out to be rather handy to have around," she breathed, gasping as he stroked the velvety skin just below her ankle.

"I'm counting on that," he admitted. "I plan to be indispensable." He stroked his way up to her calf, making her suck in another quick breath. "Irresistible."

Her back arched a little at his light touch, stoking the fire in his blood. "You're devious. I think I like it."

He trapped her gaze with his, not hiding the desire that burned in his belly. "You have no idea the things I have up my sleeves."

She swung her legs off his lap and scooted up next to him, tucking herself firmly against his side. He slid his arm around her shoulders, pulling her close, loving the feel of her body pressed so intimately to his.

She flattened her hand over the center of his chest, then let it skim lightly, temptingly down until it rested just above the waistband of his jeans. "I have a few tricks of my own. Want to see one?"

More than he could say. But there was no hurry. Neither of them was going anywhere else for the foreseeable future. "Maybe later," he answered, brushing his lips against his ears. "Definitely later," he amended quickly, making her laugh.

With a little sigh that wavered somewhere between frustration and contentment, she settled her head into the curve of his neck and relaxed. "I'm holding you to that."

"I'm counting on it." He dropped a kiss on her temple. "I know you're scared of all this—"

"I'm not," she said quickly, looking up at him, her expression so earnest it made his heart hurt a little. "I mean, I was. But I'm not now. When I was down in the basement with Becky, and I had a million other things to think about, one of my worst fears what that I'd die before I got to tell you that I wasn't afraid anymore. I have…expectations of you."

He couldn't hold back a smile. "Good. I have expectations of you, too."

She grinned at him, snuggling closer. "Good. I like having goals."

He tucked her head beneath his chin and turned his gaze toward the rushing curtain of water, finding both solace and hope in the relentless pulse of Crybaby Falls as it carved its determined path through the unforgiving rock.

"So do I," he whispered into her hair.

So do I.

* * * * *

Award-winning author Paula Graves's miniseries
THE GATES *continues next month with*
BONEYARD RIDGE.

"Emma." Dante's grip tightened on her hands. **"What are you afraid of? The bad guy or me?"**

She blurted out, "I'm not afraid of either." Her head dipped and she stared at her boots. "I'm afraid of me."

His heart melted at the way her bottom lip wobbled. "Why?"

Her glance shifted to the corner of the room and she didn't say anything for a full ten seconds. "I've been independent for so long, I'm afraid of becoming dependent on anyone."

"Relying on someone else doesn't have to be a bad thing. And it's only temporary, then you can go back to being independent."

She didn't throw it back in his face, so he figured she was wavering. He went in for the clincher.

"Besides, you saved my life twice." He lifted one of her hands to his lips and pressed a kiss there. "I owe you."

CHRISTMAS AT THUNDER HORSE RANCH

BY
ELLE JAMES

Published in Great Britain 2014
by Mills & Boon, an imprint of Harlequin (UK) Limited,
Eton House, 18-24 Paradise Road, Richmond, Surrey, TW9 1SR

© 2014 Mary Jernigan

ISBN: 978-0-263-91374-3

46-1014

Harlequin (UK) Limited's policy is to use papers that are natural, renewable and recyclable products and made from wood grown in sustainable forests. The logging and manufacturing processes conform to the legal environmental regulations of the country of origin.

Printed and bound in Spain
by Blackprint CPI, Barcelona

A Golden Heart Award winner for Best Paranormal Romance in 2004, **Elle James** started writing when her sister issued a Y2K challenge to write a romance novel. She has managed a full-time job and raised three wonderful children, and she and her husband even tried their hands at ranching exotic birds (ostriches, emus and rheas) in the Texas Hill Country. Ask her, and she'll tell you what it's like to go toe-to-toe with an angry three-hundred-and-fifty-pound bird! After leaving her successful career in information technology management, Elle is now pursuing her writing full-time. Elle loves to hear from fans. You can contact her at ellejames@earthlink.net or visit her website at www. ellejames.com.

This book is dedicated to my fans who kept writing, asking when Dante would have his book. Without my fans I wouldn't be pursuing the career I love. Thank you for reading and falling in love with my characters. May all your lives be blessed!

Chapter One

Big sky…check. Flat plains…check. Storm clouds rolling in…check.

Like ticking off his preflight checklist, Dante Thunder Horse reviewed what was in front of him, a typical early winter day in North Dakota before the first real snowstorm of the season. It had been a strange December. Usually it snowed by Thanksgiving and the snow remained until well into April.

This year, the snow had come by Halloween and melted and still the ground hadn't yet grown solid with permafrost.

Based on the low temperature and the clouds rolling in, that first real snow was about to hit their area. The kids of Grand Forks would be excited. With the holidays just around the corner, they'd have their white Christmas after all.

A hundred miles away from base, flying the U.S.-Canadian border as an air interdiction agent, or pilot, for the Customs and Border Protection, Dante was on a mission to check out a possible illegal border crossing called in by a concerned citizen. A farmer had seen a man on a snowmobile coming across the Canadian border.

He figured it was someone out joyriding who didn't realize he'd done anything wrong. Still, Dante had to check.

He didn't expect anything wild or dangerously crazy to happen. The Canadian border didn't have near the illegal crossings as the southern borders of the United States. Most of his sorties were spent enjoying the scenery and observing the occasional elk, moose or bear sighting.

Chris Biacowski, scheduled to fly copilot this sortie, had come down with the flu and called in sick.

Dante was okay with flying solo. He usually liked having the quiet time. Unless he started thinking about his past and what his future might have been had things worked out differently.

Three years prior, he'd been fighting Taliban in Afghanistan. He'd been engaged to Captain Samantha Olson, a personnel officer who'd been deployed at Bagram Airfield. Every chance he got he flew over to see her. They'd been planning their wedding and talking about what they'd put on their dream sheet for their next assignments.

After flying a particularly dangerous mission where his door gunner had taken a hit, Dante came back to base shaken and worried about his crew member. He stayed with the gunner until he was out of surgery. The gunner had survived.

But Dante's life would be forever changed. When he had left on his mission, his fiancée had decided to go with a few others to visit a local orphanage.

On the way back, her vehicle hit an improvised explosive device. Three of the four people on board the military vehicle had died instantly. Samantha had survived long enough to get a call through to the base. By the time medics arrived, she'd lost too much blood.

Dante had constructed images in his mind of Samantha lying on the ground, the uniform she'd been so proud to wear torn, a pool of her own blood soaking into the desert sand.

He'd thought through the chain of events over and over, wondering if he'd gone straight from his mission to Bagram, would Samantha have stayed inside the wire instead of venturing out? Had their talk about the babies they wanted spurred her to visit the children no one wanted? Those whose parents had been collateral damage or killed by the Taliban as warning or retribution?

Today was the third anniversary of her death. When Chris had called in sick, Dante couldn't cancel the flight, and he sure as hell couldn't stay at home with his memories haunting him.

For three years, he'd pored over the events of that day, wishing he could go back and change things so that Samantha was still there. How was he expected to get on with his life when her memory haunted him?

The only place he felt any peace whatsoever was soaring above the earth. Sometimes he felt closer to Samantha, as if he was skimming the underbelly of heaven.

As he neared the general area of the farm in the report, movement brought his mind back to earth. A dark shape exploded out of a copse of trees, moving swiftly into the open. It appeared to be a man on a snowmobile. The vehicle came to a halt in the middle of a wide-open field and the man dismounted.

Dante dropped lower and circled, trying to figure out what he was up to. About the time he keyed his mic to radio back to headquarters, he saw the man unstrap what appeared to be a long pipe from the back of his snowmobile and fit something into one end of it.

Recognition hit, and Dante's blood ran cold. He jerked the aircraft up as quickly as he could. But he was too late.

The man on the ground fired a rocket-propelled grenade.

Dante dodged left, but the grenade hit the tail and exploded. The helicopter lurched and shuddered. He tried to keep it steady, but the craft went into a rapid spin. Realizing his tail rudder had probably been destroyed, Dante had to land and if he didn't land level, the blades could hit first, break off and maybe even end his life.

The chopper spun, the centrifugal force making it difficult for Dante to think and move. He reached up and switched the engines off, but not soon enough. The aircraft plummeted to the ground, a blade hit first, broke off and slammed into the next blade. The skids slammed against the ground and Dante was thrown against the straps of his harness. He flung an arm over his face as fragments of the blades acted like flying shrapnel, piercing the chopper's body and windows. The helicopter rolled onto its side and stopped.

Suspended by his harness, Dante tried to key the mic on his radio to report his aircraft down. The usual static was absent, the aircraft lying as silent as death.

Dante dragged his headset off his head. Frigid wind blew through the shattered windows and the scent of fuel stung his nostrils.

The sound of an engine revving caught Dante's attention. The engine noise grew closer, moving toward his downed aircraft. Had the predator come to finish off his prey?

He scrambled for the harness releases, finally finding and pulling on the quick-release buckles. He dropped on his left side, pain knifing through his arm. Gritting his teeth, he scrambled to his knees on the door beneath him and attempted to reach up to push against the passenger door. Burning pain stabbed his left arm again and he dropped the arm and worked with his good arm to fling the passenger-side door open. It bounced on its hinges and smashed closed again, nearly crushing his fingers with the force.

He hunched his shoulder and nudged the door with it, pushing it open with a little less force. This time, the door remained open and he stood, his head rising above the body of the craft. As he took stock of the situation, a bullet pinged against the craft's fuselage.

Dante ducked. A snowmobile had come to a stop a hundred yards away, the rider bent over the handlebars, pointing a high-powered rifle in his direction. With nothing but the body of the helicopter between him and the bullets, Dante was a sitting duck.

He sniffed the acrid scent of aviation fuel growing more potent as the time passed and more bullets riddled the exterior of the craft. If he stayed inside the helicopter, he stood a chance of the craft bursting into flames and being burned alive. If the bullets sparked a fire, the fuel would burn. If the flames reached the tanks, it would create a tremendous explosion.

Out of the corner of his eye, he could see the bright orange flicker of a flame. In seconds, the ground surrounding his helicopter was a wall of fire.

Amid the roar of flames, the snowmobile revved and swooped closer.

Debating how long he should wait before throwing himself out on the ground, Dante could feel the heat of the flames against his cheeks. If he didn't leave soon, there wouldn't be anything left for the attacker to shoot.

The engine noise faded, drowned out by the roar of the fire.

With fire burning all around him, Dante pulled himself out of the fuselage one-armed and dropped to the ground. His shoulder hit a puddle of the flaming fuel and his jumpsuit ignited.

Rolling through the wall of flames, Dante couldn't get the flame to die out. His skin heated, the fuel was thoroughly soaked into the fabric. He rolled away from the flame, onto his back, unzipped the flight suit and shimmied out of it before the burning fabric melted and stuck to his skin.

Another bullet thunked into the earth beside Dante. Wearing nothing but thermal underwear, Dante rolled over in the snow, hugging the ground, giving his attacker very little target to aim at.

Covered in snow, with nothing to defend himself, Dante awaited his fate.

EMMA JENNINGS HAD spent the morning bundled in her thermal underwear, snow pants, winter jacket, earmuffs and gloves, one of them fingerless. Yes, it was getting colder by the minute. Yes, she should have given up two days ago, but she felt like she was so close, and the longer she waited, the harder the ground got as permafrost transformed it from soft dirt to hard concrete.

The dig had been abandoned by everyone else months ago when school had started up again at the University of North Dakota. Emma came out on weekends hoping to get a little farther along. Fall had been unseasonably warm with only one snowfall in late October that had melted immediately. Six inches of snow had fallen three days ago and seemed in no hurry to melt, though the ground hadn't hardened yet. The next snowfall expected for that evening would be the clincher, with the predicted two feet of snow.

If she hadn't set up a tent around the dig site months ago, she never would have come. As it was, school was out and she'd come with her tiny trailer in tow, with the excuse that she needed to pull down the tent and stow it for the winter. If not for the steep roof, the tent would easily collapse under the twenty-four inches of white powder. Not to mention the relentless winds across the prairie would destroy the tent if it was left standing throughout the wicked North Dakota winter.

Each weekend since fall semester began had proved to be fair and Emma had gone out to dig until this weekend. Some had doubted there'd be snow for Christmas. Not Emma. She'd lived in North Dakota all her life, and never once in her twenty-six years had the snow missed North Dakota at Christmas.

So far, the dig had produced the lower jawbone of a *Tyrannosaurus rex*. Emma was certain if she kept digging, she'd find the skull of the animal nearby. The team of paleontologists and students who'd been on the dig all summer had unearthed neck bones, and near the end of the summer, the jawbone. The skull had to be close. She just needed a little more time.

There to tear down the tent before it was buried in knee-deep drifts, she'd ducked inside to find the ground smooth and dry and the dirt just as she'd left it the weekend before. She squatted to scratch away at the surface with a tool she'd left behind. Before she knew it, she'd succumbed to the lure of the dig. That had been two days ago.

Knowing she had to leave before the storm hit, she'd given herself half of the last day to dig. Immersed in her work, the sound of a helicopter cut through her intense concentration and she glanced at her watch. With a gasp, she realized just how long she'd been there and that it was nearing sunset of her last day on the site.

She still needed to get the tent down and stowed before

dark. With a regretful glance at the ground, she pushed the flap back and ducked through. High clouds blocked out any chance for warmth or glare from the sun.

The thumping sound of blades churning the air drew her attention and she glanced at the sky. About a mile away, a green-and-white helicopter hovered low over the prairie.

From where she stood, she couldn't see what it was hovering over. The ground had a gentle rise and dip, making the chopper appear to be almost on the ground. Emma recognized the craft as one belonging to the Customs and Border Protection.

There was a unit based out of Grand Forks and she knew one of the pilots, Dante Thunder Horse, from when he'd taken classes at the university. A handsome Native American, he had caught her attention crossing campus, his long strides eating up the distance.

He'd taken one of her anthropology classes and they'd met in the student commons on a couple of occasions and discussed the university hockey team games. When he'd finally asked her out, she'd screwed up enough courage to take him up on it, suggesting a coffee shop where they'd talked and seemed to hit it off.

Then nothing. He hadn't called or asked her out for another date. He must have finished his coursework at the university because she hadn't run into him again. Nor did she see him crossing campus. She'd been disappointed when he hadn't called, but that was at the end of last spring. The summer had kept her so busy on the dig, she wouldn't have had time for a relationship—not that she was any good at it anyway. Her longest one had lasted two months before her shyness had scared off the poor young man.

Emma wondered if Dante was the pilot flying today.

She marveled at how close the helicopter was. In all the vastness of the state, how likely was it that the aircraft would be hovering so near to the dig? Then again, the site was fairly close to the border and the CBP was tasked with protecting the northern border of the United States.

As Emma started to turn back to her tent to begin the job of tearing it down, a loud bang shook the air. Startled, she saw a flash in her peripheral vision from the direction of the helicopter. When she spun to see what had happened, the chopper was turning and turning. As if it was a top being spun faster and faster, it dropped lower and lower until it disappeared below the rise and a loud crunching sound ripped the air.

Her heart stopped for a second and then galloped against her ribs. The helicopter had crashed. As far away from civilization as they were, there wasn't a backup chopper that could get to the pilot faster than she could.

Abandoning her tent, she ran for the back of the trailer, flung open the utility door in the rear, dropped the ramp and climbed inside. She'd loaded the snowmobile on the off chance she couldn't get the truck all the way down the road to the dig. Fortunately, she'd been able to drive almost all the way to the site and had parked the truck and trailer on a hardstand of gravel the wind had blown free of snow near the edge of the eight-foot-deep dig site.

Praying the engine would start, she turned the key and pressed the start button. The rumble of the engine echoed off the inside of the trailer but then it died. The second time she hit the start button, the vehicle roared to life. Shifting to Reverse, she backed down the ramp and turned to face the direction the helicopter had crashed.

A tower of flames shot toward the sky, smoke rising in a plume.

Her pulse pounding, Emma raced across the snow, headed for the fire.

As she topped the rise, her heart fell to her knees. The helicopter was a battered heap, lying on its side, flames rising all around.

Gunning the throttle, Emma sped across the prairie, praying she wasn't too late. Maybe the pilot had been thrown clear of the aircraft. She hoped she was right.

As she neared the wreck, movement caught her attention. Another snowmobile was headed toward the helicopter from the north. *Good,* she thought. Maybe whoever it was had also seen the chopper crash and could help her free the pilot from the wreckage and get him to safety. She waved her hand, hoping the driver would see her and know she was there to help. He didn't give any indication he'd spotted her. But the snowmobile slowed. The rider pulled off his helmet, his dark head in sharp contrast to his white jacket. He leveled what appeared to be a rifle across the handlebars, aiming at something near the wall of flames.

Emma squinted, trying to make out what he was doing. The pop of rifle fire made her jump. That's when she noticed a dark lump on the ground in the snow, outside the ring of fire around the helicopter. The lump moved, rolling over in the snow.

The driver of the other snowmobile climbed onto the vehicle and started toward the man on the ground, moving slowly, his rifle poised to shoot.

Emma gasped.

The man was trying to shoot the guy on the ground.

With a quick twist of the throttle she sent her snowmobile skimming across the snow, headed straight for the attacker. At the angle she was traveling, the attacker wouldn't see her if he was concentrating on the man on the ground.

Unarmed, she only had her snowmobile and her wits. The man on the ground only had one chance at survival. If she didn't get to him or the other snowmobile first, he didn't stand a chance.

Coming in from the west, Emma aimed for the man with the gun. She didn't have a plan other than to ram him and hope for the best.

He didn't see her or hear her engine over the roar of his own until she was within twenty feet of him. The man turned the weapon toward her.

Emma gave the engine all it could take and raced straight for the man. He fired a shot. Something plinked against the hood of the snowmobile engine. At the last moment, she turned the handlebars. Her machine slid into the side of his and the handlebars knocked the gun from his hand.

She twisted the throttle and skidded sideways across the snow, spinning around to face him again.

Disarmed, the attacker had turned as well and raced north, away from the burning helicopter and the man on the ground.

Emma watched as the snowmobile continued into the distance. Keeping an eye on the north, she turned her snowmobile south toward the figure lying still on the ground.

She pulled up beside him and leaped off the snowmobile into the packed snow where he'd rolled.

A man in thermal underwear lay facedown in the snow, blood oozing from his left arm, dripping bright red against the pristine white snow.

Emma bent toward him, her hand reaching out to push him over.

The man moved so quickly, she didn't know what hit her. He rolled over, snatched her wrist and jerked her flat onto her belly, then straddled her, his knees planted on both sides of her hips, twisting her arm up between her shoulder blades.

Until that point, she hadn't realized just how vulnerable she was. On the snowmobile, she had a way to escape. Once she'd left the vehicle, she'd put herself at risk. What if the man shooting had been the good guy? In the middle of nowhere, with a big man towering over her, she was trapped and out of ideas.

"Let me up!" she yelled, aiming for righteous contempt. Her voice wobbled, muffled by a mouthful of snow it sounded more like a frog's croak.

She tried to twist around to face him, but he planted his fist into the middle of her back, holding her down, the cold snow biting her cheek.

"Why did you shoot down my helicopter?" he demanded, his voice rough but oddly familiar.

"I didn't, you big baboon," she insisted. "The other guy did."

His hands roved over her body, patting her sides, hips, buttocks, legs and finally slipping beneath her jacket and up to her breasts. His hands froze there and she swore.

Emma spit snow and shouted, "Hey! Hands off!"

As quickly as she'd been face-planted in the snow, the man on top of her flipped her onto her back and stared down at her with his dark green eyes.

"Dante?"

"Emma?" He shook his head. "What the hell are you doing here?"

Chapter Two

"Well, I'm sure not on a picnic," Emma said, her voice dripping with sarcasm.

Dante stared down at the pretty young college professor he'd met when he'd taken classes at the University of North Dakota, working toward a master's degree in operations management.

She stared up at him with warm, dark chocolate-colored eyes, her gaze scanning his face. "What happened to you?" She reached up to touch his temple, her fingers coming away with blood. "Why was that man shooting at you?"

"I don't know." Dante's brow furrowed. "Did you get a good look at him?"

"No, it was all a blur. I thought he was coming to help, but then he started shooting at you. I rammed into him, knocking his gun out of his hands. Then he took off."

"You shouldn't have put yourself in that kind of danger."

"What was I supposed to do, stand by and watch him kill you?"

"Thankfully, he didn't shoot *you*. And thanks for saving my butt." Dante staggered to his feet and reached down with his right hand and helped her up. "He shot down my helicopter with an RPG and would have finished me off if you hadn't come along." A bitterly cold,

Arctic breeze rippled across the prairie, blowing straight through his thermal underwear. A shiver racked his body and he gritted his teeth to keep them from chattering.

Emma stood and brushed the snow off her pants and jacket. "What happened to your clothes?"

"I fell into a puddle of flaming aviation fuel when I climbed out of the helicopter." He glanced back at the inferno. "We need to get out of here in case the fire ignites the fuel in the tank."

He climbed onto her snowmobile.

"You should take my coat. I bet you're freezing." Emma started to unzip her jacket.

He held up his hand. "Don't. I can handle it for a little while and no use in both of us being cold." He moved back on the seat and tipped his head. "Get on. I don't know where you came from, but I hope it's warmer there than it is here."

Her lips twisted, but she didn't waste time. She slipped her leg over the seat and pressed the start button. She prayed the bent skid, damaged in the collision, wouldn't slow them down.

Once she was aboard, Dante wrapped his arms around her and pressed his body against her back, letting her body block some of the bitter wind.

It wasn't enough. The cold went right through his underwear, biting at his skin. He started shaking before they'd gone twenty yards. By the time they topped a rise, he could no longer feel his fingers.

Emma drove the snowmobile along a ridge below which a tent poked up out of the snow. A truck and trailer stood on the ridge, looking to Dante like heaven.

When she pulled up beside the trailer, Emma climbed off, looped one of Dante's arms over her shoulder and helped him into the trailer. It wasn't much warmer inside, but the wind was blocked and for that Dante could be very grateful. The trailer consisted of a bed, a sink, a small refrigerator and a tiny bathroom.

"Sit." Emma pushed him onto the bed, pulled off his boots and shoved his legs under the goose down blanket and a number of well-worn quilts. She handed him a dry washcloth. "Hold this on your shoulder so you don't bleed all over everything."

"Yes, ma'am," he said with a smile.

Her brows dipped. "Stay here while I get the generator running." She opened the door, letting in a cold blast of air.

"Keep your eyes open," he said through chattering teeth.

"I will." She closed the door behind her and the room was silent.

Dante hunkered down into the blankets, feeling as though he should be the one out there stirring the generator to life. When Emma hadn't returned in five minutes, he pushed the blankets aside, wrapped one around himself and went looking for her.

He was reaching for the doorknob when the door jerked open.

Emma frowned up at him, her dark hair dusted in snowflakes. "The generator's not working."

"Let me look at it," he insisted.

She pushed past him, closing the door behind her. "It won't do any good."

"Why?"

"The fuel line is busted." She held up the offending tube and waved him toward the bed. "Get back under the covers. At least we have a gas stove we can use to warm it up a little in here. I don't recommend running it all night, but it'll do for now."

"Why don't we get out of here?"

"It's almost dark and it started snowing pretty hard, I can barely see my hand in front of my face. It's hard enough to find my way out here in daylight. I'm not trying in the dark and especially not in North Dakota blizzard conditions."

"I need to let the base know what happened." He glanced around. "Do you have any kind of radio or cell phone?"

"I have a cell phone, but it won't work out here." She shrugged. "No towers nearby."

His body shook, his head ached and his vision was hazy. "I need to get back."

"Tomorrow. Now go back to bed before you fall down. I'm strong, but not strong enough to pick up a big guy like you."

Dante let Emma guide him back to the bed and tuck him in. When she smoothed the blankets over his chest, he grabbed her hand.

Her gaze met his as he carried her hand to his lips and kissed the back of her knuckles. "Thanks for saving my life."

Her cheeks reddened and she looked away. "You'd have done the same."

"I doubt seriously you'd be shot down from the sky. Your feet are pretty firmly on the ground." He smiled. "Paleontologist, right?"

She nodded.

"Isn't it a little late in the season to be at a dig? I thought they shut them down when the fall session started."

She shrugged. "With our unseasonably warm weather, I've been working this dig every weekend since the semester started."

"Until recently."

"Since it snowed a few days ago, I figured I'd better get out here. I'd heard more snow was coming, and I needed to dismantle my tent and bring it in." She stared toward the window as if she could see through the blinding snow.

"I take it you didn't get the tent down in time."

She gave him a little crooked smile. "A downed helicopter distracted me."

"Well, thank you for sacrificing your tent to be a Good Samaritan."

Her cheeks reddened and she turned away. "Let's get that shoulder cleaned up and bandaged."

She wet a cloth and returned to the bedside. Pushing the fabric of his thermal shirt aside, she washed the blood away.

Her fingers were gentle around the gash.

"It's just a scratch."

Her lips quirked. When she'd washed away the drying blood, she applied an antiseptic ointment and a bandage. "As it is, it was just a flesh wound, but it wouldn't do to get infected." Patting the bandage, she stepped back, the color higher in her cheeks. "I'll make you a cup of hot tea, if you'd like."

Studying her face, Dante found he liked the way she blushed so easily. "Have any coffee?"

"Sorry. I didn't expect to have guests."

"In that case, tea would be nice." Dante glanced around the tiny confines of the trailer. "Aren't you afraid to come out to places like this alone?"

Emma reached for two mugs from a cabinet. "Why should I be? It's not like anyone else comes out here."

"What if you were to get hurt?"

She shrugged. "It's a chance I'm willing to take."

"As close as it is to the border, you might be subject to more than just an elk hunter or farmer."

"I have a gun." Emma opened a drawer and pulled out a long, vintage revolver.

Dante grinned. "You call that a gun?"

She stiffened. "I certainly do."

"It's an antique."

"A Colt .45 caliber, Single Action Army revolver, to be exact."

Nodding, impressed, Dante stated, "You know the name of your antiques."

Her chin tipped upward. "And I'm an expert shot."

"My apologies for doubting you."

The wind picked up outside, rocking the tiny trailer on its wheels.

Emma struck a long kitchen match on the side of a box and lit one of the two burners on the stove. A bright flame cast a rosy glow in the quickly darkening space. She filled a teakettle with water from a large water bottle and settled it over the flame. "I have canned chili, canned tuna and crackers. Again, I hadn't planned on staying more than a couple of nights. I was supposed to head out before the weather laid in."

Despite his injuries, Dante's stomach grumbled. "I don't want to take your food."

She leveled her gaze at him. "I wouldn't offer if I didn't have enough."

"Then, thank you."

She opened two cans of chili and poured them into a pot, lit the other burner and settled the food over the flame.

Before long the teakettle steamed and the rich aroma of tomato sauce and chili powder filled the air. Emma moved with grace and efficiency, the gentle swell of her hips swaying from side to side as she moved between the sink and the stove. Dante's groin tightened. Not that she was his typical type.

Emma appeared to be straitlaced and uptight with little time in her agenda for playing the field, as proved by their one date that had gone nowhere. Still, it didn't give him the right to go after her again.

He shoved aside the blanket and tried to stand. "I should be helping you." A chill hit him, penetrating his long underwear as if he wore nothing at all.

"Stay put." She waved in his direction. "There's little enough room in the trailer without two people bumping into each other. And I've got this covered." She shed her jacket and hung it on a hook on the wall.

"I can at least get the plates and utensils down and set the table." He glanced around. "Uh, where is the table?"

Emma grinned. "It's under the bed. You were lying on it."

He gave her a half bow. "Where do you propose we eat?"

"On the bed." She grinned. "Picnic-style."

"Do you always eat in the bed?" Images of the slightly stiff Emma wearing a baby-doll nightgown, sitting on the coverlet, eating chocolate-covered strawberries popped into Dante's head. He tried but failed to banish the thought, his groin tightening even more. The slim professor with the chocolate-brown hair and eyes, and luscious lips tempted the saint right out of him. And the kicker was that she didn't even know she was so very hot.

"I don't usually have company in my trailer. I can eat wherever I want. In the summertime, I sit on a camp stool outside and watch the sun set over the dig."

He could picture the brilliant red, orange and mauve skies tinting her hair. "I'll consider it an adventure." He reached around her and opened one of the overhead cabinet doors. "Where are the dishes and utensils?" As he leaned over her, the scent of roses tantalized his nostrils. Her hair shone in the light from the flame on the stove as much as he thought it might in the dying embers of a North Dakota sunset. Despite having shed her coat, the thick sweater, turtleneck and snow pants hid most of her shape. But he could remember it from the class he'd audited while attending the university in Grand Forks.

He tucked a hair behind her ear. "Why was it we only went out once?"

Her head dipped. "One has to ask for a second date."

Dante gripped her shoulders gently and turned her slowly toward him. "I didn't call, did I?" He stared down at her until she glanced up.

Her lips twisted. "It's no big deal. We only went out for coffee."

Dante swallowed hard. He remembered. It had been shortly before a particularly harsh bout of depression. One of his buddies from the army had been shot down in Afghanistan. He'd wondered if he'd stayed in the army if he could have changed the course of events, perhaps saved his friend or if he would have died in his place. Losing his fiancée and his friend so soon afterward made him question everything he'd thought he'd understood— his role in the war on terrorism, his patriotism and his faith in mankind. It had been all he could do to get out of bed each morning, go to work and fly the border missions.

"I'm sorry." He brushed a thumb across her full lower lip and then bent to follow his thumb with his mouth. He'd only meant to kiss her softly, but once his lips touched hers, he couldn't stop himself. A rush of hunger like he'd never known washed over him and before he realized it, he was crushing her mouth, his tongue darting out to take hers.

When he raised his head, he stared down at her through a haze of lust, wanting to drag her across the bed and strip her of every layer of clothing.

Her big brown eyes were wide, her lips swollen from his kiss and pink flags of color stained her cheeks.

Dante closed his eyes, forcing himself to be reasonable and controlled. "I'm sorry. I shouldn't have done that."

"I don't—" she started.

The teakettle whistled.

Emma jerked around to the stove, one hand going to the handle of the kettle, the other to her lips.

Dante retrieved bowls from the cabinet and spoons from a drawer and stepped back, giving her as much space as the interior of the trailer would allow.

The wind churned outside, wailing against the flimsy outer walls, the cold seeping through.

As she poured the water into the mugs, Emma's hand shook.

Kicking himself for his impulsive act, Dante vowed to keep his hands—and lips—to himself for the duration of their confinement in the tight space.

Since resigning his commission, Dante hadn't considered himself fit for any relationship. He'd come back to North Dakota, hoping to reclaim the life he'd known growing up. But the transition from soldier to civilian had been anything but easy. Every loud noise made him duck, expecting incoming rounds from hidden enemies. Until today, it had only been noise. Today he'd been under attack and he hadn't been prepared.

Emma dipped a tea bag in each mug until the water turned the desired shade. Then she pulled the bags out and set them in the tiny sink. "I'm sorry, I don't have milk or lemon." She held out a mug to him. "Sugar?"

The way her lips moved to say that one word had him ready to break his recent vow. "No, I'll take it straight."

When she handed him the mug, their hands touched and an electric surge zipped through him. He backed away and his knees bumped into the mattress, forcing him to sit and slosh hot tea on his hand. The scalding liquid brought him back to his senses.

Emma spooned chili into bowls and handed one to him. "Who would shoot you out of the sky?" She cradled her bowl in both hands, blowing the steam off the top.

"I have no idea."

"As a border patrol agent, have you pissed off anyone lately?"

He shook his head. "Not anyone who would have the firepower that man had. He used a Soviet-made RPG from what I could tell. How the hell he got ahold of one of those, I don't know."

"How'd he know you'd be here?"

"I was responding to a call from my base that a man had crossed the U.S.-Canadian border on a snowmobile in this area. I can only assume it was him."

"Could be someone with a gripe against the border patrol."

"Yeah. I wish I could get word to my supervisor. They'll be freaking out right about now. A missing helicopter and pilot is a big deal."

"Would they send out a rescue team?"

"In this weather, I don't see how."

"Hopefully, it'll be gone in the morning." She stirred her chili. "If they don't come looking for you, we'll do our best to drive out and find a farmer with a landline so that you can call back."

He nodded. "A lot of people will be worried. That's an expensive piece of equipment to lose."

"Seems to me that a skilled pilot is harder to replace." Emma took a bite of her chili and chewed slowly.

Dante shrugged. Everything would have to wait until tomorrow. In the meantime... "It's getting colder outside."

"I have plenty of blankets for one bed." She stared at her empty bowl and a shiver shook her body. "Without the generator, we'll have to share the warmth." Her gaze clashed with his, hers appearing reserved, wary.

His lips thinning, Dante raised his hands. "I'm sorry about the kiss. I promise to keep my hands to myself."

Before he finished talking, Emma was shaking her head. "It's going to get really cold. The only way to stay warm is to stay close and share body warmth."

Dante swallowed hard, his body warming at the thought.

He set his empty chili bowl in the sink and took hers from her, laying it on top. "We're adults. This doesn't have to be awkward or a big deal," he said while his body was telling him, *Oh, yes it does!*

Chapter Three

Emma stared at the bed, her heart thumping against her ribs, her mouth going bone-dry. If it wasn't so darned cold in the trailer, she'd sit up all night on the camp stool.

No, she wasn't afraid of Dante. Frankly, she was afraid of her body's reaction to being so close to the tall, dark Native American.

Too awkward around the opposite sex in high school, she'd focused instead on excelling in her studies. While girls her age were kissing beneath the bleachers, she was playing the French horn in band and counting the minutes until she could go back home to her books.

College had been little better. At least her freshman roommate in the dorm had seen some potential in her and shown her how to dress and do her hair and makeup. She'd even set her up on a blind date, which had ended woefully short when she had yanked her hand out of his when he'd tried to hold it.

For all her schooling, she was remarkably unschooled in the ways of love.

The wind moaned outside, sending a frigid chill raking across her body. Her hands shaking, she pushed the snow pants down over her hips and sat on the side of the bed to pull off her boots, slipping the pants off with them. Then she slid beneath the covers in her thermal underwear, sweater and turtleneck shirt and scooted all the way to the other side of the small mattress.

What man could lust after a woman covered from neck to feet? Not that she wanted him to lust after her. What would she do? Heaven help her if he should find out she was a virgin at the ripe old age of twenty-six.

Emma lay on her back, the blankets pulled up to her chin and her eyes wide in the dim glow of the stove's fire. "You'll need to turn off the flame before we go to sleep." Perhaps in the dark she'd felt less conspicuous and self-conscious.

Dante reached for the knob on the little stove and switched it off. The flame disappeared, throwing them into complete darkness.

The blanket tugged against her death grip, and the mattress sank beneath the big man's weight. "Don't worry. I promise not to touch you."

Damn, Emma thought. With a man as gorgeous as Dante Thunder Horse lying next to her, what if she wanted him to touch her? Then again, one close encounter with her bumbling, shy inexperienced self and he'd disappear, just like he had the last time she'd gotten up the courage to go out for coffee with him.

He stretched out alongside her, his shoulder and thigh bumping against her.

A ripple of anticipation fluttered through her belly, followed by a bone-rattling shiver as the cold seeped through the three blankets, her sweater and thermal underwear.

"This is foolish. We won't last the night in the frigid cold without heat." He turned on his side and reached around her.

"W-what are you doing?" she squeaked as his hand brushed across her breast.

"We're both fully clothed, which, by the way, isn't helping matters. We're both adults and we're freezing. The best way to warm up is to share heat."

"That's what we were doing."

"Not like this." He rolled her onto her side, pulled her against him and spooned her backside with his front, his arm draped around her middle. "Better?"

Her pulse pounded so loud she could barely hear him, but she nodded and whispered, "Better." Far too much better.

As she lay in the dark, cocooned in blankets and a handsome man's arms, part of her was freaking out, the other part was shouting inside, *Hallelujah!*

"Let's go to sleep and hopefully the storm will have passed by morning."

Sleep? Was he kidding? Every cell in her body was firing up, while her core was in meltdown stages. Little shivers of excitement ignited beneath her skin with his every movement. His warm breath stirred the tendrils of hair lying against the side of her throat and all she could think of was how close his lips were to her neck. How likely was he to repeat the kiss that happened just a few moments ago?

If she turned over and faced him, would he feel compelled to repeat the performance? Did she dare?

"You smell nice. Like roses." His chest rumbled against her back, his arm tightening around her middle.

"Must be my shampoo. It was a gift from a friend." As soon as she said it, she could have kicked herself. Why couldn't she just say *thank you* like any other woman paid a compliment?

"Am I making you nervous?" he asked.

"I'm not used to having a man…spoon me."

"Seriously?" His thighs pressed against the backs of

her legs and one slid across hers. "They were missing out. You're very spoonable."

She bit her bottom lip, afraid to admit she was a failure at relationships and scared off the men who'd ever made an attempt to get to know her. "I'm not good at this."

"It's as natural as breathing," he said, his big hand spanning her belly. "Speaking of which, just breathe," he whispered against her ear.

His words had the opposite effect, causing her breath to lodge in her throat, her heart to stop for a full second and then race to catch up.

Her arm lay over his and she wasn't sure what to do with her hand. When she let it relax, it fell across his big, warm one.

"Your fingers are so cold," he said.

She jerked her hand back. "I'm sorry."

"Don't be. Let me have them." He felt along her arm until he located her hand and enveloped it in his. "Tuck it beneath your shirt, like this." He slipped his hand with hers under the hems of her sweater and thermal shirt, placing them against the heat of her skin. "You're as stiff as a board. Are you still cold?" He moved his body closer.

"Yes," she lied. Inside she was on fire, her nerve synapses firing off each time he bumped against her.

His fingers curled around hers, his knuckles brushing against her belly. "You really haven't ever snuggled with a man?"

Not trusting her voice, she shook her head.

"Then you haven't found the right one." Dante's lips brushed the curl of her ear.

She lay for a while basking in the closeness, letting her senses get used to the idea of him being so near, so intimate.

Without the heat from the stove top, the trailer's

interior became steadily colder and Dante's hand holding hers inched upward beneath her shirt. "Just tell me if you want me to stop."

Oh, heck no. If anything, she wanted him to move faster and cup her breasts with that big, warm hand. A shiver of excitement shook her.

"Still cold?"

"Yes." So it was a half truth. The parts of her body against his were warm, the others were cold and getting colder.

"Sharing body heat works better when you're skin to skin." His knuckles nudged the swells of her breasts.

Her breath caught in her throat when she said, "I know." Emma bit her bottom lip, wondering if Dante would take her words as an invitation to initiate the next move.

"I don't know about you, but it's getting pretty damn cold in here. If we want to keep warm all night, we'd better do what it takes." He removed his hand from her belly and rolled onto his back.

The cold enveloped her immediately and she scooted over to lie on her back as well, tugging the blanket up to her nose.

Dante sat up next to her, tugging the blanket aside, letting even colder air beneath.

"What are you doing?" she said through chattering teeth.

"Getting naked." His movements indicated he was removing his thermal shirt and stuffing it beneath the covers down near his feet. He slid his long underwear over his hips, his hands bumping into her thigh as he pushed them all the way down to his feet.

"Now your turn." He reached for the hem of her sweater and dragged it over her head.

"Are you crazy? It's f-freezing in here." She tried to keep her turtleneck shirt on, but he was as determined to remove that as he'd been with the sweater.

"Again, we're adults. If it helps, just think of me as a big electric blanket to wrap around you." He stuffed her shirt and sweater into the space around her feet and went to work on the long thermal underwear, dragging them down over her legs.

By the time he had her stripped to her bra and panties, she was shaking uncontrollably. "I was w-warmer b-before you s-started," she said through chattering teeth.

"You'll be warm again. Come here." He dragged the blanket over them and pulled her close, crushing her breasts against his chest, his big arms wrapping around her back, tucking the blanket in as close as he could get it.

Their breath mingled, the heat of their skin, touching everywhere but her bra and panties, helped to chase away the chills. But Emma still couldn't stop shaking. She'd never lain nearly naked with a man. She had trouble breathing and couldn't figure out where her hands were supposed to be. Planting them against his chest was putting too much space between them and allowing cold air to keep her front chilled. She tried moving them down to her side, but her fingers were cold and she wanted them warm. When she slipped them around to her belly, they bumped against a hot, stiff shaft.

As soon as she touched it, she realized it was his member and before she could think, her hands wrapped around it.

"Baby, only go there if you mean it," he warned her. "As close and naked as we are, it wouldn't take much to set me off."

"I thought you were just an electric blanket," she whispered, reveling in a surge of power rolling through her.

She had caused him to be this way. Her body against his was making him desire her in a way she'd only dreamed about.

For a moment, all her awkward insecurities disappeared. Her fingers tightened around him and slid downward to the base of his shaft.

His arms squeezed around her and his hips rocked, pressing himself into her grip.

Blood hummed through her veins. For that moment, she forgot the chill in the air and the fact they could freeze to death. Her focus centered on what she had in her hands and, in connection, what it could lead to.

Dante moaned. "Do you know what you're doing to me?"

"I think so," she responded. Her hand glided up his shaft to the velvety tip, her core heating, liquid fire swirling at her center, readying her to take him.

"I didn't get us naked in order to take advantage of you."

Her hands froze. "Am I taking advantage of *you*?"

"Oh, hell no."

Her finger swirled across the tip, memorizing him by touch. "Just say so and I'll stop," she repeated his words.

"Are you sure you want to do this?" He ran his hands over her back and down to smooth over her bottom.

She laughed, emboldened by the complete darkness. "I've never been more sure of anything in my life." Something about the anonymity of the dark gave her the confidence to continue. Then she hesitated. "Unless you don't want to. You're the injured party."

"I've wanted this since I stole that kiss." He hooked the elastic of her panties and slid them down her legs.

She kicked them off, loving the way his member

pressed into her curly mound. Just a little lower and he'd be there.

"I don't have protection," he said.

"I'm clean of STDs if that's what you're saying." How could she not be when she'd never made love to a man?

"So am I." He nuzzled her neck, his lips pressing against her pounding pulse. "But we shouldn't do this without protection."

"Can't you withdraw at the last minute?"

"Withdrawal isn't one-hundred percent safe."

"You can't stop now." Surely she couldn't get pregnant on her first time. Her first time. Wow. With a man as gorgeous and gentle as Dante, maybe she'd finally overcome her awkward shyness. She trembled, her body shaking like an engine when it first starts.

"Are we going to do it?" she asked, her hand tugging on him, guiding him to her center.

He chuckled softly. "Say the word."

She inhaled and let out the single word on a breath of air, "Please."

Dante hesitated for less than a second, and then he rolled on top of her, nudged her legs apart with his knees and settled between her thighs, his member pressing to her opening.

But he didn't enter, not immediately. He started with a kiss. One similar to the one he'd stolen at the stove. This time, Emma kissed him back, finding his tongue and sliding hers along the length of his. She curled her fingers around the back of his neck and dragged him closer, loving the feel of his smooth chest against her fingers. She reached behind her and unclasped her bra, wanting her naked breasts to feel what her fingers had the pleasure of.

Dante tore it away and slid it beneath her pillow, then he pulled the blanket over their heads and moved down her body. Inch by inch, he tasted her with his tongue, nipping her with his teeth, settling first on one breast, sucking the tip into his mouth and rolling the tight bud around. He moved to the other and gave it equal attention before he inched lower, skimming across her ribs and down past her belly button to the tuft of hair at the apex of her thighs.

Emma held her breath, wondering what he would do next. His mouth so close to home, she couldn't move, frozen to the sheets, waiting.

With his big, rough fingers, he parted her folds and stroked that sensitive strip of skin.

"Oh, my!" she exclaimed, her heels digging into the mattress, raising her hips for more.

He swirled, tapped and flicked, setting her world on fire. When she thought she couldn't take any more, he moved up her body, and pressed into her.

At the barrier of her virginity, he paused.

Emma wrapped her legs around his waist and dug her heels into his buttocks, urging him deeper. "Don't stop," she pleaded.

"But…"

"Just do it. Please." She tightened her legs.

He thrust deeper, tearing through.

She must have gasped, because he pulled back a little.

"Are you all right?" Dante asked.

She laughed shakily. "I'd be better if you didn't stop."

After hesitating a moment longer, he slid slowly into her and began a steady, easy glide in and out.

The initial pain lasted but a moment, and soon Emma forgot it in the joy of the connection between them. So this was what all the fuss was about. Now she understood and dropped her feet to the mattress to better meet him thrust for thrust.

When Dante stiffened, he stopped, his hard member buried deep inside her. A moment later, he dragged himself free and lay down beside her, pulling her into the warmth of his arms.

The heat of his body and the haze of pleasurable exhaustion washed over her and she melted against him. "Mmm. I never knew it would be that good."

He lay with his arms around her, his body stiff. "You cried out. Why?"

Heat rose into her cheeks. "Did I?"

For a long moment, Dante held her without talking. "You were a virgin, weren't you?" When she refused to answer, he continued, "Why didn't you tell me?"

Emma rested her hand on his chest, feeling the swift beat of his heart against her palm. "I was embarrassed. Besides, what difference does it make?"

"We wouldn't have done it." He smoothed a hand along her lower back.

"Are you sorry you did?" she asked, her lips so close to his nipple, she tongued the hard little point, liking the way it beaded even tighter.

"No."

She smiled in the darkness and relaxed against him. "Me, either. Virginity is way overrated."

He tipped her chin up with his finger. "Then why are—*were*—you still one?" His breath warmed her.

"Like I told you. I'm not good at relationships. I could never get past a first date."

She could feel his head shaking side to side. "Inconceivable," he said, then captured her mouth with his.

When he broke the kiss, Emma lay in his arms, basking in the afterglow, their bodies generating enough combined heat that, along with the cocoon of blankets, they held off the cold.

"Just so you know, I'm not good at relationships, either," Dante said into the darkness. "I can offer you no guarantees."

"I understand." The warmth she'd been feeling chilled slightly. What did she expect? Sex was sex. No matter how good it felt, it didn't necessarily come with emotional commitment.

She couldn't expect Dante to fall in love with her just because she'd given him her virginity. "Don't worry. I won't stalk you or make any demands of you. The 'no guarantees' thing goes both ways."

His hand paused the circular motion he'd begun on her naked back.

She added to boost her own self-confidence, "Thank you for getting me over my awkwardness. I won't be so hesitant with my future dates." As soon as she said the words, she could have kicked herself. Would he consider them flippant and insensitive, or worse? Would he think she was loose and easy with her body?

Despite his announcement that he'd give no guarantees, she'd harbored a wish, a dream and a raging desire to repeat what had just happened. When the storm cleared and they made it back to civilization, she hoped he'd ask her out again. Though sex with Dante had been magical to her, he certainly wouldn't be impressed enough for a repeat performance with an awkward ex-virgin?

Chapter Four

Dante pressed himself as close as he could get to the jagged hulk of his crashed helicopter; his copilot lay at an awkward angle, still strapped to his seat, dead from a broken neck sustained upon impact. He didn't recognize the copilot, his face was hidden in shadows.

A movement at the edge of the village where he'd crashed caught Dante's eye. The flap of a dark robe fluttered in the desert breeze. There. The man he'd seen at the last minute, pointing an RPG at him, stood at the corner of a mud hut.

Staying low behind the metal wreckage, Dante leveled his 9 mm pistol, aiming at the man, waiting for him to step out of the shadows and come within range.

The sound of an engine made his blood run cold. An old, rusty truck rumbled down the middle of the street between the buildings, loaded with Taliban soldiers wielding Soviet-made rifles.

Alone, without any backup, it was him with a full clip against the Taliban. If he wanted to live, he had to make every shot count.

The truck barreled toward him and stopped short. The soldiers leaped over the side. He fired, hitting one, then another, but they kept coming as if the truck had

*an endless supply. One by one, he fired until the trigger
clicked and the clip was empty.*

*Taliban men grabbed his arms and pulled him from
the wreckage, shouting and shooting their weapons in
the air. The hum of the truck engine growled louder as
they dragged him closer.*

"Dante."

*How did they know his name? He struggled against
their hold, kicking and shoving at their hands.*

"Dante, wake up!"

He opened his eyes. The sand and desert disappeared
and dim light seeped in around the blinds over a window.

"Dante?" a soft feminine voice called out and it all
came back to him.

"Emma?" he said, his voice hoarse.

She leaned over him, her naked body pressed against
his, her breasts smashed to his chest, her thigh draped
over his. She smelled of roses mixed with the musky
scent of sex.

It took him a moment to shake the terror of being captured and dragged away by the Taliban, and even longer
to return to the camp trailer on the North Dakota tundra.

Then he noticed a red mark on Emma's cheek. "What
happened to you?" He reached up to gently brush his
thumb around the mark.

She smiled crookedly. "You were having a bad dream."

"I did that?" His chest tightened and he pushed to a
sitting position. "Oh, Emma, I'm so sorry."

"It doesn't hurt." She pressed her fingers to the red
welt. "I'm more worried about the engine noise I hear
outside."

Dante sat still and silent, focusing on the noise from
outside. Just as she'd said, an engine revved nearby.

Dante threw back the covers. "Get up. Get dressed."

"Why?" She asked, scrambling off the bed, gooseflesh rising on her naked skin.

"We don't know if the man who shot me down yesterday is back."

"Damn." Emma grabbed her sweater, tugged it over her naked breasts and slipped into her snow pants and boots.

Dante only had his thermals to pull on and his boots.

When he reached for the door handle and twisted, it didn't open. "Is there some kind of lock on this?"

"It should open when you twist the handle."

He tried again.

About that time, the trailer lurched, sending him flying across the floor, slamming into the sink.

Emma fell across the bed. "What the hell?"

"The door lock is jammed, and someone's driving your truck with the trailer still attached. Hold on!"

The vehicle lurched and bumped over the rough terrain.

"He's backing us up!" Emma shouted. "If he goes much farther, we'll end up in the ditch my team has been digging." She staggered to her feet and flung herself across the room to the door. Another bump and her forehead slammed into the wall.

She slipped, her hands grabbing for the door latch. "We have to stop him."

Dante staggered across to her. "Move!" He picked her up and shoved her to the side. Bracing himself on whatever he could hold on to, he slammed his heel into the door. The force with which he hit reverberated up his leg. The door remained secure. He kicked again. Nothing.

Emma grasped the sink and ripped the blinds from the window. "Oh, my god. We're going to fall—"

The trailer tipped wildly. Everything that wasn't nailed to the floor, including Dante and Emma, was flung to the back of the trailer as it tumbled down the near-vertical slope of the dig site. The rear end of the trailer slammed into the ground, crumpling on impact. Cold air blasted through the cracks and glass broke from the windows.

Dante landed on the mattress as it slid toward the back of the trailer. "Emma?" He couldn't see her anywhere.

"I'm okay, I think." A hand waved from beneath the mattress. "I'm just stuck."

The truck engine revved and a door slammed outside. Then the upper end of the trailer caved in, bearing down on them. Dante rolled to the side, letting the mattress take the bulk of the blow.

When the world quit shaking, Dante was jammed between the mattress and the wall. Metal squeaked against metal and the trailer seemed to groan.

"Dante?" Emma called out.

"I'm going to try to move this mattress." He squeezed himself against the wall and rolled the mattress back. "Can you get yourself out?"

"I'll try." Emma reached up, grabbed the edge of the sink and pulled herself out from beneath the mattress.

Dante let the mattress fall in place and hauled himself up on it, ducking low to keep from hitting his head on the crushed trailer. His stomach lurched when he saw the bumper of the truck through a crack in the wall. Whoever had driven them into the ditch had crashed the truck down on top of them. If it shifted even a little, they'd be stuck in there, trapped and possibly crushed.

Light and cold wind filtered through the broken window over the sink. Placing his head close to the opening, he listened.

"Is he gone?" Emma whispered.

A small engine roared above them. If he wasn't mistaken, Dante would guess it was a snowmobile. "I think that's him leaving now." And none too soon. The truck above them shifted and the walls sank closer to where he and Emma crouched on the mattress.

The door was crushed and mangled. They wouldn't be getting out that way. If they didn't leave soon, the truck would smash into them. "We have to get out of here."

"How?" Emma asked.

Dante lay back and kicked the rest of the glass out of the window over the sink. Then, using the pillow, he worked the jagged edges loose. "You go first," he said.

"And leave you to be crushed?" Emma shook her head. "No way. If you can get out, I can get out."

"If I get stuck, neither one of us will get out. If you go first and I'm trapped, you can go for help."

Emma worried her bottom lip between her teeth. "Okay. But you're not getting stuck." She edged her body through the tight opening and dropped to the ground. "Now you!" she called out. "And throw any blankets or coats you can salvage out with you."

Dante scavenged two blankets from the rubble and pushed them through the window. He followed them with Emma's winter jacket.

Metal shrieked against metal and the trailer's walls quaked.

"The truck's shifting!" Emma called out. "Get out now!"

Dante dove for the small window, wondering how he'd get his broad shoulders through the narrow opening. He squeezed one through and angled the other, the rim of the window tight around his ribs. Then he was pushing himself through.

Emma braced his hands on her shoulders and walked backward as he brought his hips and legs almost all the way out.

The entire structure wobbled and creaked, then folded like an accordion.

Emma dragged him the rest of the way, both of them falling onto the ground as the truck's weight crushed the remainder of the trailer walls beneath it.

Dante rolled off Emma and stood, pulling her up beside him. Together they stared at the wreckage.

She shook in the curve of his arm. "If one more minute had passed…"

His arm tightened around her. "We're out. That's all that matters."

"But who would do this?"

"I don't know, but I'm sure as hell going to find out."

EMMA COULDN'T REMEMBER the road leading into the dig site being as long as it was, until she had to walk through snow to get to a paved road. Her toes were frozen and her jacket barely kept the cold wind from chilling her body to the bone. But she couldn't complain when all Dante had on were his thermal underwear and the blankets he'd salvaged from the trailer before it had been crushed beneath her truck.

With the truck a total write-off, she'd hoped the snowmobile she'd left parked outside the night before would be usable.

Whoever had tried to kill them had stabbed a hole in the snowmobile's gas tank and ripped the wires loose. It wasn't going anywhere but a junkyard.

If they wanted to get help, they were forced to trudge through three feet of snow for almost two miles just to reach a paved road. And as the North Dakota countryside could be desolate, it could be hours or days before anyone passed by on the paved road.

Tired, hungry and cold, Emma formed a smile with her chapped lips. At least she wouldn't die a virgin. "Are you doing okay?" she asked. "We could stop and hunker down long enough for you to warm up."

"I'm fine." Enveloped in the two blankets he'd thrown from the wreckage, his thermal-clad legs were more exposed to the elements than anything else. "We should keep moving."

Emma could tell he was trying not to let his teeth chatter. She slipped her arm around him and leaned her body into his to block as much of the wind as she could. Blankets provided little protection against the icy Arctic winds. If they didn't find help soon, he'd freeze to death. How much could a man persevere after being shot down and nearly crushed?

Her gaze swept over him. The man, all muscle and strength, displayed no weakness. But as cold as she was, he had to be freezing.

Though the storm had moved on and the sun had come out, the wind hadn't let up, seeming to come directly from the North Pole.

When they reached pavement, Emma almost felt giddy with relief. With the gravel road she'd come in on buried in snow, she hadn't been completely sure they were headed in the right direction.

"Which way?" Dante asked.

Emma glanced right, then left, and back right again. "If I recall correctly, the man who owns this ranch lives in a house a couple of miles north of this turnoff."

A cold blast of wind sent a violent shiver across her body.

"Here." Dante peeled one of the blankets off his back and handed it to her.

"No way." She refused to take it. "I'm warm enough. You're the one who needs it."

"I'm used to this kind of cold. I grew up in the Badlands."

"I don't care where you grew up. If you drop from hypothermia, I can't carry you." She stood taller, stretching every bit of her five-foot-four-inch frame in an attempt to equal his over six-feet-tall height. "Put it back on."

He grinned, his lips as windburned as hers, and wrapped the blanket back around his shoulders. "Then let's get to it. The sooner we get there, the sooner I get my morning cup of coffee." Wrapping the blankets tightly around himself, he took off.

Emma had to hurry to keep up, shaking her head at his offer of a blanket when she had all the snow gear on and he had nothing but his underwear. Stubborn man.

Her heart warmed at his concern for her and the strength he demonstrated.

So many questions burned through her, but she saved them for when they made it to shelter and warmth. Emma focused all her energy on keeping up with the long-legged Native American marching through the snow to find help. With the sun shining brightly, the blindingly white snow made her eyes hurt and she ducked her head, her gaze on Dante's boot heels. She stepped in the tracks he left as much as possible to save energy, though his strides were far longer than hers.

After what felt like an eternity, cold to the bone, her teeth chattering so badly she couldn't hear herself think, Emma looked up and nearly cried.

A thin ribbon of smoke rose above the snow-covered landscape. Where there was smoke, there was fire and warmth. Fueled by hope, she picked up the pace, squinting at the snowy fields until the shape of a ranch house was discernible.

Less than a tenth of a mile from the house, Emma stumbled and fell into the snow. Too stiff to move quickly, she didn't get her arms up in time to keep from performing a face-plant in the icy crystals.

Before she could roll over and sit up, she was plucked from the snow and gathered in Dante's arms.

"P-put me down," she stammered, her teeth clattering so hard she was afraid she'd bite her tongue, but was too tired to care.

"Shush," he said and continued the last tenth of a mile to the front door of the house.

Her face stinging from the cold, all she could do was wrap her arms around Dante's neck and hold on while he banged on the door.

Footsteps sounded on the other side of the solid wood door and it swung open.

"Dear Lord." An older gentleman in a flannel shirt and blue jeans stood in sock feet, his mouth dropped open.

"Sir, we need help," Dante said.

"Olaf, don't just stand there, let them in and close the door. Can't let all that heat escape with the power out." An older woman hurried up behind Olaf. "Come in, come in."

Olaf's jaw snapped shut and he stepped aside, allowing Dante to carry Emma through the door.

Even before Olaf closed the door behind them, heat surrounded Emma and tears slid down her cheeks. "We made it." She buried her face against the cool blankets covering Dante's chest.

"Set her down here on the couch in front of the fire," the woman said, urging Dante forward. She waved a golden retriever out of the way and pointed to the couch she was referring to. "The storm knocked the power out last night and we've been camping out in the living room to stay warm by the fireplace. We have a generator, but we save that for emergencies."

Emma almost laughed. To most people, a power outage would constitute an emergency. The hardy folks of North Dakota had to be really down-and-out to consider power failure to be an emergency.

Dante set Emma on the sofa and immediately began pulling off her jacket.

"Let me," the woman said. She waved Dante away. "You go thaw out by the fire." As she tugged the zipper down on Emma's jacket, she introduced herself. "I'm Marge, and that's my husband, Olaf." The woman's white eyebrows furrowed. "Should I know you? You look familiar."

"I think we met last summer. My name's Emma." Emma forced a smile past her chapped lips. "Emma Jennings from the UND Paleontology Department. I was working at the dig up until yesterday."

"I thought the site had been shut down at the end of the summer," Olaf said.

Emma shrugged. "Since we've had such a mild fall I've been coming out on weekends. I'd hoped to get in one last weekend before the permafrost."

"And then the storm last night…" Marge shook her head. "You're lucky you didn't freeze to death."

"I c-can do this," Emma protested, trying to shrug out of her jacket on her own.

Marge continued to help. "Hon, your hands are like ice. It'll be a miracle if they aren't frostbitten." The woman clucked her tongue, casting a glance over her shoulder at Dante. "And him out in the cold in nothing but his underwear. What happened?"

Olaf took the blankets from Dante and gave him two warm, dry ones. "Did your truck get stuck in the snow?"

Emma's gaze shot to Dante. She didn't want to frighten these old people.

Dante took over. Holding out his hand to Olaf, he said, "I'm Dante Thunder Horse. I'm a pilot for the Customs and Border Protection unit out of Grand Forks. My helicopter was shot down several miles from here yesterday."

Olaf's eyes widened, his grip on Dante's hand tightening before he let go.

When Dante was done filling them in on what had happened, Olaf ran a hand through his scraggly gray hair and shook his head. "Don't know what's got into this world when you can't even be safe in North Dakota."

Emma laughed, more tears welling in her eyes. After their near-death experiences, she was weepier than normal. For a short time there, she had begun to wonder if they'd find shelter before they froze.

"Mind if I use your phone?" Dante asked. "I need to let the base know I'm alive."

Marge tucked a blanket around Emma. "Olaf, hand him the phone."

Olaf gave Dante a cordless phone. Dante tapped the numbers into the keypad and held the phone to his ear and frowned. "I'm not getting a dial tone."

"Sorry. I forget, without power, this one is useless." Olaf took the phone and replaced it in the powerless charger. "Let me check the one in the kitchen."

A minute later, he returned. "The phone lines are down. Must have been knocked out along with the electricity in the storm last night."

"I need to get back to Grand Forks. My people will have sent up a search and rescue unit."

"I can get you as far as Devil's Lake," Olaf said. "But

then I'll have to turn back to make sure I get home to Mamma before nightfall."

"Don't you worry about me. I can take care of myself," Marge insisted.

"We don't want to put you in danger," Emma said.

"No, we don't," Dante agreed. "If we could get as far as Devil's Lake, we can find someone heading to Grand Forks and catch a ride with them."

"I'd take you all the way to Grand Forks, but with the snow on the road and the wife here, keeping the house warm by burning firewood..."

"We wouldn't want you to leave her alone that long," Dante assured Olaf. "It'll be a long enough drive to Devil's Lake and back."

"I'll get my truck out of the barn." Olaf hurried into the hallway leading toward the back of the house. "Mamma, find the man some of my clothes. He can't go all the way to Grand Forks in his underwear." Olaf shot a grin back at them as he pulled on his heavy winter coat, hat and gloves.

Marge left them in the living room and headed the opposite direction of her husband. When she returned, she carried a pair of jeans, an older winter jacket and a flannel shirt. "These were my son's. He's a bit taller than Olaf. They should fit you better."

"I'll have them returned to you as soon as possible."

"Don't bother. He has more in the closet and he rarely makes it up here in the wintertime. We usually go stay with him and his family in January and February. They live in Florida." She grinned. "It's a lot nicer down there at this time of year than up here."

Dante smiled at the woman and accepted the clothing graciously.

"There's a bathroom in the hallway if you'd like to dress in there." Marge pointed the direction.

Dante disappeared and reappeared a few minutes later dressed in jeans that fit a little loose around his hips and were an inch or two short on his legs. The flannel shirt strained against his broad shoulders, but he didn't say a word.

Emma figured he was grateful to have anything more than just thermal underwear on his body.

He shrugged into the old jacket and zipped it. "I'll go help Olaf with the truck."

"Stay inside," Marge insisted. "You've been exposed to the weather enough for one day."

"I'm fine." He nodded toward Emma, his dark eyes smoldering. "I'll be back in a minute for you."

Emma's heart fluttered. She knew he didn't mean anything by the look, other than he'd be back to load her up in the truck.

Alone with Marge, Emma wished she was warm enough to go out and help, but the thought of going out in the cold so soon after nearly dying in it didn't appeal to her in the least. How did Dante do it?

"That's some man you have there," Marge said, fussing over the blankets in Emma's lap.

Emma started to tell Marge that he wasn't her man, but decided it didn't matter. The farmer and his wife had been very helpful, taking them in and providing them warmth and clothing.

"How long have you two been together?" Marge asked out of the blue.

Now that she hadn't refuted Marge's earlier statement, Emma didn't know whether she should tell her they weren't together. "Not very long" were the words she came up with. They were true in the simplest sense.

She and Dante had only been together since she'd found him in the snow beside the helicopter wreckage the day before and one other time when they'd had coffee together on campus.

Marge smiled. "You two make a nice couple. Now, do you want to take an extra jacket with you? Olaf keeps blankets and a sleeping bag in the backseat of the truck in case we get marooned out in bad weather. Make use of them. I know once you get cold, it's hard to warm up. Sometimes it takes me days for my old body to catch up."

Used to the North Dakota winters, Emma nodded. To think Dante was out in that cold wind helping the old man get the truck ready sent another shiver across Emma's skin.

"I've got my camp stove going and some water heating for coffee. If you're all right by yourself, I'll rustle up some breakfast for the two of you."

"You don't have to go to all that trouble." Emma's belly growled at the thought of food.

Marge laughed. "No trouble at all. We rarely have visitors so far north. It'll be a treat to get to fuss over someone." She left Emma on the couch.

The rattle of pans preceded the heavenly scent of bacon cooking. By the time the men came in from the cold, Emma's mouth was watering and she pushed aside the blankets to stand.

"Everything's ready," Dante said.

"Good. Then come have a seat at the table and eat breakfast while Olaf and I have our lunch. No use going off with an empty stomach." Marge set plates of hot food on the table and cups of steaming coffee.

"We really appreciate all you've done for us. Truthfully, we'd have been happy just to sit in front of the fire to thaw." Emma sat in the chair Dante pulled out for her and stared down at eggs, bacon, ham and biscuits. "Breakfast never looked so good," she exclaimed.

"You're an angel." Dante hugged the older woman and waited for her to sit in front of a sandwich and chips before he took his seat.

Marge's cheeks bloomed with color.

"My Marge can make most anything with a camp stove and a Dutch oven. And she can dress a mule deer like a side of beef."

Marge waved at her husband. "He only married me because I liked hunting."

Olaf grinned. "And she was the prettiest girl in the county."

Emma hid a smile. The pair clearly loved each other. "How long have you two been together?"

Olaf's head tipped to one side. "What's it been? Thirty years or more?"

Marge shook her head. "Going on forty."

"And you still don't look a day over twenty-nine."

"Big fibber."

Emma caught Dante's smile and joined him with one of her own. The warm food and good company went a long way toward restoring her stamina.

By the time Marge and Olaf bundled them into the truck, Emma was beginning to think all was right in a crazy world. She found it hard to believe that only that morning someone had tried to kill them.

As Olaf drove the long, snow-covered road to Devil's Lake, Emma had far too much time on her hands to think. Whoever had shot down Dante's helicopter hadn't been satisfied with him being injured. He'd come back to finish the job. The big question was, would he try again?

Chapter Five

At the truck stop at Devil's Lake, Dante was able to get a call through to headquarters. The dispatcher on duty was relieved to hear from him. They'd sent out several helicopters to circle the last known location of his helicopter. The snow had done a nice job of hiding the crash site and they'd just located it beneath three feet of powder when Dante had made contact.

Dante waited while the dispatcher connected him to his supervisor, Jim Kramer.

"T.H., where the hell have you been?"

Dante laughed. "Slogging through three feet of snow to get to someplace warm."

"You had us all worried out here when you didn't show up at quittin' time."

"Nice to know someone cares." Dante had been with the CBP long enough to be a part of the team. When a chopper went down, everyone took it personally. The loss of a teammate hit everyone hard. "Rest assured, I'm not dead, yet."

"Glad to hear it." Jim paused. "What happened?"

"I was shot down by a man with a Soviet-made RPG."

"What?"

"Look, I'm sitting at a truck stop in Devil's Lake. The storm hit this area pretty hard and a lot of electric and phone lines are down. I was about to hit up a few of the truck drivers to see if anyone could get us back to Grand Forks. When I get back, I'll fill you in on all the details."

"Fair enough. But I can do you one better. Biacowski is out searching for you. I'll send him over to pick you up."

"As long as he has room for two."

"What do you mean?"

"I had a little help getting away from the burning fuselage and then surviving the storm last night by someone who works out at the university."

"Thank him for me, will ya? You know how hard it is to find good pilots."

"Will do." Dante didn't bother to correct his supervisor on the gender of the person who'd helped him. After arranging a location to pick him up, Dante hung up and turned to find Emma hugging Olaf.

Something that felt oddly like jealousy tugged at his insides. Not that he had anything to fear from Olaf. The man was married and old enough to be Emma's father.

What bothered him was that she'd felt comfortable hugging the old guy and hadn't so much as touched Dante since they'd made it back to civilization.

When Samantha was alive, he'd been jealous of any man she'd so much as said hello to. Which was practically everyone in camp. She'd laughed and told him to get over it. Though he'd never told her, he never had. His love for her had bordered on obsessive. If he was honest with himself, he was certain had Samantha lived, he'd have driven her away. She had a mind of her own and resented when he told her what to do.

He'd only done so out of fear of losing her. And his fear had played out. Samantha had died outside the wire.

Glancing across at Emma, he could see very few similarities between the two women. Where Samantha had straight, sandy-blond hair and gray-blue eyes, Emma had curly dark hair and dark brown eyes.

Being a female captain in the army meant Samantha had to have a tough exterior and confidence to command the soldiers in her company. Emma appeared to be afraid of men. But she'd shown no fear when she'd used her snowmobile to ram into the guy shooting at him. Her fear was in being alone and naked with a man.

Samantha had been hot as hell in bed and liked being on top half the time. Emma…

Her soft brown eyes met his and she smiled. Though she wasn't as sexy as Samantha, she had her own sweet serenity that made him calm and excited all at once. His heartbeat fluttered and he longed to be naked with her, buried beneath the blankets, touching her, bringing her body and senses to life.

She'd been like an exotic flower opening for the first time. And she'd given him something special, something she couldn't take back. Too bad he wasn't in the market for a relationship. Emma would be well worth the trouble.

Her cheeks grew pink.

Dante realized he must have been staring and shifted his gaze to the sky. The thumping sound of helicopter blades was music to his ears. His heart was heavy at the thought of the crashed Eurocopter AS-350 lying in a burned-out heap beneath the snow on Olaf's ranch. Helicopters weren't cheap and took time to replace. He'd gone over and over in his mind what he could have or should have done in the situation, but nothing would undo what had been done.

Biacowski set the helicopter down in a field bordering the small town of Devil's Lake.

Olaf drove the pair to the edge and let them out close enough to walk to the aircraft.

Once again, Emma hugged the older man and thanked him.

Dante stuck out his hand and shook Olaf's. "Thank you for all you and your wife have done for us."

"Thank you for your service, Dante. I hope you and your girl will come visit us again." The man grinned. "Hopefully under better circumstances next time."

Emma gave him a gentle smile. "We'd like that."

The pilot remained with the aircraft as Dante and Emma approached, hunched over to avoid being hit by the still-turning rotors. Once Dante had Emma settled in the backseat and buckled in, he handed her a headset so that she could hear the conversation up front.

Finally, Dante climbed into the copilot seat.

Dante settled the spare headset over his ears.

Biacowski glared at him. "Don't ever scare me like that again."

"Sorry to inconvenience you." Dante chuckled. "I have a feeling that if you hadn't called in sick, one or both of us would have been dead in that fire. I seriously doubt that as much as Emma helped, she could have saved both of us."

Chris glanced over his shoulder at Emma and gave her a thumbs-up. "I owe you one. Emma, is it?"

She nodded.

"Hell, the CBP owes you one. Dante's one of our best pilots."

She adjusted the mic over her mouth and spoke softly. "Glad to help."

Biacowski leaned toward Dante. "Where'd you find her? She's cute."

Dante glanced back at Emma, knowing full well she

could hear what the pilot said. "I didn't find her, she found me."

"I want the whole story when we get back."

"You got it. Just get us back before nightfall. It's already been a long day for both of us."

Dante settled back in his seat, thinking he'd close his eyes and take a short nap on the way back. A glance to the rear proved Emma had nodded off. She had to be exhausted after nearly being killed and then slogging through knee-deep snow to find shelter.

Though he closed his eyes, the rumble of the engine and the thumping of the rotors made his blood pump faster and his hands itch to take the controls. Giving up on a nap, he opened his eyes and scanned the snow-covered landscape below, half expecting to find a man on a snowmobile pointing an RPG at him.

His nerves knotted and remained stretched tight until the lights of the Grand Forks International Airport blinked up at him.

Biacowski hovered over the landing area and set the helicopter down like laying a sleeping baby in its crib.

Dante climbed into the backseat before the rotors had time to stop spinning and helped Emma out of the harness.

"I'll take you home as soon as I debrief my commander." He stared into her sleepy eyes. "Will you be okay for an hour or two?"

"I can catch a taxi back. You don't have to worry about me."

"My supervisor will want to hear your story, as well. You actually saw the man who fired on my helicopter."

"I didn't see much."

"Whatever you saw, he'll want to know about." Dante

grabbed her hand and led her toward the building. Bia-cowski followed.

Jim Kramer met them at the door to his office, showed them in and offered them coffee. "Do I need to get an ambulance to have you two taken to the hospital?" Kramer frowned, staring hard at them. "You both look like you got rolled in a fight."

Dante's gaze met Emma's and he sighed. "We did get rolled and almost lost the fight." He told his side of what had happened over the past twenty-four hours and waited while Kramer questioned Emma.

"Could you describe the man on the snowmobile?"

Emma shook her head. "Other than he had black hair, no. He was seated, so I couldn't get a feel for how tall he was and it all happened so fast, I was more worried about him running over Dante than getting a clear description of him."

Kramer came around the side of his desk and held out his hand to Emma. "Thank you for saving one of my best pilots." His lips twisted. "He's also a vital member of this team and we'd have missed him."

Dante shifted in his chair, uncomfortable with the praise when he'd allowed himself to get shot down. "Sir, whoever shot me out of the sky came back to finish the job. When he finds out he wasn't successful, he could be back. And if he thinks for a moment that Emma could identify him, he'll be after her."

Kramer leaned against his government-issued metal desk and ran his hand over his chin. "You have a point. I suppose I could assign a man to keep an eye on her."

Emma leaned forward in her chair. "I don't need anyone to keep an eye on me. I'm fully capable of taking care of myself."

Kramer shook his head. "Whoever did it has to know

it's a federal crime to shoot at a government agent. If there's any chance you can identify him, he might come after you next."

Dante leaned toward her and took her hand. "Let the boss assign an agent to you. At least until we catch the bastard."

Emma's lips pressed into a tight line, her cheeks filled with color. "No, thank you. I'm off for the next four weeks on Christmas break. I'll be vigilant and watch my back. No need to tie up resources babysitting me."

Kramer glanced at Dante. "I can't force her to accept help."

Dante's gaze met Emma's. From the stubborn look on her face he could tell she didn't like having people make decisions for her. But after all she'd done for him, he needed to be sure no one would come after her. He turned back to his boss. "I have a lot of use-or-lose vacation time on the books, right?"

"Yes, you do," Kramer confirmed.

"I'd planned on spending a little time with my family at the Thunder Horse Ranch over the holidays. If it's all right by you, I'd like to take my leave now. I'll spend part of it with Emma until we figure out who was responsible for destroying a perfectly good helicopter and then tried to kill us."

"Do I have a say in any of this?" Emma asked.

Dante's lips quirked up on the corners. "Only if it's to agree."

"Well, I won't." She pushed to a standing position. "I like my solitude and I don't need someone treating me as a charity case and guarding me as if I were a child."

Admiring her gumption, but no less determined, Dante stood beside her. "If it helps, you won't even know I'm there. I'll keep an eye on you from the comfort of my vehicle outside your apartment." He knew even before he said the words that they would get her ire up. And they did.

"Like a stalker?" She straightened.

Kramer stood, chuckling. "I'll let you two duke it out. I have a schedule to juggle. As of now, you're to report to the hospital for a quick checkup, and then you're on leave until after the first of the year. You're dismissed. And, T.H., try to stay out of the cold this time. The temperature outside is minus fifteen with a windchill of minus thirty and it's supposed to drop tonight to minus forty."

"Trust us. We don't plan on spending tonight in the elements," Dante assured his boss. "Although, it wasn't all bad."

Kramer left his office and headed down the hallway to the hangar.

When Dante turned to Emma, he noted the blush rising up Emma's neck into her cheeks.

"I won't be responsible for you missing out on family time during the holidays," she muttered.

Dante's lips twitched, but he fought the smile. She was deflecting his reference to their lovemaking and he found it endearingly cute. "I promise to spend some of my leave with my family."

"And you really don't have to spend any of it with me."

"What if I like being with you?" he quipped.

"What if I don't like being with *you?*" Twin red flags flew in her cheeks and her brown eyes flashed.

This was an Emma he liked as much as the soft, sexy one he'd made love to in the little trailer. He pulled her into an empty office and lifted both of her hands in his. "Do you really mean that?"

"You said so yourself, 'no guarantees.' Don't start feeling sorry for me."

"I don't feel sorry for you. I'm worried about you."

"Well, stop. I can take care of myself. I have for years."

"Fair enough." Rubbing his thumbs over the backs of her hands, he gazed into her eyes. "You're independent and you've taken care of yourself for a while. But have you ever had someone try to kill you before today?"

She opened her mouth to retort, but nothing came out.

"No," he answered for her. "Well, I have, and it's not fun. And it's not the right time to be on your own."

"I don't need you to be my bodyguard."

"Emma." His grip tightened on her hands. "What are you afraid of? The bad guy or me?"

She blurted out, "I'm not afraid of either." Her head dipped and she stared at her boots. "I'm afraid of me."

His heart melted at the way her bottom lip wobbled. "Why?"

Her glance shifted to the corner of the room and she didn't say anything for a full ten seconds. Then she admitted, "I've been independent for so long, I'm afraid of becoming dependent on anyone."

Dante suspected there was a lot more to her fierce independence than having been that way for a long time. Someone in her past must have hurt her. "Relying on someone else doesn't have to be a bad thing. And it's only temporary. Once we catch the bad guy, you can go back to being independent."

She didn't throw it back in his face, so he figured she was wavering. He went in for the clincher.

"Besides, you saved my life twice." He lifted one of her hands to his lips and pressed a kiss there. "I owe you. And if you don't let me pay you back by providing you a little protection in the short term, I'll always owe you my life. You can't let me go through life with such a huge obligation hanging over me, can you? It will threaten my manhood."

Her brows knitted. "You don't owe me anything. And there's nothing in this world that could possibly threaten your...er...manhood."

The way she stumbled over the last word made him think back to the trailer when her soft curves had pressed against his hard body. In an instant, he was hard all over again.

Her cheeks flamed and he could swear she was there with him.

"Please." He hooked her hand through the crook of his arm. "Let me play bodyguard for a little while. You won't regret it."

She sucked in a deep breath and let it out. "Do you really think I could be in danger? Me? I live the most boring life imaginable. How could I be a threat to anyone?"

"You saw his face."

"Surely whoever it was will assume we died in the trailer," she argued.

"When he discovers the fact that we didn't, he could come back to finish the job."

"I *barely* saw his face."

"He doesn't know that. He would only know that you and I are still alive, and we could possibly identify him."

Emma heaved another sigh. "Okay. I'll let you play bodyguard, but only for a couple of days. Surely by then they'll find out who started this whole mess."

Satisfied that he had her agreement to keep an eye on her, Dante didn't tell her that the shooter might never be found. He'd take one day at a time until his leave ran out. Maybe he was overreacting. If he did nothing and something happened to Emma, he'd never forgive himself.

THE AIRPORT WAS several miles away from the city of Grand Forks. As they stepped out into the bitter wind, Emma looked around, gathering her coat around her chin. "Are we taking a cab back to Grand Forks?"

"No." Dante guided her toward the parking lot. "I parked my Jeep out here."

A shiver shook her from the tip of her head to her toes and left her teeth chattering. "By chance does it have heated seats?"

He pulled his key fob out of his pocket and hit a button. "As a matter of fact, it does."

"Thank God," she said through chattering teeth.

"And even better, it has a remote starter and should be warming up by the time we get to it."

A dark pewter Jeep Wrangler with a hard top and raised suspension roared to life a hundred yards from where they stood.

"Yours?" Emma nodded toward the sound of the engine.

"Mine." He shrugged. "I always wanted one. I'd been saving for it since I got back from the sandbox."

Emma glanced up at him. "Sandbox?"

"Afghanistan."

She pulled her collar up around her ears to keep the wind from blowing down the back of her neck. "Were you a pilot in the war?"

He nodded, his gaze on the car ahead.

That explained his nightmare when she'd woken him in the trailer. At first she'd thought it was from having crashed in the helicopter, but it had seemed even more deep-seated. He'd said he'd been shot at before. It had to have been then.

She wondered what scars he carried from his time on

active duty. Did he have post-traumatic stress disorder? Had he watched members of his unit die?

Clouds had moved back in to cover the warming sun, and the north wind blew hard enough that Emma had to lean into it to get to the Jeep. Windchill of minus thirty was hard to take even when one wasn't tired and worn down from trudging for miles in the snow and cold. By the time they reached the Jeep, she practically fell into its warmth.

The drive into Grand Forks was conducted in silence. As Dante turned left when Emma would have turned right to go to her apartment, she remembered she hadn't given him directions. "I live in an apartment close to the university."

"And I live in an apartment on the south side of town." He shot a glance her way. "I thought we'd stop there first so that I could collect some clothes that fit and a few items I'll need."

"Need for what?"

"To stay with you."

"With me?"

"Well, yes. I thought we had this all settled. I'm your bodyguard for the next few days."

"But that doesn't mean you'll be staying with me."

"How else am I supposed to guard your body if I'm not in the same building with you?"

"But…" She bit down on her lip and stared out the window. "My apartment is really small." The thought of the hulking Native American in her apartment threatened to overwhelm her. And they weren't even in her apartment yet.

"We could stay in my apartment, but I thought you'd be more comfortable in yours."

She searched for the words she needed to set her world back to rights. Emma Jennings lived an ordered existence. Ever since a certain helicopter had crash-landed close to her dig, her life had been anything but ordered. *Chaos* was the word that best described the world she'd been thrown into.

"We'll stay in my apartment," she snapped. "But that's as far as it goes. You can sleep on the couch."

Dante sat in the driver's seat, his lips quivering on the corners.

If he smiled, she'd…she'd…ah hell, she'd probably fall all over herself and drool like a fool. The man had entirely too much charm and charisma for a lonely college professor to resist.

I'm doomed.

Dante glanced her way. "Did you say something?"

"Not at all," she squeaked and clamped her lips shut tight. Just because they'd made love once, didn't mean they'd hop right back into the sack at her apartment. He wasn't into commitment, and making love more than once would be too much like commitment to Emma. No, she couldn't take it if she made the mistake of falling for the handsome border patrol agent. No, he wasn't the kind of guy to stick around. The men in her life had a way of disappearing just about the time she started to think they might stick around.

It would be better to keep her distance from Dante and save herself the trouble of a broken heart.

She swallowed a groan. How the hell was she going to keep her distance when he would be camped out in her apartment?

Chapter Six

"I'll stay here in the Jeep while you collect your belongings," Emma offered when they pulled up outside Dante's apartment building.

"Sorry." Dante tilted his head toward her. "What kind of bodyguard would I be if I left you out here in the cold, alone? Bundle up. You're coming in with me."

Emma didn't know what she expected when she entered Dante's apartment. As good as he'd been to her since she'd defended him against the shooter, she didn't know much about him. She expected his apartment to reveal something about his life. Instead, it was as stark and impersonal as a doctor's office.

Dante went to the kitchen first and grabbed a cordless phone. "I need to check in with my family in case they got word of my crash."

Dante headed for the bedroom, speaking into the telephone as he went. Apparently he got an answering machine. "Mom, it's Dante. In case you've seen the news reports about the helicopter crash involving a border patrol agent, I'm okay. Yes, it was mine, but I'm not hurt. Call me when you get a chance. Love you."

While Dante was leaving the message and packing his bag, Emma studied what little there was in the living room and kitchen.

The furniture was plain and functional with a brown leather couch and lounge chair and a rather plain coffee table and television. On the bar that separated the kitchen from the living area were two framed photos. One was of a family of six. Four brothers and their mother and father. All the men were like Dante, swarthy, black-haired and built like brick houses.

Emma peered closer. The second man from the left had to be Dante several years ago. It was him, with a few less creases around his eyes and a happy, carefree smile.

Emma found herself wishing she'd known that happier, younger Dante before he'd been jaded by a war half a world away.

"Dante, is this picture in the kitchen of your family?"

"Yes," he called out from the bedroom.

"How old is this photo? You look so much younger."

"It was taken about four years ago, when my father was still alive."

So his father was dead. Another detail of Dante's life she was learning. "I'm sorry."

"We were, too." Dresser drawers opened and closed and a closet door was opened.

Emma set the frame on the counter and lifted the other.

The other photo was of Dante in a flight suit, standing with a couple of men and one woman in desert camouflage uniforms. Dante had his arm around the woman. She wore her hair pulled back in a tight, neat bun, her makeup-free face smiling into the camera. Sandy-blond hair and light gray-blue eyes, she was a woman men could easily fall in love with. She had one of those sweet, outgoing, girl-next-door faces with an added dose of steel. She'd have to have been tough enough to handle the ten-to-one men-to-women ratio in the desert.

Emma admired women who volunteered for armed services. She herself had tried to go into ROTC, but an injury to her shoulder as a child had kept her from passing the physical.

Emma stared down at Dante's arm draped over the woman's shoulder. In her heart she knew this woman had meant something to Dante.

"What are you doing?" Dante demanded.

Emma jumped and dropped the photo frame back on the counter. She'd been so engrossed in the two photographs she hadn't noticed Dante had returned to the living area carrying a duffel bag and wearing freshly laundered jeans and a blue chambray shirt. He was even sexier in clothes that fit.

A guilty flush burned her cheeks at being caught snooping about his private life. But she refused to ignore the picture, wanting to know more about this man she'd made love to. "Who is she?"

He started to walk by, headed for the door, but stopped beside her instead. "Someone I used to know."

Lifting the frame again, she stared across the floor at him. "She's very pretty."

Dante's gaze went to the photo, his eyes staring as if looking back in time, not at the paper picture but at the memories it inspired. "Samantha made the desert bearable."

Something in his voice made Emma's heart squeeze in her chest, but she couldn't stop herself from observing, "She has a nice smile."

He nodded. "Everyone at Bagram Airfield loved Samantha."

Emma studied Dante's face, her heart settling into the pit of her belly. "Did you love her?"

His gaze shifted from the photo to Emma. "What?"

"Did you love her?"

"Yes."

"And do you still?" Emma asked quietly.

His lips thinned, his dark green eyes unreadable. "Yes."

Emma glanced around the sterile apartment. There were no signs of the woman. Surely he wouldn't have taken Emma out to have coffee if he was still involved with her. "What happened?" she dared to ask, the question burning in her heart.

"She died in an IED explosion while visiting an Afghan orphanage outside the wire."

A heavy lump settled in the pit of Emma's gut as she stared down at the beautiful face, so happy and alive. "That's terrible."

"Yeah," he said, the word clipped and as emotionless as the room they stood in. "Ready?"

Emma nodded and set the frame on the counter. "I'm sorry for your loss. She must have been a very special woman."

"She was."

And there she had it. Samantha was a very special woman. How could Emma compete with that? No wonder he'd had coffee with her one time and walked away without calling again. Emma didn't measure up to Samantha's perfection.

Her heart fell even farther, landing somewhere around her shoes. And he'd made love to her only to find out she was a pathetic virgin. Heat burned her cheeks and she ducked her head to hide her shame. "I'm ready to leave."

She led the way through the door and stopped on the threshold. "I really wish you'd just drop me off and forget about this bodyguard gig."

Dante frowned. "Why are we arguing about it again?

I thought we'd settled this. I'm going to stay with you for a few days. I promise not to get in your way."

How could he not get in her way? Dante Thunder Horse was larger than life and had given his heart to a dead woman.

Emma had to remind herself that Dante wasn't providing her protection to get closer to her. Why should he? He'd had perfection. Making love to Emma had probably been just something that had happened to keep them warm.

Pushing all thoughts of sex with Dante to the back of her mind, Emma squared her shoulders and nodded. "You're right. It's only for a few days. Then you'll be on your way home to your family and I'll go back to my work as a professor." Spending Christmas by herself as usual. How pathetic was that?

Because her mother had died and she hadn't spoken to her father since, she had no one. Christmas was one of those holidays she dreaded each year. This year would be no different.

Dante threw his duffel bag into the back of his Jeep and opened the door for Emma. She slid past him, careful not to touch him and set off all those errant nerve endings that jumped anytime he was near. He might not see her as a potential sexual partner, but Emma's body sure couldn't forget her first time making love. The man had been amazing. Her foot slipped as she stepped up on the Jeep's running board and she crashed back into Dante.

His arms surrounded her and he crushed her to his chest.

Emma's heart thundered against her ribs. His arm crossed her chest beneath her breasts, one of his big hands covering her tummy. Even through her thick winter coat, she could feel his warmth.

In that instant, in his arm, her thoughts scrambled. For a moment, she imagined him holding her because he wanted to, not because she'd practically thrown herself at him. Accidentally, of course.

Once she had her feet under her, she tried to push out of his arms.

"Steady there," he said. "That running board can get slick in the icy weather."

Now he tells her. "I'm okay. I'll be more careful next time."

"Oh, I didn't mind. I just want to make sure you're not hurt."

"Thanks." As she scrambled into the Jeep, she felt his palm on her rear, making certain she didn't fall back this time.

Embarrassed by her clumsiness and her body's instant reaction, she settled into the leather seat and turned her face away from Dante as he climbed into the driver's seat. She gave him the directions to her apartment and sat in silence as he drove across town.

She tried not to look his way, but she couldn't help it. The man had the rugged profile of his ancestors, complete with chiseled cheekbones and a strong jaw.

Several times he glanced into the rearview mirror, his brows furrowing.

"What's wrong?" Emma finally asked as they approached the street to her apartment complex. When they passed her turn, she swiveled in her seat. "You missed my turn."

"I can't swear to it, but I think someone was following us."

Emma spun to look behind her. "In Grand Forks?"

"I know it's a small city by most standards, and there aren't that many places for people to go, but the vehicle

behind me has been on my tail since I left my apartment."
Dante relaxed. "Good, he turned off." Dante sped up and
turned at the next corner, going the long way around to
circle back to her apartment complex.

"It could be my imagination, but I'd rather be safe
than sorry." He pulled into the parking lot and parked
the Jeep on the far side of a trash bin, out of visible range
of the street.

Emma thought he was taking his job as a bodyguard
to the extreme, but didn't say anything. This was Grand
Forks, North Dakota, not Chicago or Houston.

As soon as he put the Jeep in Park, Emma unbuckled
her belt and carefully climbed out to stand on the ground.
She didn't want a repeat performance of her earlier awkward actions.

"I'm on the second floor." She led the way up the outside staircase to the entrance of her apartment and bent
to retrieve her spare key from beneath a flowerpot with
a dead plant covered in a dusting of snow.

"You really shouldn't leave a key to your apartment
out here. Anyone could get in."

"I've been living by myself for years."

"I know, but still, it's not safe."

"Well, since my purse is in my crashed truck at the
dig site, I'm glad I had a key beneath the flowerpot. It's
almost impossible to catch the apartment manager in his
office on a weekend." She unlocked the door and entered,
switching on the lights.

Nothing in her apartment had changed. After all that
had happened, it seemed both anticlimactic and reassuring at the same time. "You can set your bag by the
couch," she said. "I'm sorry, but I don't have a lot of
groceries. I had planned on stocking up when I got back
from the dig site."

"We can go to the store when you want."

"I need to call my insurance agent and deal with my truck and I guess the state police to report the accident." She turned toward him shaking her head. "I'm not even sure what I'm supposed to do."

"I'll take you down to the state police station and we can give a statement. My supervisor should already have given them a heads-up. That should get the ball rolling. They might want to bring in the Feds since it was attempted murder and an attack on federal property."

"And a federal agent," Emma reminded him. He seemed more concerned about the helicopter than his own life.

He shrugged and continued. "The National Transportation Safety Board will investigate the downed helicopter. And the Department of Homeland Security will also want to get involved as it could be considered a terrorist attack since the man used a Soviet-made RPG to shoot me down."

A tremor shook Emma. "We're in North Dakota, not Afghanistan."

Dante's face grew grim. "And the attacks on the Twin Towers and the Pentagon were here in America."

"It's hard to accept that nowhere can be considered safe anymore."

A vehicle alarm system went off in the parking lot below her apartment, making Emma jump. She laughed shakily. "Guess I'm getting punchy."

Dante strode to the window, glanced out through the blinds and shook his head. "That's my Jeep. I guess someone bumped into it accidentally. The alarm is supersensitive."

Emma joined him at the window and stared down at his SUV. The lights blinked and a siren wailed.

Digging his key fob from his jeans pocket, Dante aimed it at the vehicle. The alarm and blinking lights ceased and it grew quiet again.

Emma hadn't realized just how close she was standing next to Dante until she turned to face him at the same time as he faced her.

"Better?" he asked with a smile.

She nodded, her tongue suddenly tied, words beyond her as she stared at those lips that had kissed her senseless.

He reached out to cup her cheek. "I promise I'll do my best to protect you." Then ever so gently, he brushed his mouth across hers.

Emma exhaled on a sigh, her body leaning into his as if drawn to him of its own accord.

He slipped a hand around to the small of her back, and the one cupping her cheek rounded to the back of her neck, urging her forward as he returned for a longer, deeper kiss.

His tongue thrust between her teeth, sliding along hers in a sensuous caress that left her breathless.

The hand at her back slipped beneath her sweater, fingers splaying across her naked skin.

She wished she was completely naked, lying beside his equally naked body. Though she was unskilled in the art of making love, she'd follow his lead and they'd—

A car door slammed outside, breaking through her reverie.

Dante lifted his head and glanced out the window. "I'm sorry. I promised you wouldn't even know I was here. That kiss was uncalled for."

"That's okay." She wanted to tell him that she'd liked it, but didn't want to sound too naive or desperate. Though every ounce of her being wanted him to pull her back into his arms and kiss her again.

Dante's hands fell to his sides and he stuffed them into his pockets.

Emma couldn't move away, afraid her wobbly knees wouldn't hold her up. Instead, her gaze followed his to the parking lot below where backup lights blinked bright and a truck eased out of the parking space beside Dante's SUV.

Emma tensed. The driver was turning too sharp and his tires didn't seem to be getting enough traction to straighten the vehicle.

"He's going to hit your Jeep," Emma said, diving for the door. She flung it open and started to shout to the driver to stop.

Before she could get a word out, the world seemed to explode in front of her.

EMMA WAS BLOWN backward, hitting Dante square in the chest, knocking him onto the floor of her apartment. He fell flat on his back and Emma landed on top of him. With the wind knocked out of him and his ears ringing, he lay for a moment trying to comprehend what had just happened.

Then he was scrambling to his feet and racing down the steps to the parking lot below. His Jeep was a blackened hulk with a hole blown through the driver's side.

The truck that had been backing out of the space next to his was drifting backward across the icy surface of the pavement, the hood had been blown upright and the driver was slumped at the wheel. Smoke billowed out of the engine.

Dante ran to the truck and yanked at the door. It was locked. He banged on the window and shouted to get the driver's attention, but he wasn't waking up no matter how hard Dante banged or how loud he shouted.

The truck slid back into a car and stopped, but smoke billowed from the engine compartment and then flames sprang from the source of the smoke.

Desperate to get the man out of the truck, he glanced around for something to break the window with. The ground and the sidewalks were covered in snow from the night before and nothing jumped out that would be strong enough to break the glass.

Behind him, he heard footsteps clambering down the stairs and Emma slid to a stop beside him. "Use this," she said and slapped a hammer in his palm.

Dante gave a brief grin. Emma was smart and resourceful.

He rounded to the passenger side of the vehicle and slammed the hammer into the glass. It took several attempts before he broke all the way through and could reach his hand in to hit the automatic door-lock release.

As soon as he did, Emma pulled open the driver's door and reached inside to unbuckle the seat belt.

The flame surged, the heat making Dante's face burn. "Get back!" he shouted, racing around the other side of the truck.

Emma ignored his entreaty and tugged at the driver's arm. "We have to get him out."

Dante arrived at her side. As soon as she backed away, he grabbed the man and pulled him out, draping his limp body over his shoulder. He turned and nearly ran into Emma. "Move, move, move!"

With the burden of the man weighing him down and the ice-covered pavement slowing his steps, Dante ran after Emma, barely making it to the apartment building before the flame found the truck's gas tank. The second explosion in less than ten minutes rocked the earth beneath them and he crashed to his knees on the concrete.

Emma appeared in front of him and soon other apartment dwellers emerged from their rooms to see what all the commotion was.

Emma pointed to a woman who stood in the doorway of her apartment with her hair up in a towel and yelled, "Lisa, call 9-1-1!"

The woman's eyes widened and she spun back into her apartment and reappeared with her cell phone pressed to her ear, talking rapidly to the dispatcher on the other end.

"Here, lean on me. Let me help you up." Emma slipped one of Dante's arms over her shoulder and helped him to rise with the man in tow. Grateful for her help, he tried not to put too much weight on her as he clambered to his feet.

"We should get him inside where it's warm," Emma said, angling toward the woman on the cell phone.

She stepped back and let them enter.

Dante laid the man out on the couch and straightened.

"I need blankets," Emma said.

Lisa, still holding the phone, nodded toward the hallway. "The ambulance and fire department are on their way. The dispatcher wants me to stay on the phone until they arrive. You can find blankets in the hall closet."

"I'll get them." Emma disappeared and reappeared with two thick blankets.

Sirens wailed and soon the apartment building was surrounded by emergency vehicles, lights flashing. Firemen leaped out and quickly extinguished the blaze, but not before two other cars had sustained damage.

The emergency medical technicians brought in a backboard and loaded the driver onto it and carried him out to the ambulance.

By the time city police and the state police took their statements and the tow truck came to collect the disabled vehicles, day had turned to night. Not that the days were very long during the North Dakota winters.

Emma thanked Lisa for all her help and led the way back up to her apartment.

Dante followed her in, closed the door behind him and leaned against it.

She faced him with shadows beneath her eyes and a worried frown creasing her forehead. "If you had been in your Jeep…"

"I'd be dead. And if you'd been with me in the passenger seat, you'd be either dead or severely injured. I hope that truck driver makes it."

"Toby," she said. "His name is Toby and he's a student at UND. I hope he makes it, too. He has a promising future as an aerospace engineer." Emma ran a hand through her hair and stared across at him, her eyes glassy with unshed tears.

Dante's heart squeezed at the desperation in her tone. He opened his arms and she fell into them. Wrapping her in his embrace, he leaned his cheek against the side of her head. "It's not safe here."

"If it's not safe here, it won't be any safer at your apartment." She looked up at him with those anxious brown eyes. "We have nowhere else to go."

Dante shook his head. "Yes, we do." He turned her around and gave her backside a gentle slap. "Pack your bags. We're going to the Thunder Horse Ranch. We'll leave first thing in the morning."

Chapter Seven

Emma lay in her bed with the goose down comforter pulled up to her chin and stared at the ceiling. Exhaustion should have knocked her right out, but for the life of her, she couldn't go to sleep. Too many thoughts tumbled in her mind, too many images of the past twenty-four hours kept replaying through her head like a recurring nightmare.

The only thing that kept her from having a full-blown anxiety attack was the man lying on the couch in her living room. Dante was the one island in the murky river of her thoughts keeping her afloat.

As independent as she thought she was, she'd give anything for him to lie beside her, take her into his arms and tell her everything was going to be all right.

She'd lean her face against his naked chest and breathe in the scent of him and all would be well with her world and she'd finally be able to go to sleep.

Like hell. If he was lying naked beside her, she'd be too tempted to run her hands over his body and explore all those interesting places she'd missed when they'd made love in the cold interior of her now-destroyed camp trailer.

Achingly aware of the man in the other room and too

wound up to lay still a moment longer, Emma finally gave in, flung back the covers and sat up.

A large shadow moved and Dante appeared in the doorway. "Can't sleep, either?" He leaned against the door frame, his arms crossed and his legs crossed at the ankles.

Emma couldn't see his expression, but the faint glow through the blinds from the security light outside her living room window backlit the man, making him appear larger than life and incredibly sexy. He wore nothing but gym shorts, his swarthy, Native American skin even darker in the dim lighting.

She swallowed hard. "No. I keep thinking back over everything that's happened."

"Me, too." He crossed the room to sit on the edge of her bed. "As soon as I lay my head down, my thoughts spin."

"You could have died. Four times."

"And you could have died almost as many."

Emma harrumphed. "I feel like a big wimp." She smiled, though her lips trembled.

"Do you mind?" He moved to sit beside her and pulled her into the crook of his arm.

Emma leaned into his body, feeling immediately warmer and more secure than before he showed up in her doorway.

"As I see it, you're pretty darned brave." He held up a thumb. "First, you risked your life by nearly crashing your snowmobile into the man who shot me down. A wimp wouldn't have done that."

Emma didn't think it had been at all heroic. "I didn't think. I just reacted."

"But you reacted. Most people would have hesitated. It took someone with a backbone to charge in…without thinking." He unfolded his pointer finger. "Second, you kept your head when the trailer was caving in around us and got the hell through the window fast enough so that I could get out. Then you helped me squeeze through. I doubt very seriously I would have made it out in time without your help."

"You would have," she insisted.

He unfolded another finger. "You walked several miles in frigid cold without a single complaint, when I know you had to be hurting."

She snorted. "And fell on my face before we made it to the house."

"And gave me an opportunity to be a hero. Carrying you that last little bit was nothing, and it made me look good to Olaf and Marge." He chuckled, the vibrations sending tiny electric shocks through her.

She turned her cheek into his bare chest and closed her eyes. Daring to touch him, she laid her hand on him and felt the rise and fall of each breath he took. "Keep talking. I'm still not convinced."

Another finger unfolded as he scooted down in the bed until he was lying beside her. "When the truck was on fire and an explosion was imminent, you risked your life to help get Toby out." His arm tightened around her. "Sweetheart, you're not a wimp. You're pretty impressive if you ask me."

She wanted to ask if she was anywhere near as impressive as Samantha, but knew it wouldn't be appropriate to compare herself to a dead woman. Dragging her into the conversation would only bring Dante more pain.

Instead, she settled against his side.

"Go to sleep, Emma. If you'd like, I'll stay awake to be on the lookout until morning."

"No, we have a long trip ahead of us and I'll bet you plan on doing most of the driving."

"I'm used to long stretches of sleeplessness. I can handle it."

"You might be able to, but I can't. Surely we'll be okay if we both get some sleep. I'm a light sleeper. I'll let you know if I hear anything strange."

"I suppose it will be all right. Do you want me to go back to the couch?"

"No," she said, her hand flexing against his chest as if that alone would keep him from getting up if he wanted to. "I promise not to seduce you."

He chuckled. "Okay, but I wouldn't be opposed if you did."

Though she wanted to feel gloriously satiated like she had felt in the trailer, she also didn't want him to think she was needy. For a moment she considered making the first move, but then squelched the idea.

Dante sighed and rolled her onto her side away from him, then spooned her body with his. "Sleep. It's been a long day and tomorrow promises to be equally trying."

"Let's hope not. I could do with less drama."

"You and me both." His arm tightened around her middle and he drew her close.

For a long time, Emma lay in Dante's arms, sleep eluding her. When his breathing became more regular and deeper, she relaxed, a little disappointed that he hadn't tried anything.

Exhaustion finally claimed her and she fell asleep, cocooned in the warmth of Dante's body, her last thought being that she could get used to this far too easily.

DANTE SLIPPED BACK into another nightmare when his helicopter had been attacked in Afghanistan.

Having taken hits, he was barely able to bring his helicopter back to Bagram. But he had and set it down as smoothly as if it wasn't damaged. He was congratulating himself when one of the guys in the back said, "Giddings was hit. We need an ambulance ASAP."

As he ripped his harness loose, he gave instructions to the tower, slipped from the pilot's seat and dropped to the ground. He ran around to the other side where the gunner was being unbuckled from his harness and carried out of the craft.

Giddings had volunteered to be a gunner and had competed with others to claim the position. He'd been a damned good gunner, saving their butts on more than one occasion.

At twenty-three, he was barely out of his teens, a kid. And he had a young, pregnant wife back in the United States due to give birth in less than a month. Four weeks from redeployment back to the United States, he'd insisted on flying this mission.

Dante could kick himself for letting the kid fly. The closer they came to redeployment the more superstitious they became. It seemed that only the really good guys managed to be jinxed their last month in the sandbox.

When the ambulance arrived, Dante insisted on riding with them to the hospital and he stayed until Giddings was out of surgery and out of danger. He'd make it.

It had all happened so fast. One minute they were flying a mission, the next he was waiting for the doc to tell him the verdict on one of his crew.

It wasn't until he was on his way back to his quarters that he made the turn to swing by Samantha's room. She would be off duty by now and he really needed to see her.

She shared quarters with another personnel officer, Lieutenant Mandy Brashear. He might not get her alone, but at least he could share a hug and a kiss. After nearly losing a member of his team, he really needed the reassurance of her warm body next to his.

When he stopped outside her door, he heard the sound of someone sobbing. Without hesitating, he pushed open the door and entered. "Samantha?"

Lieutenant Brashear lifted her head from her pillow and stared up at him with tear-streaked cheeks, her eyes rounding as she recognized him. "Oh, Dante," she said, ignoring the protocol of addressing a higher-ranking officer by his rank and last name. "You haven't heard?"

Dante stiffened, his heart seizing in his chest, guessing what Mandy would say before she did. "What's wrong? Where's Sam?" He looked around the small room, although he knew she wasn't there.

"Oh, God." Mandy's tears gushed from her eyes and her words became almost incoherent as she sobbed and spoke simultaneously. "She went to the orphanage today... I...can't...believe...Oh, God." She buried her face in her hands and sobbed some more.

His hands and heart going cold, Dante gripped Lieutenant Brashear's shoulders and lifted her to her feet. "Where is Sam?"

"She was in the hospital when I left her," she blurted. "Dante, she's...she's...dead."

Dante ran all the way back to the hospital where he'd been just minutes before, outside the surgical units, waiting for Giddings to be sewn up and released. He hadn't known that in the unit beside Giddings, Samantha had taken her last breath.

He got back in time to see them zip her into the body bag. They wheeled her out on a gurney. All sealed up and final. He didn't even get to say goodbye.

"Dante," a female voice called to him.

For a moment he thought it was Samantha, but she had a gravelly voice; this was a smooth, sexy voice calling his name.

"Dante, wake up." A hand shook his shoulder this time.

Dante opened his eyes and looked up into Emma's face and blinked, for a split second wondering what she was doing in Afghanistan. Then he remembered he wasn't in the Middle East, but back in North Dakota having been attacked on multiple occasions. He rolled off the side of the bed and landed on his feet. "What's wrong?"

Emma smiled. "I'm sorry, but your cell phone is ringing. That's the third time it's rung in the past fifteen minutes."

Shaking the cobwebs from his head, he hurried into the living room and grabbed his cell phone off the coffee table where he'd left it. In the display window was the word Mom.

It was two o'clock in the morning. She wouldn't call at this hour unless it was an emergency. These thoughts whisked through his mind as he hit the talk button. "Mom, what's wrong?"

"Oh, thank goodness you answered." She took a deep breath and let it out before continuing. "Pierce and Tuck were in an accident and are in the hospital in Bismarck."

His hand tightened on the phone. The last time he'd been at the hospital in Bismarck, his father had died from injuries sustained when he'd been thrown by his horse. "What happened?"

"Yesterday, they were on their way home for the weekend when Pierce's brakes gave out. From what the police said, they had been traveling pretty fast with the roads being clear still. This was before the big storm." His mother spoke to someone in the background and returned to the story. "They had come up on an accident on the interstate. That's when the brakes must have failed. Rather than slam into the vehicles stopped on the interstate, they drove off into the ditch. The truck flipped, rolled and landed upside down." Her voice broke on a sob.

Dante's heart squeezed hard. He wished he was there to comfort his mother. The woman was a rock and if she was in this much distress, it had to be bad.

She sniffed. "I'm sorry. I can't do this." The phone clattered as if it had been dropped.

"Mom?" Dante listened and could hear female voices. "Mom!"

"Dante, this is Julia." Julia was Tuck's wife and the mother of his little girl, Lily. "Tuck was thrown twenty yards and suffered a concussion, but Pierce was trapped inside the truck until the fire department could get there from Bismarck and cut him out. They didn't get him out until the storm hit. They almost didn't make it back to Bismarck in the ambulances."

"Damn." Though he'd been away fighting in the war and then living on the opposite end of the state of North Dakota, he was still very much a part of the Thunder Horse family and he loved his brothers. To be that close to having lost one hit him hard.

"Tuck's okay," Julia continued. "It's Pierce we're all worried about. When the truck flipped he sustained a couple of broken ribs, a punctured lung and we don't know what else. He's had some internal bleeding and he's still unconscious. They've sedated him into a medically induced coma until they can figure out what else is damaged."

Dante pinched the bridge of his nose, his own crash pushed to the back of his mind. Apparently his mother hadn't heard about it and hadn't received the message on her answering machine at the ranch. He'd have to contact the ranch foreman, Sean McKendrick, and have him erase it before she got home. No use worrying her more when he was fine.

"How's Mom holding up?"

"She's doing okay, but the emotional strain is wearing on her," Julia said. "We knew you'd planned to be here next week, but with Pierce and Tuck both in the hospital and Maddox on the other side of the world in Trejikistan with Katya and not due back until next week, we thought you might want to be here."

Dante straightened. "I'm coming home."

"Thank goodness." Julia's words came out in a rush. "Roxanne is here with Pierce, and with your mother here, the foremen of the two ranches are on their own. And, Dante…" Julia's voice dropped and she paused. Footsteps sounded at her end as if she was walking down a hallway. Then she continued, "There have been some suspicious accidents happening out there. Your mother thinks it's just bad luck, but Roxanne and I think someone is sabotaging things. We're afraid if we don't have a Thunder Horse out there keeping an eye on things, there won't be a ranch to come home to. Amelia has gone so far as to hire a security firm to set up surveillance cameras."

"Why didn't she tell me?"

"She knows she can't ask you guys to come home every time something goes bump in the night. With Maddox out of the country, she wanted something to make her feel safe. Thus the security system."

The thought of his mother being scared enough to hire a security firm bothered Dante more than he could believe. "I'll stop in at the hospital on my way through. It'll take me between four and five hours to get there. I can be there around seven in the morning."

"Oh, Dante," Julia begged, "please wait until morning. The last thing we need right now is another Thunder Horse in a ditch. And I don't think your mother could worry about one more thing."

"Okay. I'll wait until closer to sunup. Expect me at noon."

"Good. Just a minute. Your mother wanted to talk to you one more time."

Dante braced himself, his eyes burning as his mother got on the phone. "Dante, your brothers are going to be okay."

"I know, Mom. I'm worried about you."

She snorted, the sound hitching with what he suspected was a sob. "I'm a tough old bird. Don't you go worrying about me. And don't you come rushing out here thinking we all need saving. Maddox will be home before you know it, and Pierce and Tuck will be up and giving him hell. Take care of yourself, son."

"I will. I love you, Mom."

"I love you, too."

When he rang off, Dante stood for a long time, with the phone in his hand, his thoughts flipping through all the chapters in his life, so many of them, including the days he'd spent riding across the Badlands on wild ponies he and his brothers had tamed. Their Lakota blood had run strong through their veins and their mother had encouraged them to embrace their father's heritage.

Wakantanka, the Great Spirit, had watched over their antics, protecting them from harm.

Dante closed his eyes and lifted his face to the sky. Where was the Great Spirit when his brothers' truck had flipped? Perhaps he'd been there. Otherwise they would both be dead.

A hand on his arm brought him back to the apartment.

"What's wrong?" Emma stood beside him in a short baby-blue filmy nightgown, her pale skin practically glowing in the darkness.

"My brothers were in an accident."

She gasped. "Are they okay?"

"So far."

"You have to go to them."

"We'll leave in the morning and stop at the hospital in Bismarck on our way to the Thunder Horse Ranch."

"I meant to ask, just where is the Thunder Horse Ranch?"

"In the Badlands north of Medora."

"Okay." She smiled. "I'll be sure to pack my snow gear. In the meantime, you need sleep. It's a long way there."

He shook his head. "I can't sleep."

"Then come lay down with me. Even if you don't sleep, you can rest." She took his hand and led him back into her bedroom, offering him comfort he gladly accepted.

When he stretched out on the bed beside her, she lay in the crook of his arm, her cheek pressed to his chest, her hand draped across his belly. He lay staring at the ceiling, thinking about his brothers and his mother and wishing his father was still alive.

"Stop thinking," Emma whispered against his skin. Her warm breath stirred him, reminding him that he wasn't alone with his thoughts.

Emma skimmed her hand over his chest and down his torso and back up in soothing circles. "Think of something else," she urged as her hand drifted lower.

He captured her wrist before she bumped into the rising tent of his shorts. "Once again, don't go there unless you mean it."

She tipped her chin and stared up at him. The little bit of light shining around the edges of the blinds gave her face a light blue glow and her eyes shone in the darkness. "I mean it."

He let go of her wrist and her hand slid lower until it skimmed across his shaft, which became instantly hard and pulsing.

He drew in a slow steadying breath. "Why are you doing this?" A sudden thought reared its ugly head and he flipped her over on her back and pinned her wrists to the mattress.

Her eyes rounded and shone white in the darkness.

"Are you doing this out of some misguided sense of pity?"

Emma shook her head. "No. Not at all."

"Then why?"

"I'm sorry. I shouldn't have been so forward." Her eyelids swept low over her eyes. "I understand if you're not interested in someone so...so..."

"So what?" he asked.

"Inexperienced," she finished, a frown settling between delicate brows.

He nudged her knees apart and settled lower between her legs, letting the hard ridge of his erection brush up against the juncture of her thighs. "Oh, I'm interested all right. But why are you? I don't need anyone's pity."

She glanced away from him and he'd bet her cheeks were flaming. "I was curious," she whispered.

"About what?"

"If the second time would be as good as the first?" She stared up at him, the limited lighting making her face glow a dusky-blue.

The tension leached out of him and he dropped low to steal a kiss. Though it wasn't stealing when she gave it freely. Emma tasted of mint and smelled like roses, the scent light and fragrant but not overpowering. Samantha had reminded him of honeysuckle growing wild and untamed. The two women were as different as night and day.

Where Sam had captured his interest with her unfettered ability to grasp life by the horns and ride, Emma was like an English rosebud, waiting for the sunlight to unfurl.

He released her hands and bent to claim her lips in a crushing kiss. Partly because of the burning desire ignited inside him and partly out of anger for making him think about Sam again. He'd tried so hard to put that chapter of his life behind him, to forget what he'd lost in her and how life had stretched before him empty without her in it.

Quiet, studious Emma had been the first woman he'd even considered dating since Samantha's death. And after having coffee with her, he'd refused to see her again, afraid that being with her meant he was dishonoring the memory of Samantha. Or that he was finally starting to forget her.

The truth was that Samantha was gone forever and Emma was lying beneath him, willing to slake the hunger in his body. If he made love to her, it would mean nothing but a physical release to him. His body recognized needs his mind had refused to let him satisfy.

Once he started, he couldn't seem to stop and Emma didn't cry out or tell him no. Part of him wished she would.

He trailed kisses from her mouth to the edge of her jaw and down the long line of her throat to the pulse beating wildly at the base.

Her fingers curled around the back of his neck and

urged him to continue his downward path to the swells of her breasts beneath the sheer fabric of her nightgown.

He grabbed the hem and ripped it up over her head and tossed it aside.

She lay beneath him, bathed in the soft, gray-blue light shining around the edges of the blinds, her breasts peaked, the nipples tight little buds.

Dante swooped down to taste first one, then the other, rolling the taut buttons between his teeth and across his tongue. When he sucked it into his mouth, she arched her back off the bed, pressing it deeper into his mouth. He gladly accepted, flicking the tip with his tongue.

Slowly, he teased his way across her ribs, slid a hand between her legs, and parted her folds to stroke the strip of flesh hiding there.

Her breath caught and held.

When he started to remove his hand, she covered it with hers and pressed it down, encouraging him to continue.

For someone who'd never had a lover, she learned quickly and wasn't too shy to let him know what she liked.

Before long, her breathing grew ragged and she dug her heels into the mattress, her bottom rising above the sheets as she called out his name. "Dante!"

Her body pulsed beneath his fingers until finally the tension subsided and she fell back to the bed, with a shuddering sigh. "Amazing."

Dante cupped her sex and leaned up to kiss her full on the lips before lying on the bed beside her.

"Wait." Emma leaned up on her elbow, her hand going to the hard line of his manhood. "What about you?"

"Watching you was enough for me."

She frowned, her fingers curling around him. "But you're still…"

"Hard?" He laughed though it took a lot for him to force it out. "I could drive nails with it right now."

"Then, please." She tugged on him, but he refused to budge.

"I don't have protection."

"We didn't have it last night."

"And that was pushing the limits. I won't risk it again. Now, if you happen to have something…?" His lips twisted. "I thought not." He tucked an arm behind his head and pulled her up against him. "I'll take a rain check in the meantime. Sleep, Emma. I have a feeling tomorrow will be another long day."

Emma settled beside him, curled against his side. Whether he wanted her there or not, she wasn't too proud to take advantage of his offer to hold her until she went to sleep.

Warm, safe and satisfied, she drifted to sleep with a smile on her face. She had to remind herself she was an independent college professor and that when all this was over, Dante would move on and possibly never see her again.

But while she had the chance, she'd take whatever scraps he was willing to throw her way. If it meant she was desperate and lonely…well, then it was true. She *was* desperate and lonely, and whatever memories she stored up during her time with Dante would have to do.

In her life history, she was destined to be alone. The men who'd come and gone in her life had been prone to have an aversion to commitment. Emma had long since convinced herself it was her or at least the magnet she seemed to carry around that attracted men who refused to commit.

Tomorrow was another day and she'd better get some sleep if she wanted to be awake when they finally made it to the Thunder Horse Ranch.

Chapter Eight

Dante glanced across at Emma as she leaned back in the seat of the SUV he had rented for the next couple of weeks. She hadn't spoken much throughout the trip and the circles beneath her eyes were more pronounced. Though she'd slept part of the night, they hadn't really had a decent night's sleep in two days.

The back of Dante's neck was stiff and he could feel some of the bruises and sore muscles he'd acquired in the helicopter and trailer crashes.

He'd insisted on a four-wheel-drive SUV for the trip, knowing the roads to the ranch could be difficult during the summer and impassible in a two-wheel-drive vehicle during the harsh North Dakota winters.

The insurance company would take their time sorting out the details of replacing the Jeep. A full investigation would have to be performed by the National Transportation Safety Board on the helicopter crash and the FBI would assist the state police with the case since it involved federal equipment and personnel.

If Pierce and Tuck were in any shape to assist, theirs was the closest FBI regional office to the crash site. Though they would not be assigned the case, Dante knew they would be involved enough to keep him informed of the progress.

So far, not a single terrorist organization or survivalist group had stepped forward to claim responsibility for shooting down his helicopter.

He'd checked in with his boss, who informed him that the police and investigation team from the state crime lab had combed over the burned out hull of the helicopter finding no more evidence or gleaning any more information than he'd already imparted. The snowstorm had covered the snowmobile tracks and more snow was predicted within the next twenty-four hours.

The winter that had held off until now had set in and wouldn't loosen its hold until late April.

Emma slept for the first hour and a half of the drive to Bismarck. The road crews had worked hard to clear the interstate highways between Grand Forks and Fargo and between Fargo and Bismarck. Other than a few slick spots, they hadn't had to slow too much, but the wind blowing in from the northwest pounded the rental, forcing them to use a lot more gasoline than if it had been calm.

By the time Dante reached the hospital in Bismarck, he was ready for the break before the additional three-hour trip to Thunder Horse Ranch. The clouds were settling in, making the sky a dark gray. If they didn't get on the road soon, they might not make it to the ranch. The weather reports on the radio were predicting whiteout conditions starting after dark.

As he pulled into the hospital parking lot, he braced himself for what he'd find. Cell phone reception had been limited between Fargo and Bismarck, with long stretches without any reception whatsoever.

When they'd neared Bismarck, he'd checked his phone. No missed calls and no text messages. He prayed that no news was good news, and climbed out of the car, stretching stiff muscles.

Before he could get around to the passenger side, Emma was already on the snowy ground, pulling the collar of her coat up around her ears.

They entered the hospital together. Emma took his hand and squeezed it. "If your brothers are anything like you, they'll be fine. Thunder Horse men seem to be pretty tough."

He returned the pressure on her hand, thankful she'd come with him. Dante remembered where the ICU was located having been there when his father was taken there. He'd died in the ICU shortly after he'd been admitted to the hospital.

The acrid scent of disinfectants and rubbing alcohol still brought back bad memories and reminded him of his loss.

It was exactly noon when he stepped out of the elevator and saw his mother, surrounded by Julia and Roxanne, talking to a man in a white lab coat.

Dante hurried forward, still holding on to Emma's hand. "What's going on? How's Pierce?" he demanded.

His mother turned, her face lighting up when she saw him. "Dante." She wrapped him in her arms and hugged him so tight he could barely breathe. And it felt good. Like coming home.

After a moment, he set her away from him and asked again, "How's Pierce?"

"Oh, Dante." His mother wiped a tear from the corner of her eye and Dante's stomach fell.

Roxanne stepped forward and draped an arm around Amelia's shoulders. "He woke up." A smile spread across her face and her eyes misted. "He woke up a while ago. Briefly. The doc says that's a good sign." She bit down on her bottom lip and a tear slid from her eye and down her cheek.

For as long as Dante had known Roxanne, she'd never cried in front of him. To see her cry now was nearly his undoing. "Is he going to be okay?"

The doctor stepped forward. "As far as we can tell, he appears to be recovering. We're going to keep him a little longer to monitor his condition. If he continues to improve, he should be able to go home."

His mother smiled through her tears. "It's a miracle." She shook her head. "The news showed pictures of his truck and it's a wonder he's still alive."

"Where's Tuck?"

"Someone looking for me?" Tuck appeared behind him, carrying two cups of steaming coffee. He walked with a limp, but he was wearing jeans and a clean flannel shirt and, other than a few bruises on his face, looked like Tuck. He started to hand the coffee to Dante. "You look like you could use this more than I can. Other than a few bruises and scrapes, I'll live. What happened to you?"

Dante had forgotten the bruise at his temple until that moment. He shrugged. "I ran into the door in my apartment."

His mother's eyes narrowed. Amelia Thunder Horse had that keen sense and woman's intuition. She always knew when he was lying. For a moment she looked like she was going to call him on it, but then she noticed the woman standing behind him and raised her brows asking politely, "Are you with Dante or are you waiting to speak with the doctor?"

Emma opened her mouth to speak, but Dante jumped in before she could. "Mom, this is Emma Jennings." Rather than burden his mother with their problems, he blurted, "Emma's my fiancée. She's come to spend Christmas with us. I hope you don't mind."

The family converged on the two, shock in everyone's expressions, especially Emma's. But she recovered quickly, wiping the surprise from her face.

His mother enveloped Emma in a bear hug, her eyes wet with unshed tears. "Wow, this is a surprise. A much-needed surprise. After all the tragedy and worry…this is wonderful."

Julia took her turn hugging Emma. "Congratulations. I'm so happy for you two. I'm Julia, Tuck's wife."

"I'm Tuck, one of Dante's brothers." Tuck hugged her, looking over the top of her head at Dante, pinning Dante with his stare. "How come we haven't heard anything about her up until now?"

Roxanne shoved him aside. "I'm Roxanne, Pierce's wife. Nice to meet you."

Emma hugged one after the other, muttering her thanks, looking flustered, her cheeks bright pink.

His mother wiped another tear from her eye and sniffed. "This is all so sudden."

Dante slipped an arm around Emma's waist and pulled her up against him. "I know. Seems like only yesterday we met. But when you know, you know. Right, Emma?" He smiled down at her, praying she'd continue to go along with his ruse.

She looked up into his eyes and nodded. "That's right. You just know." She looked out at the people surrounding her and gave a shaky smile. "I hope you don't mind my showing up unannounced."

Amelia hugged her again. "Not at all. There's plenty of room at the ranch and I'm just so happy that Dante's found someone. I've been worried about him since his return from the war."

"Mom—" Dante took his mother's hand "—I'm fine. I have a great job with the CBP and I'm still flying."

"And now you have Emma." Amelia sighed. "All my boys will be happily married and giving me grandchildren."

The elevator door pinged behind Dante, and Sheriff Yost from Billings County stepped through and strode to Amelia, taking her into his arms. "Amelia, darling. I came as soon as I could get away."

Dante's back teeth ground together at the proprietary way Yost held his mother in his arms.

Tuck stepped forward, his fists clenched. "What's he doing here?"

Amelia frowned at Tuck. "It's all right. William came when I called. He's working with the Burleigh County sheriff and the state police to determine the cause of the accident."

Dante stiffened, his arm tightening around Emma. "I thought you said Pierce's brakes went out."

Amelia shot a glance at Tuck.

Tuck faced Dante. "We had the truck hauled to the forensics lab in Bismarck. A mechanic did a preliminary look at the brakes. They'd been cut almost all the way through."

"When?"

"We don't know." Tuck rubbed the back of his neck. Scratches and bruises stretched down his arm, his elbow skinned and raw.

Yost interjected, "I spoke with the mechanic myself. Since the brake lines weren't completely severed, it took a while before all the brake fluid leaked out."

"We didn't know until it was too late to do anything about it." Tuck's gaze went to the door of a room across from the nurses' station.

A nurse stood and walked their way. "If you could,

please move your family reunion to the waiting room. We don't want to disturb the other patients."

The group moved to the waiting room.

Dante glanced around the room, his gaze going from Tuck to Julia. "Where's Lily?"

Julia smiled. "When Tuck's supervisor heard he'd been in an accident, he and his wife came to the hospital. His wife is keeping Lily right now." Julia took Tuck's hand. "We were just about to leave to go pick her up now that Tuck's been released. We'd planned on going back to the ranch, but now that you're here..."

"Emma and I are headed that way."

"Then you'll want to get there before the weather," Yost said. "The reporters are predicting another twenty-four inches and whiteout conditions late this afternoon."

Tuck pulled Julia's arm through his. "If you're heading back now, I'd like to stay until Pierce comes out of it."

Dante nodded, his gaze shifting briefly to Yost and back to his brother. "I'd feel better if you stayed. I can check on things back at the ranch and over at the Carmichael Ranch, as well." The Carmichael Ranch was adjacent to the Thunder Horse Ranch. Pierce lived with Roxanne at her ranch when he wasn't on duty with the FBI in the Bismarck office. Maddox Thunder Horse usually handled the day-to-day operations of Thunder Horse Ranch while Roxanne ran the Carmichael.

"Thanks." Roxanne took his hand. "I'm not leaving here without Pierce."

Dante squeezed her hand. "I didn't expect you to."

Amelia wrapped her arms around him and hugged him. "Be careful getting there. I don't know what I'd do if another one of my boys gets hurt."

He kissed the top of her head. "I'll be fine. You guys

worry about Pierce. Emma and I will figure things out back at the ranch. I would like to visit Pierce before I leave."

"He's only allowed one visitor at a time for a few minutes only." His mother smiled apologetically at Emma. "You can stay here with us while he goes."

Dante left Emma in his mother's hands, walked across the polished tile floor to the room his mother indicated and pushed through the big swinging door.

Pierce lay on a hospital bed, his large frame stretched from the headboard to the footboard. Covered in wires and tubes, he lay still as death, his bronze skin slightly gray, cuts and bruises marring his face.

Dante had been to visit soldiers in worse shape, but seeing his brother hooked up to all the gadgets and monitors hit him hard. They'd already lost their father. This shouldn't be happening.

His own helicopter crash seemed insignificant since he'd walked away from it relatively unscathed. Pierce was strong and with the help of *Wakantanka,* the Great Spirit, he'd pull through. But a little prayer wouldn't hurt.

Dante closed his eyes and lifted his face skyward. *"Wakan tanan kici un wakina chelee,"* he spoke the words softly, feeling them in his heart and the hearts of his ancestors. May the Great Spirit bless you, Thunder Horse.

EMMA EXITED THE hospital at Dante's side, her head still spinning with the congratulatory words of Dante's family echoing in her ears. Pulling the hood of her jacket up around her ears, she waited until they got in the SUV before saying, "What was that all about?"

Dante twisted the key in the ignition and backed out of the parking space. "What was what about?"

A shot of anger burst through her. "Fiancée?" She didn't know why his lie was making her so mad. Perhaps it was because his family had welcomed her so openly and with such love…it made her mad to build up their expectations only to disappoint them.

His lips twisted and he shot a quick glance at her. "I'm sorry. It was the only thing I could think of that would keep my mother from asking too many questions about my appearance and why you were with me."

"So you told her we were engaged? I could think of a dozen other things we could have told her but that."

"It's only for the short term, just through Christmas break. Once Pierce is out of the ICU and is home and well enough, she'll quit worrying about him and we can straighten it all out."

"I don't like lying to your family." Emma glanced out the window at the bleak skyline. "Especially to your mother."

"I don't like seeing her cry," he said softly.

All the anger slid away as Emma recalled the tears in Amelia Thunder Horse's eyes and the shadows of worry over her sons' accident. If Dante had told her he'd been shot out of the sky, she might have had a heart attack or at the very least a nervous breakdown.

Emma sighed. "I guess you did the only thing you knew how. I wouldn't want to burden your mother more when your brother is in the ICU."

Dante reached across the console and squeezed Emma's hand and kept holding it for a while afterward.

She stared down at his big fingers clasped around hers, her chest tightening. "You have a nice family."

"Yeah."

"You and your brothers are close?"

"They'd do anything for me and vice versa." He turned to her. "What about you? Do you have siblings?"

"No."

"What about your folks?"

"Gone." Which was true about both. Her mother was dead and she had no idea where her father was.

"I'm sorry."

"Don't be. I'm used to being on my own."

"No one should be alone during the holidays."

She shrugged. "I don't mind." Which was another lie. She hated the holidays for just that very reason. As much as she tried to tell herself it didn't matter, watching others laughing and taking time off to spend it with their families had always been hard on her. She'd been happy to spend her weekends alone on the dig. Digging in the dirt meant she wouldn't have to spend her weekends in her empty apartment. Perhaps she'd get a cat for company.

They traveled in silence the rest of the way to the ranch. The weather held all the way up to the last turnoff leading up to the sprawling ranch house when the first snowflakes began to fall. It wasn't long before more followed, cloaking the sky. By the time Dante parked in front of the house, the wind had picked up, blasting the snow sideways.

"You can go on in," Dante shouted over the wailing Arctic blast. "I need to check on the foreman and the animals in the barn."

"I'll go with you." She zipped up her coat, pulled her hood over her ears and shoved her hands into warm gloves. The frigid wind stung her cheeks, making her blink her eyes. Snowflakes clung to her lashes in clumps.

"You should go inside. I can handle this."

"Please," she said. "I need to stretch my legs."

"In this?"

"You forget, I'm from North Dakota, too." She grinned and followed him to the barn out behind the house.

Several horses were out in a corral, their backs already covered in a thin layer of snow. They trotted along the fence as Dante and Emma approached.

Dante opened the gate and snagged the halter of a sorrel mare. "Think you can lead her into the barn?" he yelled into the wind.

Never having been around horses, Emma figured there couldn't be much to walking a horse into the barn. She reached up and slipped her gloved hand through the harness.

The mare jerked her head up, practically lifting Emma off the ground. She bit down hard on her tongue to keep from screaming and tugged on the harness, urging the horse toward the door to the barn.

Dante passed her, leading a big black horse that danced sideways, tossing its head.

Thankfully, the mare followed the black horse through the door.

Once inside, out of the wind, the horse settled into a plodding walk.

"You can let go of her, she knows which stall is hers," Dante said. "I'll get the other two."

"What can I do?"

"Fill two coffee cans with sweet feed out of that bucket." He pointed to the corner where two large trash cans stood. One had big block letters drawn on the side that spelled out SWEET FEED. The other had CORN, written in capital letters.

Taking two coffee cans from a shelf above the trash cans, Emma opened the sweet-feed bucket and filled the trash cans with the sweet mash of grain and corn and what else, she had no idea, but it smelled like molasses.

The horses already in their stalls whickered, stomping their hooves impatiently.

The barn door swung open and Dante entered leading two large horses. He took them to their stalls and came back to grab the two cans. He filled the feed troughs in two stalls and returned to fill the feed buckets with more grain for the other two horses.

"I didn't see the foreman's truck outside. I hope he gets back before the storm gets any worse." He glanced down at her. "Ready?" he asked, holding out his hand.

Emma nodded and took his hand. He had to push hard to open the door, the wind was playing hell against the barn.

Once they were outside, Dante closed the barn door and then took off at a slow jog toward the house.

The snow had thickened until she could barely see the large structure of the ranch house in front of her.

Dante led the way, holding her gloved hand. When they reached the house he twisted the doorknob on the back. It was locked. Tearing his glove off his hand, he reached into his pocket for his keys and unlocked the door, pushing Emma through first. He quickly stepped in behind her and slammed the door shut.

Emma stood in a spacious kitchen with a large table at one end and a big gas stove at the other. Red gingham curtains hung in the window over the sink, making the blustery winter weather outside look cheerful from the warmth inside. For all the beauty and hominess, something wasn't right.

As she raised her hand to push her hood off her head, she stopped and sniffed.

Dante must have sniffed it at the same time, his nose wrinkling as he unzipped his jacket.

"Gas," Emma said softly.

When Dante started to shove his jacket off, Emma's heart leaped. "Don't move!"

Immediately, his hands froze with his jacket halfway over his shoulders.

"You smell it too?" she asked. "If you take your jacket off, as dry as it is in here, it might let out a spark. My hood does it every time I push it back from my head."

"Good point." He glanced at her. "Get out."

"I'm not going without you."

"If something happens to me and you both, no one will be around to get help. Don't argue, just get out." He walked to the door, holding his arms away from his sides to keep the Gore-Tex fabric from rubbing together and potentially causing a spark.

Emma's lips pressed together. "Okay, but be careful. I'd hate for my brand-new fiancé to go up in flames before I get a ring out of it." Though her words were flippant, her voice quavered. She opened the door carefully and exited.

Dante left the door open, the wind blowing snow through the opening onto the smooth tile floor.

Emma hunched her back to the frigid cold and waited while Dante turned every knob on the stove and the one for the oven, as well. Once he'd secured the stove and checked the gas line into it, he left the kitchen, disappearing around a corner into the darkened house.

By the time he returned, Emma's teeth were chattering and her eyelids were crusted with snowflakes.

"It's safe now. I have all the exterior doors open and there's a good breeze blowing through."

Emma stepped in from the outside. Although she was out of the wind, she was still cold and shivering. The clouds had sunk low over the house, blocking out any light from the setting sun well before dusk. Darkness descended on Thunder Horse Ranch.

Dante pulled her out of the breeze blowing through the house and enveloped her in his arms. "I want to wait a few more minutes before I feel confident it's safe."

Leaning her face into the opening of his jacket, she pressed her cool cheeks to his warm flannel shirt.

He took her hands in his, unbuttoned his shirt and pushed them inside against his warm skin. He hissed at the cold but didn't remove her hands. "Warmer?" he asked.

She nodded, not certain she could talk at that point. Her teeth were still clattering like castanets.

After a good five minutes with the cold wind blowing through the house, Dante closed the back door and went around the house closing the rest, mopping the snow-drenched floor with a towel he'd grabbed out of the bathroom.

When Emma started to take off her jacket, Dante placed a hand over hers. "Wait until it warms up in here to at least sixty degrees."

Content to do as he said, Emma stuck her hands in her pockets and glanced around the kitchen. "Did you locate the source?"

His brow furrowed. "One of the stove's burners was left on."

Emma's gaze captured Dante's. The attacks on Dante's helicopter, the trailer incident, his brothers' cut brake lines and now a house filled with gas were all too close together. "Does that happen often?"

"Never. When my mother talked my dad into buying a gas stove, she promised she'd handle it with care and always turn off the burners. He didn't want a gas stove in the house, afraid one of us kids would light our hair on fire or something. Mom was cautious about the knobs. If she even suspected she might not have turned off the stove, she'd drive a hundred miles back to check."

"Could she have left it on when she rushed to the hospital after your brothers' accident?"

"Maybe, but not likely."

"Coincidence?" Emma asked, shaking her head before he answered.

"I think not." He glanced around the kitchen. "Julia had said something about Mom hiring a security team to set up surveillance around the house. She's had some incidents, as well." He nodded to the corner. "Looks like they've started the work but have yet to install the cameras.

Emma followed his gaze, noting where wires stuck out of the corners of the room.

Dante left the kitchen and strode through the rest of the house, moving from one room to another.

Emma followed. Wires stuck out of the walls in every common area and in the hallway.

"What kind of incidents were they having here?" Emma asked, trying to keep up with him, noting the homey decor and wood flooring.

"I don't know. I think she was afraid to say anything in front of my mother. I'd hoped to find out more from the foreman."

"But he's not here."

No, and Dante had a lot of questions for the man. Where the hell was he?

When Maddox had started traveling to his wife's country of Trejikistan, he and his mother had hired Sean McKendrick to manage the ranch in Maddox's absence. Amelia was capable of a lot of things, but it was a lot for a lone woman. Sean had proven himself knowledgeable about horses and cattle and a good carpenter when things needed fixing. And he seemed to have a good heart and a love for the North Dakota Badlands.

Dante stopped in the living room and glanced down at an answering machine. A light blinked three times, paused and blinked three times again.

He punched the play button and listened.

"Mom, it's Dante. In case you've seen the news reports about the helicopter crash involving a border patrol agent, I'm okay. Yes, it was mine, but I'm not hurt. Call me when you get a chance. Love you." He erased the message.

"Good thing you got home first," Emma said. "Or else the jig would be up."

The second message played. *"Amelia, Sean here. Had to go into Medora at the last minute to pick up some supplies and the Yost boy. If you get back before I do, the horses need to come into the barn before the storm hits."* Dante deleted the message and played the third.

"Amelia, Sean again. Having troubles with the truck engine. Don't think I'll make it back to the ranch before the storm. I'll get a room at the hotel for the night and be back first thing in the morning. I'm putting a call into the Carmichael Ranch to have the foreman come over and take care of the horses."

As he deleted the last message on the answering machine, the phone rang.

"This is Dante."

"Dante, I'm glad you're home. It's Jim Rausch from the Carmichael Ranch. Sean tells me he's stuck in Medora for the night and there's some horses needing put up before the storm."

"I've already taken care of them," Dante reassured the man. "How are things your way?"

"Everything's locked down. Looks like that storm's gonna last until sometime in the middle of the night. I just wanted to get everything in place so that I'm not out in the snow in my house shoes. How's Pierce doing? Your family make it back to the ranch with you?"

"No, they're staying in Bismarck, close to the hospital. Pierce is still out of it. Although he did wake briefly."

"Sorry to hear that. What about Tuck?"

"Banged up, but on his feet."

"Good," Jim said. "Glad he's okay. I saw in the news about your helicopter crash. I guess you're okay if you're at the ranch."

"I am. I left a message on Mom's answering machine about it, but since she hasn't been home, and she hasn't seen the news, I didn't bother telling her. She's got enough to worry about."

Jim snorted. "And then some."

"Tell me about it." If anything were happening at the Thunder Horse Ranch, news would have made it to the Carmichael Ranch. Though Pierce spent his weeks in Bismarck, he commuted to the Carmichael Ranch where his wife, Roxanne lived.

"There's been one accident after another. First the barn door fell off its hinges and nearly crushed your brother Maddox the day before he left with Katya. Three days later, the hay caught fire in the barn. Sean was able to put out the fire before it did any damage, but it was close."

"What do you know about the security system Mom's having installed?"

"Sheriff Yost's son has a security business. He's doing the work. From what Roxanne said, he's not finished."

"No, not even close."

"Roxanne tells me Maddox is cutting short his stay in his wife's country to come home early because of all that's been happening. Your mother tried to convince him she's fine, but none of us like what's happening. And now this crash with your brothers. It's enough to push a sane woman over the edge."

Exactly Dante's worry. "Thanks for the update."

"Glad you're there to take care of things. Let me know if you need any help."

"Thanks, Jim."

Dante hung up the telephone and stared across the floor at Emma. "I'm sorry to say, but I think by saving my life, you've walked into a bigger can of worms than we originally thought."

Chapter Nine

Emma insisted on spending the night on the couch in the living room. Being alone in the big house with Dante made her uncomfortable. After being in the presence of his family and extended family, she found herself wishing she really did belong and that was a dangerous thing to do.

She had bad luck with families. Her father had left when she was a little girl. As a single parent, her mother had left her alone since the age of twelve so that she could save money on babysitting.

To survive, she'd learned to cook and do her own laundry and that of her mother's or it wouldn't have gotten done. Her mother worked her day job and a night job to keep her in a private school.

A month after Emma graduated from high school, her mother caught a staph infection at the nursing home where she cleaned rooms. Within two weeks, she'd died.

Completely alone at eighteen, Emma had depended on herself since. Too many times when the world seemed too harsh or the tasks too hard, she'd gone back to her rented room and cried herself to sleep. She'd have given her right arm to have someone hug her and tell her everything would be all right.

She'd completed her undergraduate degree working nights washing dishes at a local restaurant. Then she worked her way through her master's degree as a teacher's assistant. She'd captured the attention of the department head and was offered a teaching position when she completed her master's and went on to get her doctorate, determined that no matter what, she would always be able to support herself without working two jobs like her mother had.

All in all, she'd had a limited family experience, whereas Dante's family was almost storybook perfect. Lucky man.

Dante had gotten up before dawn, dressed and went out to tend to the animals, leaving Emma to dress and scrounge in the kitchen for breakfast. The refrigerator was well stocked with enough food to feed an army. A freezer in the pantry was full of what looked like a half a cow's worth of packaged beef, frozen homegrown vegetables and loaves of bread.

She supposed they had to buy in bulk when they could only get to the major grocery stores once every other month and maybe not at all during the fierce winters.

Whipping up a half a dozen eggs, she chopped onions, tomatoes and black olives and tossed them in a skillet, pouring half the eggs over the top to make an omelet.

When she had two plates loaded, the back door opened and a frigid blast of air slammed into her. "Holy smokes." She danced out of the draft and grabbed the pot of coffee she'd made and poured a cup full. "Sit. I have breakfast ready."

"Thanks." Dante stomped his feet on the mat to get the snow off his boots and sniffed the air. "Smells better than gas." He winked and shrugged out of his jacket, scarf, gloves and an insulated cap. "You don't have to wait on me, you know. My mother taught us boys to cook and clean dishes."

"I know. But I was up and it gave me something to do. Besides, it's just as easy to cook for two as it is for one."

"Thanks." He pulled out her chair and waited for her to sit, before claiming one for himself. Then he wrapped his hands around the mug of coffee and let the steam warm his face. "Heaven."

His appreciation of her efforts warmed her. "Have you heard anything about your brother?"

"As a matter of fact, my mother called late last night after you were already asleep."

Emma held her breath, praying for good news after all the bad.

"Seems Pierce woke up late last night demanding dinner." Dante smiled. "He'll be okay if he's already bellowing for food."

Emma let go of the breath she'd held, a weight of dread lifting from her shoulders. She'd never met Dante's brother, but she understood how horrible it was to lose a family member and she didn't wish that kind of loss on anyone. "Thank God."

"They hope the doc will declare him fit and cut him loose today."

"That soon?"

"He's already been up and they've moved him from the ICU. It's only a matter of time before they throw him out."

"That's good news."

"I got ahold of Tuck and told him what happened to us."

Her head jerked up. "Does he know we're not really engaged?"

"No, I didn't tell him that part. I figured it would be

hard enough to keep Mom from knowing about our crash without disappointing her about seeing her last son settling down."

"Now that your brother is going to be okay, shouldn't we tell her the truth?" The thought made her belly tighten and she set down her fork, no longer hungry. Amelia had been so happy at her son's announcement.

"No. Let her enjoy her Christmas. After the holidays, when everything settles down and we've figured out what the hell's going on, we can break it to her. She'd be better prepared to handle it then. Maddox will be back with his wife, Katya. Maybe they'll have a baby or something to keep Mom from worrying about me."

"Are they expecting?"

Dante laughed. "I wouldn't be surprised. And in the meantime, Tuck works for the FBI. He's going to put feelers out on the crash, the trailer demolition that almost included us and the explosives that took care of my Jeep."

Emma's lips quirked upward. "Must be handy having a brother in the FBI."

"Even handier to have two," Dante corrected. "Pierce is also in the FBI."

"Two FBI agents and a CBP agent. Don't you have one more brother? Is he in the FBI, as well?"

"No, he's the only one who stayed to be a full-time rancher."

Emma glanced around. "Then where is he?"

"He married Katya Ivanov, a princess from Trejikistan." He raised his hand. "It's a long story, which I'm sure they'd love to tell you all about over the holiday. They're visiting her brother in her home country and should be back soon."

"You have a very interesting family. How do you keep up with them?"

"Through Mom." Dante smiled. "She's the glue that holds us all together."

Having met Amelia Thunder Horse, she could see how. The woman was open, loving and cared deeply about her boys and wanted them to be happy. And she seemed to include their wives in her circle of love.

An ache built in the center of her chest and her eyes stung. To change the subject before she actually started crying, she swallowed hard and asked, "How much snow did we get?"

"It wasn't as bad as the weatherman predicted. We only got about a foot. We should be able to make it to town and collect the foreman and whatever supplies we might need."

"I think your mother's pantry and freezer are stocked for the apocalypse."

He laughed out loud. "Just wait. You haven't seen how much the Thunder Horse men can eat."

"If they're all as big as you, I can imagine."

Dante helped her clean the kitchen, proving his mother had taught him well. If he bumped into her more than he should have and reached over her, pinning her against the counter, it was only to get to the cabinet above.

Emma didn't read anything more into it than she dared. Dante Thunder Horse was a very handsome helicopter pilot, and he could do a lot better than dating a mousey college professor like Emma Jennings.

By the time they'd finished the dishes, she was flushed and her body oversensitized to his every touch.

"I'll be ready to go as soon as I brush my teeth." Emma hurried away to lock herself in the bathroom. The woman staring back at her in the mirror was a stranger. Her cheeks were full of color and her brown eyes sparkled. Even her dark brown hair was shinier. What had gotten into her? This was all make-believe and would end when the holiday was over.

The devil on her shoulder prodded her. So what did it hurt to live the dream for a few short days?

"A lot. It could hurt a lot," she whispered to the woman in the mirror.

Herself.

And Dante's mother when they finally told her the truth. But she'd support Dante in any decision he made, as any good mother would. She'd see that Emma wasn't the right woman for Dante and accept that it was a mistake.

The warmth of the woman's arms around her still resonated with Emma, and she missed her mother all over again.

She asked herself again, what would it hurt to pretend she was a part of this family, if only for the holiday? It would help Amelia get through it without more undue stress, Emma would have Dante and his family around her for protection and she wouldn't spend Christmas alone.

She ran a toothbrush over her teeth and made a solemn vow to herself not to lose her heart to a man that was still in love with a dead woman.

Splashing her face with water and then drying it on a towel, Emma squared her shoulders, hurried out of the bathroom and slammed against a solid wall of muscle.

Dante's arms came up around her to steady her on her feet. "Are you okay?"

Her breath lodged in her throat, her body tingling everywhere he touched it from her thighs to her breasts. "Yes." Emma's fingers curled into the fabric stretched across his chest. "Yes, I'm fine." Her pulse thumping hard in her veins, she straightened and stepped back.

"I was just about to knock and see if you were going to be ready anytime soon."

"I'm ready. All I have to do is grab my coat." *And pull myself together.*

"Wear your snow pants. It's extremely cold and windy out there."

"Okay." She hurried to the living room, jammed her legs into her snow pants and dragged them up to her waist, zipping and snapping them in place. Her boots went on next and finally her jacket. So much for being sexy in the morning with Dante. Dressed up like the Michelin Man, she looked like any other guy gearing up for the North Dakota weather. Puffy and shapeless.

"I'm ready." She crossed to stand in front of him, feeling lumpy and ugly.

A smile slid across Dante's face and he cupped her chin. "Anyone ever tell you that you're cute when you're all bundled up like the kid in *A Christmas Story?*"

She stared up at him, not sure if he was serious or just pulling her leg, surprised by the gleam in his eye and even more surprised when he bent to kiss her and whispered, "I missed you last night."

Before she had time to digest his comment, he turned and walked out the door into the cold, biting wind, stopping long enough to hold the door for her.

She walked through, still wondering why he'd kissed her and what he'd meant by his words.

THE DRIVE INTO Medora took twice as long as usual with the fresh snow and the unfamiliar vehicle. Dante didn't know the full extent of the little SUV's limits and wasn't willing to test them any more than he had to. He needed to get to town, pick up the foreman and do some asking around about what was going on in the area.

Maybe someone had information that would shed light on the happenings out at the Thunder Horse Ranch. He might also find out if the accidents were limited to the Thunder Horse family or if others in the area were having similar issues.

In Medora, Dante stopped at the diner, figuring Sean would probably hang out there with nowhere else to go until the truck was running.

He parked the vehicle on the main road running through town and helped Emma down. They entered the diner together. As he suspected, Sean was seated at one of the tables with a cup of coffee, a plate with a half-eaten biscuit and one of the biggest gossips in town sitting across from him. The local feed-store owner, Hank Barkley, knew as much, if not more, about everybody's business than Florence Metzger, the owner of the diner.

Sean stood when he spotted Dante and held out his hand. "Good to see you in one piece. I heard Pierce is feeling better."

Dante almost laughed out loud at the news.

Hank rose to his feet and shook Dante's hand. "Heard he was hollering for breakfast. He had us all worried." The man's inquisitive gaze fell on Emma and he asked, "Who do you have with you?"

"Emma Jennings." He introduced the men to her and asked, "Got room for two more?"

"Sure," Hank said. "We were just killin' time."

"Yeah, looks like we have until spring." Sean glanced out the window. "I don't think this batch of snow is going to melt until April."

Emma slipped out of her jacket and took one of the seats at the table. Dante sat in the chair beside her, his leg touching hers. Even through the thick snow pants and his insulated coveralls, he got a jolt. Something about Emma made his blood hum and his libido kick into overdrive. It had been a long night alone in his bed. Between getting up to check on her and lying in his bed awake but dreaming about making love to her, he'd slept little. A twinge of guilt accompanied these feelings. Memories of Sam were fading, which caused him more pain.

"Everything holding up out at the ranch?" Sean's words broke into his thoughts.

Dante nodded. "I took care of the animals before I left for town."

Sean and Hank sat across the table from Dante and Emma, each lifting his cup of coffee.

"Mack said he'd have to order a water pump for the truck and it would take a day or two for it to get in," Sean said.

"Then it's a good thing I came to get you." Dante glanced up at Florence when she stopped at the booth.

"Dante Thunder Horse, if you aren't a sight for sore eyes." The diner owner hugged him and looked over at Emma with open curiosity. "Is this the little filly you're engaged to?"

Emma's eyes widened.

Dante pressed a hand to her leg, his lips twitching. "Who'd you hear that from?"

Florence propped a fist on her ample hip. "I have a cousin working at the hospital in Bismarck."

Sean smiled. "I got the news from Hank."

Hank's chest puffed out, proudly. "Heard from Deputy Small, who got it from Sheriff Yost."

"I suppose the whole town knows by now?" Dante sat back and glanced at Emma.

Her face was pale and she gnawed on her bottom lip.

She hated lying to people and the more folks who knew, the more she'd probably consider she was lying to.

He draped an arm over her shoulders and leaned over to kiss her cheek. "The answer to Florence's question is *yes*. This is Emma Jennings from Grand Forks. My fiancée."

Sean, Hank and Florence all congratulated them at once, shaking Dante's hand and coming around the table to hug Emma, before resuming their original positions.

"That's just wonderful." Florence clapped her hands, her eyes shining. "Young love is so beautiful. But seriously, let me see the ring. You know it's all about the ring. It tells a lot about the man giving it."

Emma's face blanched even more, and then turned a bright red.

Dante hadn't even thought about a ring until that moment and he could see how uncomfortable Emma was with all the attention the lie had brought. "Shh, Florence, you'll spoil the surprise." He gave her a conspiratorial wink.

Florence frowned at first and then slapped a hand over her mouth. "Oh, yeah. Christmas is right around the corner."

Disaster averted, Dante took Emma's hand and held it in his like a newly engaged man would. Her fingers were stiff and cold. "But enough about us." Dante leaned his other elbow on the table. "What's going on around here?"

Hank and Florence were more than willing to fill him in on all the happenings of the small community. Frank and Eliza Miller had another baby. That would make five. Jess Blount and Emily Sanders got married a couple of months ago and were already expecting. Old Vena Bradley passed in her sleep last week, and her daughters aren't talking to each other because they can't agree on who gets what of the deceased's Depression-era glass collection.

Dante listened, bearing with the litany of social gossip, recognizing most of the names.

A customer at another table waved at Florence.

"I gotta get back to work. Yell if you need anything." She hurried off to pour coffee and deliver orders for the customers.

Turning to Hank, Dante asked, "How are things in town? Any new businesses or old ones that closed? Any new people you've seen around?"

"The Taylors finally sold their hardware store to a couple from Fargo. The old sawmill closed just before Halloween, and that abandoned hotel building sold to an investor from Minneapolis, and he's been renovating it." Hank paused to breathe, then launched into more. "I think it's because of the oil speculators who've been here off and on for the past six months, trying to buy up land."

"Same oil speculators that were here last summer?" Dante asked.

"Yes, and some new ones," Hank said.

Sean's brows furrowed. "Your mother didn't tell you about them? They've been out to the ranch several times, one in particular, that Langley fellow. He's bad about showing up whenever he likes. No matter how many times she tells him she's not selling the ranch or mineral rights, he keeps coming back. It's part of the reason she's having the security cameras and an alarm system installed."

Dante leaned forward. "What about the accidents out at the ranch? Do you think the speculators are responsible? Could they be trying to scare my mother into selling?"

Sean crossed his arms. "It would take a lot more than that to scare your mother into selling. She's feisty and doesn't let much slow her down." He chuckled. "That woman has more spunk than most eighteen-year-olds."

"But the ranch is a big responsibility for a lone woman, with Maddox gone a great deal of time," Dante observed.

Sean bristled. "I'm out there as much as I can be. I guess I could insist on her coming to town with me when I go for feed and supplies. I wouldn't mind the company. And those accidents could be just that—accidents. The barn door could have been working its way loose. You know how bad the winds are out here. And the hay was green when we put it in the barn. It could have caught fire due to spontaneous combustion."

Dante knew green hay could catch fire. That's why they usually were careful to let it dry before baling. He understood the hay had to be baled sooner because, after they'd cut the hay, a rainstorm had been predicted and they had to get it baled before the rain. "But to have two accidents like that in one week…" Dante shook his head.

The foreman shrugged. "The sheriff didn't find any evidence of tampering that could account for the door or the hay. We were just lucky no one was hurt."

"No footprints or fingerprints?"

"It rained late the night before the door fell. If someone loosened the hinges, it was before the rain. All footprints would have been washed away."

"What about the fire? Anyone out at the ranch that shouldn't have been?"

Sean's lips tightened. "Your mother was out on a date, and I was on my way back from the feed store when it started."

"Whoa, whoa, whoa." Dante held up his hand. "My mother was out on a date?"

Sean didn't respond.

But Hank did. "Sheriff Yost has been courtin' your mother. I've heard him say on more than one occasion that he wants to marry her. He told Florence he's been in love with Amelia since before she married your father, back when she sang in the *Medora Musical* in the summer."

"I didn't think she was that serious about the man."

"He's persistent," Hank said. "I'll give him that."

Sean scowled. "I don't know what she sees in him. She deserves better than that."

Dante studied the foreman. Something in his tone made him sound almost jealous.

Emma, who had been sitting quietly during the entire conversation, sat forward. "Are the oil speculators still in town?"

"Yeah. Some of them have rooms in the part of the hotel that's been newly renovated."

"What do you know about the security system Mom's having installed?" Dante asked.

"All I know is that Ryan, Sheriff Yost's son, started putting it in a couple of weeks ago, but he's waiting for some cameras that were back-ordered."

"I didn't know Ryan was back in this area. Didn't his mother take him to live on the Rosebud Reservation way back when she divorced Yost?"

Hank rubbed his hands together like a man staring at a particularly tasty meal. "I spoke with Ryan myself. He left the rez when he was eighteen, spent four years enlisted in the army, deployed to Afghanistan, got out and went to work as a security guard contracted to construction teams in Afghanistan for a couple of years. When he came back to North Dakota, he went to work for a man who installed security systems. About a year ago, his boss retired. Ryan took over this region for the security company. His territory is pretty much everything from Bismarck west. I think he's even got Minot."

"Is he based out of Medora?"

"For now. But he's on the road a lot. He even bought an old plane he uses to get back and forth faster. Got his pilot license so he can fly it himself."

"That boy seems to be doing something with his life," Sean said. "Not all of the boys from the rez are equally successful."

Dante knew that. His great-grandfather had moved off the reservation when he was old enough to leave. Though his heart remained with the Lakota people, he knew he had to get away to make a life for himself and his family.

"The boy doesn't look much like Sheriff Yost. Got more of his mother in him. Some of us wondered if he really was Yost's son. When his wife left him to return to the reservation, she didn't want anything to do with Yost, and Ryan never visited his father."

"Where is Ryan now?"

"I heard he had a job in Bismarck," Hank said. "Should be back later today. He's staying at the hotel they're converting. I think that's where the oil speculator is staying, as well."

Dante sat back, digesting all the information he'd been given. "Anything else going on around here that should raise some red flags?"

Sean grinned. "We'd like to hear more about what happened to you. We saw pictures of the crashed helicopter. You know it's only a matter of time before your mother finds out about it."

"Hopefully, by being here, she won't get upset. She'll see that I'm all right and let it go."

Sean grinned. "Don't bet on it. Amelia will be calling your boss to tell him you can't fly anymore."

Dante could imagine his mother doing that. Almost. She had never been happy about the danger her sons faced in their chosen career fields, but she respected their decisions and was as proud as any mother over her sons' accomplishments.

Pushing back his chair, Dante stood and held out a hand to Emma. "I have a few errands to run before I head back."

"Anything I can do for you?" Sean rose to his feet, as well.

"If you need feed, you might want to load some in the back of the SUV I rented. Emma and I will be back shortly and we can get back to the ranch."

"We could use more feed for the horses."

Dante tossed the keys to the foreman and helped Emma into her jacket. "Good to see you, Hank."

Florence passed by and he stopped her to give her a hug. "Good to see you, too, Florence. You're as beautiful as ever."

"Oh, now, Dante, you know how to make an old woman swoon." Her cheeks were flushed and she hugged him back.

Grabbing Emma's gloved hand, he made his way through the tables to the door.

Before Dante stepped out of the diner, his cell phone rang. The caller ID screen had Mom in bright letters. He answered, "Hi, Mom. How's Pierce?"

"The doctor's already discharged him. Can you believe it? I tried to get him to keep him for another day, but he said he was too disruptive to the hospital staff and that he'd be better off recuperating at home. We're already on the interstate and should be home in less than three hours, if the Great Spirit is willing and the roads stay clear."

"Who's driving?" he asked, knowing Pierce would hate letting someone else do the driving.

"Roxanne." His mother chuckled. "Pierce wanted to, but she told him to be quiet and lie down."

"What about Tuck?"

"He's headed home as well, but later this afternoon. He had some things he wanted to check on at his office. Then he, Julia and Lily will be on their way home for the holidays."

"What are you coming in?"

"We rented a four-wheel-drive vehicle for two weeks, or until the insurance company can make heads or tails out of what happened to Pierce's truck."

"Did you test the brakes?"

His mother snorted. "Tuck got under the hood, then under the car itself to check the brakes. He reported that everything looked serviceable. No leaking fluid or broken lines."

"Good. I'd like to have all of my family home for Christmas."

"Yes, and won't it be wonderful with everyone there. And now that you have Emma, our little family is complete and growing."

Dante's teeth ground together, but he held his tongue. Why ruin his mother's Christmas? She seemed thrilled that he'd found a woman to share his life.

His gaze shot to Emma walking beside him, her collar pulled up, her long brown curls whipping around her face. He was certain she didn't have a clue how beautiful she was.

She turned her head, catching him staring at her and she stumbled on the sidewalk. "What?" she asked.

"Nothing," he said. "I was just thinking how glad I am you decided to come with me. I hope you enjoy my family as much as they're sure to enjoy you."

Emma blinked up at him, long strands of rich chocolate hair dancing around her face. "You think they will?"

"Positive." He took her gloved hand in his and pulled her into the curve of his arm.

They walked the rest of the way to the little hotel which exterior looked brand-new. Once they entered the lobby area, Emma realized it still had a lot of work to go on the interior.

"May I help you?" a bored young woman asked.

"Can you tell me if Ryan Yost is in his room?"

"No." The woman smacked her gum, gave Dante a sweeping glance and smiled up at him. "I have empty rooms. Need one?"

Dante gave her his most charming smile. "Maybe."

Chapter Ten

The young lady's face flushed with pleasure and she batted her eyes.

Emma's own knees weakened when Dante turned up the wattage on his smile. Normally dark and intense, when he smiled it changed his entire appearance.

In his photo with Samantha, he'd smiled like this. Emma found herself wishing she could bring back the happiness he'd felt before he'd lost the love of his life. What would it be like to be loved so completely by a man like Dante?

Dante leaned over the counter toward the blushing girl. "Nicole? Is that your name?"

She nodded. "Yes."

"Such a pretty name for a pretty girl."

Nicole pressed one hand to her chest and brushed her long blond hair back behind her ear. "Thank you."

"I'm—"

Nicole raised her hand. "Don't tell me. You're a Thunder Horse. I can tell by your features. You look a lot like Maddox."

Dante inclined his head. "That's right, Maddox is my brother. I'm Dante." He turned toward Emma. "And this is Emma. We're Ryan's friends," Dante said, twisting the pen on the counter between his long, dark fingers.

"It's been a long time since we've seen him and we just wanted to say hello."

"Oh, is that all?" Her lips spread in a smile and she played with the ends of her hair. "He's been living here since they got room 207 finished. But he's not there right now. When he left this morning, he said he wouldn't be back until around noon."

"That's all we needed to know." Dante straightened and winked at the girl. "If you have a pen and a little piece of paper, I could leave a note on his door to contact us when he gets back in."

Nicole immediately dug beneath the counter and surfaced a pad of sticky notes and an extra pen, scribbling something on the top note. "Will this do?" She slid the pad and pen across the counter.

She'd written her phone number on the top page and the words *call me* beneath.

"Perfectly." Dante winked again, gathered the items and looked around.

"The stairs are behind the potted plant." Nicole pointed to a fake ficus tree in the corner of the lobby. "First floor up, second door on the right."

"Thank you." He turned to Emma. "Do you mind waiting here, sweetheart? I'll only be a minute."

Her heart skipped a couple of beats at the endearment before she remembered it was all part of the ruse. "I'll wait here." Emma darted a glance at the blonde.

Nicole watched Dante disappear around the corner before she turned her attention back to Emma. The young lady's brows rose and her lip curled in a little sneer. "Dante's from here. I'd recognize the Thunder Horse name and those beautiful cheekbones anywhere." Her gaze slid over Emma. "But you must be new around here."

Emma nodded. "I live in Grand Forks. I'm…" She didn't know whether or not to announce that she was Dante's fiancée. The lie didn't come easily to her lips. "I'm here visiting the Thunder Horse family."

Her brows furrowing, Nicole tilted her head. "Is Dante the Thunder Horse brother that just got engaged?" Her eyes narrowed as she surveyed Emma anew. "Are you the fiancée?"

Damn, word spread like wildfire in the small town. "Y-yes," Emma acknowledged. Then she straightened her shoulders and spoke with more conviction. "It was so sudden. He surprised me yesterday with his proposal. I'm still getting used to the idea." Forcing a smile to her lips, she pretended to be the giddy bride. Okay, so he hadn't proposed, but had gone directly to announcing their engagement. But she had been surprised. "I was so shocked, I barely knew what to say."

Nicole snorted. "Obviously you said yes." Her gaze shifted to Emma's hand. "What? No ring? What a shame."

Emma's cheeks heated and she stuffed her hand in her pocket. "Not yet." She leaned forward, her voice dropping to a whisper as she used Florence's supposition. "Could be what he's planning for Christmas." There, it wasn't a complete lie. By the time the holidays were over, the engagement would be broken.

But for now, she could pretend, and Nicole could back off her flirting with Emma's pretend fiancé.

Two workmen entered the lobby carrying a heavy roll of carpet.

Nicole left her position and hurried down the hallway to open a door for them.

Two more men entered the lobby, both wearing suits

and expensive-looking trench coats. When they spotted Emma, the first man smiled.

"Well, what have we here?" The man stuck out his hand. "I'm Monty Langley, my partner here is Theron Price. And you are?"

Emma ignored the outstretched hand still encased in black leather gloves. "I'm Emma."

"Emma, Emma, Emma." The man leaned on the counter, his gaze traveling from the tip of her head to the snow boots on her feet. Glad she wore several layers of clothes, she raised her brows.

"Are you checking in to the hotel?" Monty asked.

"No."

"No? Well, would you care to have a drink with me later? I'm sure we can find a bar around here somewhere."

"No, thank you." She hoped he'd get the hint.

"Well darn, and here I thought things were looking up in this godforsaken little hellhole."

"I guess you were wrong." She smiled and turned away, watching his movements through her peripheral vision.

The man's eyes narrowed and he glanced at his partner. "Come on, Theron. I have a bottle of whiskey in my room." As he walked down the first floor corridor, he shot back over his shoulder. "And they say the people are friendly in North Dakota."

"To friendly people, not jackasses," Emma muttered.

"I heard that," Langley said.

Once the two men disappeared into a room down the hall, Emma took the opportunity to escape up the stairs to room 207.

Dante wasn't anywhere in sight, and the door to room 207 was slightly ajar.

She pushed through and entered. "Dante?" she whispered. The room was dark, the drapes pulled over the window. Clothes were strewn across the floor and bed, and the trash can was overflowing with empty food containers. She couldn't make out Dante's form in the shadowy interior.

A hand clamped over her mouth from behind and she was pulled back against a hard chest.

Emma's pulse leaped and she drew her arm forward to slam into her attacker's gut. Before she could, warm breath caressed her ear.

"Shh," Dante whispered, his lips brushing the skin beneath her earlobe. He dropped his hand to her shoulder and squeezed. "I'm almost done here."

"What are you doing?" she whispered.

"Looking around."

Was he crazy? "Isn't that breaking and entering?"

"Only if you get caught." Dante shrugged. "Besides, the door wasn't locked."

"Still, Nicole could come up and find you. Or worse, what if Ryan Yost were to walk in?"

"He hasn't, has he?"

"Yet. Langley and Price, the two oil speculators, showed up downstairs."

"Really? Maybe we should talk to them."

"I have no desire to. Langley hit on me."

Dante tipped her chin. "The man has good taste."

"We should leave now."

"And we will." He checked out the door, then dragged her out behind him. He closed the door and attached a sticky note to the outside.

Dante barely gave her time to read the note before he was tugging her down the hallway and the staircase.

Langley and Price hadn't come out of their room and

Nicole was still down the hallway with the workmen when Dante and Emma headed for the exit.

A dark-skinned man with a military haircut and piercing dark eyes pushed through the door before they could escape. His eyes narrowed for such a brief moment Emma almost didn't notice.

He stopped in front of them, blocking their exit. "You're one of the Thunder Horse brothers, right?" He held out his hand. "Ryan Yost."

Emma's heart dropped into her belly. It had been this man's room they'd been in. Had he arrived a minute earlier, he'd have caught them.

Dante gripped the man's hand and gave him a cool, calm smile. How could he act so nonchalant when Emma had to clench her hands into fists to keep them from shaking?

"Last time I saw you, you were a skinny little kid in the fifth grade," Dante said.

Ryan nodded, his lips curling into a smirk. "Yeah, that would have been right before my mother divorced the sheriff and we moved to the rez. Are you back in Medora for good?"

Dante shook his head. "No, I'm only here to visit family."

"Of course." Ryan glanced around. "Were you looking for me?"

"As a matter of fact, I was. My mother wanted to know when you might be back out to finish installing her security system."

"Right. I've been waiting for the cameras I ordered to come in. I expected them today, but apparently they were delayed. I should be out there tomorrow to install them."

"That's great. I'll let her know."

"I was surprised she wanted a system installed," Ryan noted. "Most folks around here leave their doors unlocked."

"Times have changed," Dante said.

"Yes, they have. It's been good for my business, anyway."

"I suppose so." Dante glanced toward the exit. "I better let you get back to what you were doing. We'll see you at the ranch tomorrow."

Ryan stepped aside, allowing them to pass. "You can count on it."

Back outside in the cold, Emma pulled her collar up around her neck. "What the hell was that all about?"

Dante's lips firmed. "Someone's trying to hurt the Thunder Horse family. I want to know who."

"You think Ryan Yost is the man behind it?"

"I don't know at this point. That's why I wanted to talk to him. Since he wasn't around and the door was unlocked, I thought I'd check out his living quarters and get a feel for the guy."

"I thought you knew him."

"He's a year younger than me. I knew him vaguely when we were in grade school, but, like he said, his mother divorced Sheriff Yost and took him to the reservation before he left the fifth grade. I haven't seen him since."

Dante grabbed her hand and headed back toward the SUV parked in front of the diner.

Sean was waiting inside and stepped out when Dante approached. "Ready?"

"Yup." Holding up his hand, Dante said, "I'll drive."

Sean tossed the keys and Dante caught them, hit the unlock button on the fob, then helped Emma into the passenger seat before going around to the driver's side. Sean slid into the backseat.

On the drive back to the ranch, Sean filled Dante in on other information about the happenings at the ranch.

"The wild horses have moved into the canyon. I spotted a mare with a limp. I think it was the one your brother calls Sweet Jessie. I'd like to get out there and check on her sometime today if possible and bring her back if she needs doctoring."

"She had a foal last spring, didn't she?"

"Yes. He's doing good on his own, but I'm worried about her."

"Perhaps I can help out." He turned to Emma. "Have you ever ridden a horse?"

Emma shook her head. "Sorry." Life on a ranch was so far out of her league. "Isn't it kind of cold to be out riding?"

Dante's lips twisted into a wry smile. "North Dakota ranchers don't get any breaks. The animals always come first."

"You're right." Nevertheless, a chill slithered down Emma's spine. "I'd like to go. Is it hard to ride a horse if you've never done it?"

Sean laughed from the backseat and Dante smiled. "The dead of winter might not be the best time to learn. If you want to go out with us, I could take a snowmobile. Sean will need to ride a horse in order to lead Sweet Jessie back if she needs tending."

Feeling inadequate, Emma felt the heat rise in her cheeks. "I don't want to slow you down."

"Not at all. If anything, we can get out to Sweet Jessie sooner than Sean and assess the situation. By the time Sean gets there, we'll have her roped and ready for him to lead her back, if need be."

Mollified, Emma nodded. "Okay. I would like very much to go, as long as I'm not in the way."

By the time they reached the ranch, Emma was feeling more relaxed around Sean and Dante, listening to their plans for what needed done before the next big storm rolled in.

When they drove up the driveway to the ranch house, Dante said, "Oh, good. The family made it."

Three vehicles stood out front—a shiny new SUV, a big ranch truck with knobby tires and a white SUV with the markings of Billings County Sheriff written in bold letters on the side.

Once again, her nerves got the better of her and she took her time climbing out of the vehicle.

"Looks like the sheriff arrived with them." Sean headed for the house ahead of them.

"What's he doing here?" Dante muttered as he climbed out. He walked around the side of the SUV, his face tight, and hooked Emma's elbow, leaning close. "Don't worry. My family doesn't bite...much."

"I'm not worried about teeth marks. I just don't like leading them on."

"As far as they're concerned, we're engaged. I don't see any need to tell them different."

"But it's a lie."

Dante stopped and faced her, holding her gloved hands in his, smiling. "If it makes you feel any better, I'll tell them we decided to hold off on the engagement so we can spend more time getting to know each other."

Emma sighed. "I would feel a lot better. Thanks."

Dante pulled her arm through his and walked with her toward the house.

Sheriff Yost emerged from the house as they walked up the steps.

The older man stuck out his hand. "Dante, glad you could make it home."

"Sheriff." Dante shook the man's hand. "I'm glad to be home."

"I just stopped by to see that your mother made it home all right." The sheriff plunked his hat on his head. "Well, I better get back to work."

Dante stepped aside, allowing the sheriff to leave.

Emma could sense the animosity from Dante. He didn't like the sheriff and didn't want him dating his mother. She understood. He probably felt it was a betrayal to his dead father.

The sheriff climbed into his SUV and backed out of the yard, turning down the drive to the gate.

"I just don't trust that man."

"Why?"

"I don't know. Gut feel, instinct. Something." He shrugged. "Come on, let's face the gauntlet."

Before Dante could grasp the door handle, his brother Tuck threw it open. "Dante, you sly devil, get in here." Tuck embraced Dante. "I was still out of it yesterday when you made your announcement. I didn't congratulate you properly." He hugged Dante again. "Julia and I are so happy for you."

"About that—"

Julia hooked Emma's arm and drew her into the living room. "Tuck's mother was so happy, she was beside herself. I think it was the only thing that got her through the day and into the night. She'd been so worried about Pierce, I think she was on the verge of a nervous breakdown. And then you and Dante arrive with your wonderful news and it perked her right up."

Emma bit her bottom lip, wanting to say something but at a loss for what words to use.

"Speaking of Mom and Pierce, where are they? Emma and I had something to say." Dante glanced around the room.

Roxanne emerged from the hallway, her face tired but happy. "Mom was so excited to have her brood home, I had a hard time convincing her that we could feed ourselves and that she needed to rest. She tucked Pierce into his bed and crawled into her own, too tired to argue."

"You should have been there last night," Julia gushed. "She had a dozen questions about your engagement. All the possibilities kept her mind busy so that she didn't have time to dwell on Pierce. And when Pierce woke up and found out you'd gotten yourself engaged, he almost left the hospital right then and there to come shoot you for not telling us all sooner."

Emma's heart had settled like a lump in the pit of her belly. With Amelia and Pierce exhausted from their ordeal and beyond their limits, Emma couldn't break it to them that her and Dante's engagement was a sham.

"About the engagement. It's not what you think…" Dante started again.

Julia, Tuck and Roxanne all turned toward him, smiling.

Emma took Dante's hand. "What Dante is trying to say is that it was all pretty sudden and we haven't even had time to get a ring."

"No ring?" Roxanne crossed her arms over her chest. "Isn't that how you ask a woman to marry you, by offering her an engagement ring?"

Dante glanced down at Emma, his gaze questioning.

"Tell them how you proposed, Dante." Emma smiled at him, giving him a subtle wink.

Julia clasped her hands together. "This is all so romantic."

Dante's eyes widened and then narrowed slightly. He faced his brother and two sisters-in-law. "Well, we haven't known each other very long, but I knew as soon as I met her that Emma was someone special."

Emma almost snorted. He'd had coffee with her and then run like a scalded cat, never to call her later. Feeling a little guilty, but somewhat vindicated, she waited with her brows raised to see what story he'd spin about asking her to marry him.

"Go on," Tuck said, smirking. "Tell us all how it's done."

"There really wasn't much to it. One minute we were just friends and the next minute I asked her to marry me."

"Seriously?" Roxanne crossed her arms. "Did you at least get down on one knee?"

Dante tugged at the collar of his shirt. "No. I just—"

"Blurted it out," Emma finished and took his hand. "It was so spontaneous and unrehearsed." Her pulse beating hard, she raised his hand to her cheek. "I can't imagine anything more romantic." And she couldn't, because she could never imagine anyone, especially Dante Thunder Horse, asking her to marry him. And he never would, for real.

"True love." Julia sighed. "Straight from the heart."

"That's right." Dante bent and kissed Emma's cheek.

"Come on, Dante, give her a real kiss," Tuck urged.

"Yeah, Dante, show us what got her to say yes."

Dante's jaw tightened.

Emma's cheeks burned. "Really, we're not that demonstrative in public," she insisted.

"The hell we aren't." Dante swept her into his arms and kissed her long and hard.

At first she was stiff and nonresponsive, too shocked by his move to think. But as his lips softened and moved over hers, she melted against his body. He traced the seam of her lips until she opened her mouth and his tongue speared through, caressing the length of hers.

Emma rose up on her toes, lacing her fingers around his neck. The world fell away and it was only him and her, alone.

"Ahem." Tuck cleared his throat. "You've made your point."

"What a kiss." Julia wrapped her arms around Tuck's waist and leaned into him.

Dante broke the kiss and leaned his forehead against Emma's for a moment. "Are you okay?" he asked.

She nodded, her tongue still tingling from the sweet torture of his.

Finally, Dante moved away and clapped his hands together. "Now, if you'll excuse us, Emma, Sean and I were headed out to check on Sweet Jessie."

"I'm coming," Tuck said.

"You were just in a car wreck," Dante said. "Give yourself at least another day to recuperate."

Tuck's brows rose. "I would think you'd need the recuperation time more than me."

"That's right," Julia said, lowering her voice to a whisper. "We saw the news clip on your helicopter crash."

Roxanne tilted her chin, staring closely at Dante. "We also saw an article in the morning paper about an explosion in Grand Forks that put one man in the hospital. Were you part of that, as well?"

Emma's cheeks heated. If they knew about the crash and explosion, how long would it take for them to figure out that she and Dante weren't really engaged?

Roxanne's eyes widened. "You were there!" She clapped a hand over her mouth. "That was your Jeep, wasn't it? That's why you're driving a rental."

Dante raised a hand. "It was an accident and neither Emma nor I were hurt in it."

"But you could have been," Tuck reminded him.

"I'd prefer Mom didn't know about the crash or the explosion," Dante said. "She's had more than enough drama for a lifetime."

Julia pursed her lips. "It's only a matter of time before she finds out. Nothing much gets by Amelia and she's tougher than you think."

"Look—" Tuck stepped into the fray "—we've all agreed not to say anything to Mom. But if she asks, we won't deny it."

Dante inhaled and let it out. "Fair enough."

"Now, do you want me to help you with the horses?" Roxanne offered.

"I'd go," Julia said. "But I'm not much good wrangling horses, and Lily's down for her nap with your mother. I hate to leave her."

"No." Dante held up his hand. "The three of us can handle this." He nodded to Roxanne. "And I'm sure Pierce will be looking for you when he wakes."

"It's supposed to drop down to minus twenty tonight," Tuck said. "Don't stay out past four-thirty when the sun sets."

As he headed for the door, Emma's hand in his, Dante called over his shoulder, "If we're gone any longer, send out a search party."

"Will do."

Dante stopped in the kitchen to swipe a handful of baby carrots from the refrigerator and stuffed them into the pocket of his snow pants.

While Sean hurried ahead to the barn, Dante hung back in the mudroom, making certain Emma had the right winter-weather gear on to ride on the back of the snowmobile. "Standing out in that wind is bad enough, riding on the back of the snowmobile is even colder."

"I'm tougher than I look," she assured him. Emma appreciated the extra care he gave her ensuring she would be warm enough, arming her with a warm wool scarf and heavy-duty insulated gloves and an insulated helmet.

When they reached the barn, Dante went in. An engine revved and he emerged minutes later on a sleek red snowmobile. Scooting forward, he jerked his head, motioning for her to climb on the back.

Glad she didn't have to stay at the house and lie to people she barely knew, Emma climbed aboard and wrapped her arms around Dante's middle. She liked being with him, even out in the frigid cold. And when they were alone together, she could be herself. No lies. She wished they could keep going.

Chapter Eleven

Dante sped out of the yard as Sean led his horse out of the barn. Already past noon, clouds had accumulated in the western sky. The weatherman had predicted more snow that night. If nothing else, at least it would keep the saboteur from sneaking up on them and causing trouble. And if he did try something at night, he prayed the snow wouldn't hide his tracks.

Flying across the snow-covered prairie of the Badlands, he let go of the strain and pressure of the past couple of days. Out here, it was him, the sky and the incredible woman holding on to his waist. He could almost forget his life in the army, Sam and the other men of his unit.

He pushed aside the guilt of letting go. The cold reminded him of what was important—paying attention to the terrain and the time. If they were stranded out in the cold, especially near dusk, they might not be found until morning. Once the night got as cold as it would get, they wouldn't last until morning.

It took thirty minutes of steady riding to make it all the way out to the canyon. Without the added protection of foot and hand warmers, Emma's extremities would be getting pretty cold. He slowed the snowmobile and shifted her hands under his jacket, the cold gloves touching his bare skin made him jump. Unable to help her feet, he prayed the boots would keep her toes warm enough to ward off frostbite. He would have left her back at the house, but he wanted to keep a close eye on her. Not that he didn't trust his family, but they had their hands full and he figured she would have insisted on coming anyway.

When he finally made it to the edge of the canyon, he drove along the rim until he found the path leading down and stopped the snowmobile, shutting off the engine. "We walk from here."

Emma swung her leg over the back and swayed, holding on to the seat of the machine.

Dante got off and stood beside her. "How are your feet?"

"Cold. But not too bad now that we've stopped."

"I'll let you drive on the way back. There are hand and feet warmers for the driver."

"Now you tell me." She smiled. "No, really, I'm okay." She pulled off the helmet, laid it on the back of the snowmobile and secured her jacket's hood over her head. "What now?"

"We go down into the canyon and find the horses." He glanced down the path and back at her. "I should have warned you there would be hiking involved. If you're not up to it, you can stay here and wait for Sean."

"I told you, I'm tougher than I look. Lead the way."

He liked her spunky attitude and willingness to pitch in. For a college professor, she was a lot more apt and able than he'd originally given her credit. Still, it was a steep climb down into the canyon and even more difficult coming out on the snow and ice. If he saw that she was having any trouble, he'd turn back and get her out of the canyon.

They made it to the bottom with little trouble and the

sound of the snowmobile engine had alerted the wild ponies. They'd come to see if he had brought them treats.

Sweet Jessie, the tamest of the herd, led the way, favoring her right front leg with a decided limp, but no less determined to get to them ahead of the herd. She loved carrots and would follow him anywhere for the tasty treat. Especially in the dead of winter when food was scarce.

Her foal followed, his coat thick and fuzzy.

Emma's eyes widened. "They're so beautiful. Are they yours?"

"No, they're the wild ponies of the Badlands. They don't belong to anyone."

"Then why are you out here?"

"My family has always taken care of them, looking out for them and providing the Bureau of Land Management with an accurate annual count. When one is sick, we help if we can."

Dante pulled off his glove and fished in his pocket for the carrots. Already the cold wind bit at his fingers. When he had the carrots in hand, he gave half of them to Emma. "Hold these out in your hand."

"She won't bite me?"

"She might nibble a little, just keep your hand flat and she won't hurt you."

Emma held out her hand as he'd instructed, the carrots in the palm of her glove.

Dante slid his glove back on and kept his carrots out of sight.

Sweet Jessie trotted to within twenty feet of them and stopped.

"Why did she stop?" Emma whispered.

"She doesn't know you." Dante spoke softly to keep

from startling the other horses. "Give her time to learn you aren't a threat to her."

"She's so much bigger than I am. How could I be a threat?"

"You'd be surprised how threatening humans can be to the wild horses."

Sweet Jessie inched forward a little at a time, her neck stretching, her nostrils flaring, steam rising from her nose with each breath. When she was within three feet of Emma, she lifted her chin and nuzzled the carrots out of Emma's gloved hand.

Emma let out a soft gasp, a smile spreading across her face as she glanced up at Dante.

In that moment, the sun broke through the clouds and shone down on her face. Her dark hair framed her cheeks, the cool air making them rosy. But it was the flash of teeth and the excited gleam in her eyes that hit Dante like a punch to the gut.

Emma Jennings was a beautiful woman. So full of life, so innocent in many ways and strong and daring in others. This was the woman who'd ridden her snowmobile straight into danger to save him and then had given her virginity to him in the middle of a blizzard.

He reached for her, without realizing that was what he was doing.

Her smile slipped from her lips and her eyelids drifted halfway closed, her lips puckering slightly to receive his kiss.

In the frigid cold of the North Dakota Badlands, Dante Thunder Horse found himself on the slippery slope of possibly falling for a woman he'd only been around for a grand total of four days.

He pressed his lips to hers, taking them slowly at first. But as he deepened the kiss, his hunger grew and he crushed her to his body, frustrated by the amount of clothes standing between them.

Emma lurched, knocking into him and the moment was lost.

Sweet Jessie, impatient with their kissing, had sniffed out his other stash in the palm of his hand. The one fisted and holding Emma close.

The mare nudged him again, pushing Emma against Dante.

He laughed and set Emma to the side, offering the carrots up to the horse.

While Jessie's lips snuffled for the treat, Dante reached up and wrapped his hand around her frayed halter.

When the last of the carrots were gone, Sweet Jessie tossed her head, trying to loosen Dante's hold on her.

"You might want to step back," he told Emma.

She slipped from his arms and pressed a gloved hand to her swollen lips, her eyes bright and shimmering in the fleeting sunlight.

Dante held tight to Sweet Jessie, refusing to let loose.

After several attempts to shake him off, Jessie nuzzled his jacket, looking for more carrots.

Dante smoothed a hand over Jessie's nose and spoke softly. "Emma, could you hand me the lead rope?"

Emma scooped the rope from the ground and laid it across his open palm.

He snapped the lead on one of the metal rings in the halter. "Come on, Sweet Jessie. Let's see what's going on." He edged closer and pressed his shoulder to hers, then eased down to the leg she'd favored as she'd trotted up to them.

At first, she refused to let him lift the hoof. As he leaned harder against her, she shifted her weight to the other foot and he was able to raise the injured one.

As he'd suspected, the tender pad of her foot had been cut, and was infected and swollen with pus. She needed it drained and to have a poultice applied. And she needed to be kept in a clean, dry environment until the injury was well on its way to healing.

"Is it bad?" Emma asked.

"If we leave it alone, it might heal on its own."

Emma frowned. "And if it doesn't?"

"The infection could spread and she might die."

"Are we going to take her back to the barn?"

"That's what Sean will do when he gets here." Dante straightened and glanced up at the path. "You should go first. I'm going to lead Sweet Jessie out. I don't want you to be in danger if she spooks and tries to break away."

"Okay." Emma turned toward the path and started up the hill, climbing with quick, measured steps, pacing herself for the steep ascent out of the canyon. Every few steps she glanced over her shoulder to make sure Dante was still behind her.

Holding the halter in one hand and the lead in another, Dante led the horse up the narrow trail.

Every time rocks skittered down the slope, Emma's pulse leaped and she swung around, only to see the man and horse steadily climbing behind her.

Halfway up the hill, Emma was breathing hard, but confident she wouldn't have to stop before she made it to the top.

Head down, eyes forward, she took another step.

A loud blast cracked the frigid air and the earth beneath her feet shifted; gravel slid over the edge of the path and tumbled down the hill.

When she glanced up, the entire hillside seemed to be sliding downward toward her. "Landslide!" she cried out and turned back.

Sweet Jessie reared and nearly knocked Dante over the side of the trail. He let go of the lead and dropped to his knees.

The horse spun, lost her foot and slipped a hoof over the edge before she got her balance and raced back down the hill.

Higher up and closer to the source of the landslide, Emma knew she wouldn't get out of the way fast enough. When the wave of sliding rock and gravel hit, her feet were swept out from under her and she slid down the side of the steep slope, bumping and slamming against every rock, boulder and stump along the way. Pain ripped through her arms and head as she rode the wave of earth to the bottom of the steep precipice and slid thirty feet along the base of the canyon before the world stopped moving.

Gravel and small rocks continued to pelt her as she lay still, counting her fingers and toes and flexing her arms and legs. Everything seemed to be working okay, so she sat up.

"Emma!"

Emma shifted her head and glanced up.

Thankfully Dante had been farther to the north of the source of the landslide, the trail he'd been walking on had been spared. But if he didn't slow down in his race to the floor of the canyon, he'd end up causing a landslide of his own.

"I'm okay," Emma called out, the sound barely making it past her lips. Had she not been so bundled in snow pants and thick clothing, she might have more cuts and broken bones.

She rolled to her side, starting to feel the bumps and bruises she'd acquired in her pell-mell slide down the canyon wall.

"Don't move," Dante yelled. "You could have a spinal cord injury."

Ignoring him, Emma pushed to her hands and knees and stood. Her ankle hurt and she'd be a mass of bruises, but she was alive.

Dante arrived at her side, his dark face pale, his eyes wild. "You shouldn't have moved." He pulled her into his arms and held her. "Thank the spirits, you're alive." He continued to crush her to his chest, his arms so tight around her she could barely breathe without pain knifing through her.

"Careful there, Dante, I think one of my ribs is broken."

"Is that all?" He laughed, pushed her to arm's length and smiled down at her, running his hands through her hair, brushing the dirt off her face. He cupped her cheeks in his palms and bent to touch her lips with his. "You scared me."

"I scared you?" She chuckled, wincing with the effort. "I was pretty scared myself." She glanced around. "Where's Sweet Jessie?"

"Probably halfway to Fargo." He hugged her again, more gently this time, and then frowned, his gaze shooting back to where the trail had been. "What I want to know is how that landslide started in the first place."

Dante scanned the rim of the canyon above, searching for movement. Nothing but a few pieces of loose gravel moved between him and the top. Based on the loud crack he'd heard before the ground shifted, someone had set off a small explosion that started the landslide that almost killed Emma.

His jaw tight, anger rippling through him, Dante slipped an arm around Emma's waist and draped hers over his shoulder. He moved her to a safe location in the shadow of a huge overhang of solid rock.

"I'm going up to get the snowmobile."

"I didn't think you could get it down the trail."

"Not that trail, and definitely not now. But there's a wider one farther along the top of the canyon. I didn't want to bring it down here and have the noise frighten the horses."

"But that's already happened with the noise and the falling rock."

"Will you be all right staying here for a few minutes by yourself?"

She nodded, a shiver shaking her frame.

Dante needed to get her back to the ranch. Even though she hadn't had any major breaks, with a fall as frightening as that and all the bruises she'd probably acquired, she could go into shock. He hated leaving her, but it would take longer for him to carry her out of the canyon than to climb out and come back for her on the snowmobile.

"Go. I'll be okay." She wrapped her arms around herself and pulled her hood close around her face and smiled.

Dante ran across the rocks, headed north to the trail he knew was farther along the steep sides of the canyon walls. Hidden by a huge boulder, it was hard to spot until he passed it.

Soon he was on his way up the wider trail, breathing hard and worried about leaving Emma in the canyon.

What seemed like an hour later, he emerged on the rim of the canyon and glanced around for the person responsible for causing the landslide.

Nothing stood out on the flat landscape except the snowmobile he'd arrived on. He hurried toward it, praying whoever had set off the landslide hadn't damaged the snowmobile or wired it for explosives.

Desperate to get back to Emma before she went into shock, he shifted to sling his leg over the top and stopped short. Something stuck out from beneath the hood of the engine compartment. It looked like a strip of black electrical tape. Careful not to apply undue pressure, he lifted the hood and stared down at what looked like a lump of clay with a mechanical device stuck in the middle. A wire led from the device to the vehicle's starter switch.

He'd seen C-4 explosives before, but not on a snowmobile. The way he saw it, he had two choices. He could walk away and leave the snowmobile out there and wait for Sean to arrive on horseback. That would mean putting Emma on the back of the horse to transport her to the ranch at a very slow pace while one of them stayed out in the cold until help could return. It would be dark soon and the temperature would drop rapidly.

Or he could take his chances, disarm the bomb and be on his way. He studied the mechanism and the wire leading to the starter. It looked like the electrical charge from the starter would be the catalyst to detonate the bomb. If he pulled the wire off the starter wire, it should disarm the bomb.

Then again, he wasn't a bomb expert and he could blow himself up if he wasn't careful.

Dante stared out across the land and there was no sign of Sean. He sent a prayer to *Wakantanka,* reached in, gripped the wire and pulled it loose. Blessed silence met him and he released the breath he'd been holding.

Carefully, so as not to bump the C-4 and the device, he lifted it off the engine and walked a hundred yards away from the snowmobile and set the explosives on the ground. When he returned to the snowmobile, he checked the ground for tracks.

Another snowmobile had been there, one with a

chipped track. There was also a dark spot on the snow. He touched it with his finger and lifted it to his nose. Oil. The machine had been leaking oil.

Too worried about Emma to look further, he hurried back to his vehicle and went over it one more time with a very critical eye. Confident he hadn't missed another cache of explosives, he climbed on, grit his teeth and hit the starter switch. The engine roared to life. Shifting into forward, he drove the vehicle along the rim of the canyon to the wider trail leading down to the bottom.

Emma was hunched over at the base of the overhang where he'd left her. Her cheeks were pale and her lips were turning blue. "Come on, sweetheart." He helped her onto the seat and climbed in front of her. "Can you hold on?"

"I'll do my b-best," she said, her teeth chattering so hard it shook her entire body.

Slowly, he climbed the trail out of the canyon, holding on to her arm with one hand, steering the snowmobile with the other. When they reached the top, he realized Sweet Jessie had followed.

Dante left Emma on the snowmobile and tied the lead rope to the back of the vehicle. Moving slowly enough the horse could keep up on her sore hoof, he limped to-ward the ranch, a little at a time.

Fifteen minutes into their long trek back, snow began to fall. Out of the snow and clouds, Sean appeared on horseback.

Dante gave him a brief rundown of what had hap-pened, speaking quietly enough so that Emma couldn't overhear him. Then he passed Sweet Jessie's lead rope to Sean and climbed onboard the snowmobile.

Emma leaned into him, her arms not nearly as tight, her face frighteningly pale. Dante drove as fast as he could without losing Emma off the back and pulled up in front of the house.

Rather than beep the little horn and upset his mother or brother, Dante dismounted, gathered Emma in his arms and carried her into the house.

Tuck met him at the door. "I thought I heard the snowmobile." When he saw Dante was carrying Emma, he moved back. "What happened?"

"Trouble," Dante said. "I'll tell you all about it once I get her warm and dry. Is Mom awake?"

"Dante?" His mother appeared behind Tuck. "Oh, dear. What's happened to Emma? Did she fall off the back of the snowmobile?"

Dante's teeth ground together. "No, she slid into the canyon on a landslide. Someone call the sheriff."

Chapter Twelve

She must have passed out on the way back to the ranch house. Once inside, the warmth surrounded her and she swam to the surface, nestled in Dante's arms, a crowd of his family gathered around. Immediately embarrassed at being the center of attention, she struggled weakly against Dante's hold.

"I can stand on my own," she insisted. "Please, put me down."

"Not happening," Dante responded.

"Want to lay her on the couch?" his mother asked.

"No, she's been through too much, riding a landslide all the way to the floor of the canyon."

"Wow, and no broken bones?" Tuck shook his head. "She's tough. Emma, you'll fit right in around here."

"Thanks," she said, her heart warming along with her cheeks.

"Yeah, well, I can't tell if anything is broken until we get her out of these clothes," Dante said.

"Nothing's broken," Emma maintained. "Put me down. I can take care of myself."

Dante's mother clucked her tongue. "Now, Emma, sweetie, you're practically family and you've been hurt. Let us fuss."

"You've already had more than your share of injured

family. You don't need to worry about me. Pierce needs you more."

"Someone call my name?" Pierce Thunder Horse appeared in the hallway holding an ice bag to his forehead.

"Pierce, what are you doing out of bed?" Roxanne hurried toward him, grabbed his arm and tried to steer him back down the hallway.

"I'm just fine, except for this knot on my head." He removed the ice bag to display a goose egg–size lump on his forehead along with several other cuts and bruises and a black eye.

Emma felt like *he* looked and she almost laughed, but couldn't because her ribs hurt and her lip was split. "If you'll put me down, I'll crawl into a shower and bed."

"Dante, honey, carry her to the bathroom. I can help her out of that snowsuit and into a nice warm bath."

At that moment, a warm bath sounded like heaven. Emma almost cried.

"I'll take care of her," Dante said.

"I'll get her some hot cocoa, painkillers and warm a blanket." Amelia whirled away.

The remaining members of his family and extended family stepped aside to allow Dante down the hallway. Too exhausted to argue, Emma leaned her cheek on his chest and closed her eyes.

"I'm going to set you on your feet. Think you can stand?" Dante asked.

Emma opened her eyes to discover they were in a bathroom with marble counters and a big mirror. One look at her wild, tangled hair and she groaned. "I'm a mess."

A chuckle rose up his chest and shook against her body. "How are you supposed to look after falling off a cliff?"

She sighed, tilting her head toward the mirror. "Better than this."

"I happen to think you look great. Here, let me have your coat." He unzipped the insulated jacket and eased it off her arms. "Okay so far?"

She smiled. "So far so good." Reaching for the waistband of her snow pants she tried to unzip them, her fingers fumbling with the zipper.

"Let me." He took over, sliding the zipper down and then shoving the pants off her legs, leaving her standing in jeans with her thermal underwear beneath.

Emma closed her eyes again and laughed. "Nothing says sexy like nine layers of clothing and thermal underwear."

Dante removed the jeans, slipping them down over her long johns "I happen to find women in thermal underwear very sexy." As if to prove it, he skimmed a hand along the side of her legs from her calves all the way up the outside of her thighs as he rose from helping her out of her jeans. When he straightened, he rested his hands on her hips. "Ready to take off the rest?"

Exhaustion disappeared as a blast of adrenaline-powered lust ripped through her, making her pulse race and her blood burn through her body.

"Shower or bath?" he asked, his hand on the hem of her shirt.

The tub was barely big enough for one person to stretch out, but plenty big enough if they stood. "Shower."

She lifted her arms, grimacing at the twinge of pain in her ribs. Her shirt and undershirt slid up over her head and then was dropped to the floor.

Dante turned to switch the water on in the shower and adjusted the temperature. Then he helped her out of her thermal underwear. When she finally stood in nothing but her bra and panties, Dante's gaze swept over her from head to toe.

"Oh, baby, you really did get beat up."

It wasn't what she wanted to hear. His words only meant she looked like hell.

But he bent to kiss a bruise on her shoulder that was already turning a deep shade of purple. He shifted to kiss another bruise on her arm, and across to press a kiss to the swell of her right breast where a strawberry mark indicated yet another.

"They don't hurt," she assured him.

When he straightened and stared down at her, Emma's heart sank.

"Much as I'd love to kiss you all over, you need your rest."

"I'm okay, really." Afraid she might sound too needy, she tried to reach behind her to unhook her bra and winced.

Dante turned her around and flipped the hooks open.

Her breasts spilled free and she let the straps slide down her arms. "Join me," she whispered.

His hand slid up her arms and cupped her cheeks. "Not tonight. I couldn't bear it if I hurt you more. I really think we should take you to Bismarck to the hospital and have them look you over."

Emma shook her head. "I'm only bruised."

He stared hard at her, his eyes narrowed. Finally he sighed. "You're very tempting, do you know that?"

She shook her head.

"But you've been through hell." He backed toward the door, his lips firming into a straight line. "Get in there and get your shower while I find something for you to wear."

Emma slid out of her underwear in front of him. Still,

he didn't take her up on the invitation. Instead, he turned and walked out, closing the door firmly behind him.

Disgruntled and too tired to do anything about it, Emma stepped behind the shower curtain, washed and rinsed her hair and ran a soapy washcloth over her entire body until she had all the grit washed away.

When she stepped out of the shower to dry off, a flannel pajama top lay on the counter. The top was big enough to fit several of her in it. She lifted it to her nose and sniffed. It smelled like Dante. Quickly slipping into it, she discovered why there were no pants to go with it. The shirt hung down past her buttocks and halfway down her thighs. A pair of her panties and her brush lay beside the shirt. Soon, she had brushed the tangles out of her hair and was dressed enough to leave the bathroom and step out into the hallway.

Several doors lined the wall. Dressed in nothing more than a big shirt, she didn't feel up to facing the family, but she didn't know where else to go but the living room where she'd slept the night before.

"Oh, good, you're out." Amelia appeared at the end of the hallway. She hurried to Emma's side and wrapped an arm around her waist. "Come on, let's get you into bed. I'm sure you're past exhausted."

Hustled to the second door on the right, Emma went with the woman, thankful she didn't have to face the rest of the family. All she wanted was a big painkiller and a really soft bed.

And if she had all her wishes…Dante lying beside her, holding her.

Amelia flung open the door and ushered her into the room. The bed was a big four-poster with a goose down comforter and a handmade quilt folded at the foot of the bed. The blankets were pulled back and crisp white sheets beckoned to her.

"Climb in, sweetie. There's a glass of water on the nightstand and a couple of pain pills to ease your discomfort."

"Thank you." Emma crawled into the bed and lay back on the pillows.

Amelia tucked the blanket around her and smoothed her damp hair back from her face. "You poor thing. What a way to start your visit on the ranch. Don't be too put off. It's not always so crazy around here. We go for years without any excitement."

Emma touched the woman's hand, a wave of longing washing over her. She missed having a mother and being taken care of. If she wasn't careful, it would be too easy to get used to it. "I'm sure it's lovely."

"There now, get some rest."

"Mrs. Thunder Horse?"

"Please, call me Amelia. All my daughters-in-law call me that."

A guilty twinge lodged in her throat. Emma swallowed hard. "Where's Dante?"

"Sean got back with Sweet Jessie. He and Tuck are helping doctor her hoof."

"Oh, good."

"He'll be in as soon as they have her settled." Amelia turned out the overhead light, leaving the lamp lit on the nightstand. "If you need anything, just yell."

"Thank you, Mrs. Thunder Horse."

She smiled. "Amelia. Please, call me Amelia. 'Mrs. Thunder Horse' is a mouthful."

"Amelia," Emma complied, liking the woman's open friendliness.

When Dante's mother left her alone, she took the pain

pills and washed them down with water, then lay back, wishing she felt good enough to go out to the barn and watch as they helped the injured horse.

She assumed she was in Dante's room. The sheets smelled like him and the decor was subtle shades of blues and browns. Very masculine, yet homey.

Several pictures lined the walls of Dante and his brothers at various ages. One was of all four boys holding up fishing poles and their catches. Another was of Dante, rifle in hand, kneeling on one knee next to what appeared to be a mule deer he'd bagged. He had a serious look on his face, but she could see the happiness and triumph in his eyes.

The last picture was of Dante wearing army dress blues, his back straight, shoulders squared, hair short and an American flag in the background. He looked proud, and so handsome Emma's heart pounded.

As the time passed, her pulse slowed, her eyelids drifted closed and she wondered where Dante would be sleeping when he finally came in.

DANTE DRAGGED HIMSELF into the house well after ten o'clock. The sheriff had come and Dante gave his statement about the explosion, the landslide and the explosives he found in his snowmobile. Once Yost left, Dante, Sean and Tuck had spent the next couple of hours working in the barn with the injured mare.

Sweet Jessie had been spooked about being herded into a stall when she'd been used to roaming the plains free. They had finally given her a mild sedative so that he and Sean could work on her sore hoof pad while Tuck held her head. Once they'd drained the abscess, they applied a poultice, gave her feed and water, and watched for a while to ensure she didn't kick the poultice loose.

All the while he'd been concentrating on healing the horse, Dante pushed what had happened that day in the canyon to the back of his mind.

Now that he was done and on his way back to the house, memories of the day flooded him. The one that stood out most in his mind was of Emma tumbling down the very steep wall of the canyon all the way to the bottom.

He hurried into the house.

His mother met him in the kitchen with a plate of food and a mug of coffee. "She's in your bed, asleep. You might as well eat and shower."

Tuck and Sean joined him at the table and he gave them the more detailed description of what had happened, and about the explosives still sitting out on the plains. By the time the sheriff had arrived at the ranch house, darkness had settled in and the snow was falling in earnest. He'd determined it was too dangerous to go hunting for explosives that could be buried under the snow by now. Especially in the dark. He'd call the state police and ask for the assistance of a bomb-sniffing dog. Hopefully, they'd get out there the next day and retrieve the explosive device before anyone else was hurt.

"Want me to call in the FBI bomb squad?" Tuck asked.

Dante considered his offer. "It might not be a bad idea. Is there any way to trace the C-4?"

"Not if they pulled all the packaging off it before deploying it."

Dante shook his head. "It was all clay."

"Maybe we can pull fingerprints from the clay, the detonation device or your snowmobile."

"Did you run the names I gave you by your guys at the bureau?" Dante asked.

"They're conducting a background check on Monty

Langley and Theron Price, the two speculators Hank mentioned, I'm having them run a check on Ryan Yost, the sheriff's son. I haven't heard anything yet."

"Yost has a plane. Have them run a check on flight plans in and out of Grand Forks." Dante's hand tightened around his coffee mug. "We have to find who's doing this before someone gets killed." Especially if that someone was Emma. "I think it's pretty apparent that whoever's doing this is targeting the Thunder Horses."

Tuck nodded. "Unfortunately, Emma was collateral damage."

That's what had Dante worried. "Who else is going to be caught in the cross fire until we resolve this situation?"

"I don't know, but I'm as afraid for Julia and Lily as you are for Emma. I keep wondering if I should send them away until all this dies down."

"What about your mother?" Sean added. "She's liable to get hurt, too."

Amelia entered the room. "Who's liable to get hurt?"

Sean leaped to his feet and offered her his chair. "Please, sit."

"Thank you." She smiled up at him as she took the seat. "You're such a gentleman."

Sean winked at her. "I only offer my seat to beautiful women."

Dante was stunned to see his mother's face flush a pretty pink. It made her appear twenty years younger.

She jumped right into their conversation with "Are you three talking about all that's been happening?"

"Yes, we have," Tuck said. "We think you and the ladies should leave the ranch until this situation is resolved."

She glared at the men. "I'll do no such thing. This is my home. I won't be run out of it."

"Amelia, we don't want you hurt," Sean said. "We think the boys are being targeted for some reason. The women might get caught in between."

"Well, I think it's up to us to decide what we want to do about it." Dante's mother lifted her chin and challenged the others with a pointed stare. "I've lived more than half my life here on this ranch. I won't be bought out, sold out or forced off by anyone. This little piece of heaven is my sons' heritage. Their father and I held on to it for them."

"Nothing's worth losing you, Mom," Dante said. "Or losing Emma."

"Or Julia and Lily," Tuck said.

"Or Roxanne," Sean added.

"I'm not going anywhere," Amelia stated. "So what are we going to do about this?"

Dante chuckled. "We got our pride from our father, but we got our fierce determination from you, Mom."

"Darn right you did." Her stern expression dissolved into a worried frown. "I hate seeing my boys injured. We have to put a stop to this. If only we knew who was doing it."

"And why." Dante pushed away from the table and stood. "Right now, I'm going to get a shower and then I'm going to check on Emma. Do you think we should take shifts through the night?"

Sean nodded. "I'll take the first one. You've been through a lot these past couple of days. Get some sleep."

Dante shot a glance at his mother to see if she reacted to Sean's statement.

Amelia crossed her arms over her chest. "If you're wondering whether or not I know about your helicopter crash, rest assured. I do. I've known since shortly after you visited Pierce in the hospital. You know a thing like that can't be kept a secret."

"I'd hate to know what other so-called secrets you know."

"I know more than you think. I might be getting older, but I know when my sons are keeping things from me." She gave him a grim smile. "It comes from years of practice. Anything you want to tell me?" She pinned him with her stare.

Dante almost blurted out that his engagement to Emma was a sham, but he bit down hard on his tongue to keep at least that little tidbit from her. The only two people who knew the truth were himself and Emma. No gossip would be able to pass it along to his mother. "No, Mother, I don't have anything else to tell you."

She snorted, her eyes narrowing slightly. "Well, get some sleep. I'll stay up with Sean for a while. I'm too wound up to sleep, anyway."

Dante ducked his head into his room. Emma was curled on her side, sound asleep, looking so small and fragile in his big bed. She didn't deserve to be hurt like she had. The fall could have broken every bone in her body or killed her.

She slept with her hand tucked beneath her cheek. She'd rolled up the sleeves of the big pajama shirt he never wore and looked even sexier in it than in a bikini.

Desire stirred inside him. Knowing he would do nothing to quench it that night, Dante slipped into the bathroom, stripped off his smelly clothes and turned on the cool water. After a quick scrub, he wrapped a towel around his waist, crossed the hallway and entered his room.

Normally he slept in the buff. To spare Emma some embarrassment, he slipped into the pajama bottoms that matched the top that she wore. He bent over her to check her breathing.

Emma rolled to her back and her eyes blinked open, two beautiful brown eyes that stared up at him sleepily. "Are you coming to bed?"

"I'll sleep on the couch."

"Please." She reached up and wrapped her arms around his neck, her lips soft and enticing.

He bent to brush his against them.

"Stay," she entreated, tightening her hold.

Knowing it would be difficult to lie in bed beside her and not touch her or make love to her, Dante heard himself agreeing before he'd thought it all the way through. "Okay, but just until you go back to sleep."

"No. All night." She scooted over, making room for his big body.

When he lay down beside her, she snuggled close, resting her head in the crook of his arm.

With a soft sigh, she closed her eyes and her breathing deepened.

Dante lay still for a long time, studying Emma in the light from the lamp on the nightstand.

Her dark hair lay in soft waves around her face, emphasizing her pale skin and the angry bruises.

She'd saved his life, only to put her own in danger. She didn't deserve it. Tomorrow, he'd get her out of there. Maybe the FBI had a safe house he could send her to until the trouble blew over.

And when they found the saboteur, he could resume his life as a CBP officer and maybe he'd look her up for a cup of coffee. If she dared see him again.

After all that had happened, he hadn't thought as much about Sam or the war that had taken her life. All his focus had gradually shifted to Emma.

Maybe it was time to let go of Sam and get on with his life.

Emma moaned in her sleep, her brow furrowing as if she were caught in a nightmare.

Dante gathered her close and pressed his lips to an uninjured spot. "It's okay," he whispered against her hair. "You're safe."

She settled against him and grew still, a smile tilting the corners of her lips.

Dante fell asleep with Emma in his arms, praying to the Great Spirit for her protection. He wasn't absolutely certain she was safe and that had him very concerned.

Chapter Thirteen

Emma woke the next morning to sunlight pouring in through the window onto the bed, warming the blankets. Even before she opened her eyes, she reached out for the warm body beside her.

The spot next to her was empty, the sheets still warm. Dante hadn't been up long. The sheets still carried his scent and heat.

Emma rolled over onto her back and winced. Yes, she had some bumps and bruises, but it could have been so much worse.

Throwing back the covers, she eased out of the bed, her muscles sore and stiff. Someone had brought her bag into the room the night before. She rummaged for something to wear and unearthed a pretty red sweater and jeans.

Dressing quickly, she ran her brush through her hair and pulled it back, securing it with an elastic band. A quick peek out in the hallway and she padded across to the bathroom to relieve herself, wash her face and brush her teeth.

She left the bathroom and followed the sounds of voices down the hallway to the big kitchen where the Thunder Horse men sat around the table with their spouses.

Amelia stood by the stove, stirring fluffy yellow

scrambled eggs. "Sit, Emma. We were just talking about what happened yesterday and what the boys think we should do today. You might want to weigh in."

Roxanne sat beside Pierce, her dark red hair curling down around her shoulders, her arms crossed over her chest, green eyes flashing. "I'm not leaving. So you can get that thought right out of your mind, right now."

"Me, neither," Julia agreed. Lily ate slices of banana beside her in her high chair.

"Who's leaving?" Emma asked.

"Not us!" Amelia, Julia and Roxanne said as one.

Emma smiled. "I'm sorry, but I don't have a clue what you're talking about."

Dante stood and offered her his chair.

Pierce spoke up. "We were saying that it would be best for all the ladies to pack up and leave until we figure out who has been trying to hurt the Thunder Horse brothers." He tried to frown but winced for the effort.

Amelia scooped scrambled eggs onto a plate and set it on the table in front of Emma. "The men, bless their hearts, think they'd be doing us a favor by sending us off to the cities to shop until they can get to the bottom of the attacks on all of them."

Emma stared up at Dante. "Is that true?"

Dante's brows furrowed. "No. At least not the part about the shopping. However, we discussed it. After all that has happened, it's not safe for the women to be here."

Emma's eyes widened. "So you think we'll just pack up and leave because you men think that's the best thing for us?"

Dante's frown deepened. "Well, yes."

Emma fought the smile threatening to curl her lips. She liked seeing the consternation clearly written on

Dante's face and mirrored in Tuck's and Pierce's expressions. "Without giving any of us a choice?"

"It's the only way to keep you all safe," Dante said.

"Since I'm a guest here, I'll do whatever you say. But if I'm going to be booted out of the house, you should at least know my opinion of the ruling." She spoke quietly but with conviction that had the men listening. Heat rose up her cheeks as all gazes fixed on her. She crossed her arms and tilted her chin up. "I think it stinks."

The women all clapped their hands.

Roxanne took up the cause. "As Emma, the college professor, so eloquently put it, your idea stinks. So, get used to it. We're staying put until this storm blows over."

"And what if one of you gets hurt?" Pierce demanded. "Had that truck landed any other way, I'd be a dead man."

"We'll take our chances," Amelia said. "It's not for any one of you to make that decision for us. I can shoot just as well as any one of you boys. I know how to defend what is mine."

Emma let go of the smile that had been creeping up around the corners of her lips. She could just picture Amelia Thunder Horse wielding a rifle, loaded for bear. Her smile faded and she glanced up at Dante. "Again, I'm just a guest here. If you ask me to leave, I'll go back to my apartment in Grand Forks."

Dante's lips firmed. "No. Whoever shot down my helicopter knows you saw him. He might come after you in Grand Forks to eliminate any witnesses."

"That's the only other place I'd go."

"I'm still the head of this household." Amelia stood with her shoulders squared, holding her spatula like a scepter. "If Emma wants to stay, she can stay."

Emma smiled at the older woman, knowing that if Dante told her he wanted her to leave, she would. She was there because of him. As much as she appreciated Amelia's invitation, she wouldn't feel right staying if Dante wanted her gone.

The telephone hanging on the wall beside Tuck rang. He turned and answered it, walking out of the room with the cordless handset.

Dante pulled up a chair beside her. "You should eat. You missed dinner last night."

Emma lifted her fork, amazed at how hungry she was. She had a forkful of steaming eggs halfway to her mouth when Dante asked, "How are you feeling today?"

"I'm fine. A bit stiff and sore, but I'll live." She popped the eggs in her mouth and chewed.

"I wish you would let me take you to see the local doctor."

Emma swallowed. "Really, I'm okay." Then to end the argument, she shoved more eggs into her mouth. She wanted to be mad at his insistence on seeing a doctor, but it was nice for a change that someone was concerned about her health after her fall. Living so long on her own, she'd had to weather her illnesses alone.

Tuck returned to the kitchen and replaced the phone in its charger. "That was my buddy at the FBI. He ran that background check on Langley, Price and Ryan Yost." Tuck paused, frowning, his gaze going to his mother. "Price is clean of any criminal record. Langley had an assault on his record from a couple of years ago, but the woman who filed the complaint retracted it."

"The two of them showed up together on the property two weeks ago," Amelia said. "I told them then that I wasn't interested in discussing the sale of the land or the mineral rights."

"And they left?" Tuck asked.

"Yes." Amelia's brows dipped. "Then Monty Langley

came back the next day to ask if I'd consider leasing the mineral rights. He said he had some big oil company wanting to tap into the oil reserves beneath our property."

Roxanne nodded. "They hit me up for it, as well. I did some reading. As you're all aware, the oil industry is booming in North Dakota since they discovered the Bakken formation stretches from Canada all the way to Bismarck. This isn't the first time speculators have been to the ranch."

"Maddox handled them last summer," Amelia said. "Since Maddox has been gone, they might think they can coerce me into signing something."

Julia laughed. "They obviously don't know anything about you."

Amelia smiled, then said, "I need to talk to the lawyer and have each of my sons added as co-owners of the property. That way no one person—namely me—can sell without the permission of the other."

"I don't think any of us want the property sold or split up," Dante said. "This is our home. It wouldn't be right to break it up."

His mother pressed a hand to his shoulder. "Exactly."

Tuck cleared his throat. "Mom, you know how all of us brothers feel about Sheriff Yost."

"I know that you don't care for him." Her eyes narrowed. "Why?"

"It might be none of our business, but what is your relationship with the man?"

She looked away. "You know I've been going out to dinner with him. He's been a perfect gentleman with me."

Emma studied the looks on the Thunder Horse brothers' faces. Apparently they didn't trust the sheriff and found it troublesome that their mother did.

Amelia continued, "Though you're right, it's none of

your business who I date, I'm still young enough to appreciate being treated like a woman, not just someone's mother or grandmother." She smiled at Lily, who was happily smearing banana on her face.

When the men all stared at her as if she'd lost her marbles, Emma almost laughed. They only saw their mother.

Amelia Thunder Horse was still a beautiful woman with needs and desires of her own.

"Of course you're a woman," Tuck said. "And I have no problem with you dating. Dad's been gone for nearly three years now. You should get out and have some fun. Our concern is Yost. I had my buddy at the bureau run a check on Ryan Yost."

"He's the boy installing the security system in and around the house," she confirmed.

Tuck stared at his mother. "Do you trust him?"

Their mother's brows drew together. "I trust his father."

Pierce snorted a rude word beneath his breath.

Tuck continued, "Ryan had some scuffles with the law before he became of legal age and joined the military. After he served his time, he went back to Afghanistan as a civilian contractor for a couple of years."

"I know all that. He comes highly recommended by the security firm he works for." Amelia rested her hands on her hips. "I didn't hire him because he was William's son."

Tuck raised his hands. "Okay. I just want you to be cautious about the people you allow inside the house."

"I am. No one knows better than I do that a lone woman on a ranch out in the middle of nowhere is an easy target. Especially when Maddox is out of the country. That's why Maddox hired Sean. Having him here has been a godsend."

Sean nodded. "It's a pleasure to be here as protection for a beautiful woman who is nowhere past her prime."

All the Thunder Horse family stared at Sean in shock.

Sean held up his hands. "Just telling it like I see it. I'll shut up now." He leaned his back against the wall, a ruddy blush sneaking up beneath the tan on his cheeks.

Amelia's eyes flared and she glanced down, her lips curling. "Did you find anything else about Ryan Yost I should be concerned about?"

Tuck shook his head, almost as if he was disappointed. "Not yet."

Amelia lifted her head and stared at Tuck. "Then leave the boy alone. I want that system installed sometime in the near future." She folded a dishtowel over the handle of the oven and smoothed her blouse. "Now if you'll excuse me, I'd like to steal the ladies away from you." She raised her hand. "Not to take them on a shopping trip to the cities, but to help me sort through some things I want to box up and give to charity."

Emma finished her breakfast, washed her plate in the sink and left it to dry on the rack. She followed the sound of female voices to the last doorway at the end of the hallway. It opened into a large room with a massive bed positioned at the center of one wall and a fireplace in the corner with a cheery fire burning.

"We're in here," Julia called out.

Feeling like an outsider, Emma paused at the doorway into a large walk-in closet.

Amelia sat cross-legged on the floor in front of an old trunk filled with letters, photographs and scrapbooks. If not for the strands of gray hair among the darker ones, she could have been a woman half her age.

"You have to see these pictures." Julia patted the floor

beside her. "Look at Dante at five years old. Wasn't he a cutie?"

She handed Emma a picture of a little boy with dark hair hanging down to his shoulders.

"I let them wear their hair long during the summer. The boys liked pretending they were wild Indians in the Old West." Amelia chuckled. "They'd spend the summers shirtless and mostly barefoot, riding horses and helping their father as much as they could." She handed a photo to Julia. "This is Tuck when he was ten. All legs and skinny as a rail."

Julia laughed. "He was so thin."

Amelia reached for another stack of photos. "I couldn't keep meat on their bones. They ran it all off." She leafed through the pictures and handed them over to Roxanne. "There are so many of the boys hunting and fishing. We spent a lot of the summer camping out in the canyon. We'd count the wild ponies during the days and pick out the constellations in the stars at night."

Emma enjoyed hearing stories about the boys growing up on a ranch, spending their summers running around in the sun. She loved the outdoors. As a paleontologist she spent much of her time outside digging in the dirt. At night she'd lay out under the stars, dreaming about other people who'd lived long ago, staring up at the stars, just like she was.

Roxanne held out a photo. "Is this Pierce's father when he was young? Pierce looks just like him."

Emma leaned over at the same time as Julia and Amelia. The man in the picture looked much like Pierce, but he was standing with his arm around a young woman with midnight black hair, dark eyes and the high cheekbones of the Lakota.

"Yes, that's my John, before we met. He dated a young

woman from the reservation up until a week before we met. They had just broken up when he met me. I guess I caught him on the rebound." She tapped her finger to the picture. "She ended up marrying William Yost within a month of breaking up with John. She's Ryan Yost's mother. I believe her name was Mika, the Lakota name for *raccoon*."

Emma stared down at the woman with the dark eyes and sultry look. "She was pretty."

"I know." Amelia laughed. "I don't know what John saw in me."

"A beautiful woman with a big heart." Julia leaned over and hugged her mother-in-law. "I'm so glad I married into such a wonderful family."

Amelia kissed Julia's cheeks. "I love my sons, and I always wanted daughters. I couldn't have picked better ones than all of you."

Roxanne reached out to clasp Amelia's hand. "We love you."

Having just met the woman, Emma sat silent. She didn't feel as though she had the right to say anything, even if deep in her heart she knew the woman was genuinely good and loving. So she sat staring at the photo of the woman and Amelia's dead husband who looked very much like Dante.

How different would the family have been had John Thunder Horse married Mika?

And now Amelia had Mika's son working for her.

Amelia sighed. "How much of this stuff should I get rid of?"

Julia clasped the pile of photos to her chest. "None of the pictures."

"No, none of the photos." Amelia glanced at the clothing hanging above her head and stood. "I should give his clothes away. It isn't as if he'll need them anymore." She ran her hands along the rows of jeans and flannel shirts neatly hung by type and color. "He could wear overalls and look so handsome. I will always love John. But now that he's been gone for three years, it's time to let go of some of him to make room for the rest of my life."

"You're still so young. You deserve to find happiness." Julia stood and put her arm around Amelia.

"Is it wrong for me to think that way? Is it possible to find the love of your life twice in one lifetime?" Amelia laughed, her hand shifting to the opposite side of the closet. "For that matter, I should toss half of my clothes, as well. They remind me too much of my life with John. If I'm going to make a fresh start, I should start with a fresh wardrobe."

"That's the spirit." Roxanne fished a dress out off the rail. "Stay or throw?"

Amelia smiled. "I wore that the day John took me to Minneapolis to see *Cats* at the theater." She chuckled. "He hated sitting through all that singing, but he knew how much I loved it."

Roxanne's brows rose. "Does it stay or go?"

Amelia sucked in a deep breath and tilted her head sharply. "Go." She selected several more dresses and passed them to Julia, who set them on a chair outside the closet. Amelia made her way to the back of the closet and stopped, her hand freezing on a white garment bag hidden behind some old coats.

Roxanne reached over her head. "Let me." She unhooked the hanger from the rail and carried the garment bag out of the closet and laid it on the bed.

Emma followed her, wondering what was in the bag.

"With all my sons married or getting married, it brings back memories of my wedding to their father." Amelia emerged from the closet carrying a white hatbox slightly yellowed with age.

Julia perched on the edge of the bed beside the garment bag and made room for the hatbox. "How long did you know Tuck's father before you married?"

Amelia smiled. "Two weeks. He found me the last week of the *Medora Musical* in the Burning Hills Amphitheatre. I was one of the singers in the show. He stayed until all the guests had left and the cast was cleaning the theater afterward."

"I can't imagine John Thunder Horse sitting through the entire show." Roxanne's lips quirked upward. "I don't think I ever saw him when he wasn't riding a horse. He was always all about his horses and the ranch."

"Not that week. He asked me to marry him at the end of our first week together when I was supposed to head back to Bismarck where I was to start college that fall. I never went back to Bismarck to college. We eloped to Vegas a week later. He bought me this dress for our wedding in a little chapel on the strip." She unzipped the garment bag.

Inside was a timeless wedding dress made of soft, pearl-white satin. The V-shaped neckline was simple with a few lace and pearl embellishments. The back dropped low in an elegant scooped neckline. Understated and formfitting, the dress was perfect.

Emma's heart squeezed tight in her chest.

"I love this dress," Julia sighed. "I so wished it would have fit me when I married Tuck for the second time."

"I bet you were a beautiful bride." Roxanne ran her hand over the satin. "It's a gorgeous dress."

Amelia smiled at the gown. "I had hoped that one day my daughter would be able to wear my gown for her own wedding." The older woman chuckled.

"But you had four sons," Emma added, her own eyes misting. "Speaking as an only child, they were very lucky to have each other."

"Yes. My boys have had their differences, but for the most part, they would do anything for each other." Amelia lifted the dress out of the garment bag and held it up to Emma. "You and I are about the same height, and I was once about the same size as you, though you would never guess it now." She smiled up at Emma, her eyes shimmering with moisture. "I would be honored if you'd wear it for your wedding to Dante."

Emma held up her hands, horrified that this woman would offer this lovely dress to her when their engagement was fake. "I couldn't."

Amelia pulled the dress back. "Of course, you might have something altogether different in mind for your wedding. I'm sorry, I'm just a sentimental old fool."

Amelia looked anything but old, and Emma couldn't bear to break her heart. "No, I think the dress is absolutely perfect in every way. It's just…" What could she say? That she'd lied all along, that she never intended to marry her son? "It's just that I hadn't even thought that far ahead." She gave Dante's mother a weak smile. "But when I do marry, that dress would be exactly the kind of dress I'd always dreamed of."

"Try it on," Julia insisted. "We want to see you in it, don't we, Roxanne?"

"You bet." Roxanne sat on the edge of the bed. "Go on. If you're embarrassed about changing in front of us, you can go into the closet and close the door. It's big enough for an army to change in."

Before she could protest, Amelia laid the dress across her arms and turned her toward the closet door. "Do you need help getting into it?"

"No, I can manage." Emma needed help getting out of the big fat lie she'd told. With the three women waiting in the bedroom for her to come out in the wedding dress, Emma had no choice. She stripped out of her jeans and the sweater she'd put on that morning, unhooked her bra and stepped into the gown.

The satin slipped across her skin, light and smooth, gliding over her hips so easily it felt like air. She reached behind her and zipped the back, a little apprehensive about how low the neckline dipped down her back, almost to her waist.

The dress could have been tailored for her; it fit perfectly, hugging her hips and breasts like a second skin. The skirt fell in an A-line, pooling at her feet, the train stretching out three feet behind her. A full-length mirror hung on the back of the door. When Emma looked up and caught a glimpse of her reflection, she gasped and froze, tears welling in her eyes.

It was absolutely exquisite.

"Come out, we want to see!" Julia called.

Hating herself for the lie she was perpetuating, Emma opened the door and stepped out of the closet.

The women had been talking, but when they spotted her standing there, the room grew so silent Emma could hear the crackle of the fire in the fireplace.

Amelia covered her mouth with her hands and tears slipped down her cheeks. "Emma," she said, her voice cracking.

"You're beautiful," Julia said, her voice barely a whisper.

"Wait." Amelia opened the hatbox and pulled out a bridal veil, unfolding the lengths of lace-trimmed tulle. She pressed the comb into Emma's hair and turned her toward a full-length mirror.

The woman staring back at her was a stranger. Dressed as a bride, her hair around her shoulders, the veil framing her pale face, she wanted to cry.

"I'm no expert, but I think you found your dress," Roxanne announced, clapping her hands together. "It couldn't be more perfect if you'd had it designed for you."

Amelia reached for Emma and hugged her. "Dante is a very lucky man to have found you."

What could Emma say to that? Nothing. He hadn't actually found her. She'd found him dragging himself out of his burning aircraft.

"Do you like it?" Amelia held her at arm's length, her gaze searching Emma's face. "You can tell me if you don't. I won't be offended."

Emma glanced down at the satin dress and nodded. "I love it." Feeling more of a heel by the minute, Emma backed out of Amelia's arms. "I'm sorry. But I think the fall yesterday took its toll on me. If you don't mind, I need to go lie down."

Amelia's eyes widened. "Of course, dear. How inconsiderate of me. I should have known better than to keep you rummaging through my closets. Here, let me unzip you." She helped unzip the dress and Emma ran for the closet where she removed the veil, stripped out of the beautiful dress and put her own clothes back on.

When she was finished, she emerged from the closet. The women were busy folding the clothes that would go to charity. Emma laid the veil and dress on the bed, her fingers skimming across the smooth satin fabric, regret tugging at her.

"Please excuse me," she said and hurried from the room.

She ran for the bedroom she and Dante had slept in the night before and crawled up in the bed, pulling the blanket around her. It still smelled of Dante. As she lay there, she thought of Dante helping her out of the collapsing trailer first, when it meant he might not make it out at all. She thought of how he'd helped an injured horse out of the canyon in the frigid cold, of how he'd risked his life rather than leave her in the canyon any longer than he had to.

She still tingled all over when she thought of the way it felt when Dante wrapped her in his arms, and how gentle he'd been when they'd made love for her first time, and then again in her apartment. She remembered their first kiss and the way it felt to lie in bed beside him.

Then she thought of how beautiful she felt in his mother's wedding dress and of the lies she'd told these good people. Of how they'd hate her when they learned the truth.

Tears slid down her cheeks as she realized what had happened in the short amount of time she'd been with Dante. No matter how much she'd told herself not to get involved, she'd done it. She'd fallen head over heels in love with the big Lakota man.

And no matter how much she might love him, Dante was in love with a dead woman and had told her up front he wasn't looking for a relationship. He wasn't ready.

Her chest hollow, Emma curled into a ball, buried her face in the pillow and cried.

When she could cry no more, she promised herself to leave at the first opportunity. She couldn't stay there, in love with Dante and his family, when it would all end. The sooner she severed the ties, the sooner she could start getting over him.

Chapter Fourteen

Dante, Pierce, Tuck and Sean fed the horses and worked with Sweet Jessie's sore foot. The swelling was down and the horse was impatient to be outside. They all agreed it would be better to keep her in the warm, dry barn until the wound had scabbed over a bit.

Dante gave the horse sweet feed and water and ran a currycomb over her fuzzy coat.

When he and his brothers stepped out of the barn, they noticed a vehicle pulling up in front of the house. After all that had happened, Dante wasn't comfortable with anyone driving up to the ranch house that didn't have an appointment or who hadn't called first. He hurried to the house, bursting through the kitchen door.

Following the voices, he found his mother, Roxanne and Julia in the front foyer, talking to a young man with jet-black hair and dark skin, about Dante's own age.

Julia turned to Dante. "You remember Ryan Yost, don't you?"

Dante nodded. "We spoke yesterday."

Ryan shifted the box he carried from one hand to the other and held out his hand. "Dante."

Dante shook his hand. "Ryan."

The other man held up a box. "Those cameras came in like I thought they would."

Amelia waved him inside. "Let me know if you need anything."

"Thank you, ma'am. I think I have all that I need, except a ladder."

"I'll get it," Sean offered and headed for the back door. Moments later, he came in dusting snow off his jacket and carrying a ladder.

Dante watched as Ryan set the ladder up in the living room, attach a camera to the wires in the corner and screw the mount into the wall.

Tuck joined Dante at the edge of the room. "I think Sean and Pierce can handle things here. Why don't you and I go to Medora and question the oil speculators?"

Dante nodded. "Let me check in on Emma."

His mother stopped him in the hallway. "Don't forget tonight is the kickoff of the Cowboy Christmas events in Medora. It's a tradition for the family to attend. I'd like to take Emma, as well."

"She'd like that." Dante smiled. "Tuck and I can meet you in town so you don't have to wait on us."

His mother nodded. "That's a good idea."

Dante stepped into the room where Emma lay sleeping, the blankets pulled up around her. He tiptoed to the bed and stared down at her face. Her dark hair splayed across the white pillowcase and her cheeks appeared to be streaked with tears.

Why would she be crying? Were her injuries more than she was letting on? Did she miss her home in Grand Forks?

His chest tightened. He found himself wanting to take away her pain. Dante brushed the hair from her face and bent to kiss her cheek.

Emma turned her face at the last minute and their lips

brushed together. Her arm slid up around his neck, dragging him closer.

"I'm heading to town to question the speculators. Will you meet me at the diner later when the family comes to town for the festival?"

"Mmm."

He kissed her again, this time, deepening the kiss, his tongue sliding between her teeth to caress hers.

She returned the pressure, her response stronger this time.

When he reluctantly broke away, she looked up at him with dark brown eyes, the shadows beneath them making her appear sad. "Be careful," she said.

"You, too." He brushed his knuckles against the softness of her face. "I'll see you later."

"Goodbye," she whispered.

Dante left the room, feeling as though he should stay and spend the afternoon holding Emma. He hadn't thought much about Sam since Emma had come into his life. Even the guilt he'd experienced at first was fading. He finally realized Sam would have wanted him to get on with his life.

With Emma he could see a future.

His mother followed him to the front door where he dressed for the outdoors and waited for his brother to appear.

"You know she's special, don't you?" his mother said as she held his coat for him while he slipped his arms into the sleeves.

"Who, Emma?" He chuckled. "Yeah. I know."

"Then don't let her get away."

He paused and stared down at his mother. "Why would I?"

She snorted softly, holding on to his gloves. "How

many times have you successfully lied to me, Dante Thunder Horse?" she demanded.

He thought back over the years and his lips twisted. "Never."

"That's right." She handed the gloves over. "I knew when you made the announcement at the hospital that you were lying."

"I'm sorry, Mom. I shouldn't have. But I didn't want to worry you more with Pierce lying in ICU."

"Actually, I'm glad you did. It gave *you* time to get to know her better and to see how much you really care about her."

"Mom, I've only known her a few days. That's not enough to base a lifetime of marriage on."

His mother shook her head. "That's all it took for me and your father. We knew within the first hour of talking. He proposed after a week and we were married for thirty years before he passed."

"I didn't think I could love again."

"Sam was a different chapter in your life. Emma is a fresh beginning."

"I'll always love Sam."

"Son, that's the beauty of the human heart. You don't have to stop loving Sam, just like I'll never stop loving your father. But there is someone else out there you could love, as well. And I'm hoping that there might be someone out there for me. I'm not too old to want someone else in my life. I have you boys, but you have your own families."

He squeezed her hand gently. "And you deserve to love again."

"As do you."

Dante pulled his mother into his arms and hugged her. "Please tell me you're not considering Sheriff Yost."

She laughed. "I had, but I'm not so sure anymore. I think I'll keep my options open."

Sean appeared from the direction of the kitchen. "I put a pot of coffee on, care to join me?"

Amelia smiled up at Dante. "I do have options, you know."

Dante grinned as his mother left him to join Sean for that cup of coffee in the kitchen.

"Ready?" Tuck asked as he pushed past him to exit out the front door. "We're going in my truck. And we'd better hurry if we want to talk to the oil speculators before the town gets crowded for the Cowboy Christmas kickoff."

Dante almost told Tuck he'd question the men tomorrow. He wanted to go back into the room with Emma, pull her into his arms and tell her...

Tell her what?

That he could be well on his way to falling in love with her and would she give him a chance to find out?

With the idea too new to him, he decided he'd be better off waiting until later that night to hold her in his arms and make it right.

EMMA MUST HAVE fallen back asleep after Dante left. She didn't wake until Amelia poked her head in the doorway a couple of hours later.

"Emma, it's time to get ready. We're all heading into Medora for the kickoff of the annual Cowboy Christmas festivities. We leave in thirty minutes."

"I'm awake," she assured the woman. She sat up, feeling every bruise and bump and stiff muscle in her body, along with the deep sadness of knowing she'd be leaving. On the nightstand beside a glass of water, lay the keys to the SUV Dante had rented in Grand Forks.

If she really was leaving, now would be the best time

to do it. With Dante in town, the rest of the members of his household leaving for Medora, she could sneak away. She slipped into her snow gear and pulled on her boots.

Stuffing her toothbrush, hairbrush and a change of clothes in her purse, she left the rest of the contents of her bag in the bedroom and stepped out in the hallway.

"Look at you, all ready to go," Julia said, hurrying to one of the bedrooms. "We'll be a few more minutes. We had to wait for Ryan to leave before we could begin getting ready."

"He was here?"

"While you were asleep. Got half of the cameras wired. He's supposed to be back tomorrow to finish the job."

"I didn't even hear him working," Emma said.

"We had him work on the installation of the cameras at the other end of the house so that he wouldn't disturb you and Lily while you both napped." A tiny cry came from down the hallway. "That's my cue. All I have to do is get Lily dressed and I'll be ready."

Amelia emerged from her bedroom, wearing a bright red Christmas sweater. "I had a call from Maddox while you were sleeping. He and Katya flew into Bismarck over an hour ago. They're on their way and should be to Medora in time for the festivities. Isn't that wonderful?" The older woman beamed. "All my children home for Christmas." She wrapped her arms around Emma and hugged her tight. "I'm so glad you're here with us."

Guilt tugged at Emma as she returned the hug. "Thank you for all you've done for me," she said, fighting back tears. "I'm supposed to meet Dante at the diner. Do you mind if I leave a little early? I have a few things I want to pick up at the store before it closes."

Amelia's brows furrowed. "Is that a good idea to go off on your own with all that's happened?"

Emma forced a smile to her stiff lips. "I'll be fine. If I have any trouble on the road, all of you will be behind me shortly. I'll just wait until you come along."

"I could be ready to go in five minutes," Amelia assured her. "Just let me touch up my makeup and grab my purse."

"No hurry. I really can manage this on my own." Emma hugged Amelia one more time. "Goodbye." Before Amelia could come up with another argument to keep her there or go with her, Emma hurried out the door to the SUV and climbed in.

The vehicle started right up, of course. It couldn't be cranky and die to keep her from making her break from the Thunder Horses. Deep down, she wanted to stay and become a part of this family. But she couldn't make Dante love her and she wouldn't stay knowing he didn't and never would.

The stolen kisses and making love had only been a passing fancy to him. His heart would always belong to Sam.

Shifting into Reverse, she backed up, turned and drove down the long driveway toward the highway. She took one last glance in her rearview mirror before the ranch house blended into the snow and all she could see was the thin wisp of smoke from the fireplace.

She turned onto the highway headed toward Medora and the interstate highway that would take her back east. She could stop in Bismarck and stay the night or push through and arrive in Grand Forks around midnight.

Snow fell in big, fluffy flakes, thickening the farther she drove from the Thunder Horse Ranch, making it difficult to see the road in front of her. As she came to a crossroad with a stop sign, she pressed her foot to the brake.

The tires skidded and she started sliding toward the ditch.

Heart pumping, she turned into the skid and righted the vehicle, just in time to see the form of a man walking alongside the road ahead, headed toward her.

As her lights caught him in their beams, he lifted his head and waved her down.

Carefully applying her breaks, she slowed and rolled down the passenger window.

"Thank goodness you stopped." Ryan Yost poked his head through the window. "I thought I'd have to walk all the way back to the ranch house."

"What happened to your truck?" Emma asked.

"It slid into the ditch about half a mile ahead. The roads are pretty tricky."

"Are you headed back to the ranch or to town?"

"To Medora, if you don't mind."

She popped the locks on the SUV and the man climbed into the passenger seat.

"Where is the rest of the Thunder Horse clan?"

"They should be right behind me."

"In that case, turn here," Ryan said.

"What?" Emma glanced at the dirt track leading off the road. "Why?"

"Because I said so." Ryan grabbed the steering wheel and yanked it to the right.

Emma held on as the SUV bumped off the road onto the narrow strip of dirt lightly covered in snow. Pulse pounding, she fought to right the vehicle. When she had the SUV under control, she braked to a stop and shot an angry glance at Ryan. "What the hell are you doing?"

That's when she saw the dark, hard form of the gun

in his hand pointed at her head, and a rush of icy-cold dread washed over her.

"I'm taking what should have been mine."

Knowing she could be a victim or she could try to escape, Emma chose to try rather than go along with whatever Ryan had in mind. "Why do you say that? What should have been yours? Surely not me." She spoke calmly while her left hand inched toward the door handle.

Ryan laughed. "It's not you, but I've learned that to get to them, you have to go through the ones they love."

"Are you talking about the Thunder Horses?" she asked.

"Of course I'm talking about the Thunder Horses. Keep driving," he commanded. "Far enough off the road they won't see you when they drive by."

Emma eased her foot off the brake but didn't apply her foot to the accelerator. The vehicle inched forward along the bumpy road.

"Faster!" Ryan yelled and leaned across to slam his own foot down on hers. The vehicle leaped forward.

At that moment, Emma flung the door open, elbowed the man in the face and threw herself out of the vehicle. She hit the rocky ground hard and rolled out of the way of the tires.

Pain shot through the arm she'd landed on, but she scrambled to her feet and ran as fast as she could in the snow and her clunky boots.

A car door slammed and gravel crunched behind her.

By the time she reached the paved road, her lungs burned from breathing the frigid air and her muscles were screaming, but she pushed forward. Her foot hit the icy surface and she skidded and slammed onto the pavement flat on her back, the wind knocked out of her lungs.

Lights blinked far down the road toward the ranch

house. If only she could get up and keep running. They'd find her.

Emma sucked in a breath, rolled over onto her hands and knees and tried to get up.

Ryan hit her like a linebacker, plowing into her and knocking her into the ditch on the other side of the road. He landed on top of her and covered her with his body, pressing her face into the snow and ice.

She struggled, but he weighed more than she did and he had her arms and legs pinned beneath his.

The muffled sound of a vehicle engine came and went. Though she tried to scream out, she knew she wouldn't be heard. Even if she was, he might still have his gun on him. What would happen if they stopped? Would he shoot Amelia, Julia or Lily before the men took him down?

Emma wouldn't be able to live with herself if he did, so she lay quietly, no longer fighting to free herself. Once the vehicle drove by, she'd come up with another plan. If she lived long enough.

Chapter Fifteen

Dante and Tuck stopped at the hotel where the oil speculators were staying. Nicole was on duty, looking as bored as usual. "Ah, the Thunder Horse brothers. Here to see Ryan, again?"

"We're not here to see Ryan. We'd like to talk with Monty Langley and Theron Price."

"Sorry, unless you have an appointment, they've asked not to be disturbed."

Tuck pulled out his FBI credentials. "What room are they in?"

Nicole stared at the big *F-B-I* letters and nodded. "Impressive." She jerked her head toward the hallway. "They have rooms 109 and 110."

As Tuck and Dante took off in that direction, she called out, "But they aren't there."

"Any idea where they are?"

"Why do you want to know?"

"I can't answer that."

"They just got back from a ride on their snowmobiles." She snorted. "They usually have dinner at the diner around this time every day, like clockwork. I'd check there."

"They own snowmobiles?" Dante asked.

"Yeah, they keep them out back in the storage shed."

"How do we get inside the shed?"

Nicole shrugged. "Open it. We don't lock it."

Dante left the hotel and ran around the outside to the back where a weathered storage shed stood in the corner of the lot. He pushed the door open and stepped inside. The light from the doorway splashed across two fairly new snowmobiles.

"So, they own snowmobiles," Tuck said. "So do most of the people in this area."

"The one that was out by the canyon had a broken track and was leaking oil." He studied the one closest to him while Tuck dropped to his haunches beside the other.

After a moment, Tuck straightened. "This one doesn't have a broken track or an oil leakage."

The lighting wasn't the best, so Dante skimmed his hand along the top of the vehicle closest to him, feeling the tracks for any inconsistencies. One of the tracks had a notch chipped out of it. Ducking his head, Dante saw something shiny on the ground beneath the engine. He reached his hand beneath it and felt warm, sticky oil.

"A lot of snowmobiles have chinks out of their tracks and leak oil."

"Yeah, but I don't believe in coincidence." Dante left the storage shed.

"Where to?" Tuck asked.

"The diner, to find us some oil speculators."

He and Tuck climbed in the truck and drove the block to the diner, parking in front.

Through the windows Dante could see Hank and Florence at the bar counter. At a table on the south side of the diner, two men sat drinking coffee.

Dante was first out of the truck and into the diner. He marched up to the two men. "Monty Langley and Theron Price?"

The younger one with sandy-blond hair raised his eyebrows. "I'm Monty, he's Theron. What can we do for you?"

"Where were you two yesterday around three o'clock in the afternoon?"

"Why?" Monty asked.

Tuck stepped up beside Dante and flashed his FBI badge. "Just answer the question."

Monty raised his hands. "We were here in the diner with Mr. Plessinger for most of the afternoon. About have him ready to lease his mineral rights." He dropped his arms and smiled. "Are you two ready to talk money?"

"Hell no," Dante responded.

Theron frowned. "Then what's this all about?"

"Someone tried to kill me and my fiancée yesterday out at the canyon. He used C-4 explosives. The kind people might have access to if connected with an oil drilling operation."

Monty stood, his hands raised. "Whoa there, cowboy. I'm a lover, not a killer. The closest I get to the oil is when I take my car in for an oil change."

Florence stepped into the conversation. "I can vouch for the two of them. They worked over poor ol' Fred Plessinger all afternoon, drank two pots of coffee between them and ate an entire coconut cream pie."

Tuck's cell phone buzzed and he stepped away from the group to answer it.

"Where were you two four days ago? Were you anywhere near Grand Forks?"

"We've been here in Medora the entire week," Price said. "We're not scheduled to head back to Minneapolis until the end of the month."

"Do you have proof?" Dante asked.

Monty pulled a pocket-size day planner out of his

jacket and handed it to Dante. "Look at my schedule. Any one of these people I've had appointments with can vouch for my whereabouts."

Dante glanced at the names on the man's minicalendar. He recognized many of them. The men seemed slimy but legit in their alibis. He handed the planner to Monty. "I'm sorry to have bothered you."

"Sounds like someone is out to get the Thunder Horse clan. What with your brothers' brakes going out, your helicopter going down and now the explosives. Do you all have good insurance policies?" Monty held out a card. "I have a friend who sells life insurance."

Dante walked away and joined Tuck near the door.

"Are you sure?" Tuck ran a hand through his hair, his face pale. "Thanks. I'm on it." As soon as Tuck hung up, he pushed through the door. "Come on, we have to go."

"What's wrong?"

Tuck climbed into his truck and started the engine as Dante slid into the passenger seat. "I had my contact at the FBI run a check on flight plans for Grand Forks and Bismarck to see if Ryan Yost's name or plane came up. They had a couple of hits. He flew into Bismarck two days before your crash and out the next day, landing in Grand Forks the day before your crash. Then he flew out of Grand Forks a couple of days after your crash."

Dante's blood ran cold. "It adds up all too well. He could have cut your brakes and left them to bleed out, hopped in his plane to Grand Forks to target me. Now he's out at the house with the family."

"Pierce and Sean are there," Tuck said, pulling out of the diner parking lot onto the highway.

"But they're not suspecting anything." Dante hit the speed-dial number for home and pressed his cell phone to his ear. It rang five times before he gave up. "No answer."

"They could be on their way to town for Cowboy Christmas." Tuck glanced ahead as they approached the edge of town. "As a matter of fact, isn't that Pierce's SUV?"

The SUV pulled up beside them, the window rolled down and Pierce stuck his head out. "You're headed the wrong way."

"Where's Ryan Yost?"

"He left thirty minutes before us. I figure he's back at his hotel," Pierce said. "Why?"

"Do you have everyone with you?"

His mother answered, "Yes, we do. Except Emma. She was on her way to meet you at the diner." She unbuckled her seat belt and leaned over Pierce's shoulder. "Emma's not with you? She left ten minutes before we did."

Dante's heart fell down around his knees. Emma was missing and Ryan Yost might be the one responsible. Where would he take her? And why?

His cell phone buzzed in his hand and he glanced down. A text message came through with a number he didn't recognize in the display screen.

If you want to see Emma alive, come to the ranch. Alone.

Dante's hand shook as he held out the phone to Tuck.

Tuck read the message and glanced over at Pierce. "We have a problem."

Pierce pulled off the road, climbed out of the SUV and walked over to Tuck's truck. The three brothers read the message again.

"He's at the ranch with Emma," Dante said. "I have to go."

"Who's at the ranch with Emma?" Pierce asked.

"Ryan Yost."

"Where's Emma?" Dante's mother pushed her way through her sons. "And why are you concerned about Ryan?"

Dante debated telling her something to pacify her, but the look on her face was enough. "We think Ryan Yost has her. I just got this text." He showed his mother the cell phone.

"Oh, dear Lord. I knew I should have insisted she ride with us."

"If she had, you all might be the ones he's holding hostage."

Amelia stared up at her sons. "But why?"

"Good question. Only Ryan can answer that. For now, I have to go." Dante held out his hands to his brother Tuck. "Give me the keys."

"You're not going alone."

"I have to. If I don't, he might kill Emma."

"He might kill her anyway. Why not let us come with you? We're the ones trained for this."

"You forget I fought in the war."

"Yeah, but you have no training in hostage negotiation."

"I can't risk it." Dante climbed into the truck and stuck the key in the ignition.

"We're coming with you." Pierce opened the back door and got in the crew cab.

Tuck climbed into the passenger seat. "What he doesn't know won't hurt. We have your back."

"What about me?" Amelia asked.

"Maddox is supposed to arrive about now. Send him out when he does. And, Mom, I need you to stay in town and keep Lily and Julia safe," Tuck said. "Promise me."

Amelia nodded. "And promise me that you three won't do anything stupid and get yourselves shot."

"We promise," they said as one.

"Want me to notify the sheriff's department?" she asked.

"No!" they said in unison. "If it's his son, he might take sides. The wrong side."

"Got it." Amelia stepped away from the truck and raised her hand. *"Wakan tanan kici un wakina chelee."*

Dante drove toward the ranch, his foot heavy on the accelerator. He appreciated his mother's prayer to the Great Spirit, but he wasn't the one who needed it.

Emma was.

Chapter Sixteen

Emma came to and blinked at the lights shining from the lamps on end tables above her. For a moment she was disoriented, her vision blurred and pain throbbed at her temple.

The last thing she remembered was fighting to stand after the SUV full of the Thunder Horse family had passed by. One moment she'd gotten a good kick at his shins, the next moment she was awake in the living room of the Thunder Horse ranch house.

"Looks like you'll be around for the fireworks after all," a voice said.

She turned her head, a flash of pain making her close her eyes until it passed. When she opened them again, she could see Ryan Yost standing beside the window, peering through a crack in the blinds.

"Someone's coming. Let's hope it's the people I specifically requested and not any more." He clapped his hands together. "Today, I finally get my revenge on the people I hate the most."

Emma struggled to push to a sitting position, realizing that her hands were secured behind her back by something that felt like duct tape. Using her elbow, she pushed up and drew her legs under her, sitting up. Thankfully, he hadn't tied her feet together. She glanced around for something sharp to rub the tape on. Every edge seemed to be soft or rounded. "Why are you doing this?"

"I'll tell you why. For years, my father hated me, hated my mother and hated everything about our lives together. When my mother couldn't take it any longer, she jerked me out of my school here in Medora and hauled me back to the reservation where I would have rotted in hell."

Emma's head ached, but she had to keep the man talking. Maybe she could reason with him. "And what does that have to do with the Thunder Horses?"

"On one of her normal drunken binges, she let slip a secret she'd kept from me and from my father. A secret that made everything perfectly clear. William Yost was in love with the woman who married John Thunder Horse, not my mother."

"So?"

"And my mother was in love with John Thunder Horse and they'd been dating up until John met Amelia and dumped my mother. My pregnant mother."

Emma's mind cleared and focused on what the man had just said. "Are you saying John Thunder Horse was your father?"

"Damn right he was. He left my mother when she was pregnant. She was forced to marry Yost and had me eight months later."

Ryan slapped a hand to his chest. "I should have grown up on the Thunder Horse Ranch, not that hellhole of a reservation. I should have had the best of everything they had."

"Are you certain? Have you done a DNA test?"

"I look like a Thunder Horse, damn it!" He jerked Emma up by her arm and glared into her face. "I've never looked anything like William Yost."

"Because you look like your mother." Sheriff Yost

stepped into the house, gun drawn, closing the door behind him. "Ryan, what are you doing?"

"Daddy." Ryan practically spit the word out. "So glad you could come to your *son's* coming out party. Pull up a seat. We're waiting for the other main player to arrive."

Footsteps pounded on the porch outside and a voice shouted, "Emma!"

"Dante, don't come in!" Emma cried.

Ryan looped his arm around her neck and yanked her up by the throat. "Shut up."

Dante flung the door open and entered, his eyes blazing. "Leave her out of this, Ryan."

"Oh, no. I wouldn't dream of it. I've worked too hard setting this all up to end it here."

"What do you want? The ranch? Money? You name it." Dante stepped closer.

"Stop right there." Ryan pointed his gun at Emma's temple. "Another step closer and I'll shoot her."

"Why are you doing this, son?"

"Because I'm not your son."

"What are you talking about?"

"My mother told me her secret. A secret I suspect you always knew. She had an affair with John Thunder Horse before she married you, and before *he* married Amelia. She was pregnant when you married her. That's why I was born eight months after your wedding."

Sheriff Yost raised a hand. "Whoa, son, where did you hear such an idiotic story?"

"From my mother. The woman you kicked out of your house and sent back to live on the reservation. If I had been your son, you wouldn't have let her take me." Ryan's lip curled back, baring his teeth. "It all made sense when she told me I was John Thunder Horse's son. You hated me, and you hated my mother for what she did."

Ryan's arm tightened around Emma's neck. She struggled, unable to get air past her vocal cords to utter a protest.

"Let go of Emma," Dante pleaded. Emma's face was beet-red and starting to turn blue. "She had nothing to do with what happened between your father and mother."

"No way. While you and your brothers lived the life *I* should have, I wallowed in a broken-down trailer while my mother drank herself into oblivion every night. When she wasn't slapping me around, she was telling me what a failure I was compared to the four of you."

"Ryan, I don't know what your mother told you, but it was a pack of lies. I tried to get you back, but the court didn't want to go up against the tribal council. Your mother told them she wanted you to grow up knowing the way of your ancestors. They wouldn't listen to me. I loved you. I wanted you to live with me."

"Then why did you kick us out?"

"I didn't." Yost stepped closer. "You have to believe me. Your mother had problems. She was delusional. I think her breakup with John was the last straw. I didn't see it until we'd already married. And with you on the way, I couldn't divorce her."

"Lies!" Ryan dragged Emma back toward the hallway. "You threw us out."

"She told you that, didn't she?" William said quietly. "The truth was that she left me and took you with her to punish me."

"No. That's not how it was. You hated me and ruined my life. Now I'm going to ruin yours." Ryan's hand shook as he held it to Emma's head. "If you don't shoot Dante right now, I'll put a bullet through Emma's head."

"What will shooting Dante gain for you?"

"It'll be one Thunder Horse down and you will have

killed him. Amelia will never love you after you've killed her precious son." Ryan's face turned red, his eyes bulging. "Shoot him now or I swear the woman dies!"

Dante turned to the sheriff. "Do it. Shoot me if that's what it'll take to free Emma. She'll die anyway if he doesn't loosen his hold soon."

"I can't shoot you." The sheriff held his gun to the side. "I won't."

"I've never trusted you. Never thought you were man enough to fill my father's shoes or deserve to be with my mother. If ever there's a time to prove me wrong, now is it. Shoot me." Dante held his arms out to his sides, glancing over at Emma's face turning purple. "Now!" He prayed Yost would do it, but that he'd graze him, not hit him in a place that would be fatal. If Ryan thought him dead, he might let go of Emma long enough for her to breathe, buying time.

Sheriff Yost raised his 9 mm pistol and aimed. "God have mercy on my soul." He pulled the trigger.

The bullet's impact jerked Dante's arm back and he was flung to the side, angling toward Ryan Yost.

As Dante crashed to the floor, Ryan loosened his hold on Emma's neck.

Her knees buckled and she slipped to the floor.

Ryan raised his gun, pointing it at Sheriff Yost. "Now I'll be the hero for shooting the man who killed Amelia's son, and you will be blamed for setting off the explosives I have positioned around the house." Before he could pull the trigger, Dante swung his leg, sweeping Ryan's feet out from under him. His shot hit the ceiling and he landed hard on his back, his gun skidding across the hardwood floor out of his reach.

Emma, having caught her breath, spun around on her hip and kicked the gun farther away from him.

"No! You'll ruin everything." Ryan grabbed her hair and yanked hard.

Dante, his arm bleeding and his vision getting gray and fuzzy around the edges, flung himself on top of Ryan, pinning him down with his good hand, keeping him from digging the detonator out of his pocket.

Then everything seemed to happen at once. Tuck and Pierce stormed into the house, followed by Maddox and the rest of the family.

Tuck pulled Dante off Ryan.

"Don't let him get his hands in his pockets. He has a detonator in it and he says he has the house rigged to explode."

Tuck rolled Ryan onto his belly and slapped a zip tie around his wrists, then carefully dug the detonation device from his pocket and set it aside for the bomb squad. "You have the right to remain silent..."

As Tuck read Ryan his Miranda rights, Dante crawled over to where Emma was struggling to get up with her wrists still bound behind her back with duct tape.

Maddox leaned over Dante. "Let me get her." He pulled a pocketknife out of his pocket and sliced through the tape, freeing her wrists.

As soon as she was free, Emma flung her arms around Dante's shoulders. "I thought you were dead. Why the hell did you tell the sheriff to shoot you?"

"Sweetheart, you were turning a pretty shade of blueberry. Another minute and you wouldn't have made it." He winced, pain slicing through him where she hugged his injured arm. "I'm getting blood on your clothes."

"Oh, my God. Lie down. Someone call an ambulance."

Pierce handed her a towel. "Apply pressure to the wound to slow the bleeding."

Tuck placed a call to 9-1-1, requesting an ambulance and bomb-sniffing dogs.

While Maddox helped Dante out of his jacket, Emma folded the hand towel into a wad. Once Dante was out of the jacket, the wound bled freely. Emma eased Dante onto his back and applied pressure to the wound.

"Emma." Dante grasped the wrist holding the towel in place.

"Am I hurting you?"

"More than you'll ever know."

"I'm sorry, but if I let up, you'll start bleeding again."

He chuckled. "Not the arm." He laid his other hand over her chest. "Here. You're hurting my heart."

"I don't understand."

"You made me feel again." He lifted her empty hand and pressed it to his chest. "You made me ache so bad I thought I was going to die."

Her eyes misted. "I'm sorry, I don't want to cause you any pain. I know how much you loved Sam. I was leaving to go back to Grand Forks so that I wouldn't make you feel like you had to choose."

"That's the point. I didn't want to love anyone else. I didn't want to choose between you and her. But then you ran your snowmobile into a man who tried to kill me not once but three times.

"I'd have done it for anyone."

"I know. That's what I love about you. You're selfless, endearing and beautiful in so many ways."

"No, I'm just me. A college professor with very few social skills."

"You have all the skills I need, and you're the most beautiful woman I know. Because you're beautiful inside and out. You showed me that I didn't have to choose. That I could love you both."

Emma laughed, the sound catching on a sob. "You've been talking to your mother, haven't you?"

"She's smarter than I ever gave her credit for." Dante pressed her hand to his lips kissing her knuckles. "I'll never underestimate her again. Nor you."

As Tuck dragged Ryan to his feet and shoved him toward the door, the rest of the Thunder Horse family arrived with the ambulance, a state policeman and the only other deputy on duty in Billings County. Rather than risk anyone else being hurt, the party was moved out of the house.

Ryan was bundled into the state police car and carted off to Bismarck where he would face a multitude of charges.

Sheriff Yost hung around to make sure no one went inside the house his son had rigged with explosives.

Dante let the medics bandage his wound but refused to go with them to the hospital in Dickinson. "I want to make sure my fiancée doesn't run out on me." He held on to Emma's hand as he sat on the gurney, his legs dangling over the side.

Emma smiled sadly. "But don't you see? It's over. You don't have to protect me anymore. I can go back to Grand Forks."

"Is that what you want?" he asked.

Her head dipped and she stared at her feet, which were up to her ankles in snow. "You said no guarantees."

"Yeah, well, I was wrong."

His mother walked up to him where he sat and laid a hand on his shoulder. "Dante."

"Just a minute, Mother."

"No, really, if you want to do this right, take this." She removed the glove from his hand and one of hers. Then she slipped the diamond engagement ring off her finger.

The ring his father had given her when he'd asked her to marry him over thirty years ago. She pressed it into his bare palm. "Now do it right."

Dante glanced down at the ring, a flood of emotions rising up his throat. When he turned to Emma, he knew what he had to do.

Emma stared at the ring in his hand, her eyes wet with tears, her head shaking back and forth. "Don't. I don't need your pity."

"Pity? You think I'd get down on my knees in the snow because I pity you?" Dante slid off the gurney and dropped to one knee. "Emma Jennings, in the short time we've been together, we've been through a lot. You've saved my life more than once and you've shown me that I have so much more life to look forward to and I can't think of anyone I'd rather spend it with. Will you marry me?"

Emma's knees buckled and she dropped to the ground beside him. "Are you sure this is what you want?"

"I've never been more sure." He took her hand in his and removed her glove. "Marry me."

Tears slipped down her cheek even as snowflakes clung to her eyelashes and she nodded. He slipped the ring on her finger, feeling happiness bubble up inside him. He rose to his feet and lifted her up in his arms. "Mom, Pierce, Tuck, Maddox, meet my fiancée, the beautiful Emma Jennings. We're getting married."

"I thought you were already engaged," Pierce said.

Dante grinned and hugged Emma close. "Brother, in case you didn't know it already, it's all about the ring."

Chapter Seventeen

Emma's pulse pounded and her hands shook as she stood in the hallway of the ranch house, wearing Amelia's beautiful wedding dress, awaiting her cue. When the strains of Mendelssohn's "Wedding March" blared over the sound system, she stepped forward.

Maddox, dressed in a black tuxedo, offered her his arm and walked her into the living room toward the big stone fireplace at the center, where Dante stood with his brothers on the left and his brothers' wives on the right, and the justice of the peace they'd brought in from Medora in the center.

Christmas morning was bright with sunshine and it promised to be the best day of Emma's life. Her heart was so full, she could barely breathe. It had all happened so fast. The entire Thunder Horse clan had pulled together to make the wedding happen in an incredibly short amount of time.

This was it. She was about to become Mrs. Thunder Horse.

Dante stood tall, his gunshot wound bandaged and hidden beneath the sleeve of his tuxedo. He'd combed his dark hair back and his green eyes flashed when she'd appeared.

Amelia sat in a front row chair with Sean sitting to

her right and what seemed like half of the Medora citizens seated in the other chairs filling the room. A huge Christmas tree stood in the corner, lights shining and a bright star crowning the top.

Through the window she could see fat white snowflakes falling and frost making pretty designs on the glass. The day couldn't have been more beautiful and the man she was about to marry more perfect.

Emma walked toward him wondering if this was all a dream and she'd wake up in her apartment cold and alone. But when Dante smiled, his green eyes shiny, she knew it was real.

He held out his hand and she took it, knowing he'd always be there for her.

"Emma Jennings, do you take Dante to be your husband? To love, honor and cherish so long as you both shall live?"

Emma spoke in clear voice, never more certain in her life of her answer, "I do."

"And, Dante, do you take Emma to be your wife—"

Dante lifted her hands and held them tight. "I do, to love honor and cherish so long as we both shall live. Can we wrap this up? I want to kiss my wife."

Laughter rose from the crowd as Dante did just that, kissing Emma in front of everyone. When he finally let her up for air, her cheeks were warm and she couldn't stop smiling.

The justice of the peace shrugged. "They said yes. Folks, meet Mr. and Mrs. Dante Thunder Horse. May the Great Spirit bless you both."

"You heard the man, the last Thunder Horse brother is hitched," Tuck said. "Our family is growing."

"Yeah, and it's about to get even bigger." Maddox slid an arm around Katya and grinned. "Katya's pregnant."

Tuck whooped. "I don't know how you found time, gallivanting all over the globe. And don't that just beat all?" He lifted his Lily in his arms and held her up. "Lily's going to be a sister. Julia and I are expecting our second."

"Uh—" Pierce raised a hand "—I was saving it until after the wedding, but Roxy and I are expecting, too."

Amelia clapped her hands to her mouth, her eyes alight. "All those grandbabies. I am truly blessed."

Everyone turned to Emma and Dante.

Tuck spoke. "Well? What are you two waiting for? Get busy so our kids can all grow up together."

"You heard them, Wife. Let's get crackin'." Dante swung Emma up in his arms and marched her out of the room.

Her heart swelled with the love she felt for this man and his entire family. Being married to a Thunder Horse was going to be everything she ever dreamed of and more. The Great Spirit had truly blessed them.

* * * * *

MILLS & BOON®

Why not subscribe?
Never miss a title and save money too!

Here's what's available to you if you join the exclusive **Mills & Boon Book Club** today:

✦ *Titles up to a month ahead of the shops*
✦ *Amazing discounts*
✦ *Free P&P*
✦ *Earn Bonus Book points that can be redeemed against other titles and gifts*
✦ *Choose from monthly or pre-paid plans*

Still want more?
Well, if you join today we'll even give you
50% OFF your first parcel!

So visit **www.millsandboon.co.uk/subs**
or call Customer Relations on 020 8288 2888
to be a part of this exclusive Book Club!

Snow, sleigh bells and a hint of seduction

Find your perfect Christmas reads at
millsandboon.co.uk/Christmas

MILLS & BOON®

Why shop at millsandboon.co.uk?

Each year, thousands of romance readers find their perfect read at millsandboon.co.uk. That's because we're passionate about bringing you the very best romantic fiction. Here are some of the advantages of shopping at www.millsandboon.co.uk:

* **Get new books first**—you'll be able to buy your favourite books one month before they hit the shops

* **Get exclusive discounts**—you'll also be able to buy our specially created monthly collections, with up to 50% off the RRP

* **Find your favourite authors**—latest news, interviews and new releases for all your favourite authors and series on our website, plus ideas for what to try next

* **Join in**—once you've bought your favourite books, don't forget to register with us to rate, review and join in the discussions

Visit **www.millsandboon.co.uk**
for all this and more today!